BIRDS OF PREY

Robert Abatti

AuthorHouse™ LLC
1663 Liberty Drive
Bloomington, IN 47403
www.authorhouse.com
Phone: 1-800-839-8640

Published by AuthorHouse 06/03/2014

ISBN: 978-1-4969-1761-4 (sc)
ISBN: 978-1-4969-1760-7 (e)

Library of Congress Control Number: 2014910245

This book is printed on acid-free paper.

To my wife, Tanya, for her unwavering support and understanding while I was hunched over a computer after a long day's work; and to all of my children for being there during the hard times. Lastly, I wish to remember my only older brother, Philip Mark Abatecola, MD, a great orthopedic surgeon who died way too young and whose death left a void in every life he touched.

CHAPTER 1

The shadow that was cast off of the predator fleeted across the barren desert floor as it searched for anything out of the ordinary on the dry sands below that might resemble something edible. The large, black-winged creature with the small, ugly pink head had traveled over forty miles in search of its next meal and would not be denied. In the old western movies, the circling of vultures or buzzards always signaled that an Indian attack had occurred and that freshly killed food was waiting below. Being carnivorous, these birds of prey would circle, as they flew in the cooler, higher altitudes and waited for any sign of life to be gone while the sun partially cooked their dinner. They would glide along the jet streams' thermals, their six-foot wingspan and feathers fully extended, which allowed them to utilize hardly any energy. This maneuver also allowed them to stay in one area for hours. Once the feasting began, however, they would attack the remains viciously in flocks of up to eight at one time. Being extremely territorial, they prevented any outsiders from joining the party while they feasted upon their prey, usually leaving nothing but the bones behind.

The forty-nine-mile stretch of Old Historic US Route 66 from the Mountain Spring Road exit off of Interstate 40, near thc city of Needles, California, on the Arizona border, to the town of Amboy, California, was a straight run through the floor of the Mojave Desert and Death Valley. The two-lane highway, well-known to most Southern Californians as Amboy Road, was used mostly as a shortcut between the cities of the Inland Empire valleys and the Colorado River, which is the border between the two neighboring states. "The River," as most locals refer to the mighty stream that carved out the Grand Canyon as it made its course to the Baja Sea in Mexico, was a recreational haven for boaters and fishermen. It was also the artery and lifeline to some of the most fertile soil in the Imperial Valley, an agricultural mecca.

Amboy Road was often driven by vehicles at speeds exceeding one hundred miles per hour, including trucks hauling trailers with forty-foot cigar boats, due to the lack of California Highway Patrol presence. Temperatures in this desert basin in the summer often exceeded 135 degrees on the pavement, which caused sneaker soles to melt if a person were standing more than five minutes on the asphalt. The surrounding area was void of any vegetation except the occasional cactus and tumbleweed, which were scattered through the mounds of sand. Mountains rich in iron ore, which gave them a reddish hue, rose to about 7,000 feet from the sea-level desert floor. They ran parallel to the road's entire length and caused a baking effect in the center. Multiple old volcanoes dotted the landscape, with some of their lava rock strewn across the desert floor near their bases from blasts thousands of years ago.

The only living creatures that inhabited this barren territory were either reptilian or arthropod. Most of them were venomous. Farther up in the lower foothills were the few human inhabitants, who worked and lived in either Amboy (population 100) or its sister village Essex (population 127). They were the only two towns along this forgotten route. Few came out of their homes during the heat of the summer. Instead, they tended to do most of their wandering at night, when it dropped a whole fifty degrees to a cool eighty-five. If your vehicle broke down on this route, you were better off staying with your vehicle. Most people, even traveling at over one hundred miles per hour, stopped to help a stranded motorist. If one should wander into the desert, the only remains that would be found would be the bones after the vultures visited.

He looked up at the shadows circling above and could have sworn that not only five minutes ago, there were only two, but now he counted four. He looked off in all directions, scanned the desert floor for miles, and did not see any more, or anyone. It was absolutely barren. He resumed his digging, making sure the hole was at least six feet deep. At that depth the remains would never be found, not even by the buzzards above. He knew. He had done this so many times that he could do it in his sleep. Unlike others, he didn't keep any records or any trophies, just as he had been trained to do so many years ago. Always eliminate the evidence.

So he kept digging.

Finally, with his six-foot-five-inch frame standing at chin height to the top of the hole, he knew it was deep enough. He hoisted himself out of the hole with ease, dusted off, smiled at his good work, and walked over to his truck. He opened up the bed hood and lowered the tailgate. Finding the cooler, he took out a thirty-two-ounce water bottle and chugged half of it down in the first gulp. He wiped off his mouth, took off his cowboy hat, removed the bandana from his head, and drenched it with the ice water. Replacing the bandana cooled his head immediately. He finished the water and fanned himself before placing the hat back on his head. He stretched his arms, rotated his shoulders, and admired the sight of his muscles, which were taut and defined. His hair was cut to a number one on the sides, two on top, as it had been since boot camp, so many years ago. His skin was tanned a bronze color. His entire back, neck, and arms were covered by a full-body tattoo of his own bird of prey, a red-tailed hawk. His wingspan was seven feet.

Feeling reenergized, he picked up the body bag lying in the bed of the truck and threw it over his shoulder like a sack of potatoes. He walked back to the grave site whistling "If I Only Had a Brain," from the movie *The Wizard of Oz.* When he reached the edge, he hurled the bag into the bottom of the newly dug grave, picked up the shovel, and immediately began filling the dirt back in, still whistling. He finished within thirty minutes, took a rake from the truck bed, and covered up any remnants of the grave's outline. "Just like raking a giant sand trap on a golf course," he said to no one.

He replaced the tools from his truck, pulled out a water bottle from the cooler, and sat on the tailgate. Lighting up a joint he saved for the occasion, he took in the splendor of the desert in the late afternoon sun. Finally feeling the buzz at its pinnacle, he locked up the truck's bed, climbed into the cab, and started the engine. With the air-conditioner blasting and the speakers off his MP3 player blasting "Alive" by Pearl Jam, he drove three miles over packed desert floor toward the highway and home. Pleased with another mission completed, he felt absolutely no remorse. He just wanted to get home, take a good shower, watch a ball game, and eat some munchies. *Going to be a wonderful night*, he thought as he turned onto Amboy Road.

Up in the sky, the vultures had disappeared. The waning sun had begun to cast its myriad of colors one last time over the desert floor as it set. The mountains, now a magenta color, cast their long shadows over the grave site. A kangaroo mouse took his normal path home as any other evening. As it ran across the grave, it stopped. Its nose and whiskers twitched rapidly as it inhaled repeatedly. It had run across the same smell multiple times and places across this stretch of the Mojave, but never found the source. After about two minutes, it scurried along and left the victim in her final resting place alone. No service, no headstone, not even a cross, so often seen along the roads at other sites of death. Never to be found.

Just as it should be.

CHAPTER 2

Phil could see the headlights from five miles away in his rearview mirror. *Halogen lights,* he thought, *and closing extremely fast.* He pulled his vehicle over to the shoulder and sat waiting. Within less than two minutes, the 740i BMW flew past him at a whopping 125 miles per hour. The fool didn't slow down, even with the CHP chase car sitting on the shoulder, the golden HIGHWAY PATROL across the upper trunk of the black vehicle. Phil was tired and wanted nothing better than to get home and catch a replay of the Dodgers/Giants ball game. *But this asshole was doing 125,* he thought. *He's going to kill someone.*

The small-block Chevy engine, which Phil personally upgraded to bring over 500 horsepower at top acceleration, could keep up with or overtake anything on the road except a Lamborghini Contache. This was just a Beemer. He wasn't worried about catching the idiot, but the paperwork that would follow, especially if he had to impound the vehicle. He shook his head at the stupidity of it all. The engine roared to life and the desert creatures got a rude awakening as his twenty-inch tires dug into the shoulder dirt, spraying rocks for hundreds of feet. His 2010 Z28 CHP vehicle was up to 140 miles per hour in less than a minute, reflectors in the road whizzing by at light speed.

Within five minutes, he overtook the BMW. The driver must have figured something was up, since his speed had decreased rapidly to the mid-nineties. Phil turned on his light bar and three red lights in the front grill. The red taillights lit up ahead, and the speeding car decelerated evenly, coming to a stop without incident one-quarter mile up the road. With the bright lights illuminating the cab of the BMW, Phil immediately checked his computer for any outstanding warrants on either the vehicle or its occupant. Seeing a couple only in the car, Phil figured this was going to be just a routine speeding ticket. By the time he had caught up to them, they were only doing ninety-two miles per hour he rationalized. The owner of the vehicle was one Aaron Rosenstein from Bel-Air and an attorney. *Ah shit*, Phil thought. Here comes the bull of both of them being in law, or some kind of excuse. All attorneys would do anything to get out of a ticket.

Phil slowly made his way around the passenger side of the vehicle, hand on gun, just in case. The passenger window rolled down, revealing the two most beautiful blue eyes he had ever seen staring back at him. Phil, at first, was unnerved, but regained his composure quickly.

"License, registration, and proof of insurance, please," Phil said flatly.

"Sure, officer; honey, everything is in the glove compartment. Could you get them for the officer?" the slick lawyer, probably sixty-five to seventy years old, said too sweetly to his companion.

His "friend" was probably in her upper thirties, maybe early forties. She was an absolutely stunning blond with a low-cut top of very thin beige chemise, revealing plenty of cleavage. She leaned forward in an exaggerated manner, giving further exposure, which left Phil perspiring on his forehead; otherwise he stayed calm.

"Here they are, Lieutenant P. DiMarco," she said, reading his nameplate, her voice similar to Marilyn Monroe's, especially accentuating the lips with her pronunciation of his last name. "What does the P stand for, Lieutenant DiMarco?" she asked with a childlike giggle.

"Philip," he said matter-of-factly. "I'll be back with your citation for speeding. I clocked you at ninety-two miles per hour."

"Isn't there something we could do, Lieutenant? This is Candy Stripe, famous porn star. We are on our way to Laughlin for a celebration of her new contract. Why don't you join us? I'm sure she would rather be with someone in their forties than someone in their sixties." The attorney made his case.

"First off, I'm fifty-five, not in my thirties; second, what you are suggesting could be considered bribery and prostitution, and I could have you arrested," Phil shot back.

"You can't be fifty-five; you look fifteen years younger," Candy purred while licking her lips with her tongue. Phil felt himself aroused and tried to hide the effect. Candy's eyes drifted downward, and her smile increased.

"My daughter is older than you," Phil replied with a slight growl, as his patience was wearing thin. "I'll be back with your citation." Muttering under his breath as he walked back to his vehicle, his semierect third leg was causing mild discomfort as he opened up the door in time to hear the dispatcher calling, her voice sounding extremely anxious.

"Unit 19, please respond; Phil, it's urgent," she said repeatedly.

"Unit 19 here. Where's the fire, Maribel?" he asked as he settled down on the seat.

His voice, one of fatigue and a little edginess, came through too clearly to his favorite dispatcher for seven of his past ten years on the force. Part mother hen, part office daughter, but most of all, she was his one true friend that he could tell anything. Even though she was twenty-eight to his fifty-five years, she was much wiser. She worked the swing shift at night while still in graduate school going for her PhD in humanities. She won all of their debates.

"Aren't we all a little testy this fine summer night?" she said sarcastically with a fake southern drawl on top of her Spanish accent.

"Sorry, long day; just want to get home and watch the Dodger game; gotta bust some asshole shyster from Bel-Air. Has some porn star with him, flying below the radar. Probably can't wait to get to Laughlin so he can screw her," he said with true contriteness.

"That's better," she said. "You're just horny, Mr. Spock. It gets to you after a while." She was referring to the original *Star Trek* series of the 1960s, when Mr. Spock, a Vulcan, would wait seven years between sexual encounters. Then he would go crazy until getting laid. "Getting back to business, we have an Amber Alert issued by Arizona State Police for a nine-year-old girl abducted by her father. The father murdered his ex-wife in Tucson about six hours ago. They just found the body about an hour ago. Captain Palmer from Kingman called personally to notify you. I'm just getting the report now on-screen, and…"

"Why would he call instead of using the normal channels? And why is he calling me personally? We're 345 miles northwest of Tucson." Phil's curiosity and agitation increased.

"It's Danny Petrino." Maribel's voice cracked with emotion. "Cindy was murdered about six hours ago, and Danny's on the run with his daughter."

The shock in Phil was evident as he froze in mid-breath. Danny Petrino was the star quarterback for Twentynine Palms High School, with a cannon for an arm and a coach's perception of the game. Six foot four, 225 pounds, recruited by no less than fifty Division IA NCAA colleges. He settled on the University of Michigan, where his girlfriend, Cindy Marino, was going to attend. Cindy was Mirabel's best friend growing up. Maribel always had a crush on Danny but had hid it very well. Unfortunately in the final game of his freshmen year, after setting all kinds of NCAA records for a rookie while leading the Wolverines to a 10-0 start, he got buried by a 320-pound defensive tackle for the hated Ohio State Buckeyes. He blew out his throwing shoulder, torn to absolute shreds according to the leading orthopedic surgeon at the Mayo Clinic. He never played again. Cindy got pregnant in their junior year, and both of them quit school. Danny bounced from one job to another. Then they had a baby girl, who was named Gina Marie Petrino. The three of them ended up in Tucson, with Danny working as a car salesman for Ford.

"Has Mike been notified?" Phil asked as he rubbed his face. *The day just got longer*, he thought. Mike Petrino and Phil were old Marine buddies, who got each other through a year of hell in Viet Nam. Mike settled in Twentynine Palms after discharge. "Mad Max" Mike became Michael Petrino, attorney-at-law, and now was mayor of the city. Phil went to the Bay Area, where he joined and served with the San Francisco Police Department for fifteen years. He made it to homicide detective, and then his partner was fatally shot walking out of the precinct, ten feet in front of him. It was sniper fire, but the suspect was never caught. Phil knew who it was, and it drove him to obsession. It cost him his marriage, and finally his job. He eventually wound up with the California Highway Patrol, transferring to be near his old buddy and working his way up to lieutenant. Danny was Phil's godchild and like a son to him.

"No," Mirabel replied.

"Okay, I'll take care of it. You okay?" Phil asked.

"Just as numb as you are. He had everything," Mirabel said, choking back the tears. "Why?"

"He lost everything and snapped," Phil said. "Some people can handle defeat; others can't, I guess."

"Pot calling the kettle black?" Mandy assumed the moral high ground.

"Yeah, I've had enough of my own defeats, but I'm still sane," Phil said. He heard laughter and said, "I'll call him now; talk to you later."

Sitting there like a robot, he couldn't begin to think of what to tell his best friend of thirty-five years: that his daughter-in-law was murdered by his only child. Mike loved Cindy like his own, the Italian in him, like Phil, very family-oriented. He did everything for Danny growing up. Not only was he his father, but his first coach, mentor, and finally his best friend. That all changed over time, as Danny changed. Mike's wife, Kathy, had died three years earlier of breast cancer and never lived to see what Danny had become. Phil always maintained that her death was one of the contributing factors in Danny's fall from grace. Thank God she was not around to see this.

After three rings, Mike answered with his patented New York "Yello."

"Mike, what are ya doin'?" Phil's heavy Bronx accent was coming out.

"Hey, Phillie, what's goin' on? D'you catch the Dodger game?" Mike asked.

"I'm still on the job, Mikey." Phil's voice became quiet, almost somber.

The use of his seldom-used nickname sent up a red flag in Mike's brain. "What's going on, Phil?" His voice was now dead serious, instant lawyer/politician.

"It's got to do with Danny," Phil started slowly.

"Yeah? What's Danny done now?" His voice settled into one of annoyance, having dealt with his son's digressions into drugs, lost jobs, multiple loans never paid back—the shining light as a younger person now gone.

"Cindy is dead. Danny may have killed her, and he's on the run with Brittany," Phil's voice deadpanned for the Joe Friday effect.

A long inhalation could be heard through the phone, then "Oh my God." The reality hit Mike like a 60 mm howitzer.

"How, what, where?" The shock in his quiet voice was clearly evident.

"I don't have the details. The murder occurred approximately six hours ago; they just found her a short time ago. I have no other details. An Amber Alert was issued by Arizona State Police. Chris Palmer called Maribel directly."

"He's never been the same, Phil, ever since that hit," Mike replied, regaining his composure. "I let Kathy down. The last thing she asked me was to protect Danny and I failed." Resignation was in his voice. "Ah shit, I better wake up my secretary; let her prepare for the onslaught of the media, and in an election year to boot."

"Mike, you know if there is anything I can do, please…" Phil's voice trailed off.

"Doesn't need to be said between us, Phil, you know that, but thanks, buddy," Mike replied. "I better start making those calls. If he makes it this far, take care of them, Phil. They're all I have left." And the line went dead.

Phil hung up and looked at the BMW in front of him. The thoughts that ran through his mind were suddenly changed into a review of his own life. He looked at the silhouette of Candy through the rear window. He realized how alone he truly was. Suddenly the last rays of the desert sunset struck him in the rearview mirror. He turned to see the last remnants light up the sky with radiant beauty, and again thanked God for allowing him to survive another day.

He walked back to the car, this time to the driver's side. The window slowly rolled down. Phil looked directly into the sleazy attorney's eyes and said, "Your luck continues. I have an emergency and need to leave, so here's ya stuff and yur outta here," he said, still in his New York mode.

"Thank you," he said and nodded.

As Phil stood back, he saw one more eyeful of Candy's upper thigh and left buttock cheek, perfectly shaped and conveniently exposed. The car started up and pulled away slowly. Phil noticed a small piece of paper fly out the passenger's window. He laughed as he thought he could have added littering to the charges and pulled them over again, but decided not. He walked over, reached down, picked up the note, and read, "Call me, if you dare" and her cell number after, with her signature. He smelled the paper, perfume and body sweat, probably from between her breasts. He shook his head, walked back to the car, uncomfortably with another erection. He looked up at the sky, the early night beginning to display its jewels, as both Polaris and Venus could be seen. He sighed deeply as he watched the taillights of the BMW disappear, knowing how much he missed companionship beyond friends. But he still wasn't ready to trust, not yet. He still had that acid taste in his mouth from the last relationship.

He got into his vehicle, roared the engine to life, made a U-turn, and headed back to headquarters, realizing it wasn't dirty sex he wanted.

He wanted to feel loved again.

CHAPTER 3

She was perfect.

Frank had watched her for the past fifteen minutes as she took her time filling up her vehicle, spending most of the time on her cell phone. His eyes were focused like laser beams hidden behind his dark Oakley sunglasses, following her every move. She was oblivious to her surroundings, making her a kidnapper's dream. She stood five foot seven inches, probably 140 pounds, solid muscles, tight ass, dirty strawberry blond hair with hints of lighter shades, curled, shoulder length, bounced when she walked. Strode was a better description, like a thoroughbred. Head held erect as she went inside to pay her bill. *She has that "look all you want, but you can't touch" type of attitude probably*, he thought to himself. Her bag, the newest short-strapped light mauve-colored Dooney & Bourke, hung over her right shoulder just barely jutting out farther than her breasts. As she passed, the perfect booty-type ass with thong was evident under tight white petal jumpers, tanned buns in contrast. His heart skipped two beats. He began salivating and was instantly hard. He had to have her.

She casually raised her left hand, which was holding a keyless remote to her champagne-colored Infiniti FX35 as she exited the store. She opened her door and leaned slightly over, placing her purse on the passenger seat. She stayed in that position a little longer than expected. Was she teasing him already? As she began to climb into her vehicle by grabbing the steering wheel with her right hand, she hesitated again. She looked back toward his truck and smiled, flipping her hair as she closed the door. He waited for her to back up and start on her way before firing up his truck. There were only three ways out of this town. The way she was going was the only way east. She was going toward Amboy Road, probably heading toward Laughlin. Suddenly it was his lucky day.

He spotted her Infiniti up ahead about three quarters of a mile. She was in a hurry, oblivious to the posted speed of fifty-five. He slowly accelerated so as not to attract attention. She took the right-hand turn onto the first stretch of ninety-eight miles of road from Twentynine Palms to Needles. They entered the beginning of the barren desert. He accelerated and began to slowly close the distance. He saw her about half a mile ahead and decided to maintain that distance. They had at least an hour before they hit any meaningful civilization—just the way he liked it. It was time to relax and wait for the most opportune time. He slipped in a CD of Pink Floyd's live version of "The Wall; Is There Anybody Out There?" and kept the same distance from the Infinti by matching her speed. The 5.9-liter Hemi engine was purring at only 2,600 rpms, with the special overdrive built into the Borg/Warner transmission. He listened to Roger Waters's lyrics about a rock band member's tenuous psychiatric life, especially in the song "Mother," in which the star's mother psychologically tortured the star through adolescence and the consequences afterward. "I will give you all of my nightmares," David Gilmour's voice of the mother told a young Roger Waters.

Just like his mother had done to him as a child.

He reached into his little tin, took out his joint, and fired it up.

He looked ahead and saw that she was now past Amboy, a couple of miles before the Kilbaker Road cutoff that takes the inexperienced driver to Interstate 40. All of the locals knew that route added fifteen miles to the drive. If she continued on Amboy Road past the cutoff, there were thirty-nine more miles of absolutely nothing but straight road and desert, until the Mountain Springs Road entrance to the same Interstate 40. This was his playground and cemetery all rolled into one. For a moment, he had a sudden feeling of melancholy. For a split second, a vision of his having to leave his territory appeared in his mind, causing a visceral reaction. He shook his head and noticed he had dropped back while preoccupied. He took another couple of tokes and raised the volume up to earsplitting levels as the song "Comfortably Numb" began. He began to accelerate and reached 115 miles per hour with ease. He put the window down and took a blast of hot air, which increased his rush tremendously. He focused on the Infiniti, which was now less than a third of a mile away. Suddenly he saw brake lights from the distance, with the vehicle slowing down quickly. Then it veered to the right off the shoulder and onto the desert floor, with sand and cacti flying into the air as the vehicle came to a dead stop.

He lowered the radio to less than jet-level decibels and switched on his emergency blinkers. He slowed down and pulled off the road. He saw that the right front tire of the Infiniti was shredded, with the rim in the soft sand. It had probably saved her from rolling over. *Maybe the engineering wasn't so bad after all*, he thought. He shut the engine off and stepped out of his truck slowly. He walked to the driver's door, and the window slowly rolled down. He took his sunglasses off, revealing his soft, baby blue eyes, rugged face, and strong chin. His muscles, taut and well-defined, exploded from his T-shirt.

"Oh thank God, you stopped," she began almost hysterically. "The tire blew, and I don't know how I didn't roll. This isn't my vehicle. My sister is going to kill me."

"Let me take a look, see if it's just a blown tire, make sure there is no structural damage," he replied as he walked by the window around the front of the hood. She watched every move that he made, and he enjoyed the attention. He instinctively tightened his muscles more, causing the feathers in his sleeves of color to have the appearance of movement. His six-foot-five-inch frame was always a blessing when it came to women, as long as he stayed in shape like he was now. He knew she wanted him badly He was her knight in shining armor. He tightened his forearm muscles more and watched her eyes follow. He stood in front of the tire and saw that half of the rim was buried in sand. What was left of the cheap Continental tire was shredded. The rim, drum, and front-end chassis were undamaged.

He heard the driver's door open and close on the SUV. Then her footsteps in the sand came around the back end. He stood up to meet her, standing a good ten inches above her. He put his hands in his front pockets as she came closer.

"Ummm… did you f-f-find anything?" She stuttered at first, trying to catch her composure.

"It's just a blown tire. I can get it fixed for you in no time. Why don't you take the keys to my vehicle, climb in, start her up, and get the AC running while I take care of things?" he said to her so sincerely while dangling the keys.

"My name is Cherie." She extended her hand. "I don't know how to begin to thank you." She was now openly flirting as she plucked the keys from his hand.

"We'll figure that out later. Let me get done before it gets any hotter out here." Never giving his name, and she didn't pursue it.

"Okay" was all she said as she almost skipped back to her door, opened it, and pulled the keys out of the ignition. She threw them playfully over the hood, and he caught them with ease, smiling back at her. "The Dodgers could use you," she said, biting her lower lip.

"I'm a Giants fan" was all he said.

"Not everyone is perfect." She almost giggled as she easily climbed into his cab. God, the firmness of her thighs could be seen through her pants. She smiled. "Like I gave a shit about your fucking smile," he said under his breath. But he smiled back with an Eric Estrada smile and a wave. He was absolutely amazed how easy it was to lure prey into his domain.

Without touching her vehicle, he went to the bed of his truck and opened up the bed cover. He opened his ice cooler and pulled out two liter bottles of water. He walked back around to the passenger's side, and she opened the door, a blast of cold air hitting him. "Thought you'd be thirsty," he said as he handed her the water.

"Thanks so much, for everything. It smells like a roach in here," Cherie began. "Do you have some weed?"

He reached into his pocket, removed his tin box, and pulled out a perfectly rolled "fattie."

"Train wreck," he said, alluding to the species of marijuana. She took the joint and he pulled out his Zippo lighter. "Two tokes and you're good," he said as she inhaled a third of the joint on the first toke. "I see you've done this before," he said with a sexy grin. She bit her lower lip, then let out a cloud of bluish smoke, followed by coughing spasms.

She raised both thumbs, the universal sign for "good shit," as she coughed again, more fiercely. "Whoa," she said as she slowly caught her breath. She leaned back in the seat and closed the door. He turned around and felt the blast of the day's heat again. He knew it would hit greater than 115 today, which would cut his day short. He made his way to the front of her Infiniti and bent down in the shade of the vehicle, looking at the right front suspension again; he noticed the crack in the tie-rod. This vehicle wasn't going anywhere without a tow. The sweat began to form on his brow as he stood up again and made a disappointed gesture by shaking his head. He made his way back to his truck and climbed into his seat.

"There's more damage than I first noticed," he said flatly, but with a hint of understanding.

"What does that mean?" she asked as she leaned back against the passenger seat, relaxed.

"It means you need a tow," he said.

"Shit, that's what I thought you meant. It's my sister's SUV, and I'm driving it to Laughlin, where she's getting married," she said, now tearing up. "I'm her maid of honor, and I have her wedding dress and all of the bridesmaid's gowns with me. I need to get them there. To add insult to injury, there's no cell-phone service out here."

He shook his head in agreement. "Listen, I just live up the hill above Amboy," he said. "I have a landline there. You can call for a tow and call your sister. Then we'll come back for the gowns, and I'll drive you to Laughlin."

Her face lit up like the sun. "You would do that for me?" she asked. "What's the price?" she asked with a sly grin on her face.

"My price just went up, I figure," he said as he put the truck in gear and pulled forward slowly, making sure not to get buried in any soft areas of the desert. He also had a smile on his face, but the bright façade could not hide the evil burning inside of him, screaming to come out. She leaned toward him as she began the sexual ritual dance. What she didn't see coming was his huge right fist as he threw a short straight right jab, which caught her flush on the left side of her chin. The blow knocked her unconscious as she slammed back against the passenger door. He proceeded to drive to his special area. As he looked up into the bright hot sky, he noticed the first two birds of prey hovering above. He shook his head in amazement, as if they knew what was going to happen. But then again, they probably knew by seeing it so many times before.

CHAPTER 4

Phil's eyes were tired. Fourteen-hour days, getting paid for eight, was starting to wear thin on him. He still loved the job, but the loss of both his mother and father within the past two years had taken a lot of the wind out of his sails. He oftentimes dreaded that something bad was going to happen just as he was about to finally retire. He was within five years to full retirement; with the pension from the CHP and the living trust left from his parents, he could live the rest of his life in comfort. He would never be rich. His divorce took care of that. He always felt as if he were one inch away from the brass ring on the merry-go-round of life. His father put it best: "You were always a day late and a dollar short." He referred to Phil being born on January 1, so his father lost a full year of tax exemption, and therefore, a day late. When he was born, the doctor had turned out of his catcher's crouch for one minute to joke with the nurse, and out he popped. He hit the bucket, rim first.

Phil instinctively reached up to the small dent in the top of his head, a remnant of the fateful day. He smiled at the thought of his parents, old-fashioned Italians. He missed them, even though they often butted heads. He was never as good as his older brother, Tony, the doctor. An orthopedic surgeon to be exact, until a heart attack killed him at age forty-two. Or was it the cocaine that he began using again? Something his mother never knew about. Phil had made sure she never did, even on her deathbed when she wanted to know everything. He never ratted out his brother. It wasn't the way brothers were, especially Italians. That was twenty years ago.

His daydreaming was broken suddenly by a flash from his left, something off the road. He slowed the vehicle down and looked in the rearview mirror to make sure there were no oncoming cars.

He turned on the spotlight and pointed it at the vehicle that appeared to be embedded in the desert sand. Hanging from the rearview mirror was a heart-shaped crystal. He now knew where the flash came from. He pulled his vehicle off the road and as far as he could on the hard desert floor until the sand began to soften, and stopped. The last thing he wanted was to have to call for a tow for his own car. He got out and focused the spotlight so that the entire vehicle was glowing. He pulled out his big Maglite and focused on the tire tracks in the sand. The first thing he noticed was the different, larger set that appeared about thirty feet from the embedded SUV and headed back toward the road. Hopefully a Good Samaritan had stopped and aided the stranded motorist. He walked around the vehicle and saw the right front tire shredded, with the wheel drum deep in the sand. *Lucky it didn't roll over*, he thought as he stood up.

He walked around the rear of the vehicle and stopped dead in his tracks as his flashlight shone into the back compartment. There were suitcases and garment bags still inside. But what caught his eye was a large white box with the name "Vera Wang," which had all of the appearance of something important, like a wedding gown. No woman in her right mind would leave it behind. He tried the doors, all locked. Using the other end of the flashlight, he broke the passenger side window and opened up the door, avoiding the shattered glass. He entered and looked around; sweet fragrance confirmed his suspicions of this being a woman's vehicle. He opened up the glove compartment and found the registration. Lisa Stevens from Grenada Hills was what the registration said. He closed the door and went back to his vehicle. He cued up his laptop and entered the name and address. The license popped up with the picture. He was struck with how beautiful she was. Now he was really worried. He picked up the mike and called dispatch. "This is Lieutenant DiMarco. I have a disabled Infiniti FX35, eight miles east of Kilbaker Road on Amboy Road," Phil said. "This may be a crime scene. Wait to tow it in the morning; for now have a crew come out and take a look. Tell them the broken window is on me."

"I'll let them know, Lieutenant" Molly's joyful voice at night was a blessing. "And I won't tell you the score of the game."

"Thank you," he said, wanting to not know so he could watch his DVR when he got home. He sat there entering a short version of a D5 form, detailing his findings, so the

CSI crew would know what they were looking for, especially any information on the second vehicle. It had to be a raised pickup with oversized tires, just by the depth and width of the tire size compared to the Infiniti's. He stepped out again to take a look at the tracks and noticed two sets of footprints near the tire tracks. While bending down to further inspect, he heard the roar of an approaching engine, a throaty sound, but saw nothing. He ran back to his vehicle just in time to feel and finally see the black Shelby Cobra 500 roar past him at over one hundred miles per hour, with no lights on.

"Danny," he yelled out to the shadow of the car as if he could hear him. Then Phil jumped into his vehicle, started it up, and slowly turned around so as not to disturb a possible crime scene. Within seconds he was topping the century number himself, his high beams and light bar flashing as he climbed above 110 miles per hour, but still could not close the distance. He knew that Danny knew this road better than anyone, but this was beyond crazy. He grabbed the mike, steadying the car with his left hand only, and immediately had Molly on the other end. "I have Danny flying westbound on Amboy Road," he shouted with the adrenaline rush. "Black Cobra 500, lights off. I need someone from the other direction, and see if the helicopter can get up in the air." He threw the mike down as Molly replied, "Got it, Lieutenant"

His eyes focused now at the dark shadow as he closed the distance finally. After seven miles, he was now only a quarter mile behind. Suddenly the lights on the Cobra came on, and Phil knew why. This part of Amboy was overdue for repairs and had some pretty good-sized potholes. That was something you didn't want to hit at over a hundred, especially in the dark. Danny's speed slowed down to a reasonable eighty as he passed Roy's Café, made famous by an amputated finger found in French fries in the movie *The Hitcher* starring Rutger Hauer. He took the left turn at the outskirts of town onto Twentynine Palms Highway. *He's going home*, Phil thought. With the slowed speed as they began the three-thousand-foot ascent over the mountains surrounding the desert floor, Phil was able to get his cell phone out and called Mike.

"Mike, I got him in my headlights; we're just beginning the climb over the Sleep Hole Mountains," Phil said.

"He's coming home, Phillie boy," Mike said. The use of Phil's boyhood nickname meant "Don't hurt him" in his old Bronx neighborhood.

"I won't try to hurt him, but he's going too fast for this road, so I'm going to have to hang up now." Phil saw the Cobra starting up the tortuous turns at the crest of the road. What he didn't see was any brake lights, and that really scared him. Phil was doing ninety-five on the straightaway past the old salt fields just before the crest, but already was decelerating to sixty-five to take the upcoming snake turns. He had closed within one-eighth mile of Danny, but then began losing ground as Danny continued at eighty. At the last second he saw Gina Marie's head pop up in the rear window, facing backward, grabbing onto seat-belt straps, a look of total fear on her face.

"Oh my God," Phil yelled as he saw her body suddenly tossed like a rag doll as Danny whipped suddenly to the right, inertia taking her the opposite way. He knew the back end of the car was just a drop-down platform seat, with no comfort or padding for what was happening. Visions of ejection flew through his mind. He almost put his fingernails through the steering wheel. The intensity of the situation was beyond any realm of sanity. The hairs on the back of Phil's neck were all at attention, something not good at his age.

Clearing the S-curves, Phil's fears increased as Danny began the descent down the other side of the mountains, gaining speed rapidly. He was definitely back above a hundred, and the lights went off again. "Shit," Phil said as he floored the gas pedal. The front end reared up, and the engine's response was immediate, with the digital speedometer going through numbers at warp speed until settling on 115. At that point Phil felt a slight shimmy in the front and backed off the gas pedal until the car felt more solid. He was losing ground to the Cobra, however, and there was nothing he could do to improve his speed without risking going airborne.

"Shit," he barked as he pounded his left foot on the floor in frustration.

Suddenly in the dark miles ahead, multiple flashing lights could be seen as the cavalry was coming from Twentynine Palms. They were about ten miles away, but they were a sight for sore eyes, lighting up the desert floor like reflections off a disco ball, dancing about as the cars closed fast. But what made Phil's heart pound was the sight of the two Bell helicopters, intense magnesium searchlights glowing, zooming past the ground patrol. It felt like Viet Nam all over again.

Suddenly the Cobra's brakes lit up the road almost three-quarters of a mile ahead as Danny probably realized he was screwed, Phil thought. "Oh shit, what's he doing now?" Phil screamed as he saw the headlights turn on and the car make a sharp left turn and disappear from sight.

"Charlie 5 to 1 Baker 9, come in, Phil," the radio squawked with Mike McDougal's voice. Mike was the best helicopter pilot in Nam. He had pulled many men out of the shit when others wouldn't dare. He had taken some hits and was wounded twice by enemy fire, but gave more back by completing all of his missions. He ended the war highly decorated, but disillusioned with the entire war, as most veterans were. As soon as his two-year hitch was up, he left the Marines and never looked back. He never stopped flying, just either did it on his own or with the CHP. In between, he rode his long board at Oceanside Beach, known as the "Great Wise One" to the much younger surfers. Always knew exactly which wave was the best and hardly ever wiped out. "Where the hell is he going?" Mike asked.

Phil grabbed the microphone. "I think he's in one of the washes, heading south toward Joshua Tree National Park."

"I'll find him and hold him for you, Phil. I don't want to see anything happen to Danny, either," Mike said.

"It's Gina Marie I'm worried about," Phil said. "If Danny wants to kill himself, that's between him and God, but don't involve her," he growled through clenched teeth.

"Gotcha. Let me shank out of here; yak at ya later." Mike signed off as Phil watched him bank the helicopter in a left-to-right arc, the second chopper flanking him to the left. Phil slowed down as he approached the spot where Danny had turned, and waited for the other vehicles to arrive. When they were within a quarter mile, he slowly made the same left turn and entered one of the hundred dry washes formed over years by flash floods, and baked in the summer by 125-degree heat. Some of them were as wide as fifty feet, with the bed of the wash harder and flatter than cement roads. Phil turned on his bright lights and pointed his own spotlight straight ahead, watching for any sudden potholes, surprisingly finding none. He did see the tire tracks left by the Cobra, amazingly straight, even though Danny was again driving at a markedly higher rate of speed.

Then, up ahead, Phil saw the two helicopters stop and begin hovering, slowly descending, lights all ablaze on a single point. The Cobra was at a dead stop. Phil accelerated and began leaving a large plume of dust trail, plunging the officers behind him almost blind. He didn't care. Within thirty seconds he pulled up to the black car, and the first thing he noted was the open driver's side door. No sign of Danny. Phil unhitched the pump shotgun mounted on his dashboard and slowly opened the door. He pumped the shotgun once as he called out over the thumping of the helicopter blades, "Danny, it's Phil DiMarco, can you hear me?" But no answer was heard. With the gun pointed in the direction of the car, Phil carefully approached from the passenger side. First thing he did was check the backseat, and his heart almost stopped when he saw Gina lying unconscious on the cramped floor in the back. Phil's instincts took over as he ran around to the other side, still with the shotgun pointed forward. He quickly looked in front to make sure Danny wasn't hiding. Seeing nothing, he released the latch, and the driver's seat pulled forward. He felt for a pulse, which was rapid and thready. She was in shock, and he had no time.

As gently and carefully as he could, Phil lifted Gina Marie, restraining her head and neck with his massive hands against his chest as he carried her away from the car. He immediately saw one of the helicopters descending and landing five hundred feet away to prevent a dust storm. Phil quickly paced himself, trying not to stir Gina, who had not moved, but whose breathing was shallow. Tears were forming in his eyes as he prayed for her life. Suddenly the figure of McDougal in flight helmet running from the chopper brought a surreal flashback of over thirty years ago as they carried village children from harm's way to safety, only this time there were no bullets flying. "Is she okay?" Mike shouted over the thumping of blades.

"She's in shock, can't tell about internal injuries," Phil said as Mike ran alongside back toward the helicopter, bending over as they approached. Mike opened up the bay door and put down a backboard. He strapped it in, and laid sheets and blankets down in less than a minute, as Phil made his way up into the chopper and slowly put Gina Marie down. Rapidly Mike strapped her in, including a head/neck brace and restraint. He turned to Phil and barked, "Get out of here, and go find that idiot before he hurts himself, or some desert animal eats him. I'll be on Eisenhower Medical Center's roof in fifteen minutes, best trauma center. She'll be fine."

"Promise," said Phil as he jumped out of the chopper, but not before giving Mike a bear hug.

"Love ya, man. When you going to get back on your board?" Mike said as he climbed into his seat.

"You know life, sooner or later," Phil replied, slowly backing away, hunched over.

"Make it sooner, because there is never a later," Mike said, holding up the peace sign as he accelerated the engines. The blades rotated with such force that they almost blew Phil over as he was rapidly running back to his car, which had now been joined by the other black and whites. As Mike rapidly flew southwest toward the Palm Springs area, the second chopper was slowly making sweeps of the desert floor, the white magnesium light illuminating the black night like an Ansel Adams picture. He walked over to his fellow officers. Tonight it was Ramirez and Watson. They were also known as Mutt and Jeff from their height difference of ten inches, with Watson the taller.

"How do you want to handle this, Phil" Watson asked in his baritone voice, sounding like James Earl Jones. "I already called for a team to come out here."

"Thanks, Bob," Phil said, the exhaustion in his voice evident as he tried to think of the next move. "There's over five hundred square miles of open desert, and we have one human on foot in the dead of night. Start with the car and find footprints that aren't mine pointing away from the car, Tommy," he said as he looked at Ramirez. Tommy nodded and pointed his Maglite toward the area of the car. He began to walk, slowly sweeping the light back and forth. Phil and Bob stared at the helicopter, still doing its arcing sweep, going farther away. The silence began to return.

"You okay?" Bob asked Phil as they turned back toward the Cobra, watching Ramirez do his ground sweep.

"I'm just tired, Bob," Phil said. "I just wanted to get home tonight, catch the ball game. Now I may never see my bed tonight." Phil slumped back against his car. Bob, a good three inches taller than Phil's six foot three inches, leaned his elbow on the roof and stared down at Phil.

"I feel sorry that you won't see your bed tonight, but I'm not sorry that my Giants beat the crap out of your Dodgers tonight, 10 to zip. Cain threw a two-hitter." His smile was bigger than ever.

"Fuck you, Bob," Phil said, shaking his head. "No sense going home tonight even if we catch Danny in the next five minutes, thank you very much," Phil said with a bit of anger, but Bob's laughter grew contagious, and soon they were both laughing. "By the end of the year, we'll see," Phil said finally, and their conversation was cut short by the call of Ramirez, who was about a hundred feet beyond the Cobra, to the right. "Over here," he said.

They quickly got to the spot. Ramirez was on his knees, with the flashlight pointing at a fresh sneaker print in a patch of soft sand. Ramirez was half Comanche and was known to be able to track anything.

"He's heading straight toward Joshua Tree, probably in the wash that runs directly through the Pinto Mountains," Ramirez said, pointing the flashlight toward the wash, which was about fifty feet from them. "He knows this area all too well."

Phil looked at Bob. "Go back to the car, call the chopper, tell him to fly back to us, and pick up the wash," he said. Bob ran back to the car as quickly as possible and was on the radio within seconds. Ramirez stood up. "What were you two laughing about back there?" he asked.

"He told me the score of the Dodgers game, pissed me off; he likes to get under my skin." Phil chuckled at the thought.

"He sure does," Ramirez said, smiling, "especially since the fucking game was rained out up north. He got you good."

"All I can say, Tommy, is karma," Phil said as they watched the helicopter swing around and head back their way. He swept over them as Bob joined the two of them and handed Phil the portable radio as the three stared off at the bird. Within five minutes the helicopter stopped and began hovering in a spot about a mile away. The radio squawked as Phil pressed the button to listen.

"I have a body that appears to have fallen into a ravine, about twenty-five feet deep, motionless, male, mid-twenties, long blond hair in sweats, sneakers," the pilot, John Shockey, said. "I'm going to call for a medevac from the base to come out with a rescue squad. Is that okay, Lieutenant?"

"Yeah… that's fine," Phil said quietly, rubbing the back of his neck, the tension rising rapidly with each moment.

He stared at the helicopter, its blades silhouetted against the starry sky, seeming to move in slow motion, as in the movies. Phil's mind was already preparing for the worst. If Danny has died, he had to personally tell Mike that he died while being chased by Phil. Would Mike ever forgive him? Would Phil lose another in the long line of friends and family, who had either died or considered Phil dead? He looked away from the chopper, directly above, seeking reverence and solace. "If you could grant me one wish, dear Lord, please…," and the rest of his prayer was said silently.

Within ten minutes, the unique sound of multiple military helicopters could be heard coming from behind the three cops, and they each turned in unison, but saw nothing until Ramirez shouted, "There," and pointed to three silhouettes moving rapidly about fifty feet above Amboy Road. Marine Rescue Squad from the Twentynine Palms marine base could be seen flying with night goggles only, no lights. Part rescue mission, part training exercise, or they were just playing for the crowd. "Show-offs." John's voice could be heard through the radio.

"Jealous?" Phil asked.

But he never heard the answer as the three large Sykorsky helicopters flew directly over the police cars, shaking the ground as they passed, blowing everything away in their paths. Ramirez and Watson ducked as they passed, but not Phil. He stood, admiring them, his pride swelling. Once in the corps, you are always a marine, a family unto itself. If anyone could rescue Danny and save his life, it was the marines. Suddenly his thoughts were broken as the three beasts turned on their own spotlights, bigger and brighter than John's. They slowed as they approached John's position, with John withdrawing, allowing them space to operate.

Phil watched the blades closely as the three choppers hovered, appearing like gears pushing each other along. Suddenly three lines were tossed out and dropped down into the ravine, followed by three marines rappelling into the deep pit. Phil held his breath, waiting for the news. Thirty seconds seemed like two hours, until John's excited voice could be heard: "He's alive, Phil, he's alive. They're going to board him, start an IV, and get him out of there. Hoo-rah."

"Hoo-rah," Phil answered and did a little dance. He pulled out his cell phone and dialed Mike. "Mikey..." and Phil told him what happened. "We don't know the extent of his injuries, or Gina Marie's," he finished.

"Thank you, Phillie, I owe you big-time," Mike said.

"No, Mike, tut e la familiglia," Phil said.

"Bene, graci," Mike replied.

"Ciao," Phil said and hung up. Relieved for the first time tonight, he watched the rest of the rescue unfold in awe from a mile away. He turned to Ramirez and Watson. "I'm going home; cordon off the area, and we'll finish up tomorrow." With that he turned and walked slowly to his car, the fatigue starting to settle in rapidly. His thoughts were totally focused on one thing, and that was just how good his bed would feel to him tonight.

Tomorrow he would check on Gina Marie's condition—and get even with Bob Watson.

CHAPTER 5

The morning sun was already scorching the Southern California desert, with most reptiles tucked away in their holes, avoiding the dangers of hyperthermia. Sometimes their primal instincts were smarter than the advanced brain of man. The air was at a standstill; not even a whisper of a breeze could be felt. With the stagnation, higher levels of pollution began to build, giving the air a slightly sour smell. He had noticed it earlier as he was loading up his truck with his next package to be delivered to his personal cemetery. He usually didn't hang onto the packages long, but this one was special, not because she was more beautiful or sensual than the others, but because of who she was. He was changing his method of operation by knowing the victim's identity, but in this case it was necessary.

He pulled the body bag to the left side of the truck bed and made room for his cooler, tool chest, pick, shovel, and assorted weapons. He was feeling frisky. He needed to keep up his shooting skills, especially with long-range rifles. He was the best sniper ever trained by the Marine Corps, but it had been a while since he had honed his skills. He had several targets and areas already under consideration, but the timing had to be just right. First he had to bury her remains, and he wanted to get that done before the day's heat was unbearable, even for him. He looked down at the body bag and smiled as he closed the bed cover and secured the locks.

Not only had she been enamored with his size and physique (not an ounce of fat on his body), but she had loved his "killer" blue eyes. They all did. This one had as many tattoos as he had, but done with taste. He had been impressed. But not as impressed as she was with his. When she asked him how long it took to finish, his answer shook her. "It's not done," he said as he spread his arms their full six-foot-three wingspan to his six-foot-five frame and made the hawk appear to be ready to fly, wings fully spread, feathers ruffled.

"Why is it not done?" Maria asked as he slowly turned and walked toward her, lifting her five-foot-five-inch frame off the bed gently and held her under the arms. He pulled her up toward him and stared into her dark brown eyes, smiled, and asked, "Do you really want to know?" She tilted her head slightly, naïve to a point, but she had served her purpose. "Why not?" she asked, so innocently. He laughed and held her like a fine porcelain doll. His arms were held at 105 degrees at the elbows, lessening the strain on his biceps even though his muscles were in the best shape of his life. She smiled shyly, her tongue slightly protruding. He held her there while thinking of an appropriate answer.

He knew her cousin, knew who her cousin worked for. He had told her that her cousin's boss and he had been friends from the corps. With his size and jarhead cut, she had no problems believing him, going willingly with him to his house for a "nooner" before finishing her shopping for her kid's birthday party. He'd make sure she'd make it in time. She was Hispanic, late twenties, with that pear-shaped Mexican ass, and was wilder than most of his conquests. He had actually enjoyed it and wished he didn't have to do what he had to do. She was going to be his biggest prize so far in his game that had been going on for years. It would send a bewildering message to any profiler, and especially to her cousin's boss—Lieutenant Philip DiMarco.

He refocused his thoughts, and his smile quickly disappeared, replaced by a face of stone, eyes staring through her. She tensed immediately, realizing her worst nightmare and the huge mistake she had made. He smiled again, but this time an evil one as he said in a hushed voice, "Because each feather represents someone I have killed." His eyes turned dark with evil, a scowl on his face. "And I'm not done killing yet." Her eyes were wide in fear as he said, "You'll make number 162."

Before she could scream, he jerked her body like a rag doll, forcefully forward first, then reversing, the head snapping backward. With more force, he repeated the human press seven times. Finally he heard the telltale snap as the spinal cord severed off of the brain. Her body went instantly into a spastic position, hands flexed at the wrist, ankles hyperextended and inverted. This was the final sign of spinal and, ultimately, human death.

He was happy with the result.

He checked his watch, a little after seven in the morning. He didn't want anyone to steal his prize. He laughed at the thought. He opened the garage door, got into the cab, and roared the Hemi engine to life. He checked the various weapons he was carrying, including his favorite, a Walther PPK 45 millimeter with silencer in the console, and just in case he felt like hunting, a vintage Henry rifle behind his seat. Finally, in the truck bed was a 50 caliber long-range sniper rifle with tripod base, courtesy of Uncle Sam, with which he could make a kill from over 1,500 yards to one and a half miles.

Satisfied with his arsenal, he pulled out of his garage and waited for the door to close before leaving his desert paradise in the hills above Twentynine Palms. Wanting to avoid the middle of town, he approached Two-Mile Road and waited to make the left-hand turn as an approaching black and white CHP vehicle passed him on the right, heading into downtown. He noticed the "Out of Service" sign on the back as it passed with a mechanic driving. He smiled to himself at the irony as he made the left turn.

Too bad it wasn't him, he thought. He could have really fucked with his head.

The more he thought about it, the more he was convinced to move his timetable up a month. The feeling of dire consequences if he didn't was starting to gnaw at him, just like it had ten years earlier. He had killed fourteen in less than one year, all long-range sniper shots. When his sixth sense hit him, like it was now, it was time to pull up camp and escape. That way someone else would take the fall, because law enforcement had to blame someone or suffer the political backlash, especially when that someone was framed. He smiled again, this time laughing, recalling the arrest, trial, conviction, and lethal injection of the East Coast Sniper.

The wrong man got the needle.

He relocated and started all over again, this time changing his targets and method of execution. Only one person over all of these years had insisted that the FBI had convicted the wrong man, but they never listened to him. So for the last ten years, he had been hunting in his enemy's backyard, which was the last place anyone would look.

He laughed as he made his turn, driving out of the city toward his personal cemetery and two hours of hard labor. At least it kept him in shape.

CHAPTER 6

"I'm so tired, I haven't slept a wink, I'm so tired, my mind is on the blink." John Lennon's voice was singing the lyrics, but Phil felt like he was speaking for him. He was exhausted, both physically and mentally. He had tossed and turned for the entire four hours of sleep that he could get. His mind kept reliving the events of the night, finally seeing his bed by 3:00 a.m. He remembered watching the red digital numbers on his alarm clock jump in sets of twenty minutes as he slept in intervals. He would jerk awake for a moment after the recurring nightmare of seeing Danny's disfigured body in the infirmary on the base. He was stabilized there before being ambulanced to Eisenhower Medical Center. The same place poor Gina Marie was. She still was in a coma, a subdural hematoma caused by her being tossed around like a dog's toy. Then he would be back asleep, but never into the deeper stages.

"I'm getting too old for this shit," he quoted Danny Glover from *Lethal Weapon*, speaking to the mirror as he shaved. He looked into his bloodshot eyes, dark circles underneath, turkey neck, and thinning salt and pepper hair, all which had come on within the last two years. Mornings like today made him wish for a faster way to retirement.

"Five more fucking years, if I make it," he said, looking up to the ceiling as he shaved his neck, talking to his late brother, who had dropped dead twenty years earlier at the age of forty-two. "God, I wish you were here," he said, and lowered his head and began to cry. It only lasted fifteen seconds, but it felt good. He still missed him dearly, especially when today would have been his sixty-fifth birthday.

He cleaned up, finished getting into his uniform, but kept the forty-pound gun and paraphernalia belt off because his lower back was killing him. As he slowly straightened up, he realized a good program of exercise was lacking as the pounds began to increase. He would start tomorrow, his official first day of a five-day holiday, his first in three years. Boy, did he need it, even if he just did all of the repairs around the house that needed attention. Suddenly he stopped in mid-thought. Murphy's Law was knocking at the back of his brain, telling Phil something was about to ruin his vacation. He shook it off and grabbed a large thermos and go-cup of coffee and left the house.

The first steps out of the front door into the morning air were like walking into an oven that was just beginning to warm. In the ten years that he had lived there, it definitely was slowly getting hotter. That also would change when he retired, as he planned to move much farther north, possibly Oregon, where he would spend his retirement golfing and fishing. His daydream was broken as he arrived at the adobe-style station house, his home away from home for the past decade. Good people worked there, from top to bottom. They truly respected their job and the law. They were truly his second family, just a little more dysfunctional than his first.

He entered the station, stopped at the desk sergeant's area, got his mail, and said hi to everyone as he went upstairs to his office, his ten-foot-by-ten-foot space with a window. He was greeted by Mirabel Santos, his office daughter. "You look like shit, Lew," she said, now acting like his office mother.

The problem was, she was right, he looked horrible. His reflection in the office glass showed his pallor color, the same color his brother had just before dropping dead.

"Any news on that abandoned Infiniti?" he asked as he ignored any further conversation about his health.

"Yes and no," Mirabel said with a one-sided frown.

"What's that supposed to mean?" he said with a scowl, as he was not in the mood for mysteries.

"We have the identity of the driver, a Cherie Morton," Mirabel said, "who is the sister of the owner, but there was no report of a stolen vehicle. However, just fifteen minutes ago, we got an update of a missing person's report for the same person, whose last whereabouts headed her in this direction."

"Who was it filed by?" Phil asked, his attention now on full alert.

"Her sister, who expected her in Laughlin two nights ago," Mirabel said.

"You mean that vehicle was sitting out there for a whole day and night and no one reported anything? Who canvassed that area the last few days?" Phil was now pissed. "The woman could be wandering the desert, or worse."

"It was…" Mirabel furiously worked the keyboard, going through yesterday's duty roster. "Ben Johanson." She hesitated, then added, "His wife had a baby girl last night; maybe he was a little preoccupied."

Phil's facial expression basically said bullshit, but his soft side surfaced and let that part slide. "Coordinate with whoever is handling missing persons; get out pictures, have an APB to all units for Cherie Morton. Has the crime scene unit been out there yet?" Mirabel shook her head no. "It's already eight fifteen, and it'll be 120 degrees out there in no time." For some reason, Phil's gut began to churn, as if he had lived through this before and worse things were about to follow. "You have any Pepto?" He looked at Mirabel, who was already opening her upper desk drawer, pulling out the tablets and handing four to Phil. "Thank you. If it wasn't for you, I'd be lost." He meant it, and she knew it, but never took advantage. Theirs was truly a father and daughter relationship, without any genetics involved. Mirabel had often told Phil that besides her own father, the only other man she respected as much was Phil. He was humbled. Her father had worked three jobs to put four kids through college. Phil had always been a cop, and his three kids had to pay their own way through school. He helped when he could, but forever felt guilty.

"I'm going to take a ride out there myself. Get the lab rats on the horn. Tell them from me that if they are not out at that Infiniti within one and a half hours and I'm baked in the heat, I'll be really pissed off," he said. "They know what happened the last time I got pissed at them." Mirabel nodded yes at the mention of Black Friday, when three people were fired, and she was on the phone as Phil was leaving.

It took Phil less than forty-five minutes to reach the abandoned vehicle, especially with his light bar flashing and his average speed of ninety miles per hour. As he approached the SUV, he parked a good five hundred feet away on the shoulder of Amboy Road. He sat in the ice-cold air-conditioned interior of his Charger, seeing the outside temperature registering at 109 degrees, and it was only 9:09 a.m. He turned the engine off and did a scientific experiment of how long it took for the heat inside to become unbearable. Within five minutes, the interior's temperature had risen ten degrees. He turned the engine and air-conditioning back on, ran it for three minutes, and shut it off one last time. From the corner of his eye, he saw the CSI crew approaching from a mile away in his side-view mirror. Phil smiled at the thought of how persuasive Mirabel could be.

He stepped out of the car and realized that no matter how many times he had experienced it, the heat blasted him within seconds, and the sweat began to pour. He went to the trunk and got out his wide-brim cavalry hat and two bottles of water from a cooler. He opened the first bottle, chugged three quarters of it down, and poured the rest over his hat and finally his head before putting the hat back on. He already felt ten degrees cooler. The crew pulled up in their Chevy Tahoe and parked twenty-five feet behind Phil. The doors opened, and both the crew chief, Don Silvestri, and the first in line for his job, Ned Bountrie, emerged from the SUV. They reacted just like Phil, each drinking water as they walked toward him.

"To what do I owe the pleasure of your distinguished service, Batman and Robin?" The reference of the well-known nicknames for the pair brought a smile from each of them.

"When Mirabel explained the circumstances, I felt it was necessary for the boss to show how it's done," Don said.

Phil laughed and patted both of them on their backs as they walked together with Phil in between toward the vehicle. They all stopped as they saw the beginning of the tire marks, and the deeper groove from the rim after the tire was shredded, heading toward the Infiniti, which stood about 250 feet away.

"It's amazing the vehicle didn't roll, going over small sand mounds like it did and at a high rate of speed," Ned said as they examined the tracks more closely.

"Good design, with proper weight distribution and better defensive suspension systems on board to help even amateur drivers," Ned continued.

"There's another set of tracks, almost parallel, to the left—monster meat tires." Phil pointed to the left. "I saw the same tracks near the Infiniti last night, but it was too dark to follow"—not to mention Danny, but Phil let that issue stay dead. They followed both tracks until they noticed the big meat tracks stopped about seventy-five feet from the Infiniti. They also saw the footprints in the sand.

"This may be the first time I don't complain about there being no breeze," Don said as they each focused and followed the different prints. "One is definitely a woman's shoe, about a seven cross-trainer, probably New Air from the design," Ned said.

"The other prints are huge, and look like boots," Don chimed in, "probably fifteens, triple E," as he and Ned followed them farther. Phil stayed frozen, staring at the huge print. "There are more coming and going from the Inf..." Don stopped mid-sentence as he saw that Phil hadn't moved, frozen in time, staring down. "Lew, you okay?" Don asked as he walked back.

"I know this footprint," Phil said quietly so Ned couldn't hear.

"What?" Don looked at Phil quizzically. "Is the heat getting to you?"

"You were right, size 15 EEE, Marine-issued boots," Phil said as he stared out into the desert and beyond. "I wonder how many he's buried out there," Phil said as he gestured toward the vast emptiness around them.

"What the hell are you talking about, Lew?" Don asked, now more worried by Phil's strange trancelike state.

"He's back, and he's hunting," Phil said as he looked straight into Don's eyes.

A lightbulb went off in Don's head; his eyes now recognized Phil's worry.

"I thought he was executed," Don said.

Phil looked at Don with disdain. "How many times have I said they juiced the wrong guy?" Phil asked.

"At least twenty times," Don replied and then lowered his head, looking at the print again. "If it is, Lew, we're in a heap of cow manure. This whole desert could be his graveyard."

"That's why he was wearing the boots; he was expecting to do some digging that day," Phil explained. "Best thing in the world is a good old Marine combat boot to push a shovel into Mother Earth."

They both looked at each other. "We're going to be in a world of hurt," Phil said as he rubbed the back of his neck, knowing his "vacation" was about to be indefinitely postponed. "This is a murder scene until proven otherwise. Get every little scrap of evidence you can, including a cement cast of this," Phil said with a growl, pointing at the perfect 15 EEE print. "I'm going to finally nail that motherfucker, and not let some bullshit judge throw a good collar out on a technicality."

Phil turned, walked back toward his car, drained the rest of the now-warm water, and took out his cell phone. It was time to call in help, so they didn't claim prejudice later. He hit the name on his list, and within three rings, a raspy voice answered. "The only time you call me is when there's bad news, so what's it this time?"

"He's back," was all Phil said.

"No fucking way. He was juiced in Ohio seven years ago," the voice replied.

"I'm sending you a picture," Phil said as he maneuvered through the picture application, sending an instant footprint three thousand miles away. It only took fifteen seconds to hear the magical words.

"Oh shit, it can't be. Tell me, Phil, you're busting my balls," the voice answered, almost pleading.

"Sorry, Tony, it's like I've said all along. He'd wait awhile, than strike again, but you never listened. This may be just the tip of the iceberg," Phil said.

"I listened, but you didn't understand," Tony said.

"I understood, Tony, and I understand politics," Phil said sarcastically. "Well, there are no politics involved now. If this motherfucker is back and he's about to go into his next phase, all hell is going to break loose. And this time, I'm not going to let you or anyone get in my way."

"You do realize who you are speaking to?" Tony said with a condescending tone.

"Yes sir, Anthony Balducci, Assistant Director, FBI, sir," Phil said with even more sarcasm. "The same little fuckwad whose ass I saved from the Canal Street Dragons over thirty years ago."

"I'll be out there tomorrow. I'll fly into Twentynine Palms," Tony said. "I'll alert my local special agents; they'll be in touch with you. I'll call you when I land," Tony said and hung up.

Phil put his phone back into his pocket slowly as he recalled how the federal government, knowingly and willfully, framed an innocent man, then put him to death, against a backdrop of political gain. Those inside the Beltway could not admit the truth about the real killer, that they had trained him in the art of killing. Phil had known all along that the true monster who committed over thirty killings near the Washington DC area had never been caught. As he looked out over the vast expanse of the desert, he knew that other victims were lying out there. The question was, how many more times and in what fashion would he leave his mark in the sands this time.

CHAPTER 7

The black and white Chevy Tahoe passed him like he was standing still, red light on its roof rotating, as he slowed down and gave the vehicle room. He smiled to himself as he pulled over to the soft shoulder. He recognized the crime lab vehicle and knew where it was going. The cat-and-mouse game had now officially begun. He had left enough hints to cause specific responses to occur, probably disbelief at first, then denial, and finally acceptance. Their ignorance would lead to their own grief, with their cries of self-righteousness that would expose their hypocrisies. His actions would reveal their stupidity, with power and corruption at the core of leadership, first at the state, and finally the federal level of law enforcement.

He turned right at the next break in the monotonous desert scenery onto another small hard-packed dry riverbed that he used for a road. Throwing the transmission into four-wheel drive, the Bridgestone Dueler M/T oversize tires dug into the ground with a vengeance. With hardly any dust lying on the surface, the amount of cloud kicked up was minimal and could be mistaken for a "dirt devil." He also knew that the Infiniti was ten miles away, and that's where the crime lab techs' main focus would be for the next few hours at least.

He'd be finished by then anyway, and onto his next project. He was taught to always stay one step ahead of your enemy. One way was to plot counter defenses for all of their prospective responses. Military training at its finest, and he had the best the US government could afford. Now he was using that training against his mentors. Almost like a son revolting against his father, using the knowledge learned to outwit the teacher.

He reflected on his own father, a blur of a memory of a tall, soft-spoken man whose sad eyes reflected his troubled soul, even noticed by a nine-year-old. Betrayed by his wife, he took his own life the next year, saying good-bye just moments before walking into his bathroom and pulling the trigger. At the age of ten, he was left alone with his alcoholic, abusive mother, who cared more about her many boyfriends than her own son. He recalled the nights being locked in his room while she "entertained," often until one or two in the morning. Other times leaving him for an entire weekend alone, while she went away with one of her boyfriends, coming home to abuse him more for leaving a mess in the house. He looked at the small cigarette burn marks hidden within the tattoos on his arms, a reminder of those days. He also remembered his first tattoo, the first feather on his left arm, covering the most frequent burn area.

He had it done right after he had killed his mother.

He was thirteen years old, but at six feet with a slight beard, he could pass for eighteen. He could also drive, which he did to dispose of his mother's body, which was never found and hindered any prosecution of himself. He remembered the first time he looked straight into the eyes of his accusers and just smiled. That upset them more than anything. They knew he did it, but couldn't prove it, displaying their impotence in court. A child had outwitted all of them; the feeling of power that day helped fuel his thirst for so much more.

Now 162 bodies later, he was thoroughly enjoying the feeling of supremacy.

He was just beginning.

Someone had to pay for every day he had to endure the brutality of his childhood, when no one listened to his pleas for help.

Now cries for help would be answered, by him, and in no uncertain terms.

He reached his turnoff to his favorite spot. The sand here was slightly looser, which eased the digging tremendously, especially in this heat. As he pulled to a stop, he looked up and noticed two vultures already circling. Either he was getting too regimented, or they were smarter than he thought. He would definitely have to change his modus operandi.

He slowly opened the truck door, absorbing the difference in temperature gradually, instead of getting blasted. He looked out over the three acres of one of his burial grounds and knew that this would probably be his last here. It definitely was time to move on as he grabbed his shovel out of the truck bed, along with three bottles of water from his cooler. The plastic bag was beginning to cook the body, so time was of the essence. With his free hand, he lifted the 120-pound bag like it was a loaf of bread, and carried it at arm's length about seventy-five feet to his already arranged spot, exactly five feet from the last dig. He placed the bag down to the side, opened up the first bottle, drank its entire contents without stopping, wiped his mouth, and belched.

He stuck the end of the shovel in the sand and pushed with his right foot. The spade slid into the desert floor with ease. After five minutes he was three feet down, and the earth was cooler. He looked up, and now saw four buzzards circling. He increased his speed of digging, playing a beat-the-clock game in his mind. Within another seven minutes, he was satisfied with the depth and width, threw his shovel out, pulled himself out of the grave, picked up the bag, and tossed it into the hole. He opened up the second bottle of water and chugged it down. He then began the rapid filling of the grave. He was done in a total of seventeen minutes, and back into the air-conditioned cab of his truck. He drank the last bottle of water and fired up a joint. With Eric Clapton playing solo on "Sweet Wine," he put the truck in drive and drove east away from the main road. He would loop back north toward the mountains to the Devil's Playground, an elevated butte 1,500 feet above and a half mile south of Interstate 40.

He needed to practice his long-range shooting.

Phil looked over the area away from the Infiniti, more toward where the second truck had been parked. He followed the pattern of the footprints. He saw the length of the stride of the man wearing the Marine-issued boots and knew the leg length was at least thirty-six inches, which made him at least six foot five, and that added fuel to his burning fire. He also noticed that the smaller footprints had taken a direct route to the area and stopped, presumably to get into the truck. He also noticed the other, larger prints went around to the left, then right, around the back end of the truck. Phil walked to the area where the driver's side was, and looked down. There was just the larger boot prints found in the sand.

Phil stiffened with the realization that the other truck and this area may be the scene of the crime, not the Infiniti. He backed up immediately so as to not contaminate the scene. He whistled to Don Silvestri and waved at him to come over. When he arrived, Phil pointed out the print patterns.

"Are you thinking what I am?" Phil asked.

"Crime scene," Don said, and began to take numerous photographs to begin his investigation.

Phil backed up even farther and started to walk back toward his vehicle to get more water. He stopped in mid-stride as a feeling of the presence of evil enveloped him, which only went to confirm his earlier suspicions. The monster had truly returned.

He turned, looked off to the southeast, and saw six vultures circling high in the sky on their thermals, but in only one area. His mind began to race at the prospect of what they were hunting. Don noticed the same thing as Phil stood like a statue staring off into the distance. "Must be something big that died out there with that many vultures circling," he said. "Like a human being."

"Like many human beings," Phil said. He turned and walked quickly back to his vehicle. He got through to dispatch and asked for a flyover with a helicopter, giving a basic estimate of where the buzzards were circling.

Satan's scavengers would lead Phil to the killer's burial ground.

CHAPTER 8

As Phil drove back toward the station to meet up with one of the helicopter pilots to take a ride back out over that spot in the desert, his mind wandered through ancient history. Like Sherlock Holmes's Professor Moriarty, Phil had his own adversary. What concerned him was that no one was going to listen to him again, leaving his foe who was a sociopath, not a psychopath, more deadly, better equipped, and well-versed in all forms of killing. Even though he had been trained by the US government, he became a mercenary for hire, first as an assassin for the CIA and Britain's MI6, and then he went to Southeast Asia, both Cambodia and Laos, where he made multiple killings and plenty of money. No one ever saw him, with most dealings completed through untraceable phone calls and third parties who had never met the man.

Phil had met him many years ago, and he would never forget the hatred in his eyes that hid behind a smile. He was only thirteen years old, arrested for the killing of his abusive mother when Phil was with SFPD as a homicide detective. He was a huge kid even at that young age. In fact, he was as big as Phil, with a thicker beard, but always wore long-sleeve shirts to hide the cigarette burn marks on his arms. He was never convicted of the crime for lack of evidence, specifically that the body was never discovered. After the acquittal he entered the foster children's circle of nightmare families, until finally joining the Marines as soon as he turned eighteen. At six foot five, they turned him into a solid killing machine. Any weapon, any distance, he was considered the best.

He returned to the Bay Area in his full formal blue uniform two years later. Unbeknownst to Phil and his partner, John Androcelli, he had been secretly communicating with Gina Androcelli, John's daughter. They had known each other since sophomore year of high school before he had enlisted. He showed up that day at their house, unannounced. Gina threw herself into his arms, announcing to her father that she loved him and always had. John finally accepted him and gave him a chance. Phil didn't. He still had those eyes and that smile. They were all brethren of the corps, but Phil had a bad feeling about this one.

Finally, the day he was "shipping out to the base on the island of Okinawa," John questioned his intention with his daughter. He never answered—just stood at attention, saluted, and stared before leaving the house.

Three days later, John was murdered by a sniper, from long range, as he walked out of the Mission District Police Station in downtown San Francisco. Phil was coming out through the same door, fifty feet behind John. It was a pure head shot. As Phil rushed to his partner's lifeless body while chaos erupted around them, the one sound Phil thought he heard was an Indian war whoop in the distance from a rooftop. He would never forget that chant as it echoed through his brain.

His phone rang at that instant, breaking his rumination. Phil looked at the number and saw the call was from his own office phone. He answered. "Hello?"

"Hi, Uncle Phil." Gina's bubbly voice came through.

"Gina, I was just thinking about you. What are you doing in town?" Phil asked. He had stayed close to Gina after John had died, became her surrogate father; his kids became her second family. But he was always Uncle Phil to her. She had become a registered nurse, now working in the field of risk management, and still lived in the Bay Area. They saw each other usually once a year around the holidays. She was married to a loser, but had no kids. It was something Phil had wanted to talk to her about, not the kids but the loser.

"I had a conference to go to in Palm Springs, thought I'd surprise you. How about lunch?" she said.

Phil looked at his watch. It was now 11:00 a.m., an hour before the chopper would be ready. He hesitated to say anything, but after a millisecond pause, decided the truth was still the best. "That would be great, but we have to talk." His voice turned serious.

"You haven't impregnated anyone lately, have you?" she said with her dad's dry sense of humor.

"Frank's back," is all Phil said, and he heard Gina suck in all of the air in Phil's office. He then heard the phone being put down, and then his office door close. "Are you sure?" she said when she came back on the line.

"Yes," Phil said without hesitation.

"When will you be here?" she said, the seriousness reflected in her voice.

Phil punched the accelerator and turned on the lights. "Twelve minutes tops; just stay there, Mirabel will take care of you."

"Thank you, love you, Uncle Phil," she said.

"Love ya, Gina Theresa Androcelli," he said and hung up.

The desert passed him by at over a hundred miles per hour, a blurring combination of sand against bright blue sky. Phil's gut began to churn acid as his worries grew with each passing mile. He knew why Frank DiMocchio was back. He had said that much to Phil when he was thirteen years old and was walking out of court as a free person. "You'll never be able to prove anything, not now and not in the future, but I will," he had said, behind those evil eyes and that smile. It had sent shivers down Phil's spine. Now, he was an extremely dangerous assassin, with every tool at his disposal, who was also a serial killer, leaving no clues behind that he didn't want to be found. Frank was too careful, too methodical, leaving not a trace of himself at any of his kills, yet he had this time. Was he getting careless, accelerating his killing spree, beyond even his control, or was he attempting to go out in a blaze of glory?

Phil pulled into the CHP parking lot within eleven minutes. After securing his weapons with the desk sergeant, he ran upstairs to his office and found Gina and Mirabel talking like two old classmates, mostly about him. He felt a little embarrassed when they both stopped talking as he came within ten feet. Then they broke into spontaneous laughter simultaneously. Gina stood up, came over, and got up on her toes to give Uncle Phil a big hug. Standing at five foot four, she was almost a full foot shorter than he. He picked her up and they held each other tight. Tears formed in Phil's eyes.

"Are you getting soft on us, Lew?" Mirabel asked as Gina turned to wipe her own tears away.

"Are you getting nosy?" Phil asked Mirabel, and she wrinkled her nose as she returned to her work.

Phil led Gina into the office and motioned her to sit down. She hopped up onto the corner of his desk as Phil sat in his chair. "You're still a kid," he said with a smile.

"I may be thirty-five, but I'm still seventeen," she said, which also was her age the year before her father died.

"We need to be serious about this, you know," Phil replied, trying to assume control.

"Don't you think I know?" she asked, somewhat hurt. Still sometimes acting like she was still seventeen. "Why is he here, Uncle Phil, and why now?"

"Because it's a perfect hunting territory for a predator, and because I'm here," he said with resignation.

She looked at him with slight exasperation. "You are not the cause of all of the world's faults, and you are not the cause of Frank's problems."

Phil smiled, leaned back in his chair, which let out a slight creak, acknowledged Gina's logic with a nod of his head, and changed the subject.

"Has Steve gotten a job yet?" he asked, referring to her husband.

Suddenly her face changed, going from the ever-cheerful to biting her lip and finally turning away as the lower lip quivered. She eased herself down off of the desk and walked toward the window as Phil watched. He knew when she was this deep in thought, that was when she had already thought things through and was about to break some news. Without turning around, she quietly said, "When he touches me, I want to vomit." She turned around, her opaline green eyes red from crying. "Does that tell you anything?" she said with a fake grin, the hurt in her eyes so deep it broke Phil's heart. He rose from his chair, went over to her, and embraced her. As she buried her face in his chest, he felt the heaves of the sobs. He just held her until she finally pushed away, wiping her eyes with her hand as Phil reached for a package of Kleenex in his drawer. She blew her nose like a foghorn.

"Do you need a place to crash?" Phil asked, knowing what was next.

"Fuck no, it's my house. That bastard will be gone by next week. That's what my attorney said," she said with daggers in her eyes.

"That's my girl," Phil said, beaming, knowing now that Gina would be fine. She had her father's *cava dosti* thickheaded attitude in Italian, and she was a survivor. She proved that by completing her dream of becoming an RN even after John had died. "Does he know yet?"

"My attorney is serving him today," she said with confidence.

Phil's look of surprise couldn't be hidden. "Good attorney," he said with sarcasm.

"It's Steve's sister, Patricia. She hates his guts more than me," Gina replied. Phil chuckled, and she smiled again.

Suddenly their brevity was broken by Mirabel's rapid knocking on the door. As Phil and Gina turned toward the door as it opened, they saw Mirabel standing in the frame, shaking, tears streaming down her face.

"Maria's missing," she said in between sobs. "She's been gone since noon yesterday, and nobody has heard from her."

"She's done this before, remember?" Phil said, trying to reassure Mirabel, referring to her cousin's previous "lost weekends," ending up in Las Vegas. She would finally show up late Sunday. But this was only Friday morning.

"Today is her son Jose's birthday," Mirabel continued. "That's where she was going yesterday, to get stuff for his party today. Her ex-husband, Thomaso, just showed up at her house, and her car is not there and there's no sign of her. Jose spent the night at his grandparents' house when she didn't come home. She usually tells her mother where she is going, even when she takes off for Vegas." This time it was Gina who went over to Mirabel and held her as she wailed.

Phil suddenly felt sick with a terrible feeling. Marine boot prints and six vultures circling in the middle of Death Valley. This was definitely escalating, but not in a way that Frank was making mistakes, as Phil had assumed. This was planned. This was also becoming personal. Frank's attacks were directed toward Phil, in a catch-me-if-you-can scenario. As he looked at Mirabel and Gina, his worst fears were churning in his mind. How close would he try to get, and how many more would die before he himself was killed? Or would it be like ten years ago, when the "East Coast Slayer" killed scores, then framed another before leaving, coming west, and starting all over again? But what bothered Phil the most was that they were probably all under surveillance without previous knowledge, and he was studying every one of their moves. Frank had to live locally, he surmised. That also meant that he might know that Gina was here.

Phil picked up his desk phone and called dispatch. "Get me the chopper to go in ten minutes," he said. Gina walked over to the desk. He hit another button and contacted the desk sergeant. "I need to have a replacement for Mirabel, ASAP, family emergency. Get me Margie; I have a job for her," he said, referring to the computer geek who did her best work searching for things on the Internet. Within a minute he heard her nasally Chicago accent and grinned. "Watcha got, boss?" Margie asked as she entered the office.

"Look for any real estate transaction for a Frank DiMocchio," which he spelled for her, "within one hundred square miles of here, bought or rented within the last ten years."

Gina looked into his worried eyes "He's been watching, hasn't he?" Phil nodded yes. "I'm going to take Mirabel to her uncle's house; I'll make sure everyone is okay before I head back to your place. Find him, Uncle Phil. This time, don't let the courts get him. Do it for Daddy." She hugged him, turned, and went out with Mirabel.

At that point Phil knew what had to be done. The day had finally come for him to settle the score. He would kill Frank DiMocchio or die trying.

From the hilltop overlooking the city, he could see Mirabel leaving the station through the Zeiss field binoculars. She was with another woman behind her, obscured by Mirabel and sunglasses, until she stopped to pick up the keys she had dropped. He couldn't believe who he was seeing from a half mile away. He put the glasses down and crawled back toward his truck. This revelation had unforeseen consequences for which he had to alter his plans. He hated audibles, and seeing Gina Androcelli was something for which he had not planned. This changed everything. Through her, he could obtain final vindication for all of his torture, his suffering. First, it was time to create a small diversion, and then he would take care of Gina.

She would make his perfect hostage, before killing her and her Uncle Phil.

CHAPTER 9

Phil never liked helicopters.

He had an innate fear of flying to begin with and was prone to air sickness, just to add insult to injury. But here he was one thousand feet above the desert floor, following Amboy Road to the spot where Phil had seen the vultures. The pilot was new to the force, having just left the navy after ten years of flying everything from Bell H-27 rescue helicopters to F-18's off flight decks of carriers. But when Lieutenant Mary McConnell wanted to have a baby at the age of twenty-eight, she decided to leave the military, had a baby girl, Candace, and joined the CHP. She knew about Phil's phobias and was more sensitive to him then his "buddies" would have been. This meant no intentional dips to play with his stomach, no sharp turns, and under no circumstances, come within five hundred feet of any mountaintops or sides. But she did have a dry sense of humor, which he found refreshing.

She turned on the CD player, and Pink Floyd's "Learning To Fly" came over the headphones. Phil looked over at her, saw a sly smile on her face, nodded his approval, and settled back as he looked out at the never-ending desert floor. Listening to his favorite rock band eased his anxiety, and he began to concentrate on the area below. He signaled Mary to slow the speed and drop her altitude, which she did with ease and with minimal notice by Phil. She was smooth, he thought.

Talking over the song, he said, "We're coming up on the area now; see if you can hover just a little lower," as he took out his Nikon D3100 with its 55/300 mm zoom lens, wanting to take pictures from above and analyze for any abnormalities in the normal landscape of the desert.

"I'll drop down to three hundred feet; should be perfect for pictures," she said, having done reconnaissance missions for the navy.

Phil's and Mary's eyes scanned the area below; hard-packed tan-colored sand with multiple different cacti spotted in between the infrequent tumbleweed were seen. Suddenly they came upon an area that appeared to be a dry wash, about thirty feet wide. They both saw the same thing at the same time—tire tracks.

Mary banked the helicopter ever so gently around and lined Phil up with the wash parallel to him on the right side. He lowered the window and leaned out, with his camera focused on the tracks, and began clicking pictures at four shots per second. He zoomed in on the tread. His heart began to pound in his chest, and his breathing quickened. He clicked off more pictures as Mary held the helicopter in one place with one hand and her foot pedals. Finally he sat back, looked at Mary, and said, "Follow the wash until the tracks disappear."

She tipped the nose ever so slightly and began a slow glide forward, giving them better vantage.

The tracks appeared to be the same as those he saw at the Infiniti crime scene, and Phil's intensity was evident in his steel blue eyes, focused as never before. They covered the next two miles slowly, anticipating the abrupt termination of the tracks at any point, but the farther they went raised doubts about the true meaning of the tracks. Were they from people four-wheeling their trucks and ATVs through the desert in the wintertime, which was a very popular recreation in this part of Southern California?

Suddenly the tracks disappeared.

Phil and Mary craned their necks as far around as they could, and then she brought the chopper slowly around, finding the wash again and hovering over the area where the tracks stopped. Phil clicked away, zooming in on the end. Suddenly he felt a tap on his shoulder, and the look in Mary's eyes told him something that was not good was about to happen.

"Look about a hundred yards to the east, up on the small mesa," she said, pointing at the same time.

Phil looked at the area she was pointing to, squinted, and realized what Mary was seeing. "Fly directly overhead and keep this same altitude," he said as he got his camera ready for more shots. Within fifteen seconds they were hovering three hundred feet above at least two freshly dug graves, each a perfect rectangle, exactly six feet apart. Just like in military cemeteries.

"Oh my God," they both said at once.

"Land us somewhere." Phil barked out the order, not realizing the force of his voice. "Sorry," he said quietly.

She smiled, nodded, and said, "Aye, aye, captain," in her best navy voice, and slowly banked to the right and found a landing spot about three hundred yards away. She slowly descended, and the helicopters' landing struts softly touched the ground.

"By the way, you can fly me anywhere, anytime, thank you," Phil said with humility.

"Do you know what the best thing for you would be?" she asked. Phil shrugged his shoulders and shook his head no. "You need to learn how to fly, just like the Floyd said, and it would be a lot different. I can teach you if you'd like," she said as she shut everything down before they opened the doors to the oppressive heat and dust.

"I'll put it on my bucket list to do," Phil said, "and I wouldn't learn from anyone else." They both smiled, than hit the heat. "Phew," Phil said as it hit him full force, like stepping into an oven. "No matter how long I've lived here, I can't get used to this heat. The Bay Area spoiled me for that," he said as they walked toward the graves.

"But it's a dry heat," Mary replied with a chuckle at the oft-used statement.

They became more serious and quiet as they approached the first spot. Phil stepped to the edge of the grave site and felt the earth, definitely looser than outside the rectangle. He stood up, looked at Mary with sad eyes, and took out his cell phone.

"Hey, Don, what are you doing?" he asked the chief of the department's lab and CSI units.

"I'm processing some of the stuff we found at the scene this morning, and cooling off from the heat stroke I suffered after you left," he said sarcastically. "What's up?"

"Get well hydrated and cooled off quickly," Phil said. "I think I found his burial ground."

Dead silence on the other end. Then Don replied, "The vultures."

Phil explained about what they had found, where he was, and what was needed.

"I'm going to bring four very capable assistants to do the hard work, like digging," Don said. "If we find a body, then we'll bring in the bigger equipment to excavate any others. How do we get to where you are at?"

"We have road markers in the bird," Mary said "We can mark the exact wash to turn onto."

Phil relayed the information, nodded his head in acknowledgment, and hung up. "They'll be here in an hour. Let's mark this area before we head up to the end of the wash."

Within the next hour, not only did they mark the grave area, but Phil learned a few things about helicopters and flying. He started the engine and felt like a kid again, then handed the controls back to Mary. For the first time in a long while, he smiled big enough to show all three of his dimples.

"That's a much better look for you, and you'll live longer," Mary said.

"Now you sound like my late mother," Phil said as they took off, flying back toward the highway. Phil's eyes were glued to the wash, more specifically the tracks. They had been used multiple times because the tracks were too deep for just one pass. How many bodies were out here? His stomach was beginning to gnaw at him, but not because of flying. He had a sudden overwhelming feeling of dread, as if multiple tortured souls were screaming out to him at once. A rift in the "Force," as Yoda would have said. But the worst thought he had was that Mirabel's cousin was the last victim and that he was the cause of her death. Not for anything he had done, just for who he was. That truly haunted him, that something so evil could direct its anger toward him. They finally reached the highway and pulled into a hovering position.

"I figured they should be getting close by now, and we can just sit up here instead of frying in the heat, and lead them in," Mary said. Phil nodded his approval and scanned the desert floor below. They didn't have to wait long, as within five minutes the flashing lights of multiple SUVs could be seen heading eastbound on Amboy Road. They slowed as they approached the helicopter, seeing the turnoff into the wash, and began the almost three-and-a-half-mile drive as they flew overhead. Phil noticed the trucks avoided the tracks as much as possible—good lab rats. Mary flew ahead, sighting the marker they had left, and landed in the exact same spot as before. Phil was kind of sorry the ride was over, not only because it was fun, but because of what he was about to find.

Phil met Don and his "crew," almost all big bruisers, as they emerged from the first SUV. They began to unload equipment, including portable sonar, metal detectors, and plenty of shovels, as the helicopter started up again. Phil put a quizzical look on his face. Don said, "She has to go back and pick up two Feds; bring them out here." They both watched her take off, waving and giving the universal signal that she was returning. Phil waved back and smiled again, actually looking ahead to the ride home.

He turned back to Don as they started the slow march toward the marker, the other four following with the load fifty feet behind. "What's up with the Feds? Why do they need to be here?" and he realized as Don said, "Your old buddy is in deep shit if Frank's back."

Basically under Anthony Balducci's direction, the FBI got an innocent man convicted and killed, knowing they were wrong, but they wouldn't listen to Phil. He didn't know if they wanted to or if they knew but didn't care. They had their killer and that was that. Soon the truth would be revealed, because this time Phil wouldn't keep his mouth shut.

"Deeper than you will ever know," Phil replied.

"Uh, Lew, just wanted to let you know; we can't start digging until the Feds arrive," Don finally confessed.

Phil stopped dead in his tracks, turned, and faced Don, who was about five inches shorter, and his steel blue eyes turned dark. "And what are we supposed to do, hold our dicks in our hands for the next hour?" he barked. "Shit," and he turned and started walking again as Don said, "We can scan the area and get a picture of what's down there."

"I know who's down there," Phil said as he stared at the marker that was now fifty feet away. They walked the rest of the way in silence, more out of respect for the dead, both deep in thought.

Don stopped at the first site, dropped his own camera case, took out his Canon EOS 1450, and began aiming and shooting, from all different angles. The other four came a few minutes later, hauling the heavier equipment. Don pointed to an area away from the graves to store the carrying cases and other objects until the Feds arrived.

"Randy, get your machine fired up and bring it over," Don said. Randy, who stood six foot four and weighed 250 pounds, stopped and unbuckled his backpack, which was carrying his portable sonar machine, weighing another one hundred. He nodded, immediately dropped down to his knees, and unloaded the unit from its container, almost looking like an upside-down periscope, with a wide sweeper at the bottom and a ten-inch LCD screen on top, with handles to hold at a forty-five-degree angle. He turned on three different switches and waited about two minutes until the indicator lights finally turned green. He easily lifted the unit up and walked directly to where Don and Phil were standing. He stopped and made the sign of the cross before walking across the grave.

"Heavy-duty Catholic upbringing, dude," Randy said as Don was waiting for him. He held the unit in position and began his sweep, slowly back and forth, just like using a metal detector. After about five minutes of silence, he turned, looked at them, and said, "Nothing up to a three-foot depth."

"Set it for six feet," Phil said without hesitation. Now both Randy and Don looked at Phil with the same quizzical look.

"Can your gadget do that?" Phil asked Randy sharply.

"Sure. It can go to at least ten feet depending upon the undersurface makeup, but 99 percent of the time, the victims are buried in less than three feet of earth," Randy said with a slight amount of arrogance.

"This motherfucker is the worst of that other 1 percent, so set that piece of shit for six feet or find another fucking job," Phil snarled.

Randy knew his match and just nodded approval. He gently set the machine down, and through his iPhone reset the depth settings. He picked it back up and began retracing his steps and sweeping, but this time much slower, allowing the sound waves to reach their appointed depth before pinging back.

He stopped within a minute, almost two feet from the edge. He backed up slowly, concentrated on that one area, hit a button on the right handle, and pinged a signal again. His hands immediately began to sweat, and he suddenly felt the weight of the machine as he quietly said a prayer, oblivious to the calls of his superiors.

"What is it?" they both asked simultaneously.

"I have something in this image," Randy said softly as he retreated off the grave. Phil and Don looked at the image, like a fuzzy X-ray. But clearly, in the left upper portion of the sandstone was the outline of something.

They knew immediately that it was an image of a human foot, ankle, and the beginning of the tibia bone before the screen cut off, which was enough to see for all of them.

Now Phil was even more pissed that he had to wait for the Feds. It was better to be angry at someone and not think of who might be buried there. He looked at Randy. "Do the other site," Phil said, "and keep going every six feet apart until you don't find any more bones," he snarled as Don pointed Randy to the other site.

Phil walked away from the grave, away from everyone, back toward the SUVs and the ever-present cooler in Don's vehicle. He liked vodka, so one had to be careful which water bottle was grabbed. Phil had to think, had to gather his thoughts and cool down before he had a coronary like his brother and dropped dead then and there. He reached Don's vehicle, opened up the back, and found the cooler. He found the water bottle with the seal already broken, pulled it out, opened, and smelled. The 90 proof hit his nostrils hard enough to make him tear. He took a swig, felt it burn all the way down his throat, waited fifteen seconds, and took a second. He wiped his mouth, replaced the cap and bottle, took out a true water bottle, opened it, and drank most of its contents in one breath. He let out a belch, as he felt the buzz settling in quickly. In this heat it would disappear in thirty minutes, but he didn't care. He needed it at that moment.

He, and only he, knew what was coming next. First the federal fools, then the media circus, then the apocalypse. Also known as the second coming of Frank DiMocchio.

CHAPTER 10

"Sugar attracts ants quicker than salt," his father used to tell him as a child. His advice on dealing with enemies, or in his case, his mother, had always impressed Frank as some of the wisest. In his many "conquests" of women, he attracted them, not only with his chiseled large physique and bright Steve McQueen blue eyes, but with a personality and charm that could melt the Titanic iceberg. His standard line of "It's absolutely no problem at all" always worked when he did favors for luscious, beautiful women, especially pent-up housewives and soccer moms, who were usually drooling by the time he completed his task.

He had kept reconnaissance on Gina over the years, either personally or through the wonderful Internet. Social networks were a serial killer's paradise, especially if the predators were also techies themselves. Facebook was his favorite. She basically spelled out her entire life to old friends, how she was unhappy, getting ready to make the move. Luckily she had no kids, was her last quote. That always meant divorce, vulnerability, extreme pent-up passion. Something he could stir in any woman.

He had followed Gina and Mirabel into Yucca Valley, a small city thirty-five miles north of Palm Springs, along California Route 62, a desert oasis rebuilt after the powerful 1992 Landers earthquake. The 7.9 temblor, whose epicenter was two miles east of Yucca Valley, had caused major damage to many buildings. Rebuilt with federal and state relief money, the city had tripled in size since the quake. It was a typical Southern California city, with fast-food restaurants, plenty of strip malls, and businesses catering to the highway traffic. The highway carved through the center of the city, with single-story desert ranch houses spreading outwardly in a wheeled design. Most of the longtime residents were older retirees, drawn to the warmth and dryness of the desert, helping their health in many ways.

Frank was about half a mile behind them when he saw their car turn into one of the newer-built developments off of Highway 62. A large cul-de-sac with about twelve split-level houses formed the entire development. He could see multiple cars parked in front of the house that Gina drove up toward, most likely Mirabel's relatives. He dared not drive into the neighborhood, so he continued on Highway 62 for about a quarter mile and made a U-turn. He pulled his Dodge Ram into the parking lot of a Stater Brothers supermarket and parked with the cab facing the only entrance to the cul-de-sac where Gina was. He shut off the engine, opened the window to the hot afternoon air, and opened up a cold bottle of water. He figured that he wouldn't have to wait too long.

He waited all of twenty-seven minutes.

He spotted Gina's car as it pulled to the light at the intersection, and her signal indicated she was going back to Twentynine Palms, not home to the Bay Area. Frank started up the Dodge, thankfully turned on the air-conditioner full force, and closed the window as he pulled forward, inching toward the exit as he kept an eye on Gina's car. Once she made the turn onto north Highway 62, he pulled out of the parking lot and resumed following her, now a quarter mile behind, staying behind a few vehicles. Luckily his raised vehicle gave him an excellent vantage point, so he dropped back a little farther. He lit a joint after they had left the city's limits and relaxed as he made the twenty-two-mile trek back toward Twentynine Palms, listening to some old Little Feat music.

As Gina entered Twentynine Palms, Frank increased his speed to close the gap, especially after seeing her make a left-hand turn onto Two-Mile Road. She wasn't going back to the CHP station. He began to laugh to himself after realizing her destination.

Uncle Phil's house up on Joshua Lane, off of Two-Mile Road, was where she was heading, which was perfect. He could fulfill the age-old saying of killing two birds with one stone. He stayed as far behind as possible and watched her turn onto Joshua Lane, heading toward the last house up on the left. He saw no other vehicle in the driveway as he continued on Two-Mile Road for about five hundred feet and parked his truck off the road in an open patch of hard desert pack. He locked the truck and nonchalantly walked back toward Uncle Phil's house, and out of reflex, felt the butt end of his Walther PPK, which was tucked into the crack of his ass under his jeans and T-shirt. Just to make sure it was easily accessible.

He walked right up the deserted street to the last house on the left, noticing the well-manicured rosebushes surrounding a small patch of lawn to the left, a desert scene to the right. It was like Lieutenant Philip DiMarco had a split personality, he thought to himself as he walked up to the door and rang the doorbell. He stood there, arms folded, as the curtain in the living room was pulled back, revealing the shocked expression of Gina. He smiled as wide as he could, and the curtain went back into place. He heard the rush of footsteps and the front door locks undone before the rush of cool air from inside escaped as the door slowly opened.

"Hi, Gina, it's been a long time," Frank said in a gentle, soothing voice. "May I come in?" he asked with perfect manners as he stood at ease. He pulled off his sunglasses, and the warmth of his soft blue eyes hit Gina like a thunderbolt.

"You know, if my uncle caught you here, he'd arrest you," Gina said, holding onto the door, staring back up at Frank, biting her lip, as she always did when she was nervous.

"No, he wouldn't," Frank said. "He'd kill me," he added flatly. "But it would be worth it seeing your eyes again." The effect was better than what he had expected. Not only did the door open up, but Gina threw her arms around Frank's neck, almost choking him, as he lifted her off the ground with ease, moved into the foyer, and closed the door behind them with his left foot. She buried her head in his chest as they embraced. When she looked up, the electricity between them was instantaneous, as it always had been, and they kissed passionately.

"We need to go somewhere," Gina said. "I can't let my uncle know you were here."

"I don't live too far from here," Frank said. "We can hang at my place for a while; get you back here before your uncle."

"Let me get my purse," she said as she went into the kitchen, shut off the coffeepot after pouring a cup to go, and came back into the foyer. "Where's your car?" she asked as they came out of the house into the blazing sun and heat. Even with sunglasses on, they both were squinting into the bright light.

"It's around the corner," he said as they walked down the driveway. They started talking to each other, filling in the years, with Gina telling the truth and Frank lying through his teeth. But he was convincing enough, at least to Gina. She had always loved him, and that hadn't changed.

He didn't love anyone.

They arrived at his truck. Gina gave her approval of the custom lift, K-Lights, and especially the monster meat tires and rims. She hopped up into the cab after he opened the door for her, like a teenager all over again. She reached across and opened Frank's door as he approached.

"Well, thank you, ma'am." His imitation of an old cowboy brought a smile to Gina's face. He opened up the console and pulled out the little tin can with his joints. He opened it and offered one to Gina. She put her hand to her mouth, hiding a big grin, then reached and took out a fatty.

"I haven't done this in years," she said sheepishly, with some trepidation.

"Enjoy," he said as he lit it for her. She toked and began the delayed retching as the smoke hit the lower portion of her lungs, waves of coughing followed by exhalation of the pungent smoke.

"Good shit," she said after wiping the spittle from her mouth with the back of her hand. She handed the joint back to Frank as she sat back and relaxed, the high level of the Train Wreck THC already taking effect.

Frank inhaled half of the joint before handing it back, and pulled back onto Two-Mile Road. He finally exhaled without any cough as Gina began another round. He laughed as she finished the roach. He put the remnants back into his tin and turned the radio on to hear Bruce Springsteen's "Lonesome Day," and they both began singing as they drove toward the foothills overlooking Twentynine Palms, toward Frank's house. As he looked at Gina dancing in her seat, he began having second thoughts about what needed to be done.

He had never felt guilty about killing anyone before, and that bothered him. He had never felt guilt about anything at any time in his life. Not even after he had killed his own mother. He gave Gina a great big smile as she began to imitate the Boss, enjoying the moment, but his focus had returned. He now knew that she would have to die, but it didn't mean he couldn't enjoy the fruits of his labor beforehand. So, he began to dance with her as he drove toward his house and Gina's destiny.

CHAPTER 11

The first buzzard arrived while Phil was walking back toward the graves. He stopped and looked up, judging the bird to be at about two thousand feet in altitude, making a very slow banking turn to the left, beginning its large circle effortlessly drifting on the breezes above. Within two minutes a five more had joined the lone vulture, almost like a troop joining its advanced scout. Phil was amazed at the sight as he joined the others again at the graves' edges. Everyone was very somber as they sat on their packs, drank more water, and waited, nodding to Phil as he arrived. He noticed that Randy and Don were not there, and that was not a good sign. It had been over twenty minutes since Phil had walked away. How many more bodies were out there? The tech they called Drake motioned to his right, pointing toward the east. Phil looked that way and saw both of them walking back, both of their heads bowed down as they trudged along very slowly.

As they arrived, both were covered in sweat, their eyes red and swollen, their faces grim, as if the knowledge they were carrying would destroy mankind.

"How bad is it?" Phil asked, his demeanor entirely compassionate now, the alcohol having taken the edge off of his stress.

Randy walked past Phil, repeating the Lord's Prayer and making the sign of the cross after the conclusion of his praying. He quietly put his sonar equipment back into its packing, sat down, and stared directly ahead, his eyes blank, reminiscent of Viet Nam's "thousand-yard" stare. Only seeing horror can make a grown man experience that feeling, as Phil knew firsthand.

Phil slowly turned back toward Don, almost not wanting to hear what he had to say. His face was exactly like Randy's, but his eyes had seen so much that they still had some life in them. But what life was there had truly been diminished by what he had seen. He looked down, slowly shook his head, and let out a slow, long sigh.

"We counted thirty-three bodies, at least, each exactly six feet apart, each buried about six feet in depth, stretching east of here," he said flatly, as if filing a report. Then his lower lip began to quiver and the tears welled up in his eyes. He dabbed his eyes with his shirtsleeve and turned away momentarily. He turned back around, anger now in his eyes. "We've got to nab this motherfucker, Lew. We have to do it by the book so the Feds can't fuck it up this time." Don was now agitated, hands and arms flying with his speech, just like any Italian.

"Do you really trust the system?" Phil asked philosophically, staring toward the graves as he spoke. "The only way to stop him is to kill him, Don, and you know it," he finished as he turned and stared straight into Don's eyes, determination and maybe something more sinister in the steel blue eyes.

"How do you kill true evil?" Don asked. "We ain't fuckin' priests."

"First we have to find him," Phil responded. "For that you have to think like him."

"I can't think crazy," Don said.

Phil looked down at Don, put both of his large hands on his shoulders, shook his head, and with a grin said, "He's not crazy. That's the thing that most people don't understand. He is not a psychopath; he's not delusional. He's a sociopath; he feels no guilt toward society, but he's as sane as you and I. The only enjoyment he probably gets out of life is sex and death." Phil paused for a moment, then concluded, "And he's a professional killer, who plans everything to the minutest detail."

Their conversation was cut short by the sound of the helicopter approaching from about two miles away. Everyone started to stir, wanting to get this done and get out of the heat. Within two hours they had each drunk four bottles of water, but no one had urinated or had the urge to do so.

"We'll dig up the last grave here," Phil said to Don, as they watched the helicopter do a slow bank toward them. "Then we'll call for someone with a backhoe to dig up the rest under our supervision."

"If the Feds let you," Don said as he spit on the ground, more symbolic than anything else.

"This is my territory, this is the State of California, and state's rights for murder trump their ego trips or cover-up schemes," Phil said with a snarl. "Plus I saved the assistant director of the FBI's life when he was thirteen, and he still fuckin' owes me," Phil said in his thickest Bronx accent as he began to walk toward the landing helicopter, leaving Don standing there with his mouth agape, arms at his side. He was the perfect picture of an Italian mute.

With each step toward the helicopter, Phil's anger began to grow, especially as the alcohol wore off and as he thought about the hours wasted. He tried to control his well-known Italian temper, but incompetence and stupidity usually put him over the edge. He could have been looking at forensic evidence by now, even beginning the arduous task of identification of the victims and notification of the next of kin. He knew in his heart that Mirabel's family would be the first, and that made him even angrier. Some of the anger was self-directed, because he knew they had convicted the wrong man as he maintained his "asked-for silence," a favor to his childhood friend. Now the favors were about to be called in, just like with la famiglia. By the time he was within fifty feet of the chopper, he was about to blow.

The blades slowly decelerated as the engine shut down. The passenger door opened, and the typically dressed FBI agent emerged, except he was the size of a middle linebacker. *Probably from the Midwest*, Phil thought, six foot four, 265 pounds, in a dark blue suit and Ray-Ban sunglasses on a square face, with a tight haircut, but not a true jarhead. He had forearms the size of Phil's calves and a neck larger than his head. "You must be Lieutenant DeMarco," the "e" drawn out with a southern drawl. "Special Agent Timmons, FBI," and he extended his hand, larger than Phil's, which he took and gripped tightly.

"Can we dig now, Special Agent Timmons?" Phil said, looking directly into the agent's shades, trying to burn a hole through them.

"You'll have to ask my boss," Timmons replied. He released his grip and pointed with his thumb over his shoulder at the helicopter. Then a huge smile appeared on his face, as if he were in on a secret that Phil would regret. Phil looked past him and saw Mary turned in her seat, talking to the other agent in back. Then he saw her laughing, and Phil's boiling point was about to be reached.

"Excuse me, we've been frying out here for the better part of two hours and would like to proceed with our investigation," Phil basically shouted toward the helicopter. Mary turned and waved. Phil flapped his arms in exasperation, turned, and said, "What the fuck?" as he walked back toward Agent Timmons.

"That will get you nowhere with Special Agent Flaherty," Timmons said as Phil approached. "She'll take even longer now," he said with a huge grin as he stood at ease.

"She…?" Phil asked as his shoulders slumped.

"Yeah," Timmons replied slowly with a nod of his large head.

"Is she just like my ex-wife and does the exact opposite thing you ask her to?" Phil inquired.

"I don't know your ex-wife, sir, but yeah," Timmons said with a slow nod of the head.

"Oh, shit, it's going to be a long day," Phil said, shaking his head, hands on hips.

"Longer than you think," Timmons replied as the smile grew bigger.

"Did you play ball?" Phil changed the subject as he tried to calm down.

"Yes, sir, army, offensive lineman 2001 to 2004," he replied.

"Are you a West Point grad?" Phil asked.

"Yes, sir, then joined the FBI," Timmons said. "You're ex-Marine, two tours in Nam, multiple medals, including Purple Heart and Bronze Star." Phil looked at him quizzically. "I read your file on the way over," he said matter-of-factly.

"Know thy enemy," Phil said. Timmons nodded as Phil chuckled. "You seem to have an advantage over me, since I know nothing about you." Timmons smiled but said nothing as Phil felt a tap on his shoulder. He turned and was suddenly looking into the shades of Special Agent Flaherty. Phil stopped breathing for about twenty seconds after she removed her sunglasses and revealed two very intense opaline green eyes, which burned right through his sunglasses. He recovered his senses, removed his own sunglasses, and stared intently back, not wanting to squander away any control. Phil noticed out of the corner of his eye that Timmons was backing up very slowly, as if he knew what was coming next. Phil made a quick decision.

He extended his hand, put on his best smile, and introduced himself, "Phil DiMarco," but she left his hand hanging in the air.

"Let's cut the bullshit, lieutenant," she began. "You don't like the Feds taking over your case, even though we have the best-trained investigators in the world, the manpower, and the funds to do what we need to solve these types of crime." She stopped for a second. Standing five foot seven in flats, she was eight inches shorter than Phil, but was nose to nose with him, looking directly into his eyes. Phil was having major flashbacks of his ex-wife. "Plus, we won't do it for the glory," she said with biting sarcasm, her hands in fists at her side, like a fighter ready to throw a sucker punch, "or the fifteen minutes of fame." She threw the last blow extremely low.

At this point when he was married and the fight would reach the insult phase, Phil would always walk away so as not to add fuel to the fire. But he wasn't married to this bitch. "If your fucking boss had listened to me ten years ago," Phil began in a growling guttural voice, holding his rage by a thread, "none of this would be happening. I wouldn't be out here in 110-degree heat, sweating my balls off, waiting for Princess Flaherty to make her royal arrival, so we may dig up thirty-three fucking graves of victims who should be alive." His voice was now beginning to rise, and he was towering over Special Agent Flaherty, but she didn't flinch. "But that little fuckwad, who calls himself Assistant FBI Director, had an innocent man killed for his own fame and glory, so stay the fuck out of my way." With that Phil abruptly did an about-face and stormed away, leaving Flaherty standing with her mouth open. To put it mildly, when he walked past Timmons, Phil thought he saw a twinkle in his eyes behind those dark shades.

CHAPTER 12

Gina was dazed and confused.

The attraction, the chemistry, was instantaneous. They had made love for hours, each climaxing multiple times, the orgasms the strongest she had ever felt in her life. Only Frank could do that to her, and it was something she finally realized. But he was this mass murderer according to her Uncle Phil. Even her father hadn't liked Frank all those years ago. Then he was killed and Frank was blamed for his death, but she had never believed them, because she had believed his tale of innocence. In spite of all of the warnings from everyone, here she lay next to him at two o'clock in the morning. The almost full moon in the clear desert night was shedding bright light to her surroundings. His house was Victorian-style, absolutely spotless and organized, set up in the foothills above Twentynine Palms with a view of the surrounding city, lights twinkling in the night like ground stars. He had been both charming, yet shy with her, treating her with respect, putting whatever she wanted first, just as he had done all of those years ago.

How could he be this monster they said he was?

Then she saw her father's face in her dreams after falling asleep in his arms. He hadn't been in her dreams for a long time. Why tonight? She felt it was a warning, or was it her own guilt that she was feeling? Thoughts were racing through her head, and she knew that further sleep would be impossible.

She slowly rolled to her right, trying not to disturb him, but he turned and mumbled, "You okay?" He never opened his eyes, so she quietly replied, "Need to pee," and he pointed to the left. Then he rolled over, exposing his full tattoo in the bright moonlight to her for the first time. The artistry was magnificent, the detail of the red-tailed hawk beautiful in its detail. But the image suddenly haunted her as she felt a cold whisper of air pass her right shoulder, causing a chill down her spine.

She remembered why.

Twenty years ago, when he had gotten his first two feathers, one on each arm, he had told her it was his way of keeping track of the number of kills he had as a marine. He had likened it to a pilot who had small plane emblems on the body of his aircraft for every kill, or the old western gunfighter with notches in his gun. His entire back was completely covered now, with the body of the hawk covering his spinal area, the wings extending over his flanks and up into his arms. The legs with the talons ran down the back of each thigh. She shuddered and then quickly picked up her clothes, shoes, and purse, quietly crept out of the room, and found her way down to the kitchen, all thanks to the moonlight. She dressed on the run, trying to figure out how to get back to her uncle's house.

On the way to Frank's house, she had sent a text to her uncle, saying she had met an old friend at the conference and had decided to go out for drinks and then head back to her own hotel room. She'd see him in the morning to pick up her car before heading home. He had been okay with the change in plans. Now her lie was not only costing her the guilt of her own conscience, but she had no easy way back to her car. She remembered seeing a Honda S2000 in the garage when they pulled his truck inside. She'd write him a note and leave the keys with the desk clerk at her hotel. She found the keys on a hook near the refrigerator, thanking God for Frank's OCD, and opened up a door to what she thought was the garage.

Her mouth dropped to the floor as the fluorescent lights went on and illuminated every type of weapon, more than she had ever known existed, all neatly displayed behind locked glass. They ranged from simple handguns to mortars. Now she was shocked beyond Jupiter. What had her first and only true love turned into? At this point she just needed to get as far away as possible—and without wasting any time. She turned around, shut off the lights, went back into the kitchen, took the note with her, and put the keys back onto the hook. She decided to take her chances with the kindness of strangers on the road, even at this time of the morning, rather than awakening Frank. So she quietly snuck out the side kitchen door into the warm desert night air.

Luckily the moon gave her a clear view of everything as she began the long walk back into the city with a rapid pace since it was virtually all downhill. Within fifteen minutes she reached a truck stop on Twentynine Palms Boulevard and found a truck with a husband and wife team. She told them her story and hitched a ride with them into Palm Springs. She arrived at her hotel totally exhausted, opened her room, ran to the shower, and washed herself until she turned into a prune. Then she put on a comfortable cotton nightie, crawled into bed, and was asleep within two minutes, her mind too exhausted to think anymore.

She would deal with Uncle Phil and Frank's whereabouts when she woke up.

Her delay would cost everyone involved dearly.

Frank woke up three hours after Gina had left. He was slightly dazed upon awakening, an aftereffect of the drugs and wine. He didn't realize she was gone as he made his way to the bathroom, stumbling slightly in the dark over bedding that was thrown about the room. Standing in the bathroom naked as he relieved himself, rubbing his face with his free hand, he began to think about Gina. His strategy had changed. Instead of using her first and then killing her, he would train her to be his partner in crime, turn her against her uncle, and ultimately her late father. He smiled at the thought and nodded to himself in approval of his decision. He finished his business, put the seat down before flushing, washed his hands, and shut the light off, feeling his way back to bed. He crawled into his side of the

California King and slid over to the other side, expecting to find Gina, only to find the cold, uninhabited half of the sheets.

He searched his memory and remembered vaguely Gina getting up earlier, but that was all. He jumped out of bed and ran naked through the house, checking every room frantically, hoping to find her cuddled up somewhere else in his large house. Maybe it was his snoring, he thought. But after making his way through each section of the house, he came to the realization that she was gone—again.

He had taken a risk by not following his own logical course and had lost. He was not used to being duped by anyone, especially someone he thought he could "trust." He had to make rapid emergency contingency plans. He knew his house was no longer secure, but he had planned for this moment, so he knew what to do and realized the time was now. Within forty-five minutes he was fully loaded with almost every weapon he could fit into the bed of his truck, and enough supplies of food, water, and dope to get him through the next week until he made it to his other residence. First, he would leave no evidence of this house, and then he would create a few diversions to keep law enforcement busy enough to allow him to sneak away. He went to his house's alarm pad and put in a special code number. Within twenty seconds, the entire system sounded like the self-destruct sequence from the movie *Alien*.

He climbed into his truck, opened up the garage door for the last time, took one last look at his S2000, but knew he had other, better vehicles waiting for him, and backed out of the garage. The door automatically closed as part of the destruct sequence. He pulled out of his driveway and drove down his street quietly, letting the truck idle so as not to wake any neighbors. They would be awakened rudely soon enough, he thought; might as well give them that last good five minutes of sleep. He finally turned north onto Twentynine Palms Boulevard and headed to his secure perch above Interstate 40. He checked his watch every so often waiting for the last thirty seconds, at which time he pulled over to the side of the road and got out of his truck. At zero a massive explosion occurred that shook the ground, and in the distance the early morning sky was aglow. The fireball was created by ten pounds of synthetic high-potency explosives that had been strategically placed throughout his house. There would be nothing left but ashes, just the way he had wanted it to end here. When the flames died down, he got back into his cab and started driving.

As far as Gina was concerned, he knew where she lived in the Bay Area. He would make his way back to his roots and surprise her there when everyone's guard was down. He just had to give it the right amount of time. She wouldn't be protected forever, even though he knew she was probably spilling her guts to her uncle as he was driving away. It didn't matter to him. He had all the time in the world and other people to kill first, before he finally settled this score. He wouldn't make the same mistake twice. Gina would certainly have to die.

CHAPTER 13

The explosion shook Phil out of a dead sleep, and the sight of the fireball made him jump out of bed. He ran to the window for a better look. He figured it was about one and a half miles away from his house in the foothills. He was immediately on the phone with the watch commander of the fire department, alerting them to the explosion. With the ferocity of the blast, he was worried about a ruptured natural gas line like the one up north in San Bruno considering its proximity to other dwellings. He then called the watch commander at the Marine Corps base, who had also heard the explosion five miles away, but assured Phil that no maneuvers were underway this early. Phil looked at the alarm clock on his nightstand, and it read 5:42 a.m. He had finally fallen asleep at three fifteen. It was going to be another long day, and he didn't know if he had the strength to survive. He was already running on high adrenaline levels, and the added stress of lack of sleep was definitely dangerous to his health.

It had killed his older and only brother at the young age of forty-two years. Phil remembered that Friday night into Saturday morning, Super Bowl weekend twenty years ago, as if it were yesterday. They had lived two blocks away from each other in San Francisco at the time. At one thirty in the morning, he received a phone call from his sister-in-law. His brother, James, the orthopedic surgeon, had been having chest pains all night while bowling. He had been chewing Tums like candy, thinking it was the hot dog that was giving him heartburn. Phil had screamed at her to hang up and call 911; he was on his way. He arrived in time to see his brother cold, clammy, ashen gray in color. He was a cop, but he knew what a heart attack looked like. The paramedics arrived right behind him and pushed him out of the way. Phil backed into a corner, watching the cardiac monitor as they worked.

His sister-in-law, nephew, and niece were in the next room; the crying could be heard above the beeping of his brother's life beat. Suddenly alarms sounded as his brother's heart rate changed into a rapid irregular rhythm and he went into a grand mal seizure. Phil heard the paramedics barking orders to zap him as he stood in the background as if watching a Stanley Kubrick movie. In slow motion, defibrillator paddles were applied as the call for "clear" came from somewhere. He watched James's body jumping with each shock as Phil began to smell the burning of skin and chest hairs from the joules of electricity being applied again and again. Finally a regular beeping returned on the monitor.

Total chaos ensued as bodies flew by as the paramedics quickly strapped James to the gurney and rushed out to the ambulance. As he passed Phil, his last words were, "I'm sorry." The craziness continued in the ER at UCSF, with more cardiac irregularities followed by more shocks. After four hours, his brother lay in an ICU bed with ten different bottles of medicine running into multiple tubes into multiple sites on his body. A tube was down his throat, hooked up to a machine. In spite of all that was done, he coded one last time while Phil watched every minute before they finally pulled the sheet over his brother's face. He remembered looking at his watch and noted that 5:42 a.m. was the time of his death.

Phil looked again at the clock and shed a quick tear as he reached for his clothes and weapon. He dressed on the run and was out of the door within a minute. He got into his vehicle and roared the engine to life, put on the lights, and drove toward the burning area. The fire was still burning but fading in the early morning light. He looked at the temperature on the car's dashboard instruments, reading that it was already ninety-two degrees outside. That was before sunrise. He turned up the air-conditioning. Within a few minutes he reached the area and saw neighbors in a development standing in the road down the street from the burning structure. As Phil pulled his black and white to a stop, the sirens of the fire trucks could be heard coming up behind.

"What happened—does anybody know?" Phil called to the bystanders as he got out of the car. An elderly gentleman came slowly over.

"It just exploded, all at once, boom," he said with a heavy German accent. "I vas going pee, and looked out the vindow," he pointed to his house behind them, "ven the house just blew up," he said with his hands going up, gesturing the upward motion of the blast.

"Did you see anybody leaving the scene?" Phil asked, and the man shook his head.

"Who lived there?" Phil asked.

"I don't know his name; he kept to himself, big guy, bigger than you," he said. "I saw him ven he used to do his yard. He had beautiful roses. He had a very short haircut, muscular, just like a soldier. But he had this tattoo of a bird, like an eagle, that covered all of his arms and back. Strangest thing I ever saw in my life," he finished, shaking his head.

"Could the tattoo have been of a hawk?" Phil's heart pounded as he asked the question.

"Ja, ja, it could have been," the man said with an acknowledging nod of his head. "Ja, a hawk. Still strange."

It was Frank! This had been his hideout away from the main drag, nestled in a quiet neighborhood. "Did you hear anything before the explosion?" Phil asked. "Like a vehicle coming or going?"

The man looked past Phil and scratched the silver stubble on his chin as he searched his memory. "I thought I heard a truck; in fact I did, that's what woke me up," he said, searching further. "Then I felt the full bladder, but didn't want to get out of bed; thought of using the urinal, but my vife hates that, you know?" he said as Phil nodded in agreement to keep him talking as he heard more sirens closing in on their location. "It took me about twenty or twenty-five minutes before I finally got up, then boom," he said.

Phil grabbed him by the shoulders with both hands and looked into his sharp eyes. "Are you sure it was about twenty to twenty-five minutes between the truck and the explosion?" The man nodded yes immediately, very sure of himself. "Thank you; what you have told me is going to help a lot in catching the person responsible." The old man smiled at the compliment, feeling important. "There may be more people coming to ask you questions; tell them everything you told me." Phil gestured to the crowd to get back as the fire trucks came around the corner; their lights bounced off of the houses, which gave a surreal appearance to the early sunrise. They rushed past the crowd, which had cleared to their respective sidewalks, and Phil followed rapidly. Within three minutes the entire fire unit was engaged with hoses, and the blaze was being attacked from four different angles. Phil watched with amazement and envy. Firemen were loved, whereas cops were hated.

Suddenly a final SUV appeared around the corner, with lights flashing. *The chief himself,* Phil thought. At this hour of the morning, he was impressed. The SUV pulled up to Phil, stopped, and Rich Valendez got out of the vehicle. He immediately came over and shook Phil's hand. "Hey, Phil, how are you doing? What are you doing here?" he asked.

"I was about to ask you the same thing," Phil said with slight sarcasm. "I don't live too far from here and was basically tossed out of bed with the blast."

"I felt the blast five miles away," Rich said, "and knew something big had happened."

"Bigger than you could ever imagine," Phil said as they watched the firemen do their job. The remaining structure was now almost reduced to ashes, but there were still hot spots with which to contend.

"Are you thinking terrorism?" Rich asked.

"Worse than that," Phil replied dryly. "It's the coming of true evil."

The chief looked at him quizzically.

Phil looked at Rich, a man he'd known since moving here, and knew he could trust his judgment, and he would keep his mouth shut. "To put it mildly, the shit is going to hit the proverbial fan," he began. "Do you remember the East Coast Slayer ten years ago?"

"Sure. He killed, what, about eleven people, sniper style wasn't it?" Rich asked.

"He also raped and killed twenty-four women; their bodies were recovered, but the evidence collected matched absolutely no one in any system. The press was never alerted to that fact," Phil said, looking Rich in the eyes.

"What does that have to do with this?" Rich asked as he pointed to the burning structure.

"He's back, and this was his house," Phil said.

"But… he was executed, I thought," Rich said. Then the realization lit up in his face against the flames. "They convicted the wrong man," he said with astonishment.

"We discovered thirty-three bodies buried a few miles south of Amboy Road," Phil began. "The method of burial was exactly the same as ten years ago. We dug up two bodies yesterday, are supposed to begin the remaining exhumations within hours."

"But there haven't been any sniper reports," Rich said.

"Not yet," Phil said. "That will come next, and it won't be pretty."

"Maybe you got lucky and he torched himself," Rich said.

"Doubt it," Phil said with conviction. "An eyewitness heard a truck leave the neighborhood approximately twenty-five minutes before the explosion. I think he detonated the house by a timer, or by remote."

"With that type of blast, and with what looks like total annihilation," Rich said, pointing at the ashes left from a three-thousand-square-foot house, "I would say your killer knew a little about explosives."

"He was trained to kill, by all means necessary, including synthetics, by the best," Phil said almost proudly, "the United States Marine Corps."

"No shit," Rich said. "Say, how do you know so much about this guy?" he asked as they started to walk toward the remnants of the fire.

"Because I've been chasing him for twenty-five years, since he killed his own mother at the age of thirteen in San Francisco," Phil said with venom through clenched teeth. "He was acquitted because the evidence was all circumstantial and the judge was a pussy. Since then, he's honed his skills."

Suddenly Phil's cell phone started buzzing. "Now what?" he asked no one. "DiMarco" is all he said. He turned away from Rich to get some privacy.

"Good morning to you too, Phil." Doc Webster, the ME, was on the other end.

"Sorry, Doc, haven't had my coffee yet, and I just figured getting called this early was not going to be good news," Phil began. "Guess I'm a little grouchy."

"You have every right to be," Doc said compassionately, "because it's going to get a lot worse before this is all over." Phil's stomach started to churn acid as the doctor went on. "I have the cause of death, and I didn't want anyone else to know before I talked to you first."

"Fracture of the cervical spine, either C2 or C3 level, with spinal cord compression, both sexually assaulted," Phil said matter-of-factly.

"Yes on both accounts," he said, "and the sexual part appeared to be animalistic, with multiple vaginal lacerations, evidence of sodomy, and bruising from a grip like a vice around the hips of both victims, but only around the throat of one. The other one was shaken like a rag doll and her neck snapped."

Phil was walking in a trance back toward his vehicle, past the onlookers, and finally sat in his car. "Who are they?" Phil asked hesitantly, not wanting to hear the answer and sighed deeply.

"The second one, with the choke hold, was Cherie Morton, the lady from the Infiniti," Doc said, and then went silent for a few seconds. His voice got quieter. "The first grave was Mirabel's cousin Maria. I'm so sorry, Phil." His voice was quivering, holding back the tears. Phil made the sign of the cross and began to pray as he listened to the rest. "Everything is identical to the ME reports from the East Coast Slayer, not hiding any evidence, especially inside the body bags. The lab rats lifted a ton of prints. I have used condoms with semen, which will be sent off, just as ten years ago."

"His DNA won't be found in the system," Phil said flatly as he rubbed his eyes. "Just like the last time."

"What did you say?" Doc was bewildered. "They convicted someone without forensic evidence? That goes against everything we do here," he finished.

"East Coast politics is all I can tell you, doc. Can I have a copy of that report sent immediately to my desk, my eyes only, and don't say anything about what we said until after my meeting with the Feds in three hours," he said as he looked at his watch, seeing it was now 7:00 a.m.

"No problem, Phil. I have a lot of other things to do so I won't be talking to anyone else real soon," he said.

"Thanks." Phil hung up and looked at the fire crew cleaning up. He had time to drive to Morongo Valley and give the bad news to Mandy and her family in person before he had to meet with the Feds. At that moment he knew that this would be his last assignment as a CHP officer—the pursuit and killing of Frank DiMocchio. There would be no capture, at least not by him. This had now become personal.

CHAPTER 14

Frank made the left-hand turn off of Route 66 at the only intersection in the town of Essex, which was about one hundred miles from what was left of his house. He started the slow winding climb toward Interstate 40. The sun was still a half hour away from rising, and the full moon had just disappeared below his view. Being the only one on this road at the darkest point of the night was perfect. It fit his persona of being a loner and of being semi-invisible. For fun, knowing the road was basically straight for the next three miles, he turned his headlights off, plunging him further into total darkness. He slowed his truck down, opened up the sun roof, and looked at the myriad of stars one last time before they would fade away with the sunrise. He became slightly melancholy at the knowledge that this would be his last night in this part of California. He saw the interstate turnoff approaching in the dim light as his eyes adjusted. He turned his headlights back on just in time to make another left-hand turn onto a fire road.

He stopped the truck momentarily to put it into four-wheel drive and then started up the winding, narrow trail.

The oversize monster meat tires threw rocks all over as they gripped the dirt road, and the engine roared as he made his way up into the Clipper Mountains. Within ten minutes of multiple hairpin turns that tested his nerves with steep drops on either side, he reached his destination. He pulled to a stop one thousand feet from the peak, immediately jumped out of the truck, reached behind his seat, and removed a special rifle case, along with his backpack. He shoved a few bottles of water and his herbal supply into the pack and made his way up the rest of the trail by foot. He reached the crest of the 3,200-foot mountain in seven minutes, and found his perch overlooking the valley and Interstate 40.

He carefully placed everything he needed on a mat he had rolled up in his backpack, and set up his tripod on its base, so as not to leave any imprints. He opened his case and pulled out his specially made weapon for a sniper. A German Luger 50 caliber long-range rifle with a two-thousand-yard Zeiss zoom scope, measured to his wing span by the maker himself. The magazine held nine cartridges, semiautomatic. Attaching it to its base and bolting it firmly, he checked the scope's accuracy, adjusting it for the five-mile wind that was blowing. Then he sat back, opened up his little tin can, lit up a joint, and took a few tokes before settling into a perfect lotus position. His gaze was turned directly eastward as he watched the first rays of the sun making its way over the distant desert mountains, the golden fingers of God beginning to illuminate another day. He did his thirty minutes of yoga to relax and to focus.

By then the sun had fully risen, and the light on his area of target practice was perfect. Now all he needed was a good target. The spot overlooked Interstate 40, which ran east to west from Wilmington, North Carolina, to Barstow, California, about seventy-five miles northeast of Los Angeles. In this part of the high desert, the four-lane highway curved around the mountains, with east- and westbound traffic separated by over two hundred feet of median, with the westbound side on a much higher plane. Frank had scouted this area for months and had practiced shooting crows in flight from here to sharpen his skills. He watched the sparse traffic wind through the canyon below, mostly semi tractor-trailers. He didn't feel like shooting a trucker today. He was a patient killer and had plenty of time on his hands. By now the idiots in law enforcement would be running around trying to locate him. The chase was on, but he knew he would win. He always had in the past, with proper planning and execution. This time would be more fun.

After about a hour he spotted the perfect target approaching the farthest distance of his viewpoint. A BMW convertible was moving along westbound at a good rate of speed. The top was down and two women were driving alone, with no one else for at least a half mile. He loved a challenge. He took ten slow deep breaths and settled himself into a trance as he followed the car through his scope, his pulse rate down to fifty-two beats per minute. He braced his right shoulder for the expected kickback. He focused on the passenger first as he waited for the perfect distance of

1,500 yards, which he had already calculated before as right after the largest yucca tree off to the right, just before a deep ravine. As the front grill passed the tree, Frank squeezed the trigger. The explosion was muffled by his iPod earphones as he listened to Dave Matthews's "Everybody Wake Up," a song about terrorism. *How appropriate*, he thought as he saw the woman's head explode in his scope. He immediately focused on the driver and squeezed the trigger. The perfect head shot to the driver caused the car to veer immediately to the right, careening over the guardrail and flipping in the air before finally descending over and down into the two-hundred-foot ravine. Frank pulled his iPod's earphones out in time to hear the crash reverberate through the canyon.

Frank stood up and began doing an old Lakota Sioux Indian war whoop, made famous at the Battle of the Little Bighorn. His sounds now echoed through the same canyon. He smiled at his accomplishment, but also realized that he could not gloat. He immediately packed everything up, including the spent cartridges, and left his perch as clean as possible. He made his way back down to his truck and was driving down the fire road within minutes. He made better time in the daylight. He reached the main road, made a left, and proceeded to the same Interstate 40. He entered the westbound entrance and saw no one as he settled back for his drive to his next target, which would be much bigger.

What Frank had not known was that a trucker traveling eastbound had stopped around the corner and out of Frank's viewpoint. He was standing near the right front of his vehicle when he heard the shots come from behind him and saw the first, then the second heads of the women explode and the car veer to the right, flip in the air, and disappear from sight into a ravine. He finally heard the crash of the car as it settled onto the desert floor. For a minute he thought that he heard an old Indian war whoop from behind. He knew it was a sniper when the shots rang out, having served with the army in the first Gulf War. He jumped into his cab and got onto his CB radio, switching to the CHP frequency.

"Mayday, mayday, I've just witnessed a shooting on I-40; come back," he said.

Within twelve minutes, the first black and white rolled into view, lights flashing, heading westbound from the Needles area. Within ninety minutes a total of twenty-two vehicles had arrived, with more departments of law enforcement represented than ever before. Not that more would ever make it better. The total chaos between all of them that ensued was the only thing that saved Frank from being caught that day. But it wouldn't save the people that would soon die.

CHAPTER 15

Phil thought yesterday had been the worst day of his life.

He was wrong, again.

The discovery of the number of graves had shaken him tremendously. Even though he had done two tours of duty in Viet Nam and had seen his share of death, this was different. War is despicable and stupid, but unavoidable. Death during battle is acceptable. As the saying goes during basic training, "Kill or be killed," and he had still been haunted with post-traumatic nightmares. But these were innocent women. Their only fault was being at the wrong place at the wrong time, fallen victim to the worst predator ever known to mankind.

Even though Maria Melendez, Mirabel's cousin, had a wild side when she was younger, she was now a devoted mother and in line for a promotion at work, almost doubling her salary. Was it random? What had happened to lure her away from what she was doing? Or was she targeted because of whom her cousin had worked for, meaning was she stalked? Did he stalk all of his victims, or were they random, or a combination? Many of these questions would be answered as the investigation unfolded. Especially when the identities of all of the victims were known, they could establish some sort of pattern to finally nail the son of a bitch to a cross and exorcise his evil.

All of this went through Phil's mind as he pulled up to the light half a mile from Maria's parents' house. As he waited for the light to turn green, he peeked at the dashboard clock. It was 8:55 a.m., and he hoped he wasn't too early and would not wake anyone up, which sounded stupid as soon as the thought occurred. They probably hadn't slept the night before. This was the worst part of his job, one of the perks that gave him more gray hairs and shortened his life span.

He pulled the black and white directly behind Mirabel's car, which meant she probably spent the night at her aunt and uncle's house and was as exhausted as Phil was. He put the car into park, shut the engine off, and looked at the house for a minute. He knew that after he delivered the news and left, life behind those walls would never be the same. He also worried whether his and Mirabel's relationship would change as much as everything else. He remembered after his own brother's death how the family splintered apart. He had tried to be the go-between, but in the end, became the scapegoat for everyone's displaced anger. Suddenly he saw the curtain in the window nearest the front door being pulled back, and Mirabel's face alongside an older gentleman looked out at him. Phil dropped his head, said a quick prayer for strength, and got out of his vehicle.

The curtain fell back into place and the front door opened immediately afterward, with Mirabel running out to meet Phil halfway, her eyes bloodshot, with dark circles and swollen from crying. She stopped in front of him and looked directly into his eyes, which could not hide the pain of the news. She threw her arms around his neck and began to sob again, shaking; all he could do was to hold and comfort her. The pain would disappear over time, but the void left behind by Maria's death would never be filled.

Not realizing he had also closed his eyes to hide the tears, he opened them in time to see Mirabel's uncle approach slowly, also knowing by what he had just witnessed that his daughter was dead. He slowly raised his hand and touched the back of Mirabel's shoulder in an attempt to comfort. Mirabel felt his presence and stopped crying, pushing back from Phil, who was also wiping his eyes.

"This is my Uncle Alberto Melendez, Maria's father." Mandy made the introductions as the two shook hands at first, then exchanged hugs.

"So one of the bodies you found was my Maria?" he asked quietly.

"Yes, I'm very sorry," Phil said with a slight bow of the head out of respect.

"Are there many others this monster has killed?" he asked with genuine concern.

"We found thirty-three bodies," Phil said and saw Mirabel gasp and put her hand over her mouth with the shock evident on her face.

"You will find the one responsible for this?" Alberto asked with sincerity, wanting the truth.

Phil looked into his sad, brown eyes, the weather-beaten skin, and worry lines on the face that told the story of a hard life of labor and toil in the hot sun. All of his hard work and dreams shattered on this Saturday morning.

"I will do better than that," Phil began. "Not only will I find him, but I will make sure that he gets the justice he so righteously deserves."

"There will be no justice if he is allowed to live and hide behind attorneys. The system will give him more rights than the victims ever had. Kill him for Maria, for the others, and for me, senor," he now pleaded.

"I will, I promise," Phil responded as they hugged again.

"I must tend to the rest of my family, deliver the news, and begin the arrangements," Alberto said as he began to back away; he motioned to Mirabel to come with him.

"Get him, Phil, and cut his balls off, for me," she whispered in Phil's ear as she hugged him one more time, "and make sure he suffers before he meets Satan in hell," she finished as she gave him a kiss on the cheek, turned, and followed her uncle back to the house.

Phil was grateful that he didn't have to face the entire family. They needed to grieve privately for now, because once this story hit the media, they would never have another moment of peace or solitude. He stood there momentarily as they entered the house and closed the door. Within fifteen seconds, the screams of the bereaved mother and siblings could be heard through the entire neighborhood. It was at that moment that he turned and walked back to his car, anger building within.

He had witnessed enough death and suffering in his lifetime to last others through eternity.

As he entered his vehicle, the dismay of feeling powerless earlier this morning had been replaced by purpose of heart and mind. Looking back at the tormented house, he knew in his soul that he would kill Frank DiMocchio and that God would not punish him. He pulled away from the curb and left the area as quickly as he could.

When he was within a mile of the precinct, an all-points bulletin was being called over the radio about a possible shooting on Interstate 40. Phil put the lights and siren on and kicked his Charger into life, flooring the pedal as the car lurched forward past cars that parted—*like Moses parting the Red Sea*, he always thought to himself. He picked up the mike and called into dispatch to get more information.

"It's a shooting on I-40 westbound through the Clipper Mountain pass, Lew; that's what we have now," Gloria told him. "Officer Morton is en route; he'll be there in about ten minutes."

"Tell Morton to observe at first, see if there are any injured that require help," Phil began. "Unfortunately, I have a feeling it's going to be a lot worse. Tell him to wait after initial inspection until I arrive, which will be in about thirty-three minutes."

"10-4, Lew," and Gloria was gone.

Phil threw the mike down and pounded his right fist on the console. The next phase of the killing spree had begun. Now the Southwest would know what the East Coast had gone through ten years earlier. Fear and paranoia would reign as the sniper increased his killings, with law enforcement unable to find him or stop him. Phil knew he would strike again, and soon. The questions were where, when, and how many kills before he stopped this time and moved on to another place. That was the method to his evilness.

Phil also realized that in order to defeat Frank, he would have to become just as evil and have to think like Frank. What he feared most was after everything was over, that he would never stop thinking that way.

CHAPTER 16

Phil looked down the embankment at the wreckage, which lay on its side 150 feet below. The remains of the victims were still inside. It had been about forty-five minutes since Phil had arrived at the scene; he was waiting for the search and rescue squad to reach the car. The three officers rappelled down the hillside, like large bugs hopping down the slope. Finally reaching the bottom, they unhitched their harnesses and made their way to the crash site. When they reached the vehicle, the lead officer, Big John Harrison, ex-Army Ranger, peered inside, immediately turned, and began to retch. The hairs on the back of Phil's neck rose up with the tension as he watched from up above as the other two rescuers backed up at the sight of John vomiting.

"John, are you okay?" Phil radioed down.

John stood up, wiped his mouth with his sleeve, and clicked on his radio. "I'm fine, just didn't expect to see…" he said, pointing to the car, "this type of carnage. I shouldn't have eaten that taco at lunch. Half of their heads are gone, and what's left is like looking at a horror picture."

Phil's gut began to churn acid as he instinctively looked at the surrounding mountains, trying to triangulate where the shots came from. "Do you think they were shot from front or behind?" he asked.

John went back and looked more closely. "Front shot, probably large caliber. Explosive tip by the amount of damage and blood splatter that I see," he said. "Motherfucker is good."

"He's the best, trained by the best," Phil said flatly. "Get the bodies out and up to the coroner's wagon before they start to cook. Then get a hook in the beast, and let's get it hauled up," Phil said and clicked off. He walked slightly east on the shoulder about two hundred feet and stopped as he spotted some red droplets on the guardrail. He walked over and inspected more closely. He concluded that they were blood splatter. *First hit was here*, he thought, *probably the passenger first*, as he began to walk back to the area of the crash site. He looked down at the ground, saw no skid marks, but found the tire tracks that crossed the shoulder leading to the dented guardrail where the vehicle struck and flipped. The driver was probably shot twenty-five to thirty feet from the point of impact, which caused the car to veer directly to the right. He figured then that the shot came from left front, and looked in that direction. There were six flat elevated zones in the mountains surrounding the area within one to one and a half miles that could have been the shooting perch. He went to his vehicle, got out a pair of Zeiss binoculars, and looked at the varying peaks. He finally focused on one in particular. The center one had a complete view of the interstate as it came winding through, which would have been perfect target practice for Frank.

To be on the safe side, Phil had ordered the interstate closed in both directions, with the traffic diverted onto Amboy Road at Mountain Springs exit from the east and Kilbaker Road from the west. Luckily it was a Saturday morning so traffic was light, but the afternoon would be different, with people coming back from the Colorado River with their boats and toys. He figured they had about six hours to get their investigation wrapped up and then they could reopen. He had four vehicles directing traffic. What he worried about was the media's response to the sniper attack. His wandering mind was suddenly broken by the sight of two CHP vehicles, lights flashing, followed by eight black Cadillac Escalade SUVs in two-by-two rows about two miles west and closing rapidly.

"Oh shit," he said to himself. He hit the radio button. "Hey, Big John, we have company coming. Eight big black Cadillac Escalades, following two black and whites and moving fast."

"Feds, come to take over the show," John said back.

"That was my thought exactly," Phil replied. "Keep doing what you can until they get here, and I will try to keep them out of our way." He clicked off after John acknowledged. Phil watched the convoy close in on them and then passed by his position, Officers McGee and Peterson in the two black and whites. They both gave a mock salute as they passed by, then turned their vehicles around at the next U-turn five hundred yards ahead, followed by the eight

SUVs. It would have been funny if Phil weren't already pissed at the fact that they needed escorts to find their way, especially with the budget deficit. But then again, they were the Feds, and they probably couldn't find their own ass with both hands.

McGee parked his vehicle behind Phil's, and the rest lined up. McGee was the first one out and approached Phil apologetically. "Sorry, Lew, some FBI bigwig ordered the watch commander, and we got chosen to guide this asshole."

"He's a fuckwad, not an asshole, McGee, which makes him even worse," Phil replied, patting McGee on his shoulder, making light of the situation. Phil leaned up against his car with arms folded as he waited for the parade of FBI agents as they exited their vehicles, led by the five-foot-six assistant FBI director, Anthony Balducci. All of the FBI agents were dressed in dark suits with Ray-Ban sunglasses. "Is this a bad scene from *The Matrix*?" Phil asked.

"Actually it looks more like a bad Blues Brothers movie," McGee answered.

"Watch this," Phil said as he pushed off the car, walked about five feet, and extended his hand as the crowd surrounded the two old friends.

"Tony, how the fuck are ya?" Phil said in his best Bronx accent as they gripped each other's hands firmly. The usage of his nickname in mixed company caught everyone by surprise; some of the agents waited for their boss to explode. Instead, he just shook his head as he released his grip, and replied, "Good to see you too, Lieutenant." Phil still was wearing a big shit-eating grin as he towered over his childhood friend, waiting for the other shoe to fall. Instead, he was hit with a big surprise.

"We are here to help you in this investigation. As you and I both know," Tony said, "this may be just the beginning of more sniper attacks, possibly more killings. We need to work together to catch this individual."

Phil's mood immediately changed with the political correctness of the statement. His smile disappeared, replaced by a nasty scowl and a look that would melt steel. "If we had worked together ten years ago, like I had suggested, this never would have happened," he growled. The crowd of FBI agents instinctively all retreated a few steps, giving the two of them more room. "You're lucky, Lefty, that I don't kick your fucking ass like I should have forty-eight years ago," he said, quietly enough but still with a growl, "but I want to nail this motherfucker to a cross more than you. So I'll be nice and work with you, but don't ever order me like some chimp on a fuckin' chain."

Tony looked Phil right in the eyes, wary of the use of his other nickname. He knew Phil well enough to know that when he got this personal, you didn't want to cross him. But he didn't want to lose face in front of the agents. So he squared his shoulders and said, "You and I both know political bureaucratic bullshit and how much comes down from above. I asked for you ten years ago, but was turned down from above," Tony said as he pulled his glasses off, looking as intense as possible with his dark brown eyes. "They had their man and that was that. What was I to say?"

"That they were wrong about the man they finally executed," Phil said flatly. "You knew it, Tony, especially after that phone call from me asking if there had been women found that had disappeared just prior to the sniper attacks. You were dead silent for a good fifteen seconds. In fact, I thought I had lost the connection. Then you said no and changed the subject."

"I was told not to divulge any facts to you or anyone," Tony insisted while waving his hands. The scene was almost comical with the two Italians expressing their anger and frustrations with facial and hand gestures.

The sincerity in Tony's eyes was enough for Phil, who extended his hand again, which was grasped immediately. "Will you listen to me this time?" he asked.

"I'm going to do more than that, Phil," Tony began. "I've started a task force across all law enforcement levels that I'm going to head. I want you to be cochief of the task force. Total transparency of where we're going, with all information shared, and of course, the resources from the FBI to help with any evidence found."

"I'm flattered," Phil replied with humility, "but I want to remain in the field, almost like lead detective on a case. I don't want to be a desk monkey," he said bluntly.

"Like me?" Tony asked with a smile, and they both shared a laugh when Phil nodded in agreement, as the other agents showed signs of relief. They inched closer, awaiting orders, now that the turmoil had passed. "Tell me what's happened here."

"Two women, driving west on I-40, were shot, probably at very long distance with a high-powered, long-range rifle. The first victim," he said as he walked toward the bloodstained section of the guardrail, "which was the passenger, was shot here." He pointed to the spatters of blood. "The driver was shot just before the point of impact of the car with the guardrail, which caused the car to flip in the air and land about 150 feet down the embankment. I have three men down there now, retrieving the remains and then the vehicle intact. Or what remains of them," he said with a somber note.

"Do you have any knowledge of the caliber bullet used?" Agent Timmons asked from the back.

"Probably a 50 caliber," Phil said, "with exploding tips."

"Why do you say that?" Tony asked.

"Because half of their heads are gone, and I only know of a few calibers that can inflict that much damage, and because it's his favorite caliber for long-range sniper kills," Phil said as a referral to Frank's past.

"Could this be a copycat?" Agent Flaherty asked.

"I doubt it," Phil said curtly as if she were dismissed.

"Why?" she retorted. She wanted a better answer than an opinion. "What facts do you have?

"Because it's the exact same pattern, I'll bet the exact same DNA, for which there will be no match anywhere in the world, and only Frank DiMocchio could shoot this good. Period," he ended emphatically.

She nodded in agreement. "Point well taken. Where do you think the shots came from?" she asked.

Phil pointed at the fifth mountain, at the flat perch area that he knew was perfect, and said, "I'll bet my house on that flat spot on that mountain. Perfect distance for a high-caliber rifle, and perfect view site for oncoming traffic," he concluded, looking east as they all turned following his logic.

Tony began giving orders to his agents as Phil and Agent Flaherty stood alone. "I wanted to apologize for yesterday," she began. "I was told this morning that the girl who was found in the first grave was almost like family to you. I am so sorry, Lieutenant," she said.

The shock of what transpired took a few seconds to wear off, leaving Phil with a slightly opened mouth and nothing to say. "It's Phil," he said, smiling.

"It's Kelly," she replied, also smiling.

Phil started to shuffle his feet a little as he became shy all of a sudden. He was relieved when Tony returned, but even more nervous when Tony announced that they would be working together until the end. Phil tried to slow his breathing down to avoid hyperventilating as he realized the physical attraction he had for Agent Kelly Flaherty. He felt his heart pounding in his chest as he pondered the problem of trying to focus on the job at hand. He couldn't afford the distraction, not now. But as he stole a glance at her, the beauty and elegance he saw made him melt like butter.

What Phil didn't know was at that very moment, she was having the very exact same thoughts.

CHAPTER 17

Phil's mood had changed so dramatically over the course of that Saturday. It had started with the early morning adrenaline rush as he investigated the interstate killings. The chemistry that existed between him and Agent Flaherty had progressed as the day wore on, causing an elevation of that mood to its highest level. All of the euphoria came crashing down by that afternoon as the revelation of Gina's "meeting" with the most wanted killer in Phil's life came to light. The feeling of betrayal had ripped through his very core. The image of someone he had considered a daughter as she sat in front of everyone and admitted her foray with the beast was enough to shatter his soul. Then she had the audacity to admit no fault of her own since she had been abducted. The Patti Hearst story did not sit well with anyone. He finally found his way home that night after Gina was escorted back to her hotel room. She was now a prisoner of the system as a material witness under constant guard.

He knew that there would be more death and that it would be sooner rather than later. What concerned him now was his own mortality. For the first time in his professional life, he feared that the deaths would also include his own. What worried him more was his apathetic feeling toward his own demise. That mind-set would only lead to mistakes. His mind was in total conflict. All of the years of training, where one learned to survive at all costs, were finally at odds with his clinical depression.

The two conflicting thoughts had created nothing but chaos at a time when he could not afford any loss of concentration.

Not since the terror of the restless nights after Viet Nam had he felt this useless and hopeless.

He knew that he needed to retire from the force. Money was not an issue. He didn't have any at hand. That was taken by his ex-wife. But he could live decently on his pensions from both the CHP and the SFPD.

But what would he do?

Fishing and playing golf were good for a while. But then what? Traveling? He saw enough of the world with the marines. Besides, he loved this beautiful country and was more of a homebody. But being home just intensified his feelings of uselessness.

He took another swig of his beer as his eyes now focused on the replay of the Dodger game. The clock on the DVR read 3:15 a.m., with the recently reinstated left fielder up at the plate. Even the legendary Vin Scully made mention of his loss of home-run power since coming off of his suspension for using steroids. The implications were obvious. It made Phil dream of the days of Willie Mays, Hank Aaron, and Mickey Mantle. The days of his youth, before the war took all of that away, were always in the back of his mind. At this time of the morning, it only made him even more depressed than before, so he downed the rest of his beer.

He couldn't get the images of the graves in the desert, or Mirabel's face when he had to inform her of her cousin's death, out of his mind.

He was tired.

But he couldn't sleep.

He hadn't slept in two days, not more than power naps. Any more would bring on the dreams, and with the dreams came the nightmares.

So he took another swig of beer, but the bottle was empty.

He reached into the ice chest next to his easy chair and took out a fresh beer. He looked at the bottle in his hand and for no reason began to cry. Within seconds, he was an uncontrollable sobbing mess. He dropped the bottle and curled up into a ball. His six-foot-three frame was reduced to a three-foot fetus. He felt that he had slipped into his own hell. He was so exhausted that he fell asleep instead.

The clouds parted, revealing a nearly full moon, a halo of moisture circling its face. The rain had stopped momentarily, but the heat and humidity were still oppressive. He leaned back in his small foxhole and stared up at the stars as more appeared. The Big Dipper poured into the Little Dipper as the two constellations appeared directly above. Having grown up in the Bronx, stars were always hard to see clearly, but not here in the bush.

Suddenly it became eerily quiet. The platoon was under a strict silence code, with the anticipation of an enemy attack high. The Claymores and wires were set in a perfect circle of their perimeter. Unless they were Tarzan, the enemy could not enter without being blown halfway to kingdom come.

Quietly he checked his weapon's magazine and recounted the number of rounds he had left. Then he began his scan of the immediate surroundings. He saw Tony in his nest about fifteen yards to the right. His big ears were like saucers that glowed in the full moon. He too was looking at the stars. To his left was Gomez, a cigarette above each ear and a lit one that always dangled from his mouth. He chain-smoked to avoid lighting a match. He always replaced the used butt with a new one from the right ear, then moved the left to the right as he completed the cycle. His stash of cigarettes was in his right boot. They had been best friends since boot camp. He still owed them thirty-five bucks each for poker losses. He had a run of bad cards, hopefully not luck.

Phil sat up quickly as he heard machine-gun fire in the distance, maybe four clicks upriver. *Must be Bravo patrol back from their scouting*, he thought. The firing intensified for a few minutes, and then larger salvo ammunition could be heard. He thought it was mortars. But what worried him was that he thought they were theirs and not ours. Explosions and fires lit up the sky. Against the clouds, the hues ranged from yellow to orange. Its beauty would be breathtaking if not for the death associated with the colors.

As quickly as it began, the battle ended. Fires were extinguished as the darkness and then the silence returned.

But with the finality came the knowledge that Bravo patrol would not return. Also, the enemy had moved closer to their position and had overwhelming power. This thrust by the enemy was larger than what had been expected by the high command. He wished he could call for an air strike and even the odds, but the flyboys hated flying sorties in the middle of the night. Too much of a chance of friendly-fire kill, was what he was told. He was just a grunt, an inch above an earthworm, was what was drilled into his head by his boot-camp sergeant. He had no opinion.

So he waited, and continued to scan the perimeter for any sign of movement. Silently, he prayed the Claymores would save his life. A chill went through him as he felt another's soul pass on the way to its final destination.

All of a sudden the silence was broken by the fires of hell as mortar shells rained down upon their positions with deadly consequences. Explosions occurred all around. Four shells landed in a pattern, with each area the size of a tennis court. The entire drop zone covered one square mile and used over 250 rounds. In that surrealistic moment, time paused as Phil looked to the right and saw Tony's head explode. The ears traveled in opposite directions as they tumbled through the lights and rolled as each hit the ground, like coins that finally came to rest heads upright.

To the left he saw Gomez's foxhole take a direct hit and launched what was left of him into the air. It finally came to rest directly on top of Phil. The stench of burned flesh, plus the feel of the bloody intestines against his arms, caused him to open his mouth to scream, but no sound was emitted. He was hysterically trying to get the remains off of him, when another blast closer to him erupted and showered him with more dirt and debris. He was buried alive with Gomez's remains. He began to get short of breath as he slowly suffocated and…

He woke up in a cold sweat and noticed that his head hung off of the couch, with his feet up above, against the wall, just below his pictures. His breathing slowly began to return to normal as he assumed the upright position. The spinning and nausea were there; the headache would come later. He shielded his eyes against the early morning sun and peered at the TV, which was still on. He saw the *Today Show*; the clock in the corner of the screen said 7:07. The host was spouting more bad economic news, so he turned the TV off.

He stood up slowly, stretching his extremely sore back, legs, and arms. He waited for all of the popping and cracking joints to end their symphony as he began to move. He went directly to the Mr. Coffee machine and made a fresh pot of coffee. While the French vanilla flavor liquid brewed, he decided to reach into the fridge. He thought of Jim Morrison's line in the Doors' song "Roadhouse Blues": "Woke up this morning, had myself a beer" as he unscrewed the cap and slowly drank his last Foster's lager. He retrieved his favorite cup and poured one and a half inches of the brewed coffee and then added two Sweet'N Lows, along with Bailey's Irish Cream. Then he let out a huge belch from the beer, and raised his cup to his fallen buddies.

"Hair of the dog," he said as he took a swig of the strong brew and felt the immediate jolt to the body as the blast of caffeine hit. "Time to go to work," he said as he headed toward the shower and prayed that today would get better.

He stubbed his toe and spilled his coffee before reaching the bathroom. His imitation of Yosemite Sam as he dealt with the two sources of pain would make Mel Blanc proud.

He then knew that his day could and would only get worse.

As the hot water ran over his entire aching body from his head to his toes, he recounted the horror that was yesterday. From the house explosion to the sniper attack, the image of the victims still ingrained in his mind, to the discovery that his "niece" Gina had been to Frank's place, but didn't think it was important enough to let him know. He felt betrayed, especially in front of the FBI, and especially Kelly. In front of Gina and Tony, in Phil's office, she questioned whether Phil could be impartial. Then she questioned Gina's loyalties. That's when Phil was like a father defending her integrity and displaying no second thoughts of his mission; his booming voice could be clearly heard through closed doors.

"I want that motherfucker more than you will ever want anything in your life, and I want him dead, period," is how he had screamed it at both Kelly and Tony. His outburst had caused him to have some chest pains, which no one knew about, but they had subsided. Despite his family history and age, he did not seek any medical attention. Instead, he finally went home and got plastered. The pounding headache was easing as he let the water run directly on the back of his neck as it massaged the tight muscles. Suddenly an overwhelming feeling of dread invaded his serenity, almost like a ripple in the Force in *Star Wars*. Something horrible was bound to happen, if not already underway; it involved Frank, and the smell of death was everywhere. The shower stall began to spin. He turned just in time to vomit directly into the drain, and sank to his hands and knees, the hot water now hitting the middle of his back. He stayed in that position for what felt like eternity as the vertigo finally stopped.

He finally looked up and said, "Please, Lord, have pity on my soul, and give me strength to rid this world of such evil." Just then his cell phone, house phone, and beeper all went off at once. He shook his head in acknowledgment of the possible emergency, looked back up as he exited the shower, and uttered, "Thanks," as he read the urgent text message. "Sniper attack on Interstate 5 north of LA; please respond," along with Kelly's cell phone number was displayed across the iPhone screen. He sank butt-naked onto his bed as he pondered what lay ahead. For the first time in his life, a large part of him was screaming to just run away from everything. Start fresh, somewhere else, where no one knew who he was, and didn't care.

He later wished that he had listened to his subconscious.

CHAPTER 18

The early morning fog appeared to resemble a thickly quilted blanket in the passes below as the fingers spread in all directions; the mountain peaks of Southern California appeared as brown cones in a sea of white. It was only 6:00 a.m. as the sun rose over the top of the Tehachapi Mountains to the east. It started to spread not only its light, but also its warmth, which began to melt away the fog as the fingers withdrew slowly to the west toward Los Padres National Forest. The sky above was bright blue, with the ever-present inversion layer of brown smog that covered the Los Angeles basin just to the south. The early-morning golden colors began to reflect off of Pyramid Lake to the west as the light danced like fireflies off of the waves.

The quiet of the night turned into the noise of the day as the traffic began to build on Interstate 5. Commuters from the Central Valley began to wind their way up, over, and down through the pass between the Tehachapi Mountains to the east and the Sierra Madre Mountains to the west. "The Grapevine," as this part of the eight-lane freeway was called, was at best a nightmare during the workweek. The mixture of large trucks and small cars at varying speeds and skill of driving was enough to cause multiple daily accidents, especially on the 6 percent downgrade. Speeds often exceeded ninety miles per hour in certain curving, downhill stretches, with inexperienced drivers believing they were NASCAR professionals. The results were often catastrophic, with multiple severe injuries and fatalities annually. Frank sat there at five thousand feet on Sawtooth Mountain, in the lotus position on his blanket, as he surveyed the chaos below in contrast to the quiet solitude of his position. His thoughts concentrated on the next phase of his life.

He had found this spot years ago and used it when he needed total peace and solitude. He was able to commune with nature as the sounds of nighttime crickets evolved into the singing of birds with each dawn. It caused a rebirth of his own being, at peace with himself. His thoughts became more focused, now with purpose to move forward and to put into motion the final plan that would end with the defeat of all of his enemies. He looked below, now seeing all of the lanes clearly as the fog had totally dissipated, giving him almost five miles of clear visibility. He slowly stood and stretched as he methodically flexed all of his muscles. He rolled up his blanket and returned it to his backpack.

He walked fifteen yards to the left and pulled the canopy off of his rifle, which was attached to its tripod. The magazine was loaded with ten 50 caliber bullets, but without explosive tips. Those were harder to make and were used only when he wanted to inflict major damage. Today was more for turmoil than damage. He focused the 2,500-meter zoom lens scope and then looked through it with his right eye for about a minute. He stopped as a shadow passed over him, and the shrill cry of the circling hawk could be heard. He looked up and saw the male red-tailed hawk as it slowly circled about two hundred feet above the mountainside. It searched for breakfast and called for its mate with wings spread, the red tail feathers acted as a rudder that steered the beautiful bird of prey. He stood up and followed the bird intensely, seemingly drawn to it, almost in reverence of its beauty and predatory instincts. Within minutes he witnessed the hawk dive at breathtaking speed as it swooped down and in seconds emerged from the brush, a small ground squirrel caught in its sharp talons. The shrill call began in earnest as it alerted its mate to the spoils of victory, and flew off to the east and its nest in the pine trees.

Frank raised his fists in excitement at what he had just witnessed and let out a shout of approval. "This is a sign," he said to himself as he picked up his binoculars that lay near the gun stand and began to scan the interstate as it started its descent near the exit for State Highway 138. He watched as traffic continued to build; more-frantic drivers were emerging as it got closer to seven thirty. People late for work were usually the craziest ones. At least that's what Frank was hoping for this morning. Within ten minutes he had the perfect scenario building in his head, but needed the right elements for it to succeed. So he waited and stared through the binoculars as the sun began to burn the back of his neck and arms. Instead of feeling the pain, he focused harder on the oncoming traffic. Then he saw the perfect combination brewing near the top of the downgrade.

A double fuel tanker was in the second lane from the right, passing a cattle truck loaded with prized Harris Ranch cattle. A half mile behind, some yahoo in a BMW 326I was thinking he was Dale Earnhardt Jr. at Daytona as he weaved in and out of lanes, twenty to thirty miles per hour faster than the existing traffic speed. Frank smiled to himself, slowly put the glasses down, and kneeled in his sniper's position. He grasped the rifle firmly, released the safety, and settled the butt end into his shoulder. He put his right eye to the scope and focused on both the BMW and the fuel tanker. He gripped the trigger gently as he began his breathing exercise. Slowly he brought his heart rate and blood pressure down to where any nervousness disappeared.

Finally, when the fuel tanker was within a mile of his position and now five hundred feet ahead of the cattle truck, the BMW made its move to pass the fuel tanker on the right. Frank squeezed the trigger. The explosion rang in his ears, even through the earplugs. Within seconds, the right front tire of the tanker blew out with the direct hit. This caused the truck driver to lose control as the double tanker veered directly to the right into the deadly jackknifed position. Frank could see the front end of the BMW dip as the inexperienced driver slammed on the brakes, but at over one hundred miles per hour, the car flipped over. The car was launched into a death spiral twenty feet into the air. It slammed into the back tanker on its descent, which ignited both the car and tanker at once. The cattle truck was unprepared for what had occurred directly in front. The driver applied the brakes, but to no avail as it slid into the belly of the burning conglomeration. A second fireball erupted as the fuel tanks of the cattle truck exploded. The screams of both man and beast reverberated through the canyon.

Frank smiled, but did not celebrate victory just yet. He wasn't done. He stayed focused as he peered at the carnage below through his scope. He was pleased that he had only used one bullet so far. The black cloud of smoke rose higher into the air as people stopped behind and realized they were going nowhere. Many exited their vehicles, looks of horror on their faces as many covered their mouths as they tried to escape from the stench. Like cattle themselves, a multitude of humans herded toward the scene. Frank smiled again.

Then he squeezed the trigger five times in succession. Five victims within forty-five feet of each other were hit in a left-to-right shoot. The time between targets was less than two seconds, with the shots all centered at the chests. The bodies flew backward from the point of impact. It was like being back at the shooting galleries at the amusement park when he was a kid, he thought, as the last person who was shot ended up on the hood of his car. He ended up spread-eagled like he was crucified as the blood poured out of the gaping chest wound with the head slumped over. The screams erupted as panic spread through the crowd of people as they stampeded over each other as they tried to either seek shelter or just run away.

Frank focused one last shot on a man who pushed an older woman down on the ground as he tried to get past her. He squeezed one more time, and within seconds the man's body was flailed forward as his back erupted; he was dead before he hit the ground. Frank immediately jumped up and began his war whoop, his arms raised high in triumph. The adrenaline rush now surged as he quickly disassembled his rifle and tripod, picked up all of the spent shells, packed his encampment away, and walked downhill toward his truck as the screams continued from below.

As he reached the truck, he could hear the wails of multiple sirens that came from both north and south. He dropped his pack and rifle bag into the bed of his truck, locked the shell cover, and slid into the cab. He lit up a joint and enjoyed the moment of victory. He thought that the I-5 might be closed for a while. It didn't matter to him since he wasn't traveling that way anyhow. He slowly descended the dirt fire trail and made his way east, away from the disaster he had created. The only problem now, he thought, was how was he ever going to top this?

It gave him food for thought as he traveled slowly over the rough terrain. The serene sounds of Aaron Copland's "Appalachian Spring" played in his headphones as he began his journey north to his old residence in the Bay Area and a new beginning.

CHAPTER 19

Phil stared out of the small window of the helicopter as he watched the topography below change as they left the desert area and began to fly through the Palm Springs pass between the San Jacinto and San Bernardino Mountains. The jagged peaks of the brown, rocky, mountains formed a passage from the barren landscape to the lush eastern portion of the Inland Empire. Following the course of Interstate 10, they crossed over small cities like Calimesa and Yucaipa. Middle-class neighborhoods, houses with manicured lawns, some with pools, slowly changed into the larger homes of Redlands, the jewel city of the Inland Empire. A lot of money was found in the city of 65,000, known for its orange groves and large Victorian-style homes.

His brother had lived there and was buried there. He could see the cemetery in the distance to the south, nestled up in the hill, where his brother was in plot number 957. His headstone had the inscription "Weep not for me, my children, for I am at peace." He had died twenty years earlier. Phil hadn't been to his grave in over two years. He thought of him every day, prayed that he was at peace, but for some reason never found the time to visit. That would be corrected, as would the schism between him and his late brother's widow. He smiled as he thought about Italian families and their petty arguments that made the famous Hatfield-McCoy feuds seem tame. After the events of the past few days, he decided to visit his brother's grave, have a talk with him, and call his widow. "Thinking of your brother?" The question from Tony startled him; he'd forgotten that Tony was there for the funeral. A gentle hand on his shoulder from behind shook him from his trance. He turned around and nodded. "It's been almost twenty years, hasn't it?" Kelly asked.

"Twenty to be exact," Phil acknowledged, not knowing how she had known, but not caring to ask.

She sensed the wall go up as Phil turned back around, so she tried to change the subject and focus on the case at hand. Tony wouldn't let it go.

"Have you spoken to her lately?" Tony pushed harder. Kelly had a quizzical look on her face.

Suddenly the entire cabin was dead silent as Phil took a deep breath, looked south again, and then responded, "No, not yet. But I intend to, once all of this is over. Life's too short," he finished while looking at the valley below. What was once farmland and citrus groves appeared to be one city after another, with every inch of earth built upon, the freeways clogged even at 10:00 a.m. It only added to his melancholy. He felt a chill go down his spine, as if someone were walking on his grave. Knowing his older brother, it was probably him.

"You're growing soft in your old age, my friend," Tony said with some compassion. "Whatever happened to that macho Italian bullshit about respect you always gave me?"

"I've mellowed with wisdom," and as soon as Phil said it, the three of them laughed heartily.

"Sir, I have LA Sheriff Villanova on the horn," the pilot said, interrupting the mood with a dose of reality.

"This is Assistant Director Balducci," Tony said, as if people were impressed by using his title. "Yes, sheriff, we're en route now; should be there in twenty minutes," he said, and then went quiet as the sheriff updated the situation. Tony made notes as he listened; he passed one to Kelly, who immediately went onto her iPad and entered her data. Phil turned and watched Tony as he nodded and wrote, his eyes intense and focused on his legal pad. Finally he said, "I have everything I need; we'll meet you there. Thank you."

He looked up at Phil and said, "We're in the shit all over again."

"What's the story?" Phil asked, anxious to hear the details. Tony was running his right hand through his dyed-black hair, a look of total desperation on his face. Instead of answering, he handed Phil his legal pad. Phil read the sheriff's account of the chain of events that started with the fuel tanker blowing a tire through the five executions, all shot within thirty seconds. Phil's stomach knot grew tighter as he continued to read about the single chest wounds of all of the victims, all with large-caliber bullets. The final sentence was a plea for federal help, both in manpower and funds, to help find the killer. The politics of law enforcement made him sicker. "He caused the perfect accident, then had a shooting gallery to follow. It was absolutely brilliant military planning. He created the diversion first, which allowed the masses to gather, and then he followed with the main barrage."

"Brilliant, my ass—he's a psychopath," Tony replied harshly, the stress showing with his response.

"Number one, he's not a psychopath, he's a sociopath. He has all of his faculties; he is not delusional nor hallucinatory," Phil said firmly. "Two, he was trained militarily by the best this country had to offer. So he will think and plan as he was taught. He just loves to kill, in any fashion, which makes him a unique serial killer. He can change his method of operation at any time and stay one step ahead of us."

"Then you think he is already gone?" This time it was Kelly who asked the question. She had come to the same conclusion.

"Absolutely," Phil said without hesitation. "This was his diversion for the main event."

"Gina and you," Kelly said flatly. "He's heading to the Bay Area."

"Beautiful and brilliant," Phil said as he nodded his head in agreement with her assessment. Kelly blushed and smiled. Tony saw the interaction and grinned himself. Phil turned slightly red, and embarrassed, he switched the conversation back to the murders.

"This has become personal," Phil said. "I tried to convince a judge when he was only thirteen years old that he was a killer. But he wouldn't listen, like some other people I know."

"Would you get off my fucking back over that?" Tony semi-exploded. "I made a mistake, but like I told you, I had my marching orders; case closed."

"You still owe me a case of Tignanello Wine, vintage 1993, and then I'll be off of your fucking back," Phil replied, looking directly at Tony. Kelly didn't know if Phil was joking or not.

"Fuck you. Do you know how much that shit costs?" Tony said, with his Bronx accent coming back stronger.

"Yeah, I know how much—$250 per bottle—but a bet is a bet," Phil said, "even in Washington."

"That's a $3,000 bet," Kelly said. "What was the wager?"

"That Frank DiMocchio was the East Coast Slayer and that he would kill again." This time it was Tony who filled in the blanks. "You'll have your case of wine as soon as this is over, I promise."

"Good enough for me," Phil said as he extended his hand. Tony took it and they went through the motions of the old neighborhood gang's shake sequence, ending with bumping elbows and heads nodding. Kelly put her hand to her mouth and laughed as she witnessed two important grown men acting like preteens from the *Little Rascals*.

"Sorry to interrupt your fun, but we will be approaching the scene in about five minutes." The pilot's voice was heard through the headphones. Phil turned around in time to see Castaic Lake in the distance to the right as they passed through Santa Clarita. They then passed over the intersection of Interstate 5 and California Route 14. The traffic was at a dead stop for miles northbound on I-5; the southbound with scant traffic came from local cities only. The main artery of California commerce was still closed in both directions at the horrific murder scene. Phil gazed at the pointed peaks of the San Gabriel Mountains, which rose up to eight thousand feet on both sides of the interstate, fluffy white clouds hovering nearby. He wished he had his camera equipment for this picture-postcard moment. To his left, multiple huge roller coasters occupied the landscape at Magic Mountain Amusement Park. He remembered riding Colossus backward with his older daughters, and vomiting afterward as they laughed. He smiled to himself as the memory flashed through his mind.

The vegetation began to change as they flew farther north past Castaic Lake to a mixture of desert brush interspersed between tall sugar pines of the mountains in this part of Southern California. The recent rains had left the hillsides greener than Phil could remember this late in the year, with wildflowers of all different colors. The short-lived pleasure that the vibrant colors brought was shattered by the initial view of the crash scene, which looked like a war zone. Tony instructed the pilot to take a few sweeps over the scene, so they could get a better image of the horror that one man had created.

The carnage was spread over all four lanes of the southbound interstate. The charred remains of the burned wreckage of both trucks lay side by side. Smoke was still rising from the smoldering embers of burned rawhide. Bodies covered with tarps lay where they were shot. An area of about a quarter mile was cordoned off by various law enforcement agencies. On the second pass, the pilot indicated that he was about to land and to expect a little bumpiness from wind turbulence through the pass—something Phil didn't need to hear, as he had braced himself when he felt the first dip that sent his stomach into his chest. Even though it only took twenty seconds to land, it felt like an eternity to him. He would have done a better job, he thought to himself as they finally touched down and the engines were cut.

As they exited the helicopter, the stench hit them like a baseball bat. Kelly and Tony put their hands over their noses as they tried to block the smell. Phil took in slow deep breaths to allow himself to get used to the smell as he stood there and scanned the mountains around the scene. He didn't need to see the wrecks and bodies to know what had happened here. He needed to focus on where Frank set up his sniper's nest. He was already gone from the area. Phil was sure of this because Frank was a creature of habit and a planner. He would have had an escape route devised way in advance. Phil focused his vision on the third mountain to the left, about a mile away, which had fire roads going up its side and was in perfect alignment with the shootings.

His concentration was broken by a hand on his shoulder. He turned in time to see Kelly. "See something interesting?" Her voice was muffled as she asked through a hand that still covered her nose.

"You'll get used to the smell a lot quicker if you just take it in. Let your body get used to it. I learned that in Nam, especially the burning bodies," Phil said nonchalantly. He pointed at the mountain in question. "That's his perch. I'm sure of it. It's the perfect distance and angle for a sniper with his talents."

"It almost sounds like you are in awe of his abilities," Kelly said.

"It's not awe—more like respect," Phil said, almost lecturing to her. "To truly know your enemy, you must respect their strengths and never underestimate their capabilities. We need to get up there and look around. We're wasting our time down here; he's long gone, but I have an idea where he went, if my hunch is right."

"I'll get a car, let Tony know what we're doing and get up there," Kelly said. "The quicker we are, the better chance to catch him."

Phil shook his head at first as he looked away, then turned back and faced her. His eyes were dark and cold, his mood entirely different. "You must stop being an FBI agent and think differently. He will never be caught. You either have to kill him, or he gets away, to start killing all over again somewhere else. Are you willing to shoot first and ask questions later?" he asked flatly. Her silence was too much for Phil. "Just as I thought," he said. "Get a four-by-four, and let's get going," he continued with some disgust in his voice. "When we catch up to him, stay out of my way, and I'll show you how to save the taxpayers millions of dollars." He turned and walked away from her. He had dismissed her as he scanned the terrain.

He looked toward Pyramid Lake and saw a bass fishing boat trolling the calm waters. He had a sudden foreboding of things to come. He now knew that this would be the last phase of his career that started so many years ago in the bushes of Viet Nam. And just like forty years ago, he questioned the chain of command, who also underestimated their enemy. The difference this time was that he didn't give a shit anymore, because after this, he was done.

He just wanted to live to see that day.

CHAPTER 20

Frank stopped at the Public Storage facility on South Bakersfield Boulevard, paid $250 for a ten-by-eight-foot unit for two months, along with a large Master Lock, and emptied the contents of his truck into the small space. When finished, he drove across town to a Maaco auto repair shop and paid $550 in cash for a paint job on the truck. He spent the three-hour wait at a dark, half-empty bar and grille around the corner. He dined on a sirloin steak with a baked potato and steamed vegetables, with a Foster's on tap, while watching the Braves vs. Phillies game on ESPN. Even though his Giants had won the World Series the previous year, everyone was still picking the Braves to win it all. *Not today*, he thought as he watched the score balloon to 10-1 as the Phillies poured it on the Braves' ace pitcher. He had to chuckle at all of the prognosticators and their predictions. Then he chuckled again as he thought what his odds of escape from the FBI would be in Las Vegas. Not too good probably, but he liked betting on the underdog.

He finished his meal and sipped his beer until the glass was empty. The waitress was cute, and if he hadn't had his fun earlier that morning, she would have been his play toy. But he was pressed for time so he thanked her for a great meal and service, left a 20 percent tip on the table, and paid his bill. He went outside, put on his Ray-Bans to block the brightness of the afternoon sun, and walked back to the paint shop. He inspected the truck, now a dark amethyst color, evenly coated, with no streaks or missed areas. He was impressed and thanked everyone there with an extra $50.00 tip. He had always appreciated hard workers, especially those that were conscientious.

He headed back to the storage unit, reloaded the truck, but left the empty space locked when he left, even though he would never return. From there he headed north on California State Route 65 through miles of farmland. The early spring days were filled with flowering nut trees, neatly aligned in rows, their branches almost touching each other, which created a tunnel effect. Memories of his father flashed before him, and images of a little boy traveling to Modesto from the Bay Area in the car. Just the two of them, a Kodak Brownie automatic on the seat between them, finding an orchard in full bloom, wandering down the rows, taking pictures as the bees buzzed in the trees above. If only he had lived, maybe things would have been different.

Probably not.

About an hour north of Bakersfield, the route began to enter the foothills of the southern Sierra Mountains. Wildflowers were beginning to blossom at the lower elevations; the hills were a combination of yellows and lavenders interspersed among the green grasses. He took a right-hand turn onto route 190 as he headed for Sequoia National Forest and the giant redwoods of King Canyon National Park. After he paid his $10.00 entrance fee, he asked the female ranger how the fishing was, and got some inside tips on the best spots to fly-fish up on the San Joaquin River, just on the eastern boundary of the park. He paid an extra $19.00 for the weekly fishing license fee under the name of Jimmie Olsen, thanked the ranger, and drove into the quiet, pine-scented forest of giants that would probably outlive mankind. The cool crisp early spring air came through the windows and rejuvenated his spirit. As he climbed farther up in altitude, remnants of this winter's snow lined the highway to the right, especially in areas that saw little sun.

He found a fire road that cut off the main highway and required four–wheel drive, which he switched to immediately. The road wound up a hill, past trees almost 750 to 1,000 feet tall, their massive trunks twice the size of his Dodge Ram. The hard-packed dirt path curled around the side of the mountain, revealing the valley below, covered with the giant trees as far as he could see. He pulled the truck over onto a flat surface off of the dirt road. He shut everything down, took his little tin box with a bottle of ice water, and walked over to the edge. He sat down on a bed of short buffalo grass and stoked up a joint. As the high hit him, the feeling of solace at that moment was profound. The seclusion in this spot increased his feeling of isolation from the rest of the world, which he craved.

His mind began to plan his next moves as he got more stoned. Every contingency would be evaluated. He would never be caught by surprise. He knew how intense the manhunt would be for him, with a multitude of law enforcement agencies involved. That pleased him immensely with the knowledge of how much competition there would be between the different departments over the opportunity to catch or kill him. That would lead to withholding valuable information from one another, all in the name of glory.

In the meantime, he would disappear from society for at least a week. He would head to his favorite place on earth, Yosemite National Park, camp out, do some fishing, and take some photos. It would give him time to change his appearance, from a clean, totally shaved Marine, to a fully bearded, short-haired redneck. Hiding the tattoos would be a piece of cake. By now they should have a description of him, by either his ex-neighbors or Gina, his own Judas. The feeling of internal peace began to fade with the thought of her betrayal, not once, but twice. He would not allow a third time. She would die by his hands, but he would make her suffer dearly, both mentally and physically, until she begged to be killed. He would decide when she would die, however—not her and not God.

The thought of her death put a smile back on his face and warmth in his heart.

A slight breeze began to blow; the whistling sound through the pine trees was replaced by a dull roar as the velocity of the wind increased. The temperature began to drop immediately, and the late afternoon sun drifted behind one of the peaks and cast a shadow onto him. He looked at his watch, 4:55 p.m., and he chuckled at the thought of having just relaxed for two hours while police were running around like the Keystone Cops that they were. He stood up, stretched his stiff muscles, put on his long-sleeve sweatshirt and Giants baseball cap, and hopped back into his truck. It was time to go find a campsite for the night and bed down before it got too dark. He was getting hungry for a peanut butter and jelly sandwich, which he had prepared in advance. He had planned for this potential turn of events and had enough supplies to last him three weeks.

Plenty of time for everyone looking for him to finally relax, thinking he had left not only the state, but maybe the country. By then security would become lax. That's when he would make his triumphant return. Just as their guards would drop, he would swoop down, snatch Gina, and take her to his nest for the final kill. Just like a bird of prey.

Phil and Kelly stood at the precise spot where earlier that morning, one man had not only caused death and destruction, but had created utter chaos in the city of Los Angeles. His actions made people fear for their lives; many stayed home with their families, locked away from society. The sick call that day rose 47 percent, as did absentees from schools. The media helped fan the flames of fear as it covered the events of the day nonstop from twenty-five different angles. People were riveted to their TVs more than at any time since the O. J. Simpson murder trial in the 1990s. Finally the comparisons to the East Coast Slayer from ten years prior began to emerge and gain strength as the day wore on.

It was perfectly quiet as they stood, both with binoculars in hand looking directly north at the entire length of the downhill lanes of Interstate 5 for at least six miles.

"From this spot, he could pick out his intended target, in this case, the fuel truck, and follow his victim all the way down," Phil continued while he pointed with his left hand, "until he reached the perfect shooting distance, took out the tire with one shot, and set the carnage in motion. This was absolutely brilliant planning on his part. He must have scouted this area for a while before acting."

"Do you really think he planned this to happen?" Kelly asked. "Most FBI profilers would say he is accelerating and this was an impulsive explosion."

"Everything he ever did had at least five plans for each scenario, from best case to worst. He always planned in advance with military precision," Phil said. "You better start to understand this very important fact. As long as he stays at least one step ahead of us, he will have planned his next move, if it has not already been made."

"That's why no one listened to you ten years ago," Kelly said. The remark caught Phil by surprise, so he lowered his glasses and looked at her.

"Why's that?" he asked.

"Because everything you just said would go against every opinion rendered by our highly trained profilers at Quantico," she said, looking directly into his eyes with compassion and an understanding of the truth. "Your opinion would mean less than nothing."

"So that's what Tony meant," Phil said with resignation, now knowing the true reasons behind the snubs. "Washington politics as usual, I guess."

"I'm not Washington," Kelly said with a slight sultry purr, "and I'm very interested in knowing what you think."

Phil looked down, blushed slightly, acted coy, then looked directly at her and said, "Thank you for being the first female in my life who ever said that." As soon as he said it, he felt like he had stepped over the line and was about to apologize, when instead, he saw a look in Kelly's eyes that he had not seen in years—that of someone who yearned for him, and for once he not only recognized the sign, but acted. They embraced as if the world had disappeared, their kiss tender at first, but then deep and passionate. He lifted her almost six inches off the ground, her knees flexed, as were her toes inside her shoes. The silence in their world was deafening, until broken by a shrill call of a golden eagle soaring five hundred feet above on the way to her nest. He gently placed her down and still held onto her, but their lips parted as he gazed into her deep green eyes while his heart pounded inside his chest.

They stood silently for a minute and looked into each other's eyes, not knowing what to say. Finally Kelly jokingly said, "Where were we?" as she smiled, reached up, and gave him a peck on the cheek. "I needed that, just like you did, so don't feel guilty," she said, and Phil relaxed a little, but was still nervous, like a teenager after his first kiss.

"Yes, yes, I did, but we need to focus on our job at hand." Phil tried to be serious.

"You mean instead of a hand job?" Kelly retorted, and they both cracked up. Once the moment passed, they realized the gravity of the situation they were in, and Kelly was the first to say so. "We do need to focus, I agree, but I won't deny the feelings I have for you. But it won't get in the way of my job."

"I agree, on both parts," he said and saw her smile back. "We need to start by tracing our steps backward and look for any clues he may have left behind."

They split up and searched the entire cliff area first, noticing nothing out of place, except an occasional boot print, the same Phil had seen in the desert near the Infiniti. He stopped and let Kelly know what he had found. She acknowledged the same boot print twenty-five feet away. They followed the occasional boot prints back away from the edge, down the hill, past their vehicle, to a small spot almost half a mile away. That's when Phil saw the same tire tracks as in the dry canal, and followed the U-turn the truck had made. "He's back," Phil said sarcastically. Kelly called Tony immediately and informed him of their discovery. A lab team would be dispatched immediately and should be there in twenty minutes, she was told.

"So, what do you want to do for twenty minutes?" she coyly asked Phil.

He smiled and blushed at the same time. He looked at the ground and kicked a stone with his right foot. "Uhm…

not on our first date," was all he came up with, which made Kelly laugh so hard she began to almost cry.

She wiped her eyes and said, "Some first date. Take me to a murder scene, no flowers or candy."

At that very moment, Phil realized he was in love with Kelly. The thought scared him tremendously. If Frank ever found out, she would be added to the top of his hit list, along with Gina. But he couldn't hide his feelings for her, knowing this might be his last chance at true love, especially at his age.

"I promise you a wonderful first date at some time in the future, I really do. You've awakened something inside of me that needs to be further explored, but I can't give you everything of me, not now," he said with sincere honesty and passion.

"That's what I love about you," she said playfully, as she caressed the side of his face with the palm of her left hand, then turned slowly away with a smirk and a gleam in her eyes that left Phil with his mouth agape as he watched her saunter away. He smelled the fragrance she left behind, still tasted her on his lips, and suddenly felt thirty years younger.

He turned and looked back at the freeway below, amazed that such a tragedy could bring two people together from afar. Then he looked to the heavens and prayed for Frank's quick death for his own selfish reasons as he turned and watched Kelly with kaleidoscope eyes.

CHAPTER 21

By the end of the third day, there was still no trace of Frank DiMocchio. Instead of being part of the force that was hunting him down, Phil stood in front of twenty-five various law enforcement officers and discussed everything he knew about the monster now known as the West Coast Slayer. Most of the information was supposed to be background only, with the remainder handled by Tony and his monkeys. He had tried to express his opinions, but had been shot down every time—just like Kelly had said would happen. The FBI went more by the book than any other law enforcement agency in the world. That had been handed down for generations from its founder, J. Edgar Hoover, who was squeaky clean on the outside, but rumbles occurred within the inner circles. The sanctity of their profilers' opinions went unquestioned. They were stated more as fact than the fictional story of statistical evidence of patterns.

His anger had been simmering for days now as everyone shifted their focus to the LA and San Diego areas, again on the advice of profilers who felt that Frank had made his way toward Mexico. They all felt that this act of total brutality would quench his thirst for killing for a while, which allowed him time to plan his escape, and that his final destination was south of the border. Phil knew better, but no one would listen. That was all about to change.

"If I may have your attention." The noise in the room quieted to a dull roar as Phil looked around to make sure he had everyone's attention, including Tony. "As all of you know, we have not been able to locate Frank DiMocchio. You have a profile in front of you, a picture from his induction into the Marines almost twenty-five years ago. He has changed tremendously since then," Phil said as he handed Kelly a stack of papers. "Could you hand these out please?" She smiled as if she knew what was coming next. She nodded and gave Phil a boost of confidence with that certain look in her eyes that said to go for the low blow if you needed. "Special Agent Flaherty is handing out a composite made by my friends at SFPD, with the aid of a reliable witness, of what he looks like today."

Tony's look of disbelief was worth a thousand words.

"The total body tattoo is that of a red-tailed hawk. It has been filled in over the past twenty years, with each feather representing someone he has killed," Phil said as the murmurs began to grow in the room, some trying to count the number. "Some of those came in the name of the US government or other governments afterward as a mercenary, for which he was paid handsomely. He is the best at what he does for a living, and that is the killing of another human being." Phil stopped, looked around the room, and noted that every pair of eyes was riveted on him.

"Contrary to the experts, he will not stop killing, and he never will until the day he succumbs to the same end. He's going to move to another area and start all over again," Phil paused for a second, "just like he did ten years ago when he left the East Coast for sunny Southern California." The connection to the East Coast Slayer was put out there, and he took hold of the moment. "Ten years ago, when his body count mounted, everyone was eager to apprehend or kill the East Coast Slayer. They did neither, because they caught the wrong man. If you compare the evidence, most, if not all, of the sniper attacks were with high-caliber, long-range rifles. Maybe two different rifles or more were used, and one was planted in the convicted man's vehicle trunk without his knowledge."

"How do you know that?" The question came from an older agent with a hint of defensiveness in his manner.

"Because he did the same thing when he was stationed in the Philippines, this time killing at least ten by sniper fire and twenty-five by rape and murder," Phil answered flatly. The murmurs began to grow louder as some faces turned red with embarrassment at the mere mention of this latest unknown fact.

"What the fuck are you talking about?" This time it was Tony who asked the question without his usual diplomacy.

"The Philippine government hired Frank DiMocchio in 1992 to kill a prominent Muslim extremist leader who had ordered bombings in and around the southern islands. Within the next three months, the murders occurred. A long-range, high-caliber rifle was found in the wrongfully convicted and executed man's car trunk," he finished as the room grew eerily quiet; the sound of the air-conditioner that hummed in the distance was the only thing heard. "Sound familiar?" he asked with a sly grin directed at Tony.

"Where did you get that information?" Tony asked. "I never knew that ten years ago; was never informed of any link to a Marine overseas. Where did you get that information?" he repeated with increased agitation.

"Good old-fashioned police work," was Phil's terse response. "I tried to get that information to you, but was stonewalled by your underlings at that time," he said, now only a few inches from Tony, openly glaring at him, "but not this time," he finished in a snarl.

Tony ran a hand through what little hair he had left and sighed deeply. He knew that he had wronged his longtime friend and that the consequences of some of his decisions would come back to haunt him. He backed away in embarrassment as Phil continued.

"This monster," Phil said to get everyone's attention, "is more qualified than any other person alive to kill another human being in any fashion, by hand or weapon. He is the best the United States Marines ever trained. Being a law enforcement agent will not stop him from killing you, so you must be vigilante at all times if you do apprehend him. At six foot five and a very solid 275 pounds, he would crush any of you in a heartbeat physically. He is also extremely intelligent. His IQ was rated at 145, which is genius territory."

"Why is there no DNA or fingerprint verification of his existence in this file?" another, younger agent in the back asked.

"When you go very deep for your buddies over at Langley, what usually happens to your identities?" Phil asked rhetorically. All of the older agents simultaneously said, "You disappear," and the younger agent looked flushed.

"Where do you think he's going?" Kelly asked, giving Phil the opening he truly needed.

"He will continue killing until he kills the final two people on his bucket list. Those two are my niece, Gina, and yours truly," Phil said. "He murdered Gina's father, my partner when I was with SFPD homicide, with a long-range sniper attack. He was eighteen at the time, five years after he killed his own mother but was acquitted by an insane system. My partner and I were the arresting officers on that case. My niece rejected his romantic advances at the behest of my partner when Frank was first in the Marines, and three days later my partner was dead. Frank doesn't take no lightly."

"So you think he's heading north?" Kelly asked.

"Eventually he will make his way to the Bay Area, where he's from and where Gina lives. I've had twenty-four-hour surveillance on her residence in Berkeley with the help of the local police. Beyond that, if he survived, I would say he's headed north, maybe Canada," Phil said thoughtfully. "His father was half Italian, half Lakota Sioux, and he always talked to my niece about settling where his ancestors came from, but I think he's lying low right now. That's been his pattern in the past. I don't see it changing anytime soon. When he feels the timing is right and our guard has relaxed, he'll attempt to abduct or kill Gina."

"We will set up round-the-clock protection for Gina," Tony said, stepping forward to assume control of the meeting and to save face. Phil knew when enough was said and retreated backward as he nodded toward Tony.

Tony discussed logistics and assigned four agents, two women, two men, to guard Gina and her husband until Frank was apprehended. They would do alternating twelve-hour shifts. They would set up state-of-the-art video equipment and sensors and create a fortress.

Phil had heard enough and took a walk out of the room for some fresh air. The Feds were going by the book, again. It was frustrating to watch, and his stomach was already churning enough acid to melt paint off of walls. He knew that he had withheld important information concerning Gina. His mind was already racing with all of the possibilities, but the more he thought of what she had told him the morning of the house explosion, the more he felt she was lying and hiding something. The father in him reacted like any father would in this circumstance. He wanted to believe her, but there was something in her eyes during their "talk" that bothered him, and he now knew what it was.

She was in love with Frank, and her delay in divulging the truth was to protect him from being discovered by Phil. If she chose Frank over Phil, the equation would change tremendously. Would she willingly go with Frank and possibly become an outlaw herself? All of the surveillance and all of the high-tech gadgets couldn't prevent anything if Gina were a willing participant. Who better to kill her soon-to-be ex-husband than the world's best killer? The thought of the two of them combining forces made him even sicker to his stomach. The thought of killing Frank was acceptable no matter the circumstances. The guilt of Phil's Catholic upbringing was nonexistent when it came to Frank's death. He became instantly nauseated and diaphoretic as another thought occurred to him as he made his way back to the meeting.

Would he be able to kill his own godchild if she did indeed join the enemy?

CHAPTER 22

The morning sun began to creep above the jagged rocks atop the peaks of the Sierra Nevada Mountains as Frank lay sprawled below on a large granite boulder that was embedded in the Tuolumne River. As he gazed upward at the crystal clear blue skies and listened to the songs of the birds, he felt at peace, as if the rest of the world had disappeared. He sat up, checked the reflection of his image in the clear water as it flowed by the boulder, and was amazed how much he had changed in five days. The only thing that bothered him was a hint of gray in his beard, but his auburn hair was the predominant color. As he looked past his image, he could see a school of minnows as they swam by his spot. He reached in, snared three of the small fish with his hand, pulled them out, and stared at them. Their eyes began to bulge and their gills flapped open as they starved for oxygen.

The power of life or death lay within his hand.

He released them out of mercy, and watched the three regain their bearings and catch up with the school, which was swimming rapidly downstream. That could only mean that the trout were not too far behind, and hungry. He jumped up and off of "his" rock, and onto the shore where his gear was stored. He grabbed his backpack, two fishing poles, and his tackle box, along with his cooler, thermos, and fold-up chair. He headed downstream a hundred yards to an area where the river formed a beautiful pool of crystal clear water, only four feet deep, perfect for either fly-fishing or casting. The flow of the river slowed at that point due to the flattening of the valley and a dam-like effect of the large boulders embedded in the river downstream. These granite behemoths, some as large as fifty feet in length and one hundred tons in weight, a product of the fragility of the surrounding mountain cliffs from where they emanated, were the gateway to the river rapids that were situated just beyond them.

He found a spot behind a smaller boulder that gave him more solitude and also hid him from unnecessary looky-loos that passed by on Highway 140. It also gave him a good view of his truck parked five hundred yards away, just in case. He set up his chair, poured himself a cup of hot coffee, and prepared his twenty-five-year-old Sears special rods that he bought for $20. "It's not the pole," his dad would tell him when they went fishing that last time. "It's the reel, the bait, and the lure that gets the best fish, not the rod." He had the best of all three, including California's biggest night crawlers. He used his lures with a single hook loaded with bait and checked the twenty-pound line along with the settings on his Pro-Bass Excel550 reel. It gave him a nice, smooth release, but good tension when he needed to reel in a big one. He took his loaded rods, coffee, and backpack to the river's edge. He pulled two pole spikes out of his pack and drove them into the hard earth. He placed one rod in the slot, while he moved to his spot to the left and checked the bait and lure for one last time before he released the reel lock. With a fluid pitcher's three-quarter motion, he cast the line almost a hundred feet upstream, the splash a beautiful sight against the glistening water with rainbow reflections in the sunlight. The point of entry was marked with a plain small, red and white bobber. The spinner lure floated fourteen inches below, pulled by the five-mile-per-hour current.

Like any good fisherman, he pulled on the line gently and tested the freedom of the lure and the tension on the fishing rod. He then stopped and waited for any pull on the line. Within a few minutes he scored his first bite; a quick and strong yank was felt as his six-foot pole bent almost in half. Quickly he released the line slightly to avoid snapping the pole, then locked the reel and yanked the pole to his right and hoped the hook dug deeper into the fish's mouth. The tension on the line continued as he slowly started to reel the fish in, and relaxed every turn of the handle while he gave a slow yank on the rod. This way he gave the fish more resistance, which would tire it more rapidly and made it easier to capture. Within two minutes he reached down and netted an eighteen-inch, five-pound rainbow trout. The fish still had some fight to it, but lost its battle within a minute. He reached into his tackle box and pulled out his needle-nose pliers and cutting knife. He quickly pulled the hook out of the trout's mouth and used a flat round river rock as a table. He decapitated and cleaned the fish within a few minutes, then washed the blood off the rock with clean river water. He opened his backpack, took out plastic resealable bags, and placed his dinner into the ice cooler.

He was about to cast the second pole when he heard off in the distance the sound of a sports car accelerating and shifting gears. The sound of the special exhaust system gave it a cheap throaty quality. At any other time, he would love that sound, but not here in this, the most peaceful place on earth. It was like the sanctity of his church as a child, always so quiet except for the sounds of nature. He automatically opened up his pack and pulled out his Walther PPK, checked the load, and put it into the waistband under his jeans in the back. His sweat jacket covered the bulge. "One should never be caught empty-handed," his drill sergeant always screamed at him in boot camp, something he never forgot. He looked south as the car drew closer, and saw the black Chrysler 300 with fully tinted glass round the bend; the bass was booming loud enough to scare the fish away. That really pissed him off as he turned and watched them drive past his spot, but then slowed down as they began to approach his truck. When he saw the brake lights appear, Frank began making his way upstream rapidly, leaving his gear behind. For a man as large as he was, he was both extremely quick and graceful. Probably genetics from his Sioux/Roman heritage, he was always told as a child.

He rapidly made his way to within a hundred feet of his truck, which was now being inspected by three chulos from LA; blue bandannas covered their heads, and tattoos extended down their arms from thick necks. They were about five-eight to five-ten, but all were built like miniature bulls, with massive upper-body strength, thin waists and legs, and half of their underwear exposed with their low-riding jeans. Chains were extending out of their pockets, but these were not attached to keys. They were attached to guns. Frank stayed behind the large boulder as two of the gangsters made their way to the doors of the truck, finding them locked. The third scanned the river to Frank's immediate left, unaware of his presence. He stood with his arms folded, toothpick hung out of his mouth, with small beady eyes behind sunglasses. Tried to look tough as he stood there and played the centurion. Frank smiled at the arrangement of the three of them as he pulled his weapon out of his pants and released the safety. He waited until he saw the slim jim in the right hand of the asshole near his truck's driver's side door. Now he was really pissed.

"Hey, what the fuck do you think you are going to do to my truck?" he barked as he stepped out from behind the boulder, holding the pistol out of sight behind his thigh as he walked toward them. They all turned at once, stunned at the loudness of the bark and apprehensive of this huge beast approaching without any fear. The two men near the truck reflexively stepped backward slightly, a sign of weakness, but the centurion pulled on his chain, revealing a 45 mm silver-plated pistol. *Nice weapon*, Frank thought as he raised his Walther PPK and shot him between his eyes before he had a chance to even put his index finger into the trigger hole. He fell backward and hit the ground with a thud as the shot reverberated through the canyon. Frank quickly approached the other two, who were now trying to plead their case, hands held up high.

"You wanted to hurt my truck?" he asked.

"We actually wanted to steal it, bro, not hurt it," the smart-ass on the right said. Frank raised his gun and shot him dead center of the chest, dropping him immediately; blood flooded his white T-shirt.

"I'm just the driver," the man with the slim Jim said timidly, hands still raised in the air.

"Yeah, right," Frank said as he raised his gun and shot the man in the hand holding the car thief's tool. "That's for trying to steal my truck." He raised the weapon and fired twice, chest first and head second, as the body fell, which caused it to buckle backward. "That's for lying to me." He went to his truck, opened the driver's door, pulled out a pair of latex gloves, put them on, and one by one lifted the bodies of the dead men and placed them back into the Chrysler. He found the keys on the twice-shot leader. Frank rolled up the windows, closed the doors, and locked the car. As he walked away from the vehicle, he looked back and saw that with the windows fully shut, no one could see inside. He figured they wouldn't be found for a while.

So he decided to go back to his spot, and hopefully, if all of the noise hadn't scared all of the fish away, score enough trout and bass to last him a few days.

CHAPTER 23

Frank sat in front of his two-man pup tent, the same one that he and his father had used all of those years ago. He still swore to himself that he could smell his father's cologne in the tent. Canoe was the last one he remembered. He sat in front of his little fire and stirred the fish stew he had in a small black Dutch kettle. He had ended up catching his limit of five rainbow trout, all gutted and wrapped on ice that was actually snow taken from the higher elevations. He had dehydrated carrots and celery, with a can of corn added to the stock, with salt, pepper, and Tabasco sauce as the only spices. He looked around at the half-empty campground in Yosemite Valley. His slot was the farthest away from the main entrance, and away from any other campers, which was just the way he preferred. In fact, it was the same campsite he used every time he came to Yosemite.

He faced El Capitan from his chair. The upper third of the mountain face was still covered in snow and void of any climbers at this time of year. To the right he could see the beauty of the Upper Yosemite Falls as the water cascaded down hundreds of feet, fed by this year's heavy rains and snow. It was much wider than anytime he could remember in the past. Behind him and to the right was Half Dome, which guarded the very north end of the valley. He took in a deep breath and slowly exhaled. He began to see his breath as the late afternoon temperature began to drop. The sun was about an hour from full sunset at 5:45 p.m., but the strength of its rays were weakened as the angle dropped further and the shadows grew longer.

He poured himself a large bowl of his fish stew, placed it on his little fold-up table, and watched the steam rise as it slowly cooled enough for him to enjoy. He had already packed up all of his gear and had loaded everything into the truck, except the tent and what was necessary to finish his stew. That would only take him a few minutes to dismantle after he finished his last supper here in the valley of his soul. At no other time in his life had he felt so at peace as he had since being here. The quiet days, lack of human contact, especially the solitude, with living off of the land and water, all had brought a calming effect onto him. But all of those feelings were shattered this morning by the violence with which he had been involved.

He had no regrets for what had to be done. He just wished it never had to happen at all. It made for an immediate change of plans, which he was finalizing in his head at that very moment. By his recollection, the park rangers made one more sweep of the roads at sundown to make sure all of the visitors were in their camps or out of the park entirely. There was no overnight parking allowed in Yosemite National Park. By his calculation, the Chrysler

300 would be found within the next hour to an hour and a half. That's when all hell would break loose, the park would be locked down, and everyone inside the park would become instant suspects. The last thing he wanted to do now was to attract any more attention. He would decide when that would happen, and now was not the best time.

He reached over, grabbed his bowl of stew, and enjoyed the aroma before he tasted it. Seasoned just the way he liked, the stew was simple, but the taste of fresh trout couldn't be beat, especially with a little kick added to the mixture. He came across only one or two small bones, which wasn't bad for trout. He sat there and consumed his dinner with a genuine feeling of contempt. He knew it might be his last good self-cooked meal for a while. It was back to rations and beans as he became a ghost on the road again.

By now, the Fumbling Bumbling Idiots, as he referred to the FBI, had taken over the case with a special task force. He had learned that much through the good old-fashioned AM radio. There was no Wi-Fi, Internet, or cell-phone service up here. It was back to the old ways. He had wished he was born in the frontier days, when the only communication was by telegraph or Pony Express. He imagined himself as an outlaw with the quickest draw, which he had practiced many times with an old-fashioned Colt 45 he had along with the gun belt. Both dated back to the late 1800s, the pearl handles similar to the Colts used by Wild Bill Hickok and General George Armstrong Custer. He had always imagined killing his worst enemies with the Colts, dropping them before they could even get a shot off, lightning-fast.

Finished with his meal, he took the coffee pot he had brewed over the fire, filled up his travel mug and thermos, and then poured the rest onto the fire. This dampened the flames. Then he put the finishing touch on the fire with dirt, until there were no hot spots left. He immediately loaded everything into the truck and was ready to bug out in six minutes. He lit a joint as the truck's engine warmed up. Next he finalized the destination into his GPS system. He would swing south on California 41 out of Yosemite, away from the dead bodies entirely, and head past Fresno. From there he would connect to California 46 outside of Paso Robles and head toward the coast. His final destination would be in the beautiful resort village of Cambria. He figured that he would do a little body surfing and get a jump start on an early tan. With the help of peroxide, his hair would become blond in no time. With the beaches being empty this time of year because the water was still cold, he could finally take his shirt off. Plus Hearst Castle was only six miles from Cambria, and he hadn't been there since he and Gina went so many years ago.

His mood shifted dramatically as he pulled out of his home away from home and looked back in the rearview mirror one last time. Bitterness turned to mild anger as he pulled onto the main road; he saw a slow-moving RV headed in his direction with ten cars following. He pulled out and squealed all four tires as the RV blasted its horn, which was greeted with Frank's extended middle finger out the driver's window as he floored the pedal. The Hemi responded with a roar and accelerated up to sixty-five miles per hour within seconds as he left the irate old-timer in the RV in a rage. It only caused the RV driver to slow even more, which gave Frank cover to put distance between him and the other drivers.

The sun began to sink rapidly ahead of him as he began the descent out of the Sierra Nevada Mountains into the lush farmland of the Central Valley of California. In his rearview mirror, he saw the convoy more than a mile behind him and smiled as he took one last look at the beauty of the mountains. The different fragrances of pine and early spring wildflowers soon turned to steer manure as he began to pass large dairy farms, then groves of the nut and fruit trees that had displaced other staples such as corn or lettuce. Once planted, maintenance and profits from the nut and fruit business were much more cost-effective than otherwise.

About fifteen miles north of Fresno, on a straight stretch of California 41, he saw headlights in his rearview mirror that were closing fast. He squinted slightly to get a better read of the type of vehicle and noticed that it was a small pick-up truck with a single occupant. Frank followed its path as it closed the distance rapidly and finally passed him as if he stood still. Then the unthinkable happened. The man in the pick-up truck flipped Frank off as he got in front of Frank, and tapped his brakes to add insult to injury.

"You motherfucker," Frank snarled, "You shouldn't have done that. You just ruined my good mood." With that said, he floored the pedal; the front of the truck lifted up as the Hemi roared to life and rapidly accelerated. The distance, which was half a mile by the time Frank punched it, was diminished quickly. He saw the male driver look in the mirror and acknowledge Frank's presence as he tried to also accelerate and outrun Frank. To no avail, as the four-cylinder Nissan was no match for his Dodge as Frank pulled up behind and drafted one inch away from the Nissan's tail end. This maneuver helped the smaller truck to go faster. The fear could now be seen in the eyes of the twenty-something-year-old, especially as he saw Frank with an evil smile. Their combined speeds were now in excess of one hundred miles per hour.

Frank let off the gas rapidly, and the Dodge fell back a hundred feet within seconds. He opened up his console, pulled out his Walther PPK, released the safety, closed the console, and slipped the gun between his legs. He accelerated again, but this time pulled alongside of the Nissan and lowered the right side window. He looked at the young Hispanic and smiled as they jockeyed for position. Their mirrors almost touched while they drove ninety-five miles per hour down the slight decline. Then he saw the man mouth the words *el cabron*, which translated to bastard. He didn't know Frank was fluent in four languages, including Spanish. "Fuck you, asshole," he roared as he lifted the gun, extended his arm rapidly, and fired. The blast rang in his ears, but the bullet hit its target above the left ear, causing the Nissan to veer directly to the right and roll multiple times on the soft shoulder before it went airborne. The already-dead passenger was ejected through the blown-out front window; his limp body landed on the ground and bounced a few times, coming to rest as the rest of the pick-up truck landed directly on top of him in a cloud of dust.

Frank captured the entire scene in his rearview mirror as he decelerated back to sixty-five miles per hour and raised his massive arms in the sign of a field goal; he let out his war whoop as his blood now burned for more excitement. The feeling of power was so intense, and the desire to kill again was orgasmic.

He pulled the visor down as the sun was directly in his eyes as it began its descent into the horizon. He removed the long-sleeve sweatshirt that he had worn since LA and exposed his feather-tattooed heavily muscled arms. He was tired of hiding. It was time to play some games, play with the authorities and ultimately pull them away from his true targets, Gina and Lieutenant DiMarco. It was time for this legendary predator to feast on his prey.

CHAPTER 24

Because of federal cutbacks, discovery of the three bodies in the Chrysler 300 in Yosemite did not occur until the following morning. The US Ranger who found them was a fifteen-year veteran, but had never experienced a murder scene, especially a multiple homicide that had cooked inside a car for twenty-four hours. Upon seeing the same car parked in the same spot two days in a row, he had pulled his vehicle over and had slowly gotten out with a large flashlight in his left hand. He approached the car from the driver's side, but could not see inside that well due to the window tint. He rapped his flashlight on the window but received no response. He moved to the front of the car, where he noticed the tint was slightly lighter on the windshield; he saw the two men in front with wounds on the bodies. He immediately went back to the driver's side and smashed in the window with his flashlight. The smell of death erupted from the inside of a car that had acted more like an oven. It made him immediately violently ill, and he vomited into the crime scene.

After he cleaned off and made it back to his own vehicle, he called the crime into the ranger station. He was instructed not to touch anything. He didn't tell the dispatcher what he had already done, and especially about the vomiting. His senior ranger immediately called the FBI office in Sacramento, which was in charge of any murder investigation. They arrived on the scene within two hours, with the rangers blocking traffic from both directions. The lead investigator was Claude Lemieux, a brilliant and handsome man of French Canadian descent, who was relentless in his search for the truth.

Claude shook his head as he saw the broken window and the vomit that covered the driver's shirt and pants. Beyond that, the first thing he noticed was the types of bullet wounds, the tattoos, the gang colors, and a lack of evidence that they were killed inside the vehicle. He stood up and began to scan the area. He saw the two pools of blood thirty feet in front of him, separated by about eight feet. He walked to the area staying on the road and off of the shoulder so as not to disturb anymore than was necessary. He called for the lab rats to come and check these pools. He stood over the thickened crimson stain on the dirt and noticed the tire marks that led away from the scene onto the road. Wide, deep tread, truck tire, used for four-wheel-drives, which was the same pattern he had seen on the alerts about the West Coast Slayer. He called over to one of the lab techs to take pictures and molds of the tracks.

"Agent Lemieux, we have another murder site over here," Agent Fred McGriff called over from the rocks near the river. Claude made his way over and looked at the spot of blood, larger in size than the other two, a shade darker but about the same consistency.

"He was killed first, then the other two," Lemieux started. "He was the lookout. The other two were near a second vehicle, probably a truck with big tires. Both were shot on each side of the truck. Possibly the un-subs were trying to steal the truck and were caught by the owner. Someone who is a marksman killed three gangbangers with precise kill shots, then was brazen enough to stuff their bodies back into their own vehicle and lock them up, knowing they wouldn't be seen." He pulled his cell phone out and called his office in Sacramento.

"Bea, put me through to Special Agent Flaherty of the West Coast Slayer Task Force immediately," he said with urgency as he turned away from Agent McGriff, the anticipation within him building rapidly at the importance of his initial findings. His mind was racing as he heard his trusty secretary come back on the line. "I have Special Agent Flaherty on the line." There was a temporary silence, then a click, then a female voice on the line: "Special Agent Flaherty." Kelly could be heard, her voice all business.

"Agent Flaherty," Claude began as he felt himself almost hyperventilating with excitement, "this is Agent Claude Lemieux from the Sacramento office. I think we've discovered the West Coast Slayer in Yosemite National Park."

"What? What are you saying?" Kelly sputtered in disbelief at first. "Hold on, I'm going to put you on speaker phone so everyone here can listen in to your report." He heard her calling everyone over and then she returned, but her voice was more distant on the speaker phone.

"Go ahead, tell us what you've found," she commanded.

"I found a murder scene of three gang members, killed professionally, all by the same person, and placed back inside of their vehicle. They were probably trying to carjack a truck, with large oversize tires with the same pattern as the West Coast Slayer," he said as he heard a male voice say something on the other end. "The one farthest away from where the truck was appears to have been a lookout, and was killed first. The other two were on each side of the vehicle when they were killed. Then all three were stuffed back into the car, and the car was locked. It had to be broken into by an inexperienced US Ranger. The scene was compromised with vomit."

"Agent Lemieux, this is Lieutenant DiMarco of the Task Force," Phil began. "How many bullet holes were in the victims, and their locations?"

"The driver had one between the eyes, the passenger up front had one through the chest, and the passenger in the back had… three wounds—right hand, chest, and head."

"The head shot was the lookout, the chest was a tagalong, and the last one, with the multiple holes, was the leader," Phil said.

"Agent Lemieux, good work. Secure that area, and I'll have the assistant director get extra men to begin searching the park for the killer. You have the update with the picture provided by Lieutenant DiMarco with this morning's briefing, correct?" Agent Flaherty asked.

"Yes, huge guy, hawk tattoo on the predominance of his torso and arms, white, blue eyes, shaved clean or jarhead style," Lemieux said.

"Watch it." Phil's voice could be heard above the hum of voices. "He may go the opposite way and grow his hair and beard."

"I doubt that, sir," Lemieux interjected; "it wouldn't fit his profile."

"Secure the area. We'll take care of the rest, thank you again," Flaherty said abruptly and hung up.

Lemieux looked at the phone, wondered why she became agitated at the mention of profiling, shrugged his shoulders, and began giving orders to make sure no one else could ruin his murder scene.

The sun was just beginning to show its outline through the thick morning fog as Frank lay thirty-five feet from the water. The dark gray clouds that were extremely thick just an hour ago had thinned to white veils of mist as the sun exuded its warmth. Frank sat on a large towel, knees bent with his arms wrapped around them, his wet suit pulled down to his waist as he watched the rhythm and size of the swells as they crashed to the shore. The sight and sound of the ocean was always mesmerizing to him. Having fallen in love with surfing while stationed at Camp Pendleton in Oceanside, he was waiting for the height of the waves to increase to at least three feet, so he could safely body surf without getting slammed into the sand. He was also waiting for the sun to rise slightly higher, which gave him less of a chance of being shark bait in the early morning hours, when the beasts of the ocean loved to feast.

Looking up and down the beach, the only other humans he could see were a young couple with a yellow Labrador retriever almost half a mile north of him. The early spring day meant school was still in session. The beaches would be deserted until the weekend, when the casual tourists coming to this cozy beach town would spend a few hours digging their toes in the warm sand. Some, usually younger in age, would challenge the cold waters up to their waist. A small flock of sandpipers and terns skittered near the water's edge as they waited for the waves to recede, and then dug quickly for the small sand crabs that burrowed in the shallow waters. Few were successful, but amazingly, none ever drowned in a massive wave, their senses keenly alert to any danger. Not like most humans, who many times are oblivious to an oncoming wave that knocks them into oblivion. They didn't know the first rule of surfing, which was to know the strength and the timing of the waves.

He had eaten breakfast earlier at the Moonstone Beach Inn, having had eggs Benedict, which was his favorite. It was done perfectly, with the right combination of a well-timed poached egg, along with thick Canadian bacon and the creamiest Hollandaise sauce he had ever tasted. He also was given a treat he hadn't expected: the waitress's phone number, written on the bottom of the tear-off portion of the check. He could still see her strawberry blond hair pulled back into a bun, thin body but a perfect hourglass figure, with small perky tits and a tight ass. She was in her late twenties and bored with the local scene. She knew of a place above the beach in the foothills that was great for stars—and other things, she had suggested with her tongue playfully between her perfect white teeth.

Frank had already memorized her phone number and would call her after 2:00 p.m., when she ended her shift, just as she had indicated. His arousal was growing, as was his thirst for adventure. He needed to satisfy both and soon. The Yosemite incident was still fresh in his mind, and the yearning for death was stronger than ever. He would limit himself to just one or two murders here in Cambria over a period of a week. It would be just enough to draw the Task Force here after he was already long gone. By then he would already be in the Bay Area, preparing for his next act of superiority—the capture and death of Gina Androcelli while under the watchful eye of the FBI.

In the meantime, he needed to work on his tan and get in some great runs if the waves ever cooperated. Death would have to come later.

CHAPTER 25

The coroner's report included a scathing indictment of the amount of incompetence that was prevalent in the Fresno County Sheriff's office. The sheriff looked at the initial accident report filed by the deputy sheriffs who were first on the scene and couldn't believe they mistook a gunshot wound for an accidental puncture wound by metal debris. The coroner described the through and through wounds of the skull and brain, concluding that they had to be caused by at least a 45 caliber bullet. The victim was dead before the accident, not because of the accident. The remainder of his injuries, including multiple cuts and bruises, were all postmortem. The coroner personally called the sheriff and let him know about his findings. The sheriff turned the case into a homicide, and put the deputy sheriff who did the initial investigation on administrative leave, pending further evaluation.

This was three days after the victim's death and three days after Yosemite. The sheriff put two and two together quickly. To be shot and killed at the speed this man was traveling meant an above-excellent shooter was involved.

He had heard about the Yosemite murders, figured it was the same shooter, and called the task force. Phil and Kelly were in his office within hours. After pleasantries they went straight to the morgue. The coroner's name was Dr. Stephen Santini, who was an old-fashioned "country doctor" with a friendly demeanor who offered them coffee and a spearmint lotion to apply to their upper lip to prevent the smells of death from reaching their stomachs.

The mutilated body of the migrant worker lay on the main examination table in the center of the autopsy room, with four other tables on each side. All were occupied, but this was the only homicide case; the rest died in hospitals of non-suspicious causes. The five halogen lights shone down on the table and gave the body an eerie glow, which highlighted his injuries. The reflection of the lights off of the stainless steel surface added to the brightness, which caused Phil and Kelly to reflexively squint. The four of them stood around the body, heads bowed out of respect for the dead, as the coroner began his dissertation.

"As you can see here," Dr. Santini said as he pointed with an old-fashioned foldable pointer, "the bullet entered the left side of the skull in the parietal area just above the left ear, went straight through the upper cerebral cortex, and caused instant death before it exited out the right parietal area. Where the bullet landed is anybody's guess. The reason I know it's a bullet," he continued, "is the neatness of the wounds and the tunnel through the brain. This indicates a Teflon-coated bullet designed to prevent major damage, but great for kill shots. They always go through and through."

"The accident scene investigation revealed that when he lost control of his vehicle," the sheriff said as he pointed at the victim, "he was traveling at over one hundred miles per hour. That means he was shot while traveling at the same speed. That's one hell of a shot."

"Not for him," Phil said quietly.

"There must have been a second person involved, a driver at least," the sheriff said.

Phil shook his head, looked straight into the sheriff's eyes, and said, "It's just one monster, who just happens to be the best marksman in the world. And yes, he can drive at one hundred miles per hour with one hand and shoot with the other. There is no doubt in my mind, it's him."

"Obviously, medically speaking," Dr. Santini said, "the wounds of the victims from Yosemite should match these if they are from the same weapon."

"The problem is," Phil replied, "he may have a mobile armory with him, with God only knows how many different types of weapons. Hopefully, he's being conservative and sticking with his favorite pistol, a Walther PPK."

"Is that a 45 caliber weapon?" Dr. Santini asked. Phil nodded yes. "This size hole is consistent with at least a 45 caliber bullet."

"Why would he kill a migrant worker?" the sheriff asked.

"You have to understand that this beast loves to kill. He doesn't need a reason, but in this case, probably something this poor soul did pissed off Frank," Phil said. "Probably something as simple as road rage was the cause."

"Most killers of this nature quench their thirst for death with each murder," Kelly interjected. "Then they stalk their next prey, building up the desire to kill again, all the while formulating a plan. What we're worried about now is that he is accelerating his killings, becoming more impulsive. This puts the general public at more of a risk than before. It also makes him more prone to a mistake that will help us nab him."

"If you don't kill him first, you mean?" the sheriff asked with a smile.

"She won't…" Phil said, pointing to Kelly, "but I'll put a bullet right between his eyes; save the taxpayers a lot of money."

"Amen to that," Dr. Santini chimed in from the background.

They all shared a brief laugh, and then the sheriff asked, "Where do you think he is now?"

"He could be anywhere in the state," Phil replied, "but we think he is heading up to the Bay Area, where he is originally from and has familiarity with the scene."

"He probably continued south until Kettleman City, then went south on I-5 back into LA," the sheriff said, as he hoped that this killer was out of his territory.

"If I was him," Dr. Santini said as he began to cover the body and lead them out of the room, "I'd be lying low, give time for my appearance to change and to ease from the memories of people, especially as the media coverage wound down. If I was him, I would have driven past Paso Robles and would be lying on the beaches of Cambria, where it's empty this time of year."

Phil looked at the old doctor and had more respect for him, as what he said hit Phil right in the gut. Suddenly Phil had an idea on how to possibly track and find Frank DiMocchio.

"We have your flyer with his updated composite. If he's around here, we'll find him." The sheriff shook their hands as he prepared to leave.

"I doubt it," Phil said sarcastically. "If the FBI couldn't find him for over ten years, you have no chance in hell."

The sheriff shrugged his shoulders with a "whatever" look and said, "See ya, doc," as he turned and walked away.

"Cambria," Dr. Santini said again after the sheriff was gone. He said his good-byes and turned to return to the morgue.

As they walked out of the building, the smell of fresh steer manure from the nearby farms actually was refreshing to both of them. The sun was setting over the Panza Range of the Sierra Madre Mountains, and dusk in the Central Valley of California in the springtime was full of fragrances from flowering agriculture, especially the citrus fruits. Phil was staring west as they strolled, each deep in their thoughts.

"For the record, Phil, I wasn't with the FBI ten years ago when they botched up," Kelly said as they neared their vehicle, which was arranged through the Fresno FBI office. "In fact, I've only been with them for three years."

"You rose up through the ranks fast, Special Agent Kelly," Phil said with a little playful jab.

"It's easy when you can sleep with your commanders," she said flatly with a counterpunch that stopped Phil dead in his tracks. She turned around and smiled at him as she said, "You are so easy." He began to pout slightly. "I was actually with the dark side, working as both an analyst and field operative working on serial killers in the armed forces overseas. What you quoted about the Philippines in front of the squad the other day was originally from my report. Knowing I knew something about Frank, I was recruited to the FBI, under Director Balducci, to help with serial killers who are either still in, or discharged from, the military in this country. I knew a lot of shit. That's why I'm here."

"I'm glad you are," Phil said with a smile as he now caught up with her. Then he blushed, and she smiled even more.

"You reacted when the doc said Cambria—why?" she asked as they got into the car.

"Because it made perfect sense, and would be almost ten days since the LA massacre. The media coverage has faded to the back, especially with the uprisings in the Middle East," Phil said. "But he wouldn't stop killing; he would adapt his methods."

"He'll start abducting, raping, and killing women again," Kelly said as she settled into the passenger seat and buckled up. Phil started the engine and nodded in agreement.

"Start tracking pockets of missing women between the ages of sixteen and forty," Phil said, "within the past three to four days, and we may get lucky. Start with Cambria."

Kelly nodded in agreement and took out her cell phone to call the task force, when she turned to Phil. "By the way, where are we going?" she asked.

"A little place called the Moonstone Beach Inn, where they have the best New England clam chowder and fireplaces in their suites and the sound of ocean waves to sleep by," he said with a sheepish grin.

"Where's that at?" she asked.

"Cambria," Phil replied as he pulled onto CA-41 heading south.

The body rested on the large beach towel, covered with a SF Giants blanket, apparently asleep in the prone position, with arms stretched out above her head, which was turned to the right. The beach was deserted. The fifteen-foot walls of sandstone still gave off heat from the day's sunlight. Fifty feet to her right, a large man was seen digging in the sand. If spotted, it would have been assumed that he was building a large sand castle. That was not unusual, not even at night. But it was unusual this particular night, especially since the woman wasn't sleeping. With the seclusion of the spot, Frank had found another perfect burial ground. With the soft sand compared to the hard-packed sand of the desert, the digging was much easier. Three in three days was good enough for one spot. He didn't want to push his luck. He had already made plans to leave after putting the finishing touches on this last grave.

He already had reservations at a Holiday Inn in Paso Robles and would get a restful night's sleep there before moving on to the Bay Area. If he hurried, he could catch the last few innings of the Giants game. The first-place Cardinals were in town seeking revenge from last year. So he dug faster.

CHAPTER 26

The stick seemed to turn end over end on its journey through the air and finally settled gently in the sand. The two-year-old Irish setter pounced on it immediately, grasped the stick in its teeth, and turned to run back toward her master, but stopped. She dropped the stick and began to sniff around the area. She snorted fiercely as the cackles on her back stood on end immediately from head to toe. She backed away from the area, whimpered at first, and then began barking viciously while she stared at her stick. She bared her teeth and snarled in between barking and pawed at the sand where she stood. Her owner, a retired US Army colonel noticed the odd behavior and rushed over.

"What's the matter, girlie, there, there," he said as he tried to calm her down. "What is it?" He picked up the stick and expected her to react. Instead, she stared at the ground just behind where he stood. He slowly turned and saw the fifteen-foot cliffs made of sandstone with areas of wildflowers that had grown. Their yellow and pink blossoms added color to the early morning. He saw nothing moving, nothing threatening, such as a snake or even a ground squirrel. He stepped back, tried to focus on what the dog stared at, and looked down. He blinked a few times, then squinted and followed the pattern. Then he noticed two similar areas to the right, and felt a chill that ran immediately down his spine. The last time he saw this was in Viet Nam forty years ago, and he never would have expected to find them here.

These were freshly dug graves.

He pulled out his cell phone and dialed 911. He gave his rank and name and explained what he and his dog had just found. When the dispatcher questioned him further, maybe doubting his story, it was met with a lecture on what he had seen in his lifetime and the need for immediate investigation. He never knew that what he had discovered would lead to the circus that would eventually occur.

Their night had been exhausting in so many ways. They arrived at 1:15 a.m. after having checked in with the county sheriff's office. Yet they both yearned for the touch of each other. Their lovemaking was gentle yet passionate, and they finally collapsed into each other's arms by four fifteen. The sound of the waves could be heard through the open window as they crashed onto the shore, which was the perfect background for sleep. Yet at 6:45 a.m., Phil was wide-awake. He looked down at the top of her dark auburn-colored head cradled in his arm. The fragrance of her lavender shampoo mixed with the scent of passionate love filled his nostrils. He had not felt this at peace, this happy, in so long and wished for it to last forever. Their bodies were entwined, but in perfect harmony. For the first time in many years, he felt the layers of his wall coming down. Feelings that had been distant memories and ones never felt exploded in his mind, his heart, and his soul.

Yet he lay there wide-awake, with his life in chaos.

He was worried that his mind would become distracted and take him away from his primary goal. This needed to be accomplished before moving on to any possible changes in his life. He had to either capture or kill Frank DiMocchio before he could find any everlasting peace. His thoughts were interrupted as Kelly stirred, turned to the right, shifted without awakening, grabbed her pillow, and curled the sheet over her left shoulder. He innocently picked up his edge of the sheet, stared at her beautiful body, and became aroused again.

Phil quickly put the sheet down.

He knew that he wouldn't get back to sleep, so he slowly got out of bed so as not to disturb Kelly. He sauntered over to the hotel room's excuse of a coffee pot. He filled the four-cup container with water and put the premeasured coffee/filter into the receptacle. He turned the machine on, and the coffee took five minutes to brew. He used the time to walk over to the window as his legs were a little wobbly, and stared out at the peace of the Pacific Ocean. Inside, he was wishing he could wake up every morning as he did today. The fog was still hugging the coast like a blanket, but there were areas of breaks in the gray, which exposed a deep blue sky. As he took in slow deep breaths, the smell of the salt air cleared his lungs of all of the pollutants to which he had been exposed.

A beep softly announced the completion of the coffee brew. He grabbed a cup of the bitter concoction and poured in three Sweet'N Lows and two packages of sugar, along with powdered creamer, to make it palatable. He headed into the bathroom, turned on the shower, and was instantly disappointed at the water pressure. Conservation was necessary, but a person needed a good shower in the morning to feel halfway human and to get him or her pumped for the day ahead. By the time he was finished with the lousy shower and the putrid coffee, his mood had deteriorated from bliss to slight agitation. He quickly dressed in Nike sweatpants, black-hooded sweatshirt, and black Nike cross-trainers, peeked in on Kelly who was still fast asleep, scribbled a note saying he went for a quick walk in case she woke up, and quietly left the hotel room. He made sure the "Do Not Disturb" sign was still there.

The cool sea air felt like walking into an air-conditioned room on a hot summer day. It offered him instant relief from his stresses. He walked on a graveled path toward the quiet beachfront road, and then toward the beach. The solitude was genuinely welcome as he took his Nikes and socks off, rolled up his pants, and walked down toward the water. He stood there looking out over the now bluish gray water with the curls about five or six feet high, and he wished he were out there. It had been over fifteen years since his last run at Half Moon Bay, when he blew out his left knee on that last big curl. He automatically looked down at the scars on the knee from the reconstruction with three cadaver ligaments that replaced his own. He slowly waded into the shallow water, with the temperature about fifty-eight degrees, which made him pause at about shin height as his bones began to hurt. He turned and got out quickly. He smiled as he thought about the abuse he would have taken if his children were here and saw him go in and out that quickly. The old-timer jokes would be coming at him fast and furiously.

Suddenly he saw three sheriff's vehicles pass by on the beach road heading south and stop a half mile away. He saw the five officers get out of their vehicles and head down toward the beach. Phil found himself breaking out into a trot as he closed the distance quickly straight down the cool smooth sands of the Central Coast. Up ahead he saw a small crowd forming in front of the cliffs. He couldn't see anything lying on the sand, such as a seal or baby whale. He saw the officers pushing back the gathering crowd as Phil came within one hundred feet. As he drew closer, he recognized the deputy sheriff who had met them last night, as he had come on at midnight.

"Hey, Lieutenant." He waved to Phil to come over. "This may be the work of your boy—looks like four graves, freshly dug within the past few days," he said as he shook Phil's hand and led him past the gawkers as three of the deputies started pushing the people back, trying to preserve what was left of the crime scene. "Sheriff Boyle, this is Lieutenant DiMarco from the FBI Task Force. He's been tracking the West Coast Slayer."

"Phil," Phil said, extending a hand.

"Ron," the sheriff said, shaking hands vigorously. "Looks like four graves."

"The graves will all be uniform, spread evenly apart; the bodies will be found at a six-foot depth," Phil said, looking into the sheriff's tired eyes. "It's his MO. Usually the bodies are in a body bag or some kind of wrapping, like a beach blanket, if necessary, almost as if trying to preserve them. Most of them are killed during sexual acts. The cause of death most of the time is severance of the cervical spine, usually at the C2-C3 level, by snapping the neck, while others were killed by simple strangulation. This guy is huge, with huge hands, inches taller than me and built like an NFL linebacker. He has a full-body tattoo of a red-tailed hawk, each feather a symbol of a person he has killed, including his own mother at the age of thirteen." Phil finished with emphasis.

"Satan himself." Ron said as they looked at the four graves quietly. "They were dug in the last three days. A retired army colonel found them; actually his dog did. Army never could find anything," Ron said.

"Amen to that. What division were you in?" Phil said.

"Second Battalion, Troop D, at the Battle of Que San, and you?" Ron replied.

"Third Battalion, Troop E, Mekong Delta, later on. Just to let you know, we trained him," Phil said.

"So he really knows how to kill," Ron replied.

"He's probably moved on from here already, if that's what you are worried about," Phil replied. "That's always been his pattern, until something inside of him explodes and he does what he did in LA. He's just tuning up with these four, I hate to say. I'll have the FBI work this scene if you don't mind."

"It would be my pleasure," Ron said with a smile and a slap on the back. "Let the Feds pay for it and face the media, that's fine by me. My only concern at this time is the safety of the citizens of Cambria."

Spoken like a true politician, Phil thought, smiled at him, and nodded in understanding. Phil turned away, took out his cell phone, and called Kelly's phone. She answered on the fourth ring.

"Agent Flaherty," she said, slightly groggy.

"Good morning," he said in an extremely sensual voice. "Be happy it's me calling, and not Tony," Phil began. "He'd want to know why you're so groggy at 7:30 a.m."

"Where are you?" she asked.

Phil imagined her reaching for him, clinging to the sheets, trying to hide that luscious body, shook his head, tried to concentrate, and said, "Houston, we've got a problem. They've discovered four freshly dug graves here on south Cambria Beach, right down the road from where we, uh… were last night."

"Oh shit, he's been here for a few days," she replied. "You think he's still here?"

"Doubt it; he's back to small hits on the run, then vanish," Phil said. "It's what he's done in the past, and he is a creature of habit."

"I'll call the lab rats, and Tony, let him know the situation, and that you have the crime scene under control," she said. "I'll meet you down there in ten minutes."

He turned back and stared at the graves as he put the phone back into his pocket. He just couldn't believe that Frank could kill four women that quickly and bury them without being seen. If it weren't for the nose of a dog here or a wake of vultures in the desert, they would never have discovered the graves. His existence would have been unknown, and the killings could have been a lot worse. Hopefully God was guiding the animal kingdom to help catch this monster, Phil thought, because the humans not only couldn't find him, but they had created their own leviathan.

CHAPTER 27

Frank had paid cash for two nights at the Travelodge in Paso Robles. He had registered under the name of Eddie Logan, who was the clubhouse manager of the World Series Champion 1954 New York Giants. He had spent the entire day after waking up at noon cleaning his various weapons, with the television tuned to CNN, MSNBC, FOX News, and the local ABC affiliate for further coverage of the discovery of the graves on Cambria Beach. At 5:00 p.m. the FBI Task Force held a news conference covered by all of the stations, with Assistant Director Anthony Balducci answering all of the questions. They had recovered four bodies, all of them young women with the same burial technique as that found in the Southern California desert.

Frank knew they were lying. He had not used body bags this time, wrapping them instead in their own beach blankets and towels. He had to conserve his supplies, and he knew that there was probably plenty of other peoples' DNA on the items besides his own. They could match someone else, but not him, since he didn't "exist" per any documents at any level of any government. He was the true "Invisible Man" and would continue to use it to his advantage.

He was finishing the last gun, his Walther PPK, when he stopped and stared at the TV set; the face of Lieutenant Philip DiMarco could be seen standing in the background. But what mesmerized Frank was the stunning brunette who stood directly in front of the lieutenant. They were carrying on a casual conversation while the briefing was occurring. Frank studied their features as the assistant director continued to speak in the foreground. He observed DiMarco bend slightly and whisper something in her right ear; a smile showed up on her face, and then a backward right elbow jab playfully aimed at DiMarco happened. His smile sealed Frank's suspicions that they had a thing going. That changed everything as far as his adversaries were concerned, with this FBI agent now added. Seeing how close the two of them were gave him a new idea as he aimed his gun and made believe he had pulled the trigger. He would have to kill this FBI agent first before killing Gina. By killing both Gina and his lover, Di Marco would be in a weakened state, and much easier prey for the final showdown.

The conference ended, and the know-it-all TV analysts were now giving their spin on the events of the day. He turned to ESPN and waited for the Monday night game between the Reds and the Braves to begin. He got up, walked over to the window, cautiously pulled the curtain back a half inch, and peered out from his room into the early evening. The sun had already set on the valley, and the tulle fog was beginning to form. He had prepared to leave at about nine o'clock, which would allow enough darkness and lack of traffic to hide his escape. With this fog that began to build rapidly, he would leave an hour earlier, especially having to go on the switchback roads through the Cholame Hills.

The game was in a rain delay, so he turned the TV off, grabbed a quick shower, and finished packing. He hated staying more than twenty-four hours in one hotel, but there were exceptions to the rules. He looked around the room, satisfied with the order he had left behind. The bed was neatly made, and everything was back in its original location, with nothing extra left behind. He opened the front door cautiously after closing all of the lights and peered out into the parking lot, which was now full of vehicles, but there was no one roaming about. He moved quietly and swiftly. The brisk cool air was invigorating and filled him with energy. The lights were shrouded in the mist, which cast an eerie golden hue to the security lights. It would help to dim the clarity of anyone's vision that night.

He quickly loaded his weapons into his truck bed, with the exception of the Walther PPK and a blue steel Smith and Wesson 37 Magnum, which were in his backpack. They would be in the cab with him, just in case. He was bored, and with boredom came avenues of escape. He was only one step ahead of his adversaries. He needed to be at least three ahead.

He laughed as he pulled slowly out of the parking lot onto east CA-41. With the past history of the knuckleheads in the FBI, staying five steps ahead wouldn't be too hard. As long as they didn't listen to DiMarco, he'd be fine and on his way to Canada, but only after they were all dead.

It was finally time to go back home and settle his business, once and for all.

Phil sat there and stared at nothing. He was seething underneath a calm exterior. It had been almost two weeks since the discovery of the bodies in the desert, one week from Yosemite, and the task force was no closer to Frank DiMocchio than it was that very first day. Every indication was that he was now heading for the Bay Area, but no one in the FBI, with the exception of Kelly, took Phil seriously. The specialists at Quantico all said the same thing. He would continue to try to stay below the radar and had probably relocated within a short distance of the Central Coast to maintain control of the situation. They treated him as every other serial killer would be treated. That was their first mistake. They went by statistical analysis, which was admirable, but that was their second mistake. Then they thought like psychologists, which was their third and fatal mistake.

Frank was foremost an extremely well-trained killer. He was methodical, and everything was planned in advance. He avoided the smallest mistakes most other killers made. He was not only an exceptional killer; he was also a military tactician, in the mold of some of the greatest generals ever known, such as Patton or Rommel. That was how he became the supreme assassin and obtained a great deal of wealth along the way. But Phil couldn't make the geniuses understand that very point. This was not your everyday psychotic, but someone who planned every move as if it were a military battle during war.

The FBI had placated Phil by providing around-the-clock protection for Gina and her soon to be ex-husband until Frank was caught. He had seen their plans of protection: four people rotating twelve-hour shifts, clearly in sight at all times, as if that would scare him. What they didn't realize was that Frank would scout them as he was taught and learn their weaknesses over a period of time. Only when he was satisfied that the odds of his success outweighed the possible loss would he proceed with his plan. They didn't stand a chance against this monster, and Phil's niece would pay for their incompetence.

He was feeling guilty. The Italian in him knew that family came first and that he should be with Gina. Instead, he was 250 miles south in the sheriff's office as he awaited the preliminary results of the autopsies on the four young women from that morning. Kelly had gone back to Los Angeles, per orders from the high command, to run the task force, since the assistant director was needed immediately back in Washington DC. He missed her already. That didn't help his sour mood, but it made him focus more on his job. Then his job became sit and wait, and that soured him even more.

Finally he saw the sheriff coming down the hallway holding a file above his head, waving it for Phil to see.

"Well, it's about fucking time," he snarled at no one in particular.

"They were all killed by the same method," the sheriff started as he walked into the office and went to sit down.

"Fractures of the C2, C3 vertebral bodies, with severance of the spinal cord, were the causes of death. All were sexually active, with no semen internally, but condoms found with the bodies will be found to have contained semen from the same perpetrator," Phil deadpanned. The sheriff stopped his seating in midair, a look of astonishment on his face. Phil stood up and said, "That's all I needed to know; it's definitely him, and now he's definitely our problem. Trust me, contrary to the fucking assholes in the FBI, he's long gone from here." He stuck his hand out. "Semper fi," he said as the sheriff stood, shook his hand, and replied, "Semper fi and happy trails." He nodded and smiled.

Phil left the bland brown building in downtown Cambria and walked along the main street, past the small shops where summer tourists poured their money into the economy. What happened here this dark day would definitely help the economy with the amount of thrill-seeking nuts that would come to this quiet beach town.

"California is nothing but the land of fruits and nuts," his father always said when he was a boy growing up in the Bronx. His father never understood how Phil could settle out here after the war. His father was US Army, out of Fort Dix, New Jersey, an infantryman who survived the D-Day landing at Omaha Beach on June 6, 1944. The only time he came to California was in 1965, when he took the family to Disneyland. The freeways were crowded even back then, the smog was horrible, and the people were "strange," according to his father. He vowed never to return and honored that wish, even though Phil tried to convince him that San Francisco was like New York west. His father and mother had settled in Las Vegas before both dying in their eighties. Phil still owned the house they lived in, kept it as it was when they died, their ashes in their respective urns in their bedroom. His dad always thought they would have beachfront property when California fell off into the sea.

Their memories made him smile, though he was melancholy at the same time. He truly missed them.

He walked back along Moonstone Beach Boulevard. The sun had been gone for hours, a thick blanket of fog had returned, and a fine mist could be felt against the skin of his face as he headed back to the hotel. His CHP comrades in the Paso Robles station had arranged for a black and white to be waiting for him. The keys were with the manager, whom Phil had already called. He watched the waves curling in, crashing much louder than earlier this morning when all hell had broken loose. The swells were up to fifteen feet every seventh wave, with straight face curls that crashed straight down at a moment's notice. Very dangerous even for veteran surfers like himself, but for every person who had ever ridden a curl on a board, the sea always beckoned. Tonight, it helped Phil think things out clearly.

He had decided to follow his own instincts and begin his own pursuit of Frank, going with the gut feeling he had. As he sat in the sheriff's office for hours, he had time to study the maps of the western United States and Canada. By the time he had left, he had a premonition of where Frank was heading. He would start in Paso Robles and move north from there. He couldn't wait for the fucking FBI anymore. He was going rogue and couldn't give a shit. Gina came first, and he was the only one who knew what Frank would do next. He would begin surveillance of her house and her life. Then after careful preparation, he would strike. Phil could outmaneuver him with similar movements, but only by anticipating instead of reacting. He felt it was similar to medicine's motto of "an ounce of prevention is equal to a pound of cure."

He entered the hotel's parking lot and saw the 2011 Camaro black and white. His heart began to race as he anticipated what the drive would feel like. He quickly grabbed the keys from the manager, thanked him for everything, threw his bags into the trunk, and climbed into the captain's seat. He looked around at the interior: state-of-the-art technology with two laptops bolted on swing gear, digital dashboard, and six-speed manual shift. He depressed the clutch as he inserted the key into the ignition and cranked it. The engine caught on the second turn of the starter. The small block Chevrolet V-8 was very similar to the old 327 cubic inch blocks from the old days as it roared to life. It had been modified to push almost 500 horsepower, with plenty of torque to help with quick acceleration. The aluminum/lead alloy used for the block was made for longer pursuits at constant high speeds to prevent the engines from seizing. The base of the vehicle was widened by an extra two inches to add stability.

He hooked his iPod to the sound system, finding the live version of Pink Floyd's "The Wall," and heard the MC's voice warning about video equipment as the band blasted into the first cords of "In the Flesh." He put the shifter into reverse and slowly let off the clutch, felt it grab within an inch of the floor plate, and the thrust backward was instantaneous. Phil smiled as he put it into first, depressed the gas pedal slightly, and felt the car lift slightly up front. He pulled out onto the boulevard, punched the gas, and popped the clutch. The car fishtailed down the street as he left twenty-five feet of rubber behind, the smoke filled his nostrils, and he was a teenager all over again. He speed shifted and threw the gears until he was doing over ninety-five miles per hour in fifth gear and the car was cruising at 3,500 rpms. He flashed his roof bar lights so any sparse traffic pulled over as he flew by with the windows down, radio blasting, as he tried to close the gap between him and Satan's protégé.

CHAPTER 28

Frank took the exit for California Route 41 off of Interstate 5 and passed underneath the green signs for both Los Angeles and Sacramento, which were illuminated against the full moonlight, as he entered the small town of Kettleman Springs in the middle of the Central Valley of California. It was just past midnight, and he was making decent time. He had left the fog on the western side of the Los Padre hills about two hours ago. The valley was crystal clear, but the millions of stars normally seen were obscured by the bright light of the spring moon. The fragrant aroma of citrus blossoms was evident with every breath he took.

Up ahead he saw the familiar red and yellow sign of his favorite midnight snack, an In-N-Out Double-Double, animal style, with fries and a root beer. His mouth began to salivate at the thought of the first bite. As he rounded the corner of the street, past a deserted McDonalds, he wasn't surprised to see the long line on the drive-through. He pulled behind a raised black Ford F-250, the young driver maybe all of seventeen, dancing in his seat to an old Bruce Springsteen song, "Living Touch"; the pungent aroma of skunkweed was emitted from their open windows. Frank laughed to himself and laughed even harder when they pulled up to the speaker and ordered four Double Doubles and four fries for two people. *Must be great weed*, he thought.

His thoughts were distracted by what appeared to be a five-year-old boy running around, chasing the blackbirds that had swooped down on discarded food. Frank looked around, couldn't see his mother or father, and wondered whom he belonged to, until he saw his mother emerge from inside the restaurant carrying a takeout bag and soda. A cell phone was glued to her right ear as she talked away, oblivious to what her child was doing as she walked to her vehicle. The child ran after her through a busy parking lot, around moving cars, and was nearly hit twice. He saw the mother raise a keyless remote and beep a Mercedes E500.

"Figures, a rich bitch, probably has a nanny watch the kid," he said to no one as he pulled forward and ordered his favorite meal. He pulled ahead, focused on the stoned teenagers in front, as he heard his stomach growl from hunger. He finally paid and received his meal, along with a root beer. He sampled the hot fresh French fries and closed up the bag. There was a rest area ten miles north on I-5, and he felt more comfortable eating in its obscurity. He sucked on his root beer to wash down the salty taste of the fries as he headed back toward the interstate. He pulled onto the northbound ramp and nailed the gas pedal as the Hemi came roaring to life and brought his truck up to seventy-five miles per hour in no time. He found the live version of Genesis's "Seconds Out" on his iPod and blasted "Squonk" while he kept time with the snare drum and bass with his right hand and left foot. He rocked in his seat as he drove faster; he topped out at ninety-five miles per hour and made the exit for the rest area by the time the song ended.

As he pulled into the rest area, he saw only three cars besides his, all of them parked near the bathrooms. He slowly pulled past and noticed the black Mercedes E500 in the middle. "Shit," he said as he pulled past the cars to the very end in the shadows of the large eucalyptus trees. The bright moon lit up the area better than any security lights, so the overhanging limbs gave him nighttime shadow. He shut the engine down, but left the key in the ignition to prevent the overhead lights from automatically coming on. He opened his bag of goodies, pulled out his Double Double first, and unwrapped enough of the burger to take his first bite. He reached for a napkin as the juices dripped into his new beard. He sat back and savored the combination of grilled onions, fresh lettuce, tomatoes, two slices of cheddar cheese, with thousand-island dressing on top of two grilled beef burgers that hit his palate. The flavors exploded in his mouth, and he moaned as if he were having an orgasm.

He finished the burger in less than two minutes, took a long slug of root beer, and was about to attack the fries when he heard engines start up. He looked into his large side-view mirrors and noticed the Mercedes was the only car that did not leave. The other two must have been traveling together, as the lead car waited for the second one to pull out, and they finally passed Frank as they left the rest area. Suddenly he noticed the overhead light in the Mercedes came on as the child climbed out of the passenger door and began to run toward the bathroom. Frank turned around in his seat and saw the child disappear into the bathroom as the mother talked on the phone.

He had seen enough.

He opened the console, pulled out his Walther PPK and silencer, pulled his keys out of the ignition, opened the door, and hopped out of the cab. He quickly screwed the silencer into the weapon as he briskly walked in the shadows and approached the car from its blind spot. He looked up to the bathroom and saw no evidence of the child. His anger grew with the amount of neglect this mother was showing. How did she know that there wasn't a pedophile lurking in one of the stalls? He walked to within ten feet of the Mercedes, lifted his arm, and fired one shot through the driver's window. The bullet went through the woman's cell phone and finally through her parietal skull, which caused instant death as she slumped to the right, blood and brains sprayed on the passenger's window. He quickly turned, still not seeing the child as he briskly walked back and climbed into his truck. He started the engine, backed up, and looked back at the lot, vacant except for the Mercedes. He started forward, and at the last minute noticed the boy running freely around behind the bathrooms, oblivious to what had just happened.

"You'll be better off without that bitch for a mother," he said to himself as he slowly entered the empty interstate, accelerated to the posted seventy miles per hour speed limit, and set the cruise control. He reopened his bag, only to find his fries now cooled off, but still devoured them within a few minutes, downed the rest of his root beer, and finished everything off with a fresh joint. He began the 176-mile trip to Berkeley, California.

He was about to visit Gina's house at a time when most people were in REM sleep, which left them vulnerable to good surveillance and maybe something extra.

CHAPTER 29

The older couple pulled their thirty-year-old Airstream RV into the rest area, weary from driving through gusty crosswinds for the past one hundred miles. The husband's arms were screaming in pain from gripping the wheel so hard the entire time and began to tremor slightly as he began to relax his hold. He noticed the vacant Mercedes SUV parked in the handicapped space without the required blue placard hanging from the rearview mirror and shook his head in contempt. He pulled ahead into the area made especially for RVs and pulled to a stop. He released his hands from the steering wheel, and his arms fell to his sides in total exhaustion. He looked over at his wife in the passenger's seat, fast asleep, and smiled. He had retired after twenty-five years as a sergeant from the Livermore Police Department to care for her. She had early Alzheimer's disease, and he had given her a sedative earlier to prevent her from getting agitated during the treacherous drive. Even with the power of the Ford F-350 to help pull the small fifth-wheel sleeper, Mother Nature's forty-mile-an-hour winds made him feel like he had been driving a Tonka toy truck instead. He had felt the back end of the trailer lift a few times, but he never lost control and his wife had slept through the whole episode.

He slowly opened his door and gingerly made his way out of the cab. Every joint in his body disagreed with his movement and let him know it as the stiffness gave way to pain. But as his father once told him, joint pain with aging just meant one was still alive. He smiled at the thought as he looked up at the dark sky. Predawn was always the darkest hour of the early morning, with very few stars shining at that time. He checked his watch against the overhanging halogen light as he made his way toward the bathrooms. It was 4:45 a.m. and he was 160 miles from his home in Livermore. At the rate of speed he normally traveled, that would mean he would hit the morning rush-hour traffic over the Altimont Pass. Commuters from the Central Valley who made their daily drive to Oakland and San Francisco over this winding eight-lane highway through the surrounding hills were always subject to traffic delays until at least 11:00 a.m. He decided to rest for a few hours after using the facilities and avoid the mess.

As he came closer to the men's room, he noticed a young child running around on the grass behind the facilities, acting as if he were an airplane, with his arms stretched out. The old man looked back over his shoulder at the Mercedes SUV and thought he saw part of a shoulder just past the steering wheel. "Jesus, she's passed out as her kid's running around in the dark," he said loud enough for the boy to hear;

the boy stopped dead in his tracks and stared at the older man. "Are you okay?" the old man asked.

"I'm not supposed to talk to strangers," he said, backing up slightly.

"How about I go wake up your mommy, okay?" the old man said as he held up his hands in a gesture to avoid scaring the child further. As he started to turn, the boy said, "She won't like it if you wake her up."

"Why's that?" the old man asked.

"She gets angry and yells when I wake her up sometimes," he said as he looked down at the ground; the universal sign of guilt hung from his neck.

"Well, I won't let her get angry," he said and began to walk toward the Mercedes. When he came within thirty-five feet of the SUV, he noticed the bullet hole in the driver's window and stopped dead in his tracks. He turned to the boy and said, "You stay here." He waited for the boy to acknowledge his command before he moved forward. He closed the distance quickly but carefully as he looked for anything out of the ordinary on the ground or the surrounding area. He approached the vehicle from the passenger's side. His worst fears were confirmed as he came closer to the vehicle and noticed the woman slumped over, blood splattered over the window, with bits of brain tissue caught in the seam of the doorframe. He didn't need to look any further. He pulled out his cell phone and dialed 911.

"911, what is your name, location, and emergency?" the friendly male voice asked.

"This is retired Sergeant Donald McMillan of the Livermore Police Department, and I've come upon a murder scene at the rest area on northbound Interstate 5 near Kettleman Springs. A woman has been murdered, and her young boy, around the age of five, is running loose here," he said matter-of-factly as he stood at attention.

"Sir, have you touched or stepped on anything? Can you describe what you saw as far as the murder?" the dispatcher said as his fingers could be heard flying across his keyboard.

"I noted the lone vehicle, a Mercedes SUV, parked in the handicapped space near the bathrooms when I pulled in with my RV. I noticed the child running loose and found the woman who I assume was the mother slumped over to the right, a single bullet hole in the driver's window." He hesitated as he made sure the child was not nearby. "There is blood and brain tissue on the passenger's window," he said more softly.

"Is the child there?" the dispatcher asked.

"He's back to running around the bathroom area. He must have ADD or something," Donald said. "I hope to God he hasn't seen anything."

"Me too," the dispatcher said. "Sergeant, a black and white is en route to your area, and ETA is less than two minutes. Can you secure the area?"

"So far there's no one else here, but I have my old badge with me and can secure if needed," Donald said.

"I figured you had your badge with you," the dispatcher said with a hint of humor.

"You just never know when you travel..." Donald said, with the implication evident.

"Nope, you never do," the dispatcher replied.

At that moment Donald looked up as the reflection of the lights off the hillsides in the dark gave an eerie surreal image. The CHP vehicle approached rapidly from the south and roared into the rest area doing almost eighty miles per hour, and then rapidly decelerated with a throaty sound of the exhaust to a stop within thirty feet of Donald. The low-pointed nose of the Camaro had four red lights that were alternately flashing in the grill, which gave it an appearance of the old video game *Pong*. The car was parked at a forty-five-degree angle to the rear end of the Mercedes, the light bar on the roof lit like a Christmas tree. The driver's door opened, and a large, older CHP officer with single bars on his lapels emerged. He quickly walked over to the driver's window of the SUV without saying a word and examined the window before he gave a quick glance at the lifeless body inside. He put his hands on his knees and bent his head down as he mumbled some words and made the sign of the cross before he stood up and walked over to Donald.

"I'm Lieutenant Philip DiMarco," he said as he extended his hand as he approached. "You must be Sergeant McMillan," he said as they shook hands.

"Retired, but yes, I was a sergeant. Twenty-five years in the Livermore force. Now I'm just Don," he said.

"Phil," he answered as they released their grip.

"You're part of the FBI Task Force on the West Coast Slayer, aren't you?" Don asked. He pointed to his RV parked about two hundred feet away. "I get over five hundred channels on satellite TV; gotta follow my A's, you know. I have been watching everything about your case. You think this was his work?"

"He was last in Cambria over the past week, so maybe. That's why I was heading up I-5 when the call came in." Phil noticed the young child running around behind the bathroom building. "First I need to close the rest area with flares and roadblocks. Could you watch over the boy while I do that, and then we'll talk further." Don nodded and made his way back toward the building as Phil popped the trunk of the Camaro. As with all CHP vehicles, the mandatory flares and portable roadblocks were always packed in the trunk. He carried the necessary material to the exit ramp and had the temporary closure of the rest area completed in less than ten minutes. He walked back to the murder scene as the first light in the eastern sky could be seen. The start of another long day, but instead of dread, Phil felt alive and energized. He knew this was Frank's work. The timing was right, as was the kill shot as he looked through the bullet hole at the female victim slumped over the console. The single-shot entrance wound on her head was the mid-parietal area, which was right above the left ear. Taking into account the suspected height of the woman as she sat in her car, where the bullet hole was, and the splatter pattern of blood and brain, Phil knew the shooter was extremely tall. The question was motive; he heard the little boy laughing as he and Donald played airplane.

Suddenly the thought hit Phil that the mother was in the car while the young child was going to the bathroom alone. The neglect of the mother, if seen by Frank, would definitely set him off considering what his childhood was like. As Phil stood near his car, he sent a text to dispatch with the license plate and VIN number to begin the identification process, while he awaited the crime scene techs and the local county sheriff. He looked at the top edge of the sun as it began its rise over the miles of fruit and nut tree orchards and said a prayer for strength in his quest to rid this world of absolute evil. His thoughts were broken by a pinging sound like the old sonar sound in the movies and realized it was his own cell phone. He located the text message.

"Vehicle owner is one Richard DiVicenza of 1135 El Portollo Drive, Rancho Santa Fe, purchased less than six months ago."

"Oh shit," Phil said as he read the message.

"What's going on?" Donald said as he appeared out of nowhere.

"Where's the boy?" Phil asked.

"Using the head," Donald replied, "and he wants to give Mommy more time to sleep."

"Great, can you keep an eye on him?" Phil asked.

"I've got to check on the wife, early Alzheimer's disease, make sure she's okay," Donald said.

Phil felt immediate compassion for the man, who worked hard for years and retired just in time to care for a dying wife. Phil had the disease on both sides of his family in his grandparents. He remembered caring for his grandmother, who was in the advanced stage of the disease, when he was seventeen years old. It was the hardest two weeks he ever had in his life. In fact, boot camp with the Marines, which occurred only three months later, was much easier. "God bless you," Phil said, "for what you are doing."

"I took a vow thirty years ago," Donald said. "She stood by all of those hard years when I came out of the navy, went through the academy, and was a beat cop in Oakland, before moving to the Livermore Police Department."

Phil extended his hand again, which Don took with a questioning look in his face. "You survived Hell's Bathroom," and they both had a laugh at the inside joke of what Oakland was called to distinguish it from Hell's Kitchen, which was the nickname of the lower west side of Manhattan, New York. "Marines, SFPD, then CHP, but divorced," Phil said. "Mine moved up to a senior partner of a big law firm, who could provide her with much more than I with my pension. I got the kids, who are now all grown and have promised to care for me in my old age. But I'm not holding my breath on that promise." They laughed again. "The car belongs to Richard DiVicenza of Rancho Santa Fe."

Donald's smile quickly disappeared at the mention of the name. "*The* Richard DiVicenza?" was all he asked.

Phil nodded slowly. "So obviously this was his wife," he pointed at the Mercedes, "and that's his little boy."

"Oh shit is right," Donald said as more flashing lights could be seen coming from the south. His look of concern was warranted, considering he was a witness to a mob wife's murder.

"Don't worry; your name will not show up in the reports because you didn't witness the actual shooting," Phil said. He looked toward the RV and said, "You have enough to worry about."

Donald took a card from his wallet and handed it to Phil. "My home phone number is on the back if you need me for anything."

Phil smiled as he saw the official card from the Livermore Police Department, which dated back to when he was on the force, and knew he would probably still be carrying his own when he retired. That and his badge would be with him until he died. "Do you still carry your piece?" Phil asked.

"Wouldn't you in this crazy world?" Donald asked as he extended his hand for their final shake. "May God give you the wisdom and strength to capture this monster before he kills again," he said as he nodded to Phil in reverence.

"You and I both know he'll never be captured," Phil said as Donald turned to head toward his RV. "The only question is how many more will die before he does." He watched Donald and the boy walk toward his RV and a life of fulfillment in a different way. It would be harder than anything he ever had done as a cop all of those years. To watch your soul mate slowly die both mentally and physically before your eyes was no way to retire. Phil respected the man more than most other men he had crossed paths with in his life, even though they had just met. Phil turned at the sight and sound of approaching vehicles as the different branches of law enforcement arrived en masse.

The first to greet him was Pete Schaefer, the sheriff of King's County. They exchanged pleasantries as he took a look at the Mercedes and the victim. Within seconds, the FBI lab techs had roped everything off and had begun their investigation. Phil backed his car away from the area as the scene exploded into controlled chaos within minutes. The sheriff approached him as he exited his vehicle. "Do you really think this is your guy?" Pete asked.

"Are you hoping it is?" Phil asked with a big grin on his face.

"Wouldn't you if you were in my shoes?" Pete asked as if for forgiveness.

"You bet your ass," and they both shared a brief laugh. "You and I both know who is in that vehicle," Phil began as Pete nodded in acknowledgment. "She's murdered in a rest area in the middle of nowhere in the early morning hours. She appears to have been on a trip with their only son. If this was an execution as a message to Mr. DiVicenza, his son would not be walking around freely. He would either be dead or kidnapped and held for ransom, or worse."

"Then why was she killed and the boy spared?" Pete asked. "He could have been in the bathroom at the time and didn't see anything."

"Exactly," Phil said. "Would you let your five-year-old go to the bathroom alone in this rest area?" Don shook his head. "Neither would I, but she did. That's just the type of brazen negligence that would set Frank off, and it wouldn't be the first time he killed a negligent or abusive parent. I'll bet a week's pay that the gun used to kill her was a 9 mm Walther PPK with a left twist on the bullet."

"But I thought the West Coast Slayer was a sniper and a rapist," Pete said, looking for a comment.

"He is a killer, period," Phil said. "He kills by any method, which is usually meticulously planned and executed. This was more of an impulsive kill, which means something set him off and reminded him of his own dark early years."

"Was he abused?" Pete asked.

"Enough to the point where his first murder victim was his own abusive mother," Phil said, and he watched Pete's mouth drop wide-open in astonishment. "Then the Marines took him under their wings and created the greatest killing machine, with the expanded knowledge of ways to execute his murders. Then the government made him a nonentity so that all records of his existence were wiped clean, so that there is no DNA evidence outside of the murder scenes to connect the dots. We have enough forensic evidence to convict thirty times over, but we need his DNA to match anything. So unless he's captured, we have no case against him."

"He knows this, of course?" Pete asked and answered his own thought. "So he won't let anyone take him alive. He'll keep going until he is dead."

Phil looked at Pete and smiled. He put a hand on Pete's shoulder and said, "My friend, I've only known you for ten minutes, but you surmised exactly what I've been telling those pinheads at the FBI for over ten years, and they have yet to listen."

"Do you mean the Fuckwad Bullshit Instigators?" Pete asked.

"Did you grow up in New York?" Phil asked after he heard his favorite expression, which was coined in New York.

"Flatbush section, Brooklyn, but I left after high school, enrolled at USC, and stayed in California when I graduated," he said. "You too?"

"Washington Heights, Bronx, settled in San Francisco after Nam," Phil said. "I only went back for funerals, last time about fifteen years ago. It's just not the same."

"It never is after you leave home," Pete said.

"Wait a minute. Are you the same Peter Schaefer who blew out his knee in his senior year when he had the chance to win the Heisman?" Phil asked. Pete dropped his head down and pulled up his right pants leg. The ugly midline scar from the thigh to the shin said it all.

"I never saw the hit coming, but I still remember the pain," Pete said.

"It was a dirty low helmet to knee hit, and they didn't even throw the flag on the play," Phil said.

"You know the SOB never apologized," Pete said, referring to LaTroy Buford, the middle linebacker at UCLA, who delivered the career-ending blow.

"God took care of it for you when he was gunned down in Watts," Phil said.

Pete was quiet at first, then said, "I felt guilty after he died because there were many nights when I prayed for bad things to happen to him."

"You were expressing normal anger," Phil said, "as the shrinks would say. Me, I probably would have pulled the trigger myself if I had the chance."

Before Pete could answer, three FBI agents came walking over. "Must be the early shift; their suits are pressed without wrinkles," Phil said.

"Fuckwads, I told ya," Pete said with a big smile. Phil had a hard time keeping a straight face when the agents came within fifteen feet.

"Lieutenant DiMarco?" the lead agent asked as he looked straight at Phil and ignored the sheriff. "I'm Special Agent Jonathan Broxton, and I've been asked by the assistant director to secure the area and assume control of the situation."

Phil looked the agent straight in the eye and said with a scowl, "This is Sheriff Peter Schaefer, who was second in voting for the Heisman Trophy in spite of blowing out a knee when you were still sucking on your mother's tits, so show him a little respect and say hello." The agent was dumbfounded and didn't know how to respond. "Just as I thought, another mouthpiece for the head fuckwad, Tony Balducci."

Pete stepped forward and tried to hide the grin as he said, "If you want to take over the crime scene, be my guest. What do you want to do with the child? My deputy sheriff just went to get him in the back of the rest room. We don't have the time or resources to babysit while you investigate."

"Well, uh… I, uh…, I'll have to find out that answer for you," Broxton replied finally.

Phil almost imploded. "Are you that fucking stupid? Didn't you get the reports of a small child who may have witnessed the murder running around unsupervised until the motorist came into the rest area?"

"Speaking of the motorist, we need to question him," Broxton replied as if everything Phil said meant nothing.

"I've already questioned him, and he saw nothing but what you see now," Phil snarled. "Plus he is a retired police sergeant with an ill wife. I told him he was free to leave. I have his address and phone number."

"You shouldn't have done that, lieutenant," Broxton said with the accent on Phil's rank, which was meant as an insult. "You didn't have the authority to…" But before the words could come out he was hit with a right cross that Phil threw with bad intentions. Broxton's knees buckled as he crumpled to the ground, and his eyes glazed over as he lost consciousness on the way down.

"And that's what you do with a fuckwad if you are from the Bronx," Phil said to Pete, who was counting down from ten. At zero, Pete said, "You're out," and raised Phil's hand in victory. "Any more questions of authority here?" Phil asked of the remaining two agents, his fists still clenched and ready to fly. There was no argument as they tended to their wounded colleague. The tension was broken by the special ring on Phil's cell phone meant for Kelly.

"Did you have to go all New York and nail the asshole?" was her greeting that caught Phil off guard and speechless.

"Yes, he was wearing a new camera device if you haven't figured that out yet," she said as Phil regained his bearings. "Don't worry; he won't bring charges—he'd be too embarrassed and he had it coming to him. His marching orders were to secure the scene and consult with both you and the local sheriff. Then he was to report back to me for further instructions. So he went rogue and may actually face disciplinary charges."

"Jesus, remind me never to piss you off," Phil said with a smile.

"By the way, nice right, straight from the shoulder," Kelly said. "My father would be proud. He was a boxing coach in the army."

"Frank was here. I know it, feel it," Phil said.

"I believe you, but you are better off heading to the Bay Area, where you felt he was going in the first place," Kelly replied. "I already notified the crew about your impending arrival."

"I owe you," Phil said.

"More than you ever know," Kelly said with a sensual hint. "Please be careful, I can't have anything happening to you right now."

Phil felt warmth in his heart that had been ice-cold for years, which brought a smile to his face. "For the first time in my life, I will be extra careful." He hung up in time to see Pete standing about ten feet away, a smile on his face.

"She must be something special," Pete said. "You don't hide your emotions too well. Don't ever play poker, or you will lose your shorts." They both laughed.

"She is special," Phil said, "and I've never hid an emotion in my life. I may live in California, but I still have a very blunt, New York personality. Anyone who knows me knows I will tell them what I feel is the truth, without hiding."

"Well, sir, it's been an honor and a pleasure to have met you, but you need to go hunt that bastard down, and leave no prisoners in the process," Pete said as he extended his hand. "I'll take care of these fuckwads."

They shook hands, and exchanged a man hug; Phil turned and made his way back to his vehicle. He fired it up, and at the urging of Pete, who was making a spinning motion with his hands, burned out of his parking area space. He couldn't contaminate any evidence, but the roar of the engine followed by the squeal of the tires caused the entire ground to shake. Rubber smoke filled the air as he accelerated to nearly ninety miles per hour by the time he reached the interstate. He was ready to push the car to its limits and make it to Gina's house within the next few hours. Deep down inside, he was worried that no matter how much protection she had, it was not enough, and that bad consequences were about to happen. Kelly asked him to be careful, but at this point he felt that he had to throw all caution to the wind. If only others would have heeded his warnings or trusted his instincts further, death might have been avoided. In his soul, however, he sensed the loss of life, while in his mind he heard their screams of agony. He knew that he would be too late.

CHAPTER 30

Frank sat at a small table on the sidewalk at the small bistro on Telegraph Avenue; an order of crepes with fresh strawberries and whipped cream had just arrived. The first bite of the sweet delicious pastry mixture was enhanced by pure maple syrup, one of the perks of eating in a smaller bistro over your commercialized restaurants like IHOP, where the syrup was flavored cornstarch. He savored every bite as he took his time and made mental notes of the morning crowds. He sipped his cup of coffee as he watched the early morning traffic passing by; the young Berkeley crowd was a true mixture of all races. The famous university, home of some of the most liberal idealism in the country, was only a few blocks away.

He had arrived at 3:00 a.m., found a parking spot on a quiet street, crawled into the back of his cab, and slept hard for three hours. He then drove past Gina's Victorian-style house on Olive Street and noted the obvious Crown Victoria with four antennae on the trunk parked three hundred feet down the street. It was not occupied, but the other one, parked 750 feet away, was. However, neither occupant paid any attention to Frank's truck as he passed them. They were too busy, as their attention was occupied by the young college student in the low-cut jeans who walked by at the same time. They would be easy to neutralize, he thought, as he turned left at the next corner and then made another left as he came around on Maple Avenue, which ran parallel to Olive Street. The third surveillance car was parked in front of a house that was the back-door neighbors to Gina. The two agents in that car were both on their respective cell phones, most likely not on company business, and did not see Frank's truck either.

Frank smiled to himself as he knew this surveillance was costing the government a lot of money and time. He had plenty of both, and they didn't. After a while the teams would get bored of babysitting and mistakes would be made, especially with the laziest of the groups. He had already witnessed their errors. This was going to be fun. He made another left at Emerald Street and passed Olive Street again as headed back to Telegraph Avenue, where he had found the bistro. He parked his truck at the BART station and walked back to the bistro for his breakfast.

He ate very slowly, which allowed him time to plan his surveillance routine and his assault on her house. He ran scenarios through his mind of entrance, neutralization of any agents or relatives, finally ending with the abduction of Gina. He didn't want her to die just yet, and definitely not in her own home. She would die when he wanted her to die. He smiled at the thought of his power.

His good mood was broken by the sight of a CHP vehicle, a Camaro, which drove north on Telegraph and was stopped by the red light at the intersection a hundred feet away from the bistro. What gave Frank pause was the silhouette of the driver. It was none other than Lieutenant Philip DiMarco, who was probably here to see Gina. Hopefully his ultimate adversary was here just to check up on her and not to protect. They needed to be killed in the order he wanted, not at the same time, and the lieutenant needed to be last. That was his designed plan all along, and it wasn't open to change. The traffic light changed, and the car roared north. Their eyes never locked, but something made the cop look toward the bistro as he disappeared from view.

Frank gulped his last cup of coffee, wiped his mouth quickly, left a five-dollar tip on the table, got up, and left. He quickly crossed the street and headed north on Telegraph about twenty-five yards before he ducked into an art gallery. He pretended to admire the paintings in the windows as he watched the street. Sure enough, within two minutes, the black and white Camaro came up Telegraph Avenue and stopped in front of the bistro. Frank smiled as he watched the cop's head swivel in all directions as he looked for a shadow that did not exist. Slowly the vehicle pulled away and proceeded back toward Gina's house. Frank turned and nonchalantly asked the owner, who was the only person in the gallery, "How much is your starting price for this Jaquel painting? I just love his work with the palette knife." His question had the owner perplexed. The androgynous, older man looked over the top of his reading glasses in a manner of condescension at the long-haired, bearded beast of a man dressed in a sweatshirt and jeans.

"That one is $55,000; we have others in the back if you'd like to see," he replied with a wave of his hand. "They may be more in your price range"

The answer agitated Frank immensely. One thing in life he hated more than abusive mothers was a person who disrespected others just because of money or race. Instead of an immediate violent reaction, as most killers at that point would have done, he calmly replied with the straightest of faces, "I would love to, if you please." Frank motioned with a nod and diplomatic wave of his hand to have the man lead the way. The man began a nonstop chatter about the different techniques used by many French artists as he strutted to the back of the gallery. Not once did he ever look back at Frank, who slowly pulled his Walther PPK from his back waistband with the silencer still in place. He flipped the safety, waited for the man to cross into the back room, lifted his arm, and fired one shot through the back of his skull. His head exploded as brain and blood splattered all over the less-expensive paintings as the man collapsed forward onto the floor. Frank turned around, locked the door from the inside, closed it, and walked out to the gallery as he put his gun away. He locked the front door from the inside as he turned the open sign to closed and shut the locked door behind him as he exited. Suddenly he felt like having an ice cream cone; he remembered the location of his favorite Haagen-Dazs ice cream shop about a mile from there.

His smile had returned.

Phil knew Frank was there. On his first time around, he had caught a glimpse of a large shaggy-appearing person seated at the outdoor bistro, but he was already through the intersection and could not turn around. It had only taken him a few minutes to make the long trip around the block with traffic flow that early in the morning. Yet when Phil returned to the spot, he noticed the man was gone. That made him think it was Frank even more for the simple reason that no man that large could move that fast or had any reason to run from the law unless he were already guilty of a crime. He slowed his vehicle down to a crawl, oblivious to the traffic he was causing, as he scanned the sidewalks on both sides of the street. He pounded his fist on the steering wheel at the frustration of being that close, yet just as far away as before. He continued his search for another ten minutes as he extended his perimeter by another four blocks without any success. Phil knew that if Frank had ducked into any of the smaller buildings or shops along Telegraph Avenue, he would have a hard time locating him from the car.

He decided to park the car at Gina's place and walk back toward the bistro. This way he could watch and canvas at the same time. Someone had to have seen a man who resembled Bigfoot in the middle of Berkeley. He made his way down Olive Street past the large Victorian houses, all three stories in height, with wraparound porches and witches' peaks. The colors ranged from subtle earth tones to the extreme pink with purple trim on one corner that made Phil cringe when he saw the monstrosity. He wondered how the neighbors could stand to see it every day. As he got closer to Gina's place, the large oaks that draped each side of the street worried him as possible hiding places, excellent for surveillance. He passed Gina's house as he looked for a parking space and spotted the FBI car with the two jerks inside preoccupied with their smartphones. They never noticed him pass by, which incensed Phil beyond belief.

He found a parking space about a block away. He slowly made his way toward Gina's house and stayed in the shadows of the giant oak trees. When he was fifty feet from the surveillance vehicle, he pulled his 45 mm Remington from its holster and walked the rest of the distance with the firearm tucked at his side. Within ten seconds he was at the right rear quarter panel of the Crown Victoria and neither agent inside had yet noticed him. His anger increased exponentially as he heard the idiots in the car talking shop about who was banging who on the side at the job. He calmly walked up to the passenger's window, rapped once on the partially open window, pointed his gun through the crack, and yelled, "Bang, you're both dead." He stepped back as he holstered his weapon, placed his hands on his hips, and waited for the FBI agents to recover from the shock, which was evident in their reactions. Neither had any chance of drawing a weapon; instead, they jumped out of their respective seats and dropped their smartphones. As they sheepishly got out of their cars, Phil screamed, "You both should be brought up on charges of dereliction of duty, you two worthless pieces of shit. If that was Frank DiMocchio, you would have been shot through your phones and never known it. He wouldn't knock first, you fucking assholes."

Phil's face was crimson red with rage, but his eyes had turned just as evil and dark as the monster he was chasing. People began looking out of their windows at the scene unfolding below as the large police officer could be seen clearly frustrated; his hands rapidly gestured as he screamed at the other two men. Then they saw the officer turn as he gave them both his large middle finger in the universal gesture of dismissal. He made his way up the block and finally disappeared out of sight. They watched the other two men get back in the Crown Victoria. The drapes closed all around as the witnesses realized the drama had ended for now.

Five hundred feet the other way and across the street, a large figure stood in the shadows of the largest oak tree. He also had witnessed the entire episode of ineptitude and smiled. What the CHP officer had said was so true and was a prophecy of events that were about to unfold. But he would wait until a better time for their execution. Frank turned and walked the two blocks to his truck unnoticed, even in broad daylight. "This is going to be a piece of cake," he said as he got in and drove away.

CHAPTER 31

Gina felt his presence. She knew he was somewhere close. She gently pulled back on the lace curtains in her front parlor room and peered out onto the early-evening sidewalk of what used to be the safest place on earth. She was born and raised in this house, had cared for her mother, dying of breast cancer, in this house. It had kept her alive after her father's tragic death, after her relationship with Frank and subsequent bad marriage to Steve. Now she felt as if not even the house could protect her from such evil.

Seeing nothing out of the ordinary, she let the drape fall back into place and turned around. She thought of her mother's last days that were spent in this room, which was turned into a hospice ward for her care. Hospital bed, oxygen concentrator, and portable heart and blood pressure monitors, their constant beep now silenced. Gina had taken three months off from work and watched her mother go from a fighter and a vocal advocate for the battle against breast cancer to one who advocated her own death in the end. She was in constant pain and anorectic and had lost thirty of her 120 pounds within two months. She survived the last few days on morphine and Ativan, with sips of chamomile tea when she briefly awoke. On her last day, she told Gina, "I love you," in a faint whispered voice, followed by "please end this for me," a pleading look in her eyes, but also one of being at peace within. Gina gave her an extra amount of both drugs, and she passed away peacefully that night.

The only person who knew was Uncle Phil, who was there helping her father at the time. He had never told a soul, not even his best friend and partner. His visit with her earlier that day to personally warn her had left her stunned. The murder of the gallery curator had all of the markings of what Frank was capable of, yet she still doubted Phil. The guilt for what she had done the night of her mother's death, along with the subsequent betrayal of her father and Uncle Phil, hit her like a hammer. Her knees weakened as she became nauseated and diaphoretic. She immediately sat in her father's favorite chair, a La-Z-Boy, elevated her feet, and put her head back. Suddenly she felt a cool breeze pass over her shoulder and noticed that the curtains where she had been standing moved slightly. Suddenly the presence of her father, with a scent of his Old Spice cologne, was now in the room. She made the sign of the cross as she felt her father's spirit draw her back to the curtains.

She slowly rose from the chair, made sure she was not going to collapse, and moved over to the window. Her hand shook as she slowly pulled back on the finely laced curtain. Even in the dim light of the early night, she saw the shadow of the back of a large man with a hooded sweatshirt as he walked past the house six doors down across the street. He stopped, turned as if drawn to her gaze, and stared directly at Gina. She felt her entire body go cold as she stared into the eyes and soul of the devil.

The room began to spin as she stopped breathing, let go of the curtain, and backed away from the window before everything went black. When she came to, she was back in the La-Z-Boy, a cold compress across her forehead. FBI agents Solmers and Martinez stood over her.

"Are you okay? What happened?" they both asked simultaneously.

"I saw him." Shaking, she pointed at the window.

Solmers moved quickly to the window and peered out. He saw nothing, then headed out of the room to the front porch while Martinez got on her cell phone to the agents posted in the cars. She asked if they saw anything and got a negative answer on both ends. They both made sure the house was secure and returned to the front parlor. Gina was now sitting upright and her color had returned to her cheeks, but the fear in her eyes was still apparent.

"What exactly did you see, Gina?" Solmers asked.

Gina's stare was focused on a point five feet in front of where she was seated, but she remained silent. Solmers and Martinez looked at each other; both shrugged their shoulders, unsure of what to do next. Gina, her gaze still focused on the floor, finally said, "I felt he was near. I kept going to the window, and finally I saw a large man in a hooded sweatshirt about five hundred feet down the street. As if drawn by divine intervention, he turned, and I saw his evil eyes. That's when everything went black." Looking up with tears streaming down her face, she blurted out, "My mom died in a hospital bed right there," and she pointed at the spot at which she had been staring. She stood up suddenly, wiped her eyes, and said, "You both think I'm crazy, but he was there." Her look was one of anger and betrayal. Both agents held up their hands as if to say "not us," which caused Gina to storm out of the room and upstairs. Finally the sound of her bedroom door as it slammed in frustration could be heard.

"Stress can do strange things," Solmers said as he looked out of the front window. "You think we should report this… incident?" he said as he turned and faced Martinez.

"What incident?" she replied as they both nodded in agreement.

That decision would cost them their lives.

Frank had stayed in the car for almost four hours, had seen the changing of the guard at exactly 6:00 p.m., and had no doubt it would change again at 6:00 a.m. Just as he had thought. They were doing twelve-hour shifts, and usually the last hour of the shift was when the greatest number of mistakes occurred. The fatigue factor happened to everyone, no matter how well-trained or how much coffee one drank. He decided right then and there that he would attack at 5:15 a.m. It was the darkest part of the day, just before dawn. With extremely small binoculars with a 1,000-meter zoom capability, he made out the acne scars on the man just coming on duty, who was driving an identical Crown Victoria. The female agent passenger with him was of Hispanic descent. They were there to take over babysitting Gina. He had to laugh. Why not hang a neon sign on the roof of the car and advertise your presence properly? They parked in front of the house and immediately exited the vehicle, with only a brief scan of the surrounding area before they bounded up the steps to the front door. The door immediately opened and they stepped inside.

Within fifteen minutes, the daytime shift agents, a short black female and a tall lanky white male, exited the house, came down the steps, had another cursory look around the neighborhood, and crossed the street to their own Crown Victoria. The car was started, and they drove past Frank's Altima without noticing anything. Again, not too obvious, he thought and laughed harder. Within fifteen minutes another female agent left the premises and walked past Frank's spot toward the BART station. Her head was down, engrossed in her smartphone, oblivious to her surroundings and never sensing Frank's presence. So they had a five-person detail, he figured, with two on the premises at all times, with a third person to escort her to and from work.

Suddenly a female agent emerged from Gina's house, being towed by a German shepherd, out for the evening walk. He zoomed in with his glasses and saw that she was definitely of Mexican descent. Early forties, but in decent shape. She walked the dog and stopped at the surveillance Crown Victoria, leaned in, and talked to the two other agents. Like Frank thought, not too obvious. Did they think that if he saw a show of force, he would abandon his plans?

He was more concerned about the dog than any of the agents he had seen so far.

The agent stood up as the dog began to pull her away from the car as it smelled a spot nearby and raised its leg to urinate. A male dog tended to be more aggressive, sometimes more protective of its master. He would definitely protect the house better than the Feds. They headed back home and back inside within a few minutes.

After another two hours, Frank decided it was time for a closer reconnaissance of the area, especially the little nooks, crannies, and alleys that ran behind many of the residences. This is where the garbage was collected. Frank knew there was an alley between Gina's house and her neighbors behind. That's why it was so stupid to post a sentry in front of the rear neighbor's house. He needed to find out if there was another sentry for whom he had not accounted. He reached up to the overhead light switch and turned it off before he opened the door and slid out into the night. He headed away from the house and car until he reached the corner, where he made a right onto the cross street. About a hundred yards ahead was the opening for the alley, and he easily slipped into its shadows.

He was dressed entirely in black, with a black sweatshirt with the hood pulled up to hide his face. Instinctively he either walked or ran in a more crouched position, trying to convey a smaller person than his six-foot-five-frame actually was. He began to quickly walk the gravel road and did not see any vehicles parked anywhere in the stretch to the next street corner, which was beyond Gina's house. Most of the houses were Victorian-style, multiple floors with porches, some that wrapped around the entire perimeter of the house. There were toolsheds in almost every yard, along with doghouses and children's toys. Frank made mental notes of everything, including the poor quality of overhead lighting in most areas, with very few large Mercury vapor lamps that could light up an entire yard.

Within thirty-five seconds he was passing the rear of Gina's house. He noted the doghouse and toolshed, but no toys. He also noticed a large metal railroad spike driven into the ground, with a large link chain attached for the dog, which indicated not only a good-sized animal, but one with a lot of strength. Frank tried to remember if Gina had said anything about the shepherd but could not recall one iota. Most dogs were good watchdogs, but the shepherd had a better sense of smell than most, which made it more of a formidable defense against break-ins. He noticed a large screened-in porch, with a swinging screen door, washer/dryer, then the regular back door entrance, probably to the kitchen, he thought. He looked to his left and saw the second Crown Victoria for a split second, but only the tail end. The rest of the car was hidden by the neighbor's house, and he wasn't noticed. They would still need to be taken out, as would the first surveillance car.

He hurried to the end of the alley and noted an empty lean-to garage on the left one hundred feet short of the street. It would definitely fit his Altima. He made a right onto the street out of the alley, crossed the intersection of Gina's street, and made a right toward her house but on the opposite side of the street. He came within two hundred feet of the first car, and then ducked to the left into another alley's driveway, which took him past the car but short of Gina's house. He emerged slowly back onto the street and hid in the shadows of the large black oaks that lined the street. He stood for almost ten minutes behind the largest tree as he surveyed Gina's house and noticed the parting of the curtain in the front room to the right. He put his back against the tree, which blocked the sight of his entire body. Luckily no one else was on the street at that time of night.

He counted to 120 before he slowly emerged from behind the tree after the curtain closed. He began his walk back to the alleyway and emerged again beyond the car. He stopped suddenly as he sensed something or someone watching. He slowly turned just in time to see Gina's face from 750 feet and locked on her eyes. The torture within him began as the anger over her betrayal fought with the love he felt for her. He turned and moved quickly to get around the next corner as he headed back toward his rental car, and to the hotel for the night. He would need his sleep and would return for his next round of fun at 5:00 a.m.

CHAPTER 32

The early morning fog hung close to the ground and created a mist, which appeared as a veil of moisture droplets in the dim streetlights. The muffling effect of the fog was profound as it amplified the silence. Without any hint of a breeze, the air hung still. With no traffic on any thoroughfares and very few lights on in the multitude of homes surrounding, he felt all alone.

Everything was perfect.

That's what had him concerned.

He had packed his backpack with enough weaponry to take out an entire platoon, not just a company of FBI agents. The most important part of his plan was the element of surprise. There had been nothing occurring for three days after he had initially arrived and created angst with the murder of the gallery curator. With inactivity, carelessness would occur, along with the ever-present fatigue factor. He had counted on a synergistic effect of the two, which gave his plan a greater than 78 percent probability of success. He would take those odds any day of the week.

Dressed entirely in black, with a black ski mask rolled up on his head like a beanie all the way down to calf-high black moccasins, he moved quickly in the shadows. He checked his watch and saw it was exactly 5:15 a.m. as he continued quickly and quietly down the alley behind Gina's house. He reached the point where he could see the surveillance car on the next street and stopped behind a shed, which held three garbage cans, blue, green, and black for different recycling purposes. He pulled out his small field glasses, zoomed in, and saw both of the agents in the car fast asleep. He rapidly retreated and found a cross alley to the back street that exited out onto the street thirty feet to the rear of the surveillance car. He stopped against a brick retainer wall just before the street and lowered his backpack slowly to the ground. Thirty pounds lighter, he moved even quicker. He pulled down his ski mask, squatted down, and moved rapidly like a large crab. He made his way to the back of the vehicle, placed his back up against the trunk, and listened to both of them snoring. He smiled as he pulled his Walther PPK with silencer attached from his shoulder holster, released the safety, took a deep breath, and stood up. He casually walked up to the open passenger window, raised the weapon, and rapidly pulled the trigger twice. The sound of the cough it made was captured within the car. Both shots hit the right temples of the two agents; their bodies jerked spasmodically with the impact, then ceased all movement. Their death was instantaneous, with blood and brains splattered throughout the rear of the car.

He quickly turned around, retreated toward his backpack, lifted it, and pulled out a raw steak wrapped in plastic bags. He began walking back to Gina's house as he replaced the Walther PPK into its holster. When he was within ten feet of the back gate, he hurled the steak toward the doghouse, and it landed three feet in front. He backed up into the shadow of the telephone pole and waited. Within twenty seconds he heard the unmistakable sound of a dog's claws walking on a hard floor. He heard the animal make its way through the house and finally out the doggie door built into the rear entrance and screen doors. Within another fifteen seconds, the animal was cradling the steak. He licked the meat at first, then began to eat, but fell asleep within thirty seconds. Using a form of liquid barbiturate that was often deployed in covert operations, Frank had applied a liberal amount as coating for the steak. The dog would sleep for hours but remain unharmed. He didn't mind killing humans, but not innocent animals.

He made his way up the back stairs and found the screen door hooked closed. He took out a Swiss Army knife and pulled out the knife-edge as thin as a scalpel. He inserted the tool into the crack between the door and jamb. With minimal upward pressure, he forced the hook out of its inlet. He pulled the door open, scanned the porch, and found the far window slightly open. It was probably used for venting while cooking. He looked inside and could see the kitchen table, with four chairs on the other side with no occupants, faintly outlined by the LED lights on the appliances. The house appeared quiet. He quickly removed the outer screen and slid the window up. With the agility of a man half his size, he easily climbed through the window and placed his soft-soled moccasins on the linoleum floor. He adjusted his eyes to the dim light that came from the stove in the kitchen, moved around the table, through the kitchen, and grabbed a thick dish towel. He reached the hallway and peered around the corner. He saw a soft light that came from under the closed door of the front left room, where he had seen Gina earlier that week. The remainder of the hallway was dark.

He slipped quickly down the hallway, weapon in hand, toward the light, past montages of pictures of Gina and her family over the years. He reached the parlor door and found it slightly ajar. He peered through the crack and saw the male agent asleep. He was lounging in a La-Z-Boy, feet up in the air, snoring loudly. He pushed the door slowly open, raised his right arm, and fired. The cough was muffled even further by wrapping the towel around the weapon. The bullet caught the agent through the left eye and killed him instantly as the blood ran down his face and dripped onto the carpeted floor. Frank turned and closed the door.

He turned and walked back down the hallway as he quickly checked the downstairs rooms and found no other occupants there. He moved quickly to the stairs; he remembered from years ago to avoid the fifth and eighth stairs, which squeaked under his weight. He made the climb up the fifteen stairs without any noise, and stood at the landing as he recalled the layout. The master bedroom was to his right, most likely where Gina was right now. There were three other bedrooms; one contained the female

Hispanic agent. He figured it would be Gina's old bedroom down at the other end of the hallway. Quickly he opened the other two bedrooms and found them empty. As he paused at Gina's old door, memories flashed in his mind. He opened the door and entered the room. The rush of air that preceded him awakened the Hispanic agent. She reached in an attempt to grab her weapon out of her shoulder holster on the end table. She never made it, as he fired one shot through the open right side of her chest; blood exploded over Gina's old bed as the agent was rocked backward. He fired one more through the heart to be sure, and backed out of the room, the smell of carbonate evident.

He checked his watch; its fluorescent hands glowed in the total darkness, now at 5:22. *Still on schedule*, he thought as he slowly made his way down the hallway to what used to be Gina's parents' bedroom, which was now hers. He wondered if the soon-to-be-ex-husband was sleeping over for added protection. Just in case, he quickly changed the magazine on his gun, now fully loaded with seven rounds and one in the chamber, but he wouldn't need that many. He was just being as cautious as ever. He slowed his approach down to a slow crawl as he finally reached the door, put his head to it, and listened. The first thing he heard was muffled voices that came from the television. As he listened more carefully, he heard movement. The older floorboards creaked ever so slightly underneath a foot as the person moved past his position on the other side, then stopped. Then came the unmistakable sound of a hammer on a Smith and Wesson 38 caliber handgun being cocked, and he knew there was a third FBI agent he had not seen that stayed with Gina twenty-four hours a day. He hated "audibles" being called at the last moment, but he had no choice. Suddenly the television voices went silent, and any light that had been seen in the crack of the doorframe was now gone.

He quietly moved back from the door, laid down on his right side with most of his body hidden by the wall, his head even with the doorjamb and the gun in his right hand. With his long left arm, he reached up, turned the handle, and gently pushed the door open. The gun blast came immediately and sailed four feet above his head. Within a second of the blast he returned fire; the cough of his Walther PPK was followed by a thud as the body hit the ground and a clank as the gun hit the bed frame. In the gray of night, Frank made out the feet of the person he had shot and knew it wasn't Gina. The feet were long and slender. Gina's were small and flat. He smiled in the dark as he slithered up the doorframe, quickly entered the room, and used the door as a shield as he hid. After the ringing in his ears dissipated, he could hear Gina's breathing to the right. He aimed the gun in that direction, but froze as she spoke.

"Get it over with." Defiance was heard in her voice.

For the first time in his life, there was sudden conflict within. The want, the desire to kill his betrayer, was at odds to an emotion he had never felt before—sympathy. He lowered the gun, stepped out from behind the door, and stood at the end of the bed as he stared toward the silhouette of her shape in the dark. His inner conflict led to confusion, which was unacceptable in his world. He shook his head like a dog in an attempt to clear his mind. The realization that his time was limited came as his watch gave his left wrist a quick, silent vibration. He had set it earlier to warn him of the upper limit of his operation time, which helped to snap him back to reality.

"You have five minutes to pack what you need in a bag that you can carry and get dressed, or I'll shoot you dead and leave you with the rest of them," he said with a snarl.

In the light of the streetlamp, he saw the edges of a large California King bed. Gina, as always, slept to the left, just like when they were together. The bed was a four-post Paul Bunyan solid oak frame bed. It must have cost a fortune, probably part of the settlement from her father's death. Frank was never the beneficiary of that incident, no matter how hard he had tried. There were matching end tables and two large dressers in the room. The scent of multiple fragrances, all female, could be smelled as he stood in the room and waited for her to move. She stood still in bed in defiance of his demand. That one act pushed him over the edge. He raised his weapon and fired a shot that whizzed by Gina's right ear. The bullet splintered the headboard right behind her as she jumped at the sound.

"I'll put the next one through your head, bitch," he growled. "Now move your fucking ass."

The use of profanity against her shocked Gina. Frank had never exhibited that much anger or hatred toward her, no matter what, in the past. She immediately became docile as she entered survival mode. Her act of rebellion had been met with a greater force in true evil. It was a scenario she could not win going toe-to-toe with Frank. He would kill her just like the federal agents who lay dead in her house. The house was no longer her sanctuary, so it was time to leave while she still could. She moved quickly out of the bed as Frank continued to glare at her. His eyes burned through her even in the darkness of the night, which caused her to shudder inside. She moved quickly as she used the light from her cell phone to help her find her necessities and threw everything in her backpack. She then grabbed her clothes, a pair of Nike sweats, and clean underwear and socks and headed for the bathroom.

"Leave the cell phone on the bed and the bathroom door open," Frank commanded.

Gina did as she was told. She quickly peed, dressed, and combed her hair, all in plain view of Frank, who continued to stare at her from the exact same spot. She was ready to leave in less than three minutes.

They quickly left the bedroom, Gina in front of Frank, the Walther PPK still pointed at her back as she walked down the stairs. "Back door and grab a coat and hat on the way out," Frank said as Gina hesitated at the bottom of the stairs. She noticed the front parlor door was closed. She knew that Agent Smalls stayed in that room. She also knew that he was dead, killed in the same room her mother had died. She had warned them, but they had paid her no heed. She passed the montages of her family's lives as a sign of her own life as it passed in front of her eyes. As they exited the rear of the house, Gina saw her dog sprawled on the ground. The anger flared immediately.

"What did you do to Buster, you motherfucker?" she snarled through gritted teeth. She went to charge Frank but was halted by the feel of the cold barrel of the silencer pressed up against the center of her forehead.

Frank looked at her with amazement as he said, "Shit, Gina, you know me. I would never hurt an innocent animal. Humans are a different story; they're fun to kill." He smiled. "He's asleep after being given a sedative." Then the smile disappeared. "You ever question anything I do again, I'll kill you on the spot. Now get going." He nodded with his head in the direction to the right as he lowered the weapon.

Her anger turned into terror as she watched Frank's eyes turn from a soft blue when he referred to her dog, to a dark black at the mention of death. Her uncle had been right all along. She knew she couldn't win, so again, she just turned and began to walk. She began to plan her survival as she walked down the dark alley. She would be totally submissive, including sexually, until the time was right.

At that moment she knew that she would do whatever it took to kill Frank DiMocchio, even if it meant sacrificing her own life.

CHAPTER 33

The sudden swiftness of the murders and the lack of response by trained special agents of the FBI in such a high-profile case left the department in an immense state of shock. Everything they had learned about dealing with serial killers was totally ineffective against the West Coast Slayer, Frank DiMocchio. They were scrambling to learn where it all went wrong and how to correct their tactics to prevent a reoccurrence. The blame game also began as soon as the initial shock dissipated. Even the two other surveillance agents down the street from Gina's house were not aware of anything that early morning until their relief appeared and found their fallen comrades. The appearance of failure by the two remaining agents resulted in their immediate suspension after being debriefed by their superiors and members of the task force. Before they left disgraced, they did indicate that three nights earlier, there was a false alarm about a possible sighting of Frank, but nothing official had been reported.

After being flown up to the Bay Area with Kelly, Phil was in no mood for any more incompetence. He had been extremely quiet the entire trip after exploding on the phone earlier when his childhood friend informed him personally what had transpired in Berkeley in gruesome detail. He had said, "Tony, you couldn't find your fucking head with both of your hands" when a promise to locate Frank and Gina was made. Then Phil had told him to basically stay out of his way and that he was going to need more leeway in the investigation. He basically wanted control of the operation on the West Coast. Finally Tony did just that and allowed Phil to lead the task force from the field. Tony was the final decision maker from central command. The kidnap/murder and subsequent change in command also had put a strain on the relationship between Phil and Kelly. She noticed the distance grow between them as the hours passed.

As they surveyed the crime scene, the acrid odor of blood and carbonate was evident throughout the house. Phil felt an overwhelming sense of sadness. He stood in the front parlor, where Agent Solmers lay in his own pool of now dark crimson. His eyes were closed and he had never seen his killer, Phil thought. "He was asleep at the time he was shot," he said to Kelly, who quietly followed Phil from the front door, visibly shaken at the sight of her dead colleague. It was one of the reasons he headed the investigation of the massacre: he had no ties to the dead victims and had investigated plenty of murders while with SFPD. "He never heard or saw anything," he acknowledged to the CSI and morgue personnel waiting for him and Kelly to make their initial sweep. "What was their shift, six to six?"

"Yes," Kelly answered as tears streamed down her face. "He just had twin baby boys almost a year ago. He couldn't wait to teach them baseball," she blurted out. "Sorry, they had twelve-hour shifts, 6:00 a.m. to 6:00 p.m.," she said. She wiped the tears, shook her head, took a deep breath, and regained her composure.

"The last hour of any shift is always the longest," Phil said, "when fatigue usually settles in and mistakes are made. Frank knew their schedule."

"But… how?" Kelly asked.

"He staked out the house for three days, plenty of time for the professional killer he is to watch the pattern and plan this attack," Phil replied as he walked out of the room. They walked down the hallway filled with the memories of a past lifetime of a family of decent people. Phil's anger grew with the knowledge of each mistake that had been made. "He used the alleyway in the back," Phil said as they stepped out onto the porch and pointed to the gravel path. "Tell me there wasn't anyone watching the alley." Kelly shook her head no in acknowledgment of his theory.

"No, I guess not," she admitted.

"Jesus fucking Christ," Phil said in disgust as he walked down the steps past the sleeping German shepherd, and out through the swinging back gate. He stood in the middle of the alley, looked right and left slowly then shook his head even more at the stupidity of it all. He turned around and walked back to the house, up the outdoor stairs, and stopped dead in his tracks as he saw the screen from the far window behind the washing machine. The window was the point of entry. Phil went over, looked at the window, and saw no marks to indicate forced entry. The window had been left open, probably during cooking or eating the night before. No one checked it before retiring. Phil was getting sicker to his stomach with every passing moment. He turned with a scowl on his face, and Kelly realized the reason for his anger. She kept her distance from Phil in fear of what he might say or do. She had not seen the true dark side of him until now, and she didn't like what she saw. He stormed past her and banged the kitchen door in anger as he went back down the hallway to the stairs and up to see the rest of the horror.

Agent Martinez was being evaluated by the coroner as Phil walked into the room that he knew as Gina's when she was a child. Tom Slater, MD, turned and said, "It's been a long time, my friend, but it never changes," as he took off his gloves and shook Phil's hand. Tom had been assistant coroner in San Francisco when Phil was on homicide and then had made coroner for Alameda County, which Berkeley was a part of.

"It only gets worse as we get older and more intolerant," Phil said sadly.

"Are you getting as cynical as I am as we get older?" Tom asked.

"Probably more than you," Phil said. "This is Special Agent Kelly Flaherty of the FBI's task force. This is Dr. Thomas Slater, distinguished coroner of Alameda County." Tom shook her hand and nodded politely. As with all local law enforcement officials, there was always a small amount of distrust with the federal agencies, which led to the politeness of most meetings. Phil looked past Tom and saw the amount of blood that had soaked what once was Gina's childhood bed. He noticed the agent's gun inside the holster on the nightstand. *Another mistake*, he thought. She should have been sleeping with her piece in the bed, ready to be fired.

"The first bullet went through the right side, probably as she reached for the gun," the coroner said as if he had read Phil's own thoughts. "That shot forced her backward, and then he finished her off with one through the heart. She never had a chance."

"Yes, she did," Phil said with bitterness in his voice as he turned and looked at Kelly. "But nobody would listen, just like thirty years ago."

Tom sensed the tension in the room between the two of them and knew from years of experience that it went further than simple turf wars. This was more personal and he didn't want to take sides, but his loyalties were to Phil from years of fighting crime together in the same sewer of life's stench. "When everyone's talking and no one is listening, how can we decide?" he said, quoting part of a line from an old Crosby, Stills, and Nash song.

Phil smiled for the first time that night. "Are you still playing?" he asked Tom.

"Once a month at Yoshi's with the band," Tom said with pride. He looked at Kelly and said, "I've played drums with a jazz group called Taz for the past thirty years. It's the only thing that's kept me sane, besides my wife and kids, of course."

"Good save," Kelly said, and they all had a lighter moment as they stood among death.

"There's a fifth agent down in the master bedroom," Tom said but couldn't finish his thought as Phil immediately turned, walked out of the room, and down the hallway toward his late partner's old bedroom. Tom and Kelly trailed behind him as he made his way through the room's double oak door entrance, then stopped dead in his tracks.

"One shot at an upward angle, with entrance just below the sternum, exit wound left upper scapular area," Tom said. They all stared down at the female agent's body, which was sprawled on the floor in death's final macabre pose. Tom looked at Kelly with concern as he saw her lower lip quiver and the tears roll down both cheeks. She closed her eyes, made the sign of the cross, and said a silent prayer, which seemed to bring her solace. She quickly wiped away the tears before Phil could see anything. Tom gently put a hand on her shoulder in consolation, and she acknowledged his gesture with an "I'm okay" mouthed in silence.

Phil turned and looked at the room's entrance, then swung back to the body. He did this three more times, and he changed the angle of his head each time. He looked at Kelly and asked, "Did you normally run a three-person routine overnight?"

"No, normally it was two agents inside, with four on the street," Kelly said. "Something must have spooked Gina and the agent decided to stay. That was standard routine in that circumstance. Frank couldn't have known that she would be spending the night."

Phil sighed deeply and closed his eyes as both his head and shoulders slumped. He was exasperated and couldn't help the display of frustration. He looked at Kelly as the anger began to rise within and said, "How many times have I told you and anyone else who would listen that it wouldn't fucking matter? He would have anticipated it and made counter maneuvers, as he was trained to do so many years ago." Phil's voice was calm but cold, with contempt a close second. "Frank was on his belly behind the doorjamb, knowing that anyone on the other side would be shooting at least waist-, if not chest-high. How many of your agents are trained to shoot at a down angle if they think someone is on the other side of a door?"

"None," she answered quietly.

"My point exactly," Phil said. "Ten years later, untold numbers of murders, and yet no one has learned that in order to beat him at his game, you need to think like him. You can't think like a profiler and try to anticipate his next move. He was trained to be two steps ahead of the best-trained enemy combatant. That would put him five steps ahead of your agents, as witnessed here," he said with reverence so as not to further upset Kelly. He knew she was not responsible for these agents' deaths. Instead, he blamed her boss. "If the great Anthony Balducci, assistant director of the FBI, had worried less about his promotional status within the bureau, the real East Coast Slayer would have been executed. Instead, an innocent man died while the true killer escaped, morphed into the West Coast Slayer, and started to perform his own executions."

"What do you want me to do?" Kelly asked.

"Stand behind me, support me, but please don't stop me from finally killing him," Phil said emphatically.

"You can't be judge, jury, and executioner, Phil," Kelly implored. "There are laws against that sort of vigilante behavior. I won't stop you from finding and capturing him if the opportunity arises so that he may be brought to justice for his crimes. If he has to be killed as a means of self-defense, so be it. But I won't let you just kill him, or you'd be just like him. I couldn't love a man like that, because that's not you—that's him." The tears streamed down her cheeks as the anguish she was feeling finally broke through the hardened facade.

The sight of the pain her tortured soul was enduring dissipated any anger or resentment that Phil had felt. He immediately put his massive arms around her, gave her a quick hug, confessed his love for her and that he would try his best to capture Frank as she wished. All of this was said in earshot of Tom, who remained skeptical of Phil. Kelly also had her doubts, but said nothing further as she finally left the room

"You just lied through your teeth to that woman who loves your ugly ass," Tom said without mincing words. "You are still going to kill Frank."

"At the first fucking chance I get," Phil growled. The look in his eyes was one of an intensity that Tom had never seen in his old friend, and it had him worried.

"Just remember what you wish for and hope that it doesn't come back to bite you in that hardheaded Italian ass," Tom said.

Phil's expression softened slightly, but he was still serious when he replied, "If I don't kill him, Tom, he's just going to continue to do what he has done over and over again. I can't let that happen… even if it means sacrificing others to stop this insanity. It's like that in any war. It's called collateral damage, and it is always acceptable to some degree."

"But this isn't a war, Phil; it is one lone psychopath that has caused the death and destruction, not an army," Tom implored, "and the death of innocent bystanders is never acceptable… at anytime."

"It may not be acceptable," Phil replied, "but sometimes, it is necessary."

"Then you are no longer the same person I knew all of those years ago, when you had grown weary of the death and violence," Tom said sadly.

"No, I'm not, Tom, as you are not also," Phil said. "Life does that to you; no matter how hard one tries to be the same old person he or she once was, we all change. If not, we grow stagnant and die."

"As you are destined to do sooner than you should," Tom said solemnly.

"As long as I die killing Frank DiMocchio. Take care, Tom; great seeing you one more time," Phil said as he nodded, turned, and left the room. Phil felt himself harden against his old comrade-in-arms, slightly irritated about the moral lecture, as he quickly descended the stairs and stormed out of the house through the front door. He needed to escape the madness as he had felt his panic increase from within. He leaned up against one of the large oak trees as he slowed his breathing rate down rapidly. The faces of the women and children that had died at his hands that day so many years ago haunted his very soul as they flashed before his eyes. Fifteen people who were in the wrong place at the wrong time paid for his anger, after his best friend was shot and killed by a sniper hiding in their village that day. They were innocent human beings caught in the throes of a killing machine who at that time had no feeling but hate left inside. He bent over and vomited rhythmically until the dry heaves ceased. He stayed still as the lightheadedness began to ease and the feeling of overwhelming nausea passed. He looked up at Gina's house and knew that he would never see it again. But he was at peace at that moment, knowing that his just retribution would soon come to fruition with the death of someone he once was.

CHAPTER 34

The shock of what had happened still was evident in Gina's blank stare as she sat on the edge of the bed in the hotel room. The effects of the Valium had caused her to be more lethargic than normal, especially at five o'clock in the afternoon. She hadn't taken any kind of anxiolytic medication in years, but she was more than willing when it was offered. After they had arrived back at Frank's hotel room at about six o'clock in the morning, she had taken a long shower to wash off any remnants of guilt, but the smell of death was ingrained into her now. She was responsible for all of those deaths as if she had been the one to pull the trigger, simply because she had let her guard down at a moment of extreme weakness and he had exploited her position. She also knew that she was sure to die, and soon, but for some reason didn't care. Finally she fell asleep without even speaking to her captor at any time since they had left her house. Now she just sat there and stared at the floor in front of her as the evening news played in the background, oblivious to what was being said.

He wasn't.

With unwavering attention, he listened intensely to every word the roving reporter had to say. Her description of him as a mad psychopath made him laugh. They still didn't understand him, he thought as he shook his head in disagreement. Then the sketch they displayed showed him almost three weeks ago with a shaved head and face, the sketch of his tattoo poorly done. He laughed again, then finally said to Gina, "At least you could have told them about the dimples on my face and ass," as he got up to urinate. He didn't make it to the bathroom.

She sprang from the bed with a primal scream that erupted from her twisted mouth as she jumped onto his back. She scratched and clawed at anything she could grab, including his hair and beard, then bit down hard on his neck. The taste of blood soured in her mouth, but she wouldn't disengage. Suddenly he roared, reached backward, grabbed her by the shoulders, and flung her across the room. She crashed into the far wall and took down a painting of a peaceful valley. He felt his neck, saw the blood on his hand, and his rage exploded. He picked her up like a rag doll and tossed her back across the room, where she hit the other wall. She crumpled to the floor unconscious. He stood over her with fists balled up and breathed hard as he finally began to calm down. He turned around and headed to the bathroom to clean up and finally urinate.

After about ten minutes, Gina began to stir and her eyes slowly fluttered open. Frank was perched on the edge of the bed as he watched her carefully. His anger had passed, and he had no desire to kill her at the present time. It took Gina another three or four minutes to fully regain consciousness, and her mood appeared to be more submissive. She finally sat up, pulled her hair back out of her face, and looked up at Frank.

"Sorry, I just lost it," she said flatly. "Are you going to kill me now, or wait until later?"

"I don't want to kill you, but I will if I have to, especially if you pull a stunt like that again," Frank said. "Go take a shower, get your head cleared, then get dressed and ready to leave."

"I'm hungry," she said as she staggered to her feet and stretched slowly to minimize the pain and stiffness; she didn't think anything was broken.

"We'll get something on the road," he said flatly as he stood and began to pack his things, which was a signal that she was dismissed. Gina lumbered into the bathroom, and within seconds, the shower was running.

"Leave the door open," he said to her as it was about to close. She gave him a vicious look but complied. "Glad to see you haven't lost your nerve," he said as she turned her back on him. He shook his head in disbelief. He remembered his father once telling him when Frank was small, after one of his mother's verbal assaults against his father, that you just couldn't change a woman's personality. A man could be "trained," but the reverse was not true. Frank firmly believed in everything that his father had taught him, but his early death had left such a void. Frank shook his head and refocused on the task at hand. He finished packing as the steam from the shower added moisture to everything in the room. He waited for Gina to finish showering and drying off before attempting to load the truck.

He loaded all of the clothing baggage first, followed by the cooler full of different beverages and water. He had enough rations packed already, just in case he really got hungry. Last to be loaded was the large duffel bag with most of his weapons, all except his 50 caliber rifle, the Henry long rifle, 2 RPGs, and one handheld SSM. Those were packed separately. All told, he had over five thousand rounds of live ammunition, with multiple loads for every weapon.

By the time he was finished, Gina was ready to leave. She appeared wearing a simple lavender-color sundress, which accentuated her hourglass figure. He stood there looking at her as if he had just seen her for the first time. "You look beautiful," he said sheepishly. Gina was pleasantly surprised by the remark and the sweet attention. Her mother always told her that one could get a lot more bees with sugar than with salt. Gina decided to play the female sweet card to the hilt, draw Frank closer, then either kill him with his own gun or get the hell out of there.

"Thank you," she replied softly as she passed him, gently touched his cheek, smiled, and eagerly climbed into the passenger side of his truck without question. As he climbed into the cab, Gina asked, "What happened to the rental car?"

"I took it back while you slept," he said blandly. What she didn't know was that he double-dosed her Valium and handcuffed her to the bed frame after she was zonked out. He wasn't about to take the chance of her running off. The stakes were too high. She was his prize, while being bait at the same time. If she had to die after his mission was accomplished, so be it. He had no guilt one way or the other. In the meantime he was going to enjoy using her and her many talents. He smiled to himself as he started the truck and lit up a joint while waiting for the engine to run through its start-up cycle. He passed it to Gina, who took a long toke and began to immediately cough and choke.

As they pulled out of the hotel parking lot, he saw an advertisement billboard for an In-N-Out Burger just two miles away. He waited for Gina to pass the joint back as she took a second, then a third hit, and finally exhaled the pungent blue smoke. "You in the mood for a Double Double?" he asked.

"I am now," she said and began to giggle as she handed the joint back. Frank looked at the remnants, now more of a roach, took the last possible toke, and put the head out between his fingertips. He enjoyed the momentary pain. "Don't bogey the joint next time or you won't get any," he said seriously, but Gina just stuck her tongue out at him and laughed. If she wasn't stoned, he would have smacked her. *There will be plenty of time for that and more*, he thought as he drove toward his dinner before they headed northwest. They would avoid any of the major cities or towns, sticking to the back roads and camping, while the incendiary that was the death of five federal agents and the kidnapping of a witness to the murders would slowly fade into the ashes of time.

CHAPTER 35

They had disappeared off the face of the earth. In spite of a media blitz with an updated picture of Gina from the hospital that she had worked at and a composite drawing of Frank, there had been no sightings. A reward of $1,000,000 was now being offered by the task force for any information that led directly to the apprehension of Frank DiMocchio. The money came straight from the FBI's coffers after every agent in the entire agency volunteered 5 percent of their current pay as a reward. After three days of an intense manhunt with over one hundred federal and local law enforcement agents, they were no closer to finding the pair than they were that fateful morning. It was inconceivable to the upper echelon of the FBI that they could not be found. The same mistakes that had been made ten years earlier were occurring again. They highly underestimated their enemy, and now even with a hostage, he couldn't be located. They had concentrated on hotels, gas stations, restaurants, and such along the possible routes out of the Bay Area.

They had never checked campsites.

After the first day in the hotel, they had driven at night only and camped out along the route in a two-man pup tent, which took all of five minutes to assemble or take down. That first day they made camp outside a small town called Pine Grove, along California Route 88 about fifty miles northeast of the city of Stockton, in the Sierra Mountain foothills.

Gina sat in a fold-up canvas chair, a handheld mirror in her hands, and looked at the new woman who stared back at her. Her long curly auburn hair had been cut extremely short and was now bleached blond. Frank had drawn a serpent's tattoo from her neck down her left arm using body paint that was part of his camouflage kit. She now looked like an older punk rocker. She was hesitant at first, but when Frank had insisted that she had to change her appearance or die, she agreed. Now she loved what she saw. Frank approached her and gave her a catcall whistle. "You look marvelous," he said with a Billy Crystal accent.

"You're looking more like Jerry Garcia of the Grateful Dead, after he died," she said with a chuckle, as his hair and beard were now totally gray and scraggly looking.

He smiled at the thought and held up his right hand backward with the middle finger bent in half to indicate the similarity to the famed rock guitarist with the deformed hand. His appearance was nothing like anything that floated around the media or through the task force. He knew it would be that way, as it was ten years prior, since the FBI always went by the book. The only person that would think outside the box was his archenemy, Lieutenant DiMarco, but he would not be listened to, as it also was ten years ago. They were in need of feminine supplies that Frank had not considered in his plans and needed to go into town to stock up. It was time to see if their appearance set off any alarms. "Time to go," was all he said as they finished loading the remainder of their camping gear into the bed of the truck.

They headed straight to a Union 76 gas station about two miles from their camp that they had passed in the middle of last night. Frank had remembered that there was a mini-mart with the station. They could stock up on most necessary staples there to keep them going without going to a true grocery store, where the risk of being recognized would have increased tremendously. He pulled in to the station and stopped at the pump farthest from the mini-mart. He used one of his many phony credit cards to pay for the gas at the pump. He stayed on the far side of the truck while Gina went inside to purchase the necessary items.

Frank watched the cost of filling up his truck as the pump closed in on $100, with the price of gas up to $4.25 a gallon. As he replaced the nozzle into its holder, a black Cadillac SUV with dark-tinted windows pulled up at the pump closest to the mini-mart. Frank looked inside the store and saw Gina at the counter as she talked away to a young female teenager behind the counter. Hurry up, he said to himself.

Then everything changed.

The two passenger doors of the SUV opened up as two large black men emerged, ski masks pulled down over their faces; they walked into the store with guns drawn. Within ten seconds, Gina was grabbed around the throat and being dragged away from the counter as the second robber held a gun to the clerk's head.

"Shit," Frank said to himself. He quickly moved from the driver's doorframe, pulled out his Walther PPK with the silencer attached, and made his way around the back of the SUV without being seen. He quickly came around the driver's side, saw the driver's head turned toward the action inside the store with the engine running and radio booming. Frank walked up, raised the weapon, fired one shot through the window and the driver's head, and killed him instantly.

He put his weapon at his side and made his way around the front of the SUV and into the entrance of the store like he was Dirty Harry. "Let go of her," he said to the man who held Gina.

"Or what, motherfucker?" the gangster said, but didn't get to hear the answer as Frank raised his gun, fired once, and hit the man in between the eyes. The man dropped to the floor immediately. Frank immediately turned and fired at his accomplice. The shot went through the middle of his chest and drove him back against the counter. The clerk, who had been in shock since the start, began to scream at the top of her lungs. Gina rushed over, hugged her, and helped to console her.

Frank looked at the total that was posted on the cash register and asked, "Is that the total for our groceries here?"

"What?" she looked at him quizzically. "You can just take what you want."

Frank pulled out $65, laid it on the counter, and picked up a few bags with one hand, motioning for Gina to get the rest. "I'm not a thief," he said, as if insulted.

Suddenly the clerk recognized who she was talking to; her face became apprehensive again. Frank noticed immediately, and his shoulders sagged as he realized what had to be done.

"Please don't shoot me," the clerk said as she began to shake; Frank looked directly at her. His eyes showed no emotion. He tightened the grip on his gun, but hesitated long enough for Gina to step in front of him, blocking his sight of the clerk. "I just had a baby two months ago, and I'm all he has." The clerk now covered her head with her arms for protection as she sobbed uncontrollably.

"Don't—for me, please," Gina said as she held her hand to his chest over his heart as her soft green eyes searched deep into his and pleaded for mercy.

Frank took a deep breath, relaxed his finger off of the trigger, and looked past Gina at the clerk. "Does this place have video cameras?" he asked her bluntly.

"No," she said.

"Good. You wait fifteen minutes before you call 911. Then tell the police that you ran into the back when you saw the SUV pull up and the men come out wearing ski masks. You locked the door, then heard yelling and gunshots, then silence, and came out to find this. Do you understand?" Frank barked the question as if still in the corps.

"Y-y-yes," she stuttered. "I don't know who shot them because I had locked myself in the back office when the shooting took place."

"Excellent," he said quietly as he walked past Gina. He pulled up his sleeves to show the tattoos, which confirmed the clerk's suspicions and worst nightmare. He stood almost one and a half feet over her, looked down at her, and snarled, "If you tell them the truth, I'll come back, kill you and your baby, and sleep very well at night. You can thank her," he said as he nodded at Gina, "for saving your sorry ass."

He turned, walked past Gina, and said, "Let's go." He exited the store, disgusted that he let Gina leave a witness behind. He had never felt compassion for an eyewitness before and wouldn't start now. He loaded the groceries into the cab of his truck and waited for Gina. She walked up to him, gave him a peck on his cheek, and said, "Thank you."

"Did you get the beer?" he asked her.

"Oh shit, I forgot," Gina said.

"I'll get it. Here," he said as he tossed her the keys, "start her up; you can drive a little." She smiled from ear to ear. He turned and walked back into the store.

"I forgot some beer," he said as he nonchalantly walked to the refrigerated section and grabbed a twelve-pack of Heineken. He came over and put a $20 bill onto the counter. Then he reached behind him, pulled out his gun, and shot her in the chest. The bullet knocked her down and she was dead before she hit the floor. He turned and walked out. He looked at his truck and saw Gina rocking out to the music, oblivious to what had just happened. *Better off that way*, he thought. He would deal with her insubordination later. At that moment, his mind was at ease and he felt much better. It was going to be a great day after all.

CHAPTER 36

The report about the killings at the Union 76 station in Pine Grove was the lead story on CNN, Fox News, MSNBC, and all of the other national news media outlets. Within hours of the first reports of the bloody rampage, scores of television satellite trucks were parked along the shoulders of California Route 88, with their dishes aimed up past the tall pine trees. The grim details of the multiple shootings shook the small conservative town of people who had lived there for generations; some traced their roots back to the gold-prospecting days of the mid-1800s. It was a peaceful town, where everyone knew each other and people still left their doors unlocked at night. The only ethnicities in the town were either white or Mexican, with no major crime of which to speak. The influx of gangs and drugs had not made its way to this part of California as of yet. The story of the deaths of the three black youths who had traveled from their homes in Vallejo, over one hundred miles away, to commit robbery and murder was portrayed as righteous retribution. That was not the case with the senseless death of the innocent, white young clerk. The story of a small-town teenage mother trying to make ends meet, and getting caught in what many said was a racially motivated gang-related robbery that went bad, was the underlying story. A memorial fund for her two-month-old child was established immediately by the Union 76 company.

Phil crossed underneath the yellow police tape and walked up to the Cadillac SUV, which was still parked at the closest pump. He looked at the bullet hole in the driver's side window and the spray pattern of the blood and brains inside. The body had already been removed. The task force had insisted upon not removing anything else but the dead when they got wind of the quadruple murder in a remote section of Northern California within four days of the Berkeley slaughter. Kelly had already gone into the mini-mart to evaluate that scene. Phil wanted to start with what he felt was the first murder, as he looked around at the bucolic area and tried to imagine what had transpired. According to most local deputy sheriffs, the amount of traffic that the gas station would have had at that time of morning would have been minor at best. It was the perfect time of the day to be robbed, since the business was closed by nine o'clock at night.

Phil played out the scene in his head. The driver had stayed behind but did not have the engine running. He was the lookout, but was found with his nine-millimeter semiautomatic weapon under his left thigh with the safety engaged. There were no other vehicles around except the slain clerk's 1999 Honda Civic, with a baby's car seat in the back. There were no video cameras anywhere. That meant the robbers were confident that they would not be bothered and could take their time. They did not anticipate any immediate threat posed by anyone at the time. That was their first mistake. Someone else was here at the time, someone who appeared to be inconsequential or was well-hidden. In Phil's mind, the tactics used to subdue the gangsters were all signs of a professional killer, who was taught to always eliminate the guard or lookout first before mounting any type of final assault—simple military training that was learned in basic training in boot camp with the marines all those years ago. Second rule of thumb was to make sure the lookout was taken by surprise, which thereby eliminated any communication with the primary target inside.

Phil went back under the tape, looked at every pump in the gas station, and checked all of the prices from the previous purchases, which were still emblazoned digitally. Assuming Frank was still driving a truck, he looked for the largest purchase and found it at the pump farthest from the mini-mart. A total of $98.25 for a little over twenty-three gallons of gas, or about what a domestic pickup truck would hold (usually twenty-six-gallon tank capacity), which gave the truck almost five hundred miles of range. Phil stood behind the pump, looked at the SUV, and then slowly made his way around the far pumps and up to the back of the SUV. All the while, he kept the driver's window in sight at all times. He replayed the maneuver, this time in a crouched position as a soldier would do when he darted from one position of cover to the next, which hopefully decreased his chances of being seen or killed.

Phil finally concluded that the lookout had seriously failed to carry out his duty. The only way Frank could have snuck up on him without being seen was if the driver was looking at what was happening inside the store. These gangsters were easy prey for a trained killer, especially against such a bunch of amateur criminals. He shook his head in disbelief and walked toward the mini-mart while he tried to imagine that scenario as it unfolded. When he entered the store, the first thing he did was to evaluate the environment; he saw where all of the different amenities were. Then he looked at the blood pools and spray pattern of the three victims. Kelly came walking over, deep in thought. Phil stood still in the spot where Frank had been standing when he shot both armed men. They had both been shot within moments of his entering the store. Phil walked toward the counter and studied the blood pattern on the glass and the computer terminal to the pumps.

The clerk had been shot last, Phil thought, *at close range and at a downward angle*. Frank had walked over just like Phil had just done and fired. She had been killed as an afterthought.

"She was shot because she was a witness to whoever killed the three men," Phil said to Kelly, who nodded in agreement. "Frank was definitely here," he said emphatically. "I'll bet my entire pension that all four victims were killed by the same gun, which will match the Berkeley, Fresno, and Yosemite murders."

"I agree," Kelly said. "How do you think it went down?"

"Gina was inside the store buying supplies, and Frank was at the far pump getting gas." Phil pointed out the window as he spoke. "You'll need to run the credit card purchase on that pump by the way. I'll bet it's a phony ID," he continued. "The two robbers walked in brandishing weapons, probably took Gina as a hostage as the clerk was forced to open the register. They didn't expect Frank DiMocchio to walk in, and they didn't expect him to be who he was."

"Do you think Frank and Gina were just passing through?" Kelly asked.

"It happened in the early morning." Phil said his thoughts aloud. He walked over to the counter, reached over, and picked up a Rand McNally foldout map of California. He opened it and found their approximate location. His eyes focused on the small green tent about three miles due east. "They were staying nearby and stopped in prior to leaving." His finger pointed to the universal symbol for a campground. "I should have known that," Phil said in frustration. "Deep down, he's still a grunt, and a grunt knows how to stay below the radar. They'll be camping wherever they stop and driving at night." He looked back at the map. "They're heading north on Route 88, which hooks up with US 395 in Nevada. From there they can head either north to Carson City and Reno, or south back toward LA."

"They're heading north," Kelly said without hesitation.

Phil was startled with the revelation. "How can you be so sure?"

"He can't top what he did in the Grapevine, so why go back? Plus he now has Gina and needs to stay toward rural areas, where it's easier to hide out and less chance of being spotted," she replied.

"Plus, pretty soon he'll need another hunting and burial ground," Phil said as they walked out of the mini-mart. "I totally agree with your evaluation. You better get on the horn and call Tony; let him know what we found and where we're going."

She began to pull her cell phone out of her pocket and stopped before calling. "You think he's looking for another hunting ground while toting Gina along?"

"That's just the point," Phil said with exasperation. "He may do just that, which would go against everything preached by your bureau's profilers. He's not going to stop being who he is because we are chasing him. At some point, Gina will become a liability. At that juncture, she's not going to be alive for long if we don't kill this motherfucker before then," he said, his voice cracking with emotion.

"Where are we heading first?" she said as she put the phone to her ear.

"The campground nearby and see if they were or still are there," Phil said as they climbed into the white Crown Victoria. "Nothing like being inconspicuous," Phil said with dry humor about their vehicle, which any ten-year-old could identify as a Fed's car. "Why can't we have a four-wheel-drive vehicle at least?" He pulled out of the gas station and headed north, but not before removing his weapon from his holster and placing it under his left thigh. Kelly did the same thing. "Just in case," he said.

They arrived at the nearest campground within five minutes and pulled up to the main entrance. As with most sites in this part of California, the entrance fee was submitted voluntarily in an envelope kindly supplied by the parks department, sealed with the required amount, into a slotted box; a tear-off tag was the camper's receipt. There was no ranger on-site, so they drove through the area, windows down, first looking for anyone remotely resembling Frank and Gina, and second, looking for potential witnesses. The campground was clean, with tall sugar pines mixed with redwoods lining the sites, some with electric hookup, but all with old used barbeque pits.

"I loved camping with my kids," Phil blurted out, nostalgic at that very moment.

"Camping out to me was no room service," Kelly said honestly. "Born and raised in Pittsburgh, the daughter of a city cop, who pampered me my entire childhood. Spoiled me to the point where no man can match his genuine love for me… before you, of course," she said, and blushed slightly.

Phil remained silent while he digested what he had just heard as they reached the main shower/bathroom area.

"I can see why they would hide out in places like this, isolated enough to slip in and then slip out without being noticed. Do you think Frank has camping equipment with him?" she finally asked to break the awkward silence.

Phil was happy to move the subject back to their pursuit, as a myriad of emotions ran through his soul at that moment that he did not want to address or was too scared to try. "He probably has enough equipment and weapons with him to support a platoon," Phil began. "Every good marine always has his pup tent with him, just in case." He stopped the car at the site that was occupied by a retired couple with an older Ford F-350, which was parked in front of a fifth wheel in the next-to-last stall in the campground. The last stall was empty. He shut the engine down, opened the car door, and placed his weapon back into his holster as he got out. His eyes darted all around as he inhaled clean air and pine-needle scent. Kelly did the same as they walked up to the door on the RV and knocked gently. Kelly stood in front. A woman officer out here would be less intimidating than someone Phil's size asking the questions. The door opened slowly; an elderly man in a T-shirt and white shorts stood in the opening.

"Can I help you?" His slight German accent could be heard.

"Special Agent Flaherty with the FBI Task Force," she introduced herself while holding up her credentials. "This is Lieutenant Philip DiMarco." Phil nodded his head and smiled politely while showing his CHP badge, then reached for the picture of Gina and the composite of Frank from his pocket. "Have you seen these two in this campground at any time this week?" she asked.

The man took the pictures, looked to his left, and called, "Wanda [which he said with a V], cumin se here," to his wife, a frail mid-eighties female dressed in a sweater in eight-five-degree weather, her skin paler than a ghost. He whispered quietly in her ear in German, and she studied the pictures. Her head turned sideways, and her facial expression frowned as she studied Gina's picture for a long time. She looked at her husband and said something to him in German. He looked at Kelly and said, "She said a girl looked a little like that, but with short blond hair, who was here earlier. She was in the last site." He pointed at the last stall, which was empty. "A big man was with her, but she never saw his face; he always had his hood up on his jacket." He handed the pictures back. "They left yesterday early morning."

"Do you know what they were driving?" Phil asked.

The old man thought for a second, then said, "A dark truck, what you call a Ram, I think. Yes, that's it. I saw the long horns on its head," he said, with his hands gesturing the emblem of the Dodge Ram truck.

"Are you sure it was dark?" Phil asked.

"Ja, almost black but not quite, like a merlot grape," the old man said with a smile.

"Thank you," Kelly said, handing the pictures back to Phil. "Is your wife okay?"

"She has leukemia, cold all of the time, wants to see all of this country before she dies," he said with pride.

"God bless both of you," Phil said as they nodded and turned to leave.

"So, they were here and left just before the murders at the gas station five minutes from here," Phil said. "They are driving an amethyst-colored Dodge Ram. I wonder if they commandeered another vehicle. And now Gina's appearance has been altered."

"Do you think voluntarily?" Kelly asked, and Phil shot her a death glare as they got into their vehicle. "Phil, be honest with not only me, but yourself." Kelly was now reading him the FBI playbook. "We have to worry that she may swing to the other side. Remember the Stockholm syndrome."

"This is Pine Grove, California, not fucking Stockholm, Sweden," he said harshly back, like a father protecting his own daughter. Then he pounded the steering wheel and shook his head. "I've worried about that since the day I knew he came back," he said more quietly. "I've prayed she didn't fall into his trap as she did years ago, but love can do weird things to any human being. I just hope she's being forced to do things as a matter of survival and not free choice," he finished.

"But then she would be suffering, probably abused, and that's not what you want either," Kelly said quietly, as she could only imagine the turmoil that existed within Phil with the revelation. What she feared most was that it would compromise his judgment and lead to a devastating mistake that would cost more lives. She had to consider talking to Assistant Director Balducci and having Phil pulled from the investigation. Would he understand why, and would it destroy their fading relationship? She had felt the distance grow between them over the past few days since the Berkeley debacle. She knew he blamed not only himself for what had happened that day. She was now the face of the dreaded FBI, not Kelly Flaherty.

"I just want this to be over," he said with a snarl, "and Frank DiMocchio to be dead. Whatever else happens is considered acceptable and inconsequential collateral damage as long as he is put six fucking feet into the ground."

At that moment Kelly looked into the eyes that used to be soft and understanding, but saw nothing but hatred and evil. She no longer feared that Phil was changing and possibly unfit to continue the investigation. She was worried that he was in some way becoming more like the killer he sought than the man he once was. That was something she would never be able to accept and something she would have to address. But now was not the time, so she remained silent as he jammed the shift into gear and stomped on the gas pedal, his anger transferred to road rage as they roared out of the campground past a waving old man. The silence was the beginning of the death spiral of their love.

CHAPTER 37

Frank and Gina were in the middle of nowhere.

They had driven all night as they took the circuitous route so they could stay only on smaller state routes and avoid the more highly patrolled interstate system. By three o'clock in the morning, they had found a campsite in the Shoshone Mountains of northern Nevada. They were the only campers at the Berlin-Ichthyosaur State Park outside the small town of Ione. They were at 6,500 feet and the air was thin and crisp in the early morning as Frank unzipped the two-man tent and stood up in the bright warm sunshine. The mountains that surrounded the site were covered with dense groves of ponderosa pines. Some of their jagged peaks rose above ten thousand feet in elevation, the tundra line where trees ceased to exist evident like an artist had drawn a fine line. Above this was remnants of the past winter's snow, especially on the north-facing peaks. The sounds of blackbirds and the squawking of blue jays could be heard high up in the trees. Frank took a few deep breaths, found his way to the other side of the tent, unzipped his pants, and relieved himself.

The total isolation of this site was a blessing. With the unforeseen events that had transpired, Frank had to change his plans. He knew of this place years ago and had always kept it in the back of his mind under contingency escape areas. He looked down at the valley below from his perch at the highest point of the campground and could see the main road that led into the park. Any visitors that came this way would be visible fifteen minutes before they arrived, which made their present site easier to defend in case of attack. Always gain and control the higher ground in any circumstance where a firefight could be anticipated. Again, basic military tactics that never went unheeded. His plan now had shifted from traveling every night to previously planned campsites, to settling here for at least three days. He figured this would allow the Feds to go crazy hunting for them while Frank further evaluated his thoughts about Gina. She was indebted to him for saving her life back at the Unocal station and had shown more than enough affection for him that night, more than ever before. But he still couldn't trust her, not until she proved herself in a different way. But in the end, he knew that she still would die. Yet he wanted to determine when her end would come, and he definitely did not want her death to be at someone else's hand.

However, at the moment, he wanted to unwind from the chaos and plan his next moves. He remembered about the Humboldt River about a mile east of the camp, which was nestled against the mountains as it flowed into the next valley. He remembered it being stocked with rainbow trout and smallmouth bass, with some nice pools of water that were perfect for either fly or cast fishing. "Nothing like a day of fishing to help a person escape from the harsh realities of life," his father always told him as they escaped the city and his mother. It was what Frank needed right now.

"What are you thinking about?" Gina's question startled him out of his daydream.

"Going fishing," he said blandly. "We need to stock up on food when we can. There's a river about a mile from here—pretty good fishing from what I remember."

"Can I go?" she asked innocently.

Frank snickered at the remark, as if he were about to leave her a mile behind and allow her to escape. "Of course you're coming," he said with a sly smile. He opened up the locked bed on his truck and retrieved his fishing gear, tackle box, and Coleman stove. "First we need to eat breakfast. I'll fire up this stove; go and get the bacon and eggs out of the cooler, along with pots and pans, and we'll eat before we go."

Phil sat despondent on a cold windblown bench, his thoughts caught in a myriad of fresh consternation. He had not been to this spot since that day in 1971, yet the memories were still fresh in his mind as if it had happened yesterday. The emotions that he had felt all of those years ago had returned in force. Being here magnified all of the failures in his life, which had changed so dramatically that warm July day. He looked up at a spot on the water some seventy-five yards out, as if the blood were still there. Instead, he saw a seagull as it circled over the pristine dark blue water of Lake Tahoe. He couldn't fathom that forty years had passed, along with so much death and sorrow that had followed hers.

They were both seventeen at the time, having grown up in the same neighborhood in the Bronx, a romance budding when they had turned thirteen. Their families waited for the wedding, which was scheduled to take place in September 1972, by which time they would both be eighteen and legal. He had been invited to join her family on vacation that summer when they traveled out west. They were discussing wedding plans as she sat on the edge of the boat and put on her skis. She kissed him on the cheek while her father stared at them, then jumped into the water, a smile from ear to ear displaying the true joy of that moment. He handed her the ski towrope; she waved good-bye and began to paddle backward as he extended out the rope slowly to prevent any snags. Her father handed him the orange flag to raise, a signal that a skier was in the water as a warning to other boaters.

Her father sat back in the captain's seat and attempted to fire up the boat's engine, but it wouldn't start. He got up cursing at the old Mercury 300 as he came to the stern and inspected the motor. In the meantime, his daughter was treading water at the end of the seventy-five-foot rope, with her skis perpendicular to the water. Suddenly Phil looked up and saw two speedboats racing around the far side of the lake, doing well over the normal allotted speed. His eyes widened as they both made the sweeping turn and headed straight toward their area. Their speed increased as the roar of both engines intensified with each passing second, their hulls only feet apart as they raced faster. Phil yelled out to Cathy, who turned just in time to see the inside boat sideswipe the outside boat, which caused it to veer directly left as it was about to pass them. The front "V" of the speedboat caught Cathy directly in the head as she tried to swim toward Phil. He still could hear the thud; it killed her instantly, her lifeless body left floating as the blood pooled around the massive wounds to her head. Phil stood in shock as Cathy's father clutched his chest and collapsed; he was dead before he hit the floor.

That one catastrophe changed his life forever; as the shock wore off in time, his grief turned to pure anger and hatred. He wanted to kill somebody in retaliation after Cathy's death was ruled an "accident" by the state of Nevada's Board of Inquiry. He sought revenge against both men who were sailing the speedboats that day. He went to the one person who he thought could help him achieve his just reward. He sat in the small booth in the restaurant on Fordham Road in the Bronx and looked directly into the eyes of Vito Genovese, capo dei capi of the Genovese crime family at that time. He asked the don for the favor as he pled his case. The don, however, was wiser than Phil ever knew. "Do you want to be owing to me for the rest of your life?" Vito had asked, the implication clear. "You are a good young man, from a good family. I know your father well, as he sold me all of my life insurance." A smile had appeared with the mention of Phil's father. "I respect him, and for that reason, I must deny your request." Finally he looked at Phil with cold eyes and said, "When you kill someone, it must be for business only, never for personal reasons. Emotions lead to mistakes, mistakes lead to witnesses, and witnesses lead to more death until the police finally capitalize on your mistake. If you want to kill, join the Marines like your father did. They will give you all of the training and plenty of *morigones* to kill." The words had hit him like a thunderbolt. He went to the recruiter's office the very next day. He remembered how proud his father was the day he enlisted, and how hard his mother had cried. But he knew that if he hadn't joined, he probably would have followed his other neighborhood friends except Tony and would have been a wise guy instead.

"Are you okay?" Kelly said as she stood directly in front of him and stared down at him. He was oblivious to her presence until that moment. "We'll find her, Phil, I promise."

He stood up, wiped his face with his sleeves, inhaled slowly, and said, "Yeah, I know, but dead or alive?" He walked away, content to keep the past within himself, to complete his grieving alone. He took one more look over his shoulder and saw Cathy's reflection in the water as she smiled back one last time. The somber mood had lifted as he remembered that last kiss. The loss of his innocence began with the loss of his one true soul mate, his true love. He also knew that the happiness he felt with Cathy was different and would never be recaptured. Beyond the sexual chemistry with Kelly, there was a feeling of a deeper connection, but he had begun to question what kind. He had finally come to realize the different forms of love that existed in life and that he couldn't compare one to the others. The problem was not one of comparison, but a question of validity of the emotion.

He looked over at Kelly as they walked back to the car. As if reading his thoughts, she interlocked her right arm with his left and smiled at him. At that moment, the sun disappeared behind the clouds and a chill was cast over them. Not a word needed to be said in Phil's mind as he felt this to be a sign of the death spiral of their love. Phil wanted their relationship to last, to bottle a feeling of serenity for eternity. Unfortunately in the back of Phil's mind was that little voice of dread as it warned him of impending doom.

That voice had never been wrong.

CHAPTER 38

The number of stars was beyond belief. Every constellation could be seen, including Orion's Belt, something Gina had never seen before growing up in the Bay Area. Even on her many trips to different cities across the country, the stars never shone like they did tonight. The absolute darkness in the middle of Nevada allowed the heavens to be the guiding light. She could only imagine what pioneers felt as they traveled across the country with only the lights from the stars and moon to guide them. Their beauty at this moment was breathtaking.

"Amazing, isn't it?" Frank asked as he sat in the chair next to her.

"Probably the most beautiful sight I have ever seen," she said without hesitation.

Over the next five minutes, Frank pointed out the five planets that could be seen that night (Jupiter, Saturn, Venus, Mercury, and Mars), the different zodiac constellations, the North Star, and the Milky Way. Gina was like a little kid all over again. While he sat there and pointed out all of these amazing sights, Gina's mind raced. She was confused about what she was feeling. She knew she loved Frank, even if he still intended to kill her. She still couldn't believe he did all of those horrible things her uncle had said he had done, even after he had killed the robbers in cold blood. Everything he had done so far was for her. If he had truly wanted for her to die, she would have been killed by the gangsters. Instead, he saved her life against all odds. She was unhappy that he had to kill the girl, but she understood why after he had explained the situation to her after their torrid love making that night.

What was starting to concern her was the excitement she felt when those men were killed. She had always been on the side of saving lives, but was ecstatic at the moment Frank raised his pistol and fired the first shot. She had made love to him afterward that night like never before, for the most part from the residual high she felt after the killings. She knew killing innocent people was wrong, but killing criminals saved the government tons of money in prosecution and jailing of those who deserved to die in the first place. She wanted to feel that rush again.

"Can you teach me how to shoot as well as you?" Gina asked. "My dad showed me when I was a kid, but he was nowhere as good as you."

Even in the dark night, there was enough light from the stars to show Frank's quizzical face. He shifted in his chair, lit up a joint, took a long toke, and then passed it to Gina. He held the smoke for almost thirty seconds, allowing the THC to escape and infiltrate his bloodstream. "For what purpose?" he finally asked after the remainder of the smoke was exhaled.

"Because if something should occur that would benefit two shooters as compared to one, such as the Feds, wouldn't you want me to at least shoot the fucking thing?" she said almost defiantly as she deeply inhaled the smoke and handed the joint back.

Frank stood up and looked down at Gina, but without saying a word, walked into the tent. Gina could hear the bags being moved around and zippers being opened and closed. He came back out and sat down in his chair, but not before he handed Gina an unloaded 9 mm Glock. "This will be yours, and training begins at first light," he said in a commanding voice. "It's not loaded, so don't get any fucking ideas," he added with a broad grin. He looked at Gina's glow in the dim light, her face with the expression of a child at Christmastime.

She shook her head as she ran her fingers over the gun, felt the coldness and the power. She felt exhilarated. "I couldn't shoot you, Frank. I love you," she said honestly to both him and herself. She now realized where she belonged and with whom. Her confused state was beginning to form new boundaries that even she would not have crossed just two days ago. Here in front of her was a man that could protect and provide better than anyone else alive. Those same words were echoed by him all of those years ago before her father's death, but she didn't listen. She hoped it wasn't too late.

Frank looked at her and was at a loss for words. He hung his head down and scraped the dirt on the ground with the toe of his shoe, like a little boy facing the principal. "I know," he said as he stole Hans Solo's line from *Star Wars*. They both laughed at his shyness and giggled from the pot, which changed into outright guffawing. Both of them held their sides as they laughed so hard that they had to wipe away tears at the same time. Their voices echoed through the valley and were met with high-pitched cries.

Gina stopped laughing at the sounds. "What's that?" she asked, scared.

"Just bats honing in on our laughter," Frank said, "so you best be quiet," and he began to laugh again. Gina got more apprehensive, scooted around in her chair, and looked skyward for any signs of the winged creatures.

"Don't worry; they won't bother you," he finally said.

Their worries were cut short by the appearance of headlights in the distance coming south on the highway. Frank stood up immediately and ran into the tent. He emerged carrying both an M-16 automatic rifle and his Walther PPK. He looked in the direction of the headlights, now about one and a half miles away, and motioned for Gina to get up. He handed her an ammo clip for her Glock and said, "Slide it in until you feel it grab and click. There's the safety." He pointed at the lever. "Pull it toward you to release; aim and shoot if you have to—just don't shoot me. Follow my every move, understood?" She nodded immediately yes. "Let's get behind the trees, across the way." He pointed to the other side of the camp. He had turned out their small electric camp light before he had exited the tent, so they were in total darkness. They quickly made their way across the encampment and found large ponderosa pines about two hundred feet away, large enough to hide the two of them.

The vehicle could now be seen half a mile away, making the left-hand turn that only led to the state park. "It's a car," Frank said to Gina.

"How can you tell?" she asked quietly.

"Too quiet," he began. "A truck pulling a fifth wheel can be heard in this still night. So could an RV, or even just a pickup truck like mine. This vehicle has a smaller engine and a quiet exhaust system—more consistent with a car."

They both focused their eyes as the vehicle approached slowly, headlights low and far apart. "State trooper," Frank whispered. "Put your gun away; it won't be needed." He raised his M-16 and sighted the vehicle as it slowly pulled toward the tent and truck. The bright blue lightning bolt through the Nevada state name on the door panel was clearly evident as it passed them. Suddenly the extremely bright searchlight on the driver's door illuminated, exploding light over the truck and tent as the car stopped, engine idling. Frank saw two troopers inside the vehicle and muttered, "Shit." Luckily he had earlier that day changed his license plates to Utah, just in case. Still, he knew Nevada state troopers were tough hombres, many of them ex-military.

The engine stopped and the night became dead silent again. Both Frank and Gina instinctively held their breaths and listened. They were talking strategy when Frank saw the driver disengage the pump shotgun from its brace in the dashboard. The driver's door opened and the trooper emerged; he put on his large cavalry hat with his left hand while holding the rifle in his right. Frank then saw the second trooper open his door wide and swing his body toward them. Frank could see that he wasn't wearing a vest.

Frank fired two rounds rapidly; the first hit the trooper still halfway in the car square in the chest, which catapulted him backward into the car. The second shot hit the driver in the back of his head before he had a chance to react, sending him reeling forward onto his face as his cavalry hat floated down to the right, unharmed.

Frank came out from behind the tree with Gina directly behind. They slowly walked over and made sure the troopers were dead. Frank picked up the hat, took a look at it in the spotlight, and saw no blood or holes so he placed it on his head. He reached inside the car and shut off the light.

"We'll put the bodies in the trunk, and then I'll drive the vehicle while you follow me," Frank said. "We'll dump it about twenty-five miles north of here, up near route 50, then return. These vehicles have GPS systems, and I don't want them tracking it here."

"You didn't even give them a chance," Gina said with a touch of anger.

"No reason to," Frank replied. "They wouldn't have given me the time of day before shooting my ass. One thing you have to remember is that we cannot be captured or cornered. In battle, when you have the opportunity to eliminate the enemy and guarantee your own survival, you take that advantage without any thought whatsoever."

"I guess you're right," Gina said quietly. "Do you have any gloves?"

Frank started to chuckle. "I forgot you are a nurse."

"Not anymore," she said. "I've helped save enough lives in my life, might as well help dispose of a few," she said with a shrug of the shoulder.

"You're starting to scare me," Frank said jokingly as he handed her a pair of disposable gloves.

What Gina didn't want to admit was that she enjoyed that power, and wanted more.

CHAPTER 39

Frank and Gina had made the most passionate, exhausting love when they returned from dumping the car and bodies. Frank had decided to dump the bodies five miles south of where they dumped the vehicle. He had found a dry ravine with enough loose brush to cover the bodies. By that time of night, the full moon had risen, which gave them plenty of light with which to work. He didn't worry about burying them in the rock-hard ground. There were plenty of hungry creatures in this part of the country to feast on the bodies. Out of respect, Gina said a few words when they had finished. Frank even said amen out of respect, but not out of guilt. He had no guilty conscience for any of the people he had ever killed.

Just short of North Summit they dumped the vehicle down a thousand-foot cliff off county route 722. It hit the bottom of the ravine with a thud and the sound of metal twisting and glass shattering, but no explosion. Frank had deliberately run the gas tank down to practically fumes before he launched the car off the cliff. He didn't want the GPS signal to be destroyed. He wanted them to find the vehicle and the blood in the car and trunk, but no bodies. Plus, by the time they found the car and retrieved any evidence, he and Gina would be long gone.

In spite of the marathon events of the past night, they both awoke at the break of dawn. They made love again before they rapidly packed and loaded the truck. Frank had told Gina that gun lessons would be put on hold until that evening, after they had found their next encampment. Upon leaving they avoided going north by looping directly west on a small one-lane county highway that was barely paved, then cut south on a hard-packed dirt road that shook the truck's suspension. The four-wheel-drive did its job; all of the tires gripped the road and blew dust behind them like a smoke screen. They drove through canyons and came out of the mountains into more open desert terrain. The road at that time actually was part of an old dried-up riverbed, with walls almost ten feet high on each side. It was great for camouflage, but one wouldn't want to be caught there during a desert thunderstorm. A flash flood would annihilate anything in its path.

After almost two hours, they emerged onto a connector road to US Route 6, and Frank headed east. He was thinking about breakfast when the news broke over the all-news AM radio station of the disappearance of the state troopers. Apparently the GPS system was still intact, based on first reports of the vehicle being located in a ravine, with rescue and retrieving squads on the way to the scene at that moment. Frank smiled and raised his right fist in a triumphant salute, knowing full well it would take hours to get down to the car. When they found it bloodied and empty, all hell would break loose.

"They are going to go fucking crazy," Frank shouted.

"Yeah," Gina shouted and whistled louder than Frank ever could. "What?" she asked. "I can call any dog in the neighborhood," she said with a smile.

"You can wake up the dead with that whistle," Frank replied. "That could be bad for business."

They both burst out laughing as the thought evoked nasty images.

"Where are we going?" Gina asked more seriously.

"There's a small camping area about 235 miles from here just south of Interstate 80, where we'll chill for a while before moving on," Frank explained.

"Where are we… you know… going?" Her question was animated with hand gestures that indicated the future.

"Do you mean our ultimate destination?" Frank asked. Gina nodded yes. "Canada is the final stop on the Magical Mystery Tour, with stops along the way," he sang to the Beatles' old tune.

"Where in Canada?" Gina asked.

"Why the sixty-four questions all of a sudden?" Frank asked, suspicious of her motives.

"Just asking; don't cop a 'tude, dude," she said with venom and looked out the passenger window, basically putting an end to their conversation.

Frank's anger brewed slowly; he was now reticent of any further communication as he concentrated on driving and looked for any signs of law enforcement. He also regretted not killing her earlier and dumping her body with the two troopers. He wouldn't make that mistake again.

Phil stood at the edge of another cliff, overlooking a scene reminiscent of the Southern California desert shooting over a month ago, at the very beginning of this nightmare. Next to him stood the Chief of Nevada state troopers, ex-Navy SEAL, who admitted to being more nervous now than during any missions with his crew. Phil knew the feeling well. The adrenaline of battle was intense but usually short-lived, as firefights tended to be. This adrenaline rush would last for days as the media crush would suffocate the bravest soul. They were helpless to change what had happened, and then would have to explain why it happened in the first place.

"I hate this shit," Chief Steven Peterson said. "I had less anxiety facing an RPG from fifty feet than this." Phil could only nod in agreement, having been through this too much lately. He was almost becoming numb to the killings. He rationalized that it was like a doctor who saw death on a regular basis and learned to accept the fate of that phase of life. That is until it's his or her own. His thoughts were interrupted by the chief's radio squawking, a high-pitched voice that screamed something.

"Calm down, Bud, I can't understand a word you're saying," the chief screamed back into his radio, the strain in his voice matching the sweat on his brow.

"There's blood all over the inside of the car, but no bodies," Bud said hurriedly, breathless.

"What about the trunk?" the chief asked.

"Blood in there too, but less and smeared; the cabin is splattered," Bud said. "We've circled about a hundred square yards looking for any remains, but they're not here," Bud added.

Phil looked at the chief sympathetically and said, "Look for the buzzards."

Steve looked at him quizzically, then a look of understanding spread. "They've been disposed of elsewhere."

Phil nodded in agreement. "They were shot elsewhere, stuffed into the trunk, dropped off, and then the vehicle was disposed of. Start by looking for the bodies here, but ultimately follow any large flock of vultures, and look there." He thought for a moment, then said, "Where was their normal patrol area?"

"They normally had the area south of here," the chief said. He brought up Google map on his iPhone and showed Phil. "There's a state park with a campsite down at the end of this road about fifty miles; they were about to look there," Steve said.

"That's where they were killed," Phil said flatly. "It's definitely him," he said, staring down into the ravine as if looking into his own life's abyss.

"Why don't we go down and take a look?" Steve asked. "I'll drive."

"Better than standing here with our thumbs up our asses," Phil said.

"Did you grow up in the Bronx?" Steve asked as they were getting into the chief's Dodge Charger.

"How dya know?" he said with a little more accent.

"I haven't heard that expression since the old days. Grew up in the Riverside section," Steve said.

"180th and Arthur Avenue near the fish market was my old stomping ground," Phil replied. For the next hour they talked about life growing up in New York, how they missed the food, the energy of the city, but not the winters. Their conversation went from there to respective service records, family, kids, retirement, and frustrations with bureaucracy, all within an hour as they passed between the same type of mountains that were near Phil's home, but the lush green valley near the river definitely was not like Twentynine Palms. They arrived within a half mile of the campsite, and Steve slowed his vehicle down as he tried to eliminate any exhaust sound. They had decided to park at the entrance and go in by foot, keeping toward the row of pine trees. They approached with Steve in the lead, weapons drawn; Phil moved out to the right flank.

To their relief there was no one at all in the campground. Phil immediately continued toward the end of the area and found the pool of dried blood. He whistled for Steve as he stood over the dark crimson stain; bluebottle flies already fed on what looked like brain matter that was dispersed in the blood. He swished them away, trying to preserve any evidence. They returned within ten seconds. Phil noted the drops of blood that led away from the pool and stopped within ten feet. He then noticed a small amount of red splatter six feet and to the right of where these bloodstains ended, with another trail of blood to the same area where he stood. He turned around and looked at the row of trees about two hundred feet away. Steve arrived, saw the blood pool, and stopped moving. His shoulders and head dropped in recognition of the murder scene.

"They were ambushed, probably from the trees," Phil began. "Probably rifle shot, just like a sniper. Two shots probably, and they never knew what hit them." He pointed to the ground and traced the blood pattern. "One shot there, the other probably as he emerged from his vehicle over there, then stuffed into the trunk of their own car." Phil shook his head in disgust. "Their tent was probably over there." He pointed beyond the crimson pool to the last stall. "They were about to investigate." His voice trailed off as he walked back toward the trees and found two sets of recent footprints. One was small, caused by tennis shoes, but the larger one stopped him dead in his tracks. There in front of him were the same marine boots as in the desert. He heard Steve call his dispatcher, telling her to send the forensic unit to the park. Phil pulled out his cell phone and called Kelly, who answered on the first ring.

"I've been worried about you." Her voice sounded hurried.

"He's been here and has added two state troopers to his repertoire," he said flatly, avoiding Kelly's remark.

"Oh shit," was all Kelly said. Finally after a long moment of silence she asked, "Where are you?"

"In the middle of the Shoshone Mountains in the state of Nevada," Phil replied." He was at another campsite and ambushed two troopers, then dumped their bodies God knows where. They probably were following our request for assistance from local authorities to check all campgrounds."

"Double oh shit," Kelly said.

"Gina's still with him," Phil said flatly.

"That's good news," Kelly said, but Phil remained silent, deep in thought. "Are you all right? I'm stuck here or I'd be there with you."

"I'm fine, just thinking, you know," he said as he again avoided any other conversation.

"Yeah, unfortunately I do know. So where do you think he's heading?" she finally asked.

"Every place we are not," he said glumly. "We'll need tech support here."

"We're stretched a little thin with our budget right now," Kelly said in a business tone, "so we'll let the state of Nevada collect the evidence and then they can ship to our labs for final analysis."

Phil bristled at the mention of finances at this juncture. "I'll let the chief know. Thanks," he said with a bit of sarcasm. He felt the rift building between them, something Phil had dreaded from the start, but somehow knew would happen. For some reason any relationship after his marriage of twenty years ended in failure. This one was heading in the same direction, but he didn't want to deal with this now. "I gotta get going," he said briskly. "I'll call when I have more information." He ended the call before hearing any response. The funny thing was, instead of feeling guilty, he actually didn't give a shit. He was in the middle of his own life's crusade, the death of Frank DiMocchio, which needed to be completed alone.

CHAPTER 40

It took three days to finally locate the bodies of the Nevada state troopers, and true to what Phil had said earlier, a hiker noticed almost a dozen vultures circling in one spot from a mile away. He and his newlywed wife decided to investigate the area and came upon the bodies by their smell as they decayed in the heat. To say the incident ruined the young couple's honeymoon was an understatement. The autopsies also proved Phil's theory of how they died to be correct, as did the forensic evidence that was found at the campsite crime scene. Unfortunately no shell casings or bullet fragments were ever found to determine the type of weapon, but by the amount of damage done, the assumption of a high-powered rifle shot was confirmed.

The Nevada State Troopers put up a $250,000 reward for the arrest and conviction of the perpetrator. The FBI did the same on top of what they had already offered, more to save face than to help find the killer. They already knew who it was; the problem was finding him. Within hours of the findings, every campground in four neighboring states was flooded with state and federal officials hunting for

Frank and Gina. More than five hundred law enforcement agents joined in the largest joint sweep in decades, but to no avail. There was no sign of the two fugitives; Gina was now suspected of aiding and abetting, and was not considered just a kidnap victim anymore.

What everyone in law enforcement failed to realize was that Frank had already adapted his method of evasion. They were no longer staying in any designated campground or state park. Instead, they used the open wilderness of the west. They had driven nonstop after they had dumped the car and bodies up into the East Humboldt Mountains of northeastern Nevada. Frank had found an old fire road that took them two miles away from any of the main roads. He stopped at an elevation of 6,700 feet on the north side of Hole in the Wall Mountain, within half a mile of Angel Lake. They had set up the small pup tent just in front of the truck under a canopy of thick pine trees. For five days Frank would hike up and down to the southern part of the lake at dawn with his fishing gear. He caught at least three or four fish daily, from catfish to largemouth bass, with a few trout and northern pike in the mix.

Frank also decided to fully educate Gina about the weaponry he carried. Gina became quite proficient within the five-day stay with every weapon, including the fully automatic M-16 and the long-range Henry rifle. She pleaded to be allowed to shoot with Frank's silenced Walther PPK so as not to attract attention. That was the one gun he had refused to let her try. She didn't press the issue when his eyes became dark and ominous. She also changed her appearance again. This time she adapted the aging gray look of Frank, which made her look ten years older. By now Frank's beard was extremely full and thick. Along with his gray hair in a ponytail, the effect made him look like an old hippie. To add effect, Gina applied slight amounts of actor's makeup to both of them, which gave them more noticeable crow's-feet and worry lines. It became a daily routine to "age," just in case they were spotted.

After five days of fish for dinner, Gina looked at Frank and said bluntly, "I need to taste a good steak before I go fucking crazy." Frank was in the middle of cooking their dinner of trout on the Coleman stove that evening. There was the hint of a storm coming in the distance. Hopefully they were below the snow level, which could sometimes drop as low as 2,500 feet, but rarely this time of May. He looked down at the filets, which took him forever to debone, as they cooked in a light olive oil with a hint of freshly picked wild Spanish rosemary, salt, and pepper. He thought for a second and finally nodded in agreement.

"Yeah, it's time to move on. First we need to restock our supplies, including a good steak or two," he said with a hint of a smile. "Then we need to get out of Nevada."

"Idaho?" Gina asked. The question caught Frank a little off guard. He nodded in agreement, with a frown of concern.

"Got a house up there—most beautiful view out of the front window," he said. The look in his eyes and face brightened. Now Gina was the one who was befuddled.

"How many houses do you own?" she asked with a slight sarcastic edge.

"Down to six after the loss of my desert home," he said flatly as he turned the filets over as he tried to ensure thorough cooking to avoid any parasitic infections.

"So where do we stock up on supplies?" Gina kept prodding as Frank added a small amount of ground pepper jack at the end. "We can't just walk into a Safeway."

"Snowbirds," Frank said, "are the easiest prey this time of year." He pulled the filets off of the open flame and shut off the burner. "You just follow my lead. Trust me, by this time tomorrow night, you'll have a thick juicy steak done to perfection," and with that he blew a kiss like a chef. "Now no more questions; it's time to mangiare."

Assistant director of the FBI, Anthony Balducci, sat in the conference room in the Reno, Nevada, field office and looked absolutely exhausted. He had deep, dark bags under both eyes, which had lost their sparkle with each passing day. There had again been no sign of Frank or Gina. The death of the troopers added more fuel to the fire of his failure, and Washington was not pleased at all. If he did not capture Frank within the next fifteen days, his career was over. And like most Italians, he couldn't hide his emotions. Phil actually felt guilty for all of the times he had berated Tony, knowing now how his childhood friend was suffering. Tony looked at Phil, who stood leaning up against a file cabinet, the darkness of his mood evident in his quiet question "So, where do you think he is?"

Phil looked down at Tony, whose shoulders seemed to sag with the weight of stress he was carrying and said, "He's changed the script, Tony, again staying one step ahead. They are somewhere in the vast open wilderness, probably in a secluded spot, but within reach of some form of food, such as a lake or river."

"You mean he's fishing?" Tony asked as if he never took survival training in the navy.

"And hunting if possible, living off of wild berries, whatever he can find," Phil said. "But at some point he'll need to restock things you can't get out in the wild, especially with a woman in tow."

"Do you really think she's teamed up with him?" Tony asked. He looked directly into Phil's eyes, whose anger was evident from across the room.

"She's acting the same way she did after Frank killed her own father, taking his side instead of facing the truth," Phil said with a hint of exasperation in his voice. "So yes, I think she betrayed us, and ultimately me, so in case you're asking, I have no trouble treating her as a suspect." Tony waved his hand as if the thought never had crossed his mind. "Plus it's been too long without any killings or missing raped women. His urges are bound to kick in at some point."

"Are you actually hoping he either kills or rapes again?" Tony now shouted as he stood up and walked toward Phil.

"I'm not hoping or wishing anything, you fucking asshole," Phil said as he started to get mad at himself for feeling any guilt for Tony's plight in life. He stood six inches taller than Tony and was not intimidated by any of Tony's reactions. "But unfortunately, I'm a realist, and the odds are good that he will strike again, somewhere. What I'm worried about is whether Gina is going to help him more than just emotionally."

"Do you think she would kill also?" Tony asked incredulously.

"I know she can shoot; I was with her father many times when she would tag along and take shots herself," Phil said. "She was taught the necessary basics by her dad and me, but she's with the best shot in the Marines. So God knows how well she can shoot now." He paused for a moment and rubbed the back of his head. "I don't think she would kill in cold blood, but she would shoot to defend probably."

"What if she does kill in cold blood, then what?" Tony asked as he approached more slowly over to where Phil was standing.

"Then she's no longer the Gina I knew, and I'll stop worrying about her. *Il boccia di morte*," the universal Italian saying for the kiss of death, was all Phil had to say, and Tony understood. They hugged each other as a sign of respect.

"I've gotta fly to DC; they want to measure my ass first before they bury it," Tony joked and clapped Phil on the back of his shoulder. "I'm leaving Kelly and you in charge in my absence. She has final say on everything that's to do with the task force, so don't let your pride get in the way," he said with a wink as Phil chuckled. "Plus I think she really likes you, so don't fuck this one up." That statement made Phil stop and think. "What, did you think I didn't know?" Tony asked as Phil instinctively shook his head no. Tony came closer to Phil and whispered, "We're the FBI; we know everything." They both let out loud laughs as they exited the building into the blinding Reno sun and shaded their eyes as they walked toward their respective vehicles. Phil felt unhinged by Tony's last remark. Phil couldn't give a shit that Tony knew about him and Kelly. What bothered him most was that nagging doubt deep down inside that kept rearing its ugly head, which was distrust of any woman to keep a commitment. He would not survive another rejection, so he kept his guard held high.

"Good luck, Lefty," Phil called out.

Tony raised his middle finger to Phil and said as he was getting into the car, "Do me a favor. Kill that son of a bitch for both of us."

With that notion, Phil came to attention and gave Tony his best marine salute "Sir, yes, sir." He smiled and turned. As he was getting into his car, Phil had a sense of foreboding. He watched as Tony drove away, knowing that would be the last time he would ever see his friend of over fifty years. He shook his head as if to clear away that thought, but his intuition haunted him nevertheless.

As did his feelings toward Kelly.

CHAPTER 41

Gina slowly drove the truck with the lights off in the predawn hours through the nearly empty RV camp. Frank was slumped down in the passenger seat. His eyes darted back and forth as he surveyed the four campsites that were occupied, each separated by about five hundred yards. All of the sites had fifth wheels that sat on their supports, with their specially designed pickup trucks parked separately. All were relatively new. In this economy that usually meant semi-wealthy retirees, who usually stocked enough supplies for Patton's Third Army. Frank smiled, sat up, and motioned at the RV farthest away.

"Why are we going after old folks; they're usually defenseless," Gina said.

"Exactly. I don't prefer getting shot at, and I never, ever want to kill a child. They haven't had a chance in life yet, whereas old folks, as you say, have lived theirs," Frank said bluntly.

"If your folks were alive, they would be the same age as these people," Gina said.

"We'll start at the end, work our way back," he said icily and ignored her last remark entirely as he checked the loads on the guns.

"We're only going to do one place, aren't we?" she asked nervously.

"Actually I'd prefer not to leave any witnesses," he said without a hint of sarcasm.

Gina remained quiet for a minute as they pulled up to the last stall, trying to remember her lines that they had rehearsed while driving. Her pulse was racing as she felt her heart pounding in her chest. The adrenaline rush was almost overwhelming until she felt a cool hand on her right forearm; she looked over at Frank.

"It'll be fine, trust me," he began. He stopped and looked up ahead as he saw an older gentleman already coming down the stairs of his RV with a twelve-gauge pump shotgun in his right hand held high across his chest and a flashlight in his left as it guided his way. "On second thought, just let me handle this," Frank said. Gina stopped the truck, and Frank sprung out and in one motion came around the hood of the truck.

"What do you think you are..." the old man began but never got to finish. He saw the arm come up, heard the cough, saw the flash, then saw black as the bullet caught him squarely in the heart and killed him instantly and his body crumpled to the ground. Frank stepped over his body as he continued to the front door, kicked it open, and found an old woman trying to speak but couldn't because of the effects of a previous stroke. He looked directly into her eyes and saw them turn angry at the point of recognition. She was about to scream when Frank shot her in between the eyes. The bullet rocked her head back in the wheelchair, and her body slumped toward her stroke-affected side. He walked past her body straight to the refrigerator/freezer and found it loaded with plenty of different cuts of beef, chicken, and pork, but no fish. He grabbed some plastic shopping bags and stuffed five of them with all of the frozen meat, ice, and a bottle of Tres Generacion Tequila stuffed in the back.

With four more plastic bags, he stuffed canned goods, cereal, rice, pasta, canned tomatoes, and condiments. He shoved the silenced Walther PPK into his back waistband, the metal finally cool enough to not burn him after being fired twice. With five bags in the right hand and four in the left, he made his way out of the trailer. His confidence that they were done eroded when he was within twenty-five feet of the truck and he heard, "Hey, what are you doing there? We've already called the sheriff's department, so you..." The shot erupted from Gina's Glock, which was extended outside of the cab to minimize noise damage to her ears and to have her forearm braced against the doorframe. The bullet caught the neighbor in the right shoulder, spun him away from Frank, and caused him to drop his snub-nose 38 special.

"What the fuck?" Frank said in exasperation as he dropped the bags, spun, and dropped to one knee. The right hand came up rapidly with the Walther from his waistband and fired. The shot hit the neighbor just below his left scapula from behind, punctured the aorta as it bent behind the heart, and killed him within seconds. Frank grabbed the groceries, threw them into the backseat of the truck, and jumped into the passenger seat as Gina started the engine. "What? Is everybody out here fucking Wyatt Earp?" Frank said through heavy breathing. "Great shot, I owe you one, but it's time to finish this," he said as his breathing began to return to normal. "We have enough food here to last us at least three weeks, so we just need to eliminate this little village." Gina nodded and knew he was right. "We have less than five minutes, so let's get 'er done."

They made their way back to each RV and killed another five people, with Gina killing the three women as each pleaded for their lives. By the end she just laughed at the plea before shooting. To make sure, she always shot them twice, first in the chest, then in the head.

"Try not to waste any bullets; if you hit them right the first time, they're usually dead; save the second shot," Frank said as he was driving the truck rapidly away from the last trailer. The entire killing spree actually took a total of six minutes, but Frank knew that the closest sheriff or state troopers' station was over sixty miles away in West Wendover. He had planned to hit this campground, not only for the probability of senior citizens, but also for its proximity to the Idaho border, which was three miles away, just past the small town of Jackpot, Nevada. Having driven this way before many times from his second house in Idaho, he knew there was no local law enforcement in Jackpot. The town, which had grown from a general store and a post office with a casino behind to a small thriving border town off of US Route 93, relied upon the county's sheriffs to patrol. It was no secret that law enforcement was stretched pretty thin in this part of the state.

He maintained a constant speed of seventy-three miles per hour, with the speed limit at seventy-five; his chances of being pulled over at 6:00 a.m. were slim, but nothing was guaranteed. There was practically no traffic on the two-lane highway that connected northeastern Nevada with southeastern Idaho, where Frank had his second safe house/home. The sun was just rising in the east; its fingers of light cascaded down, which caused a golden hue to the landscape, which at that moment was a typical desert with very little vegetation, similar to where he had lived in Southern California. As the highway climbed up into the high mesas of Idaho, the landscape changed to one of dense areas of sagebrush; their pungent aroma reminded Frank of the liniment witch hazel, which his father used after shaving and for antiseptic purposes. The smell always eased his tensions, with its reminder of the fonder memories of his childhood.

Finally the road began to wind through canyons with tree-lined mountains that stared down at them. Gina loved the scenery, having never been in Idaho before. Many times she pointed out various birds of prey. Frank would then lecture her on their names, species, and habits. Within minutes she knew how to tell an osprey from a Swainson's hawk or a golden eagle. By the time the first deputy sheriff pulled into the campground outside of Jackpot, Nevada, and found the massacre of all of the senior citizens, Frank and Gina were pulling into the long treelined driveway of his home outside of Ketchum, Idaho. The large log cabin-style A-frame house was tucked away 750 feet above US 93 and totally hidden from view from the highway.

"Obviously we'll lay low for a while, but you'll enjoy it here," Frank said with pride as they entered through a large heavy solid oak door into the upper floor of the two-thousand-square-foot house. A smell of previous fireplace activity gave the house a rustic effect, but then she noticed the kitchen with granite countertops and a seven-burner Viking stove that had a double oven. "I learned how to cook really well over the years," he said, seeing Gina's inquisitive look. "Might as well have the best," he added as she walked past every top-line kitchen appliance from coffeepot to a huge side-by-side refrigerator. Past the kitchen was the living room, with a comfortable leather sectional couch, a sixty-inch LED/LCD TV and theater sound system, and a large granite fireplace that was fully stocked with chopped wood and kindling. The view of the Sawtooth Mountains out of the large picture window left her breathless. "If you think that's something, come downstairs and see the master suite," Frank said.

By the time they finished the tour of the bathroom with the dual-head shower/sauna, two-person sunken Jacuzzi tub, and multiple sinks with large mirrors all around, they were too excited to unload the truck after their long journey. Gina was absolutely happy at that moment, the memories of the recent bloodbath pushed to the back recesses of her mind. "I love you" was the only thing she said as she turned to face him, threw her arms around his neck, and kissed him with deep passion. She felt herself effortlessly lifted off of her feet as he carried her to the California King bed, where they disappeared for hours.

CHAPTER 42

Phil and Kelly ducked under the yellow police tape that stretched 175 feet across the entrance to the RV park/campground. Each end was wrapped around the trunk of a tall ponderosa pine. The dispatcher who originally received the 911 call from the now-dead neighbor was intelligent enough to listen to the description of the intruder with a female driver and figured it to be Frank and Gina. She alerted her watch commander, who notified the sheriff. Once the first deputy reached the campsite and saw the carnage, the sheriff then called the task force. The FBI then had Phil and Kelly flown out by helicopter from Reno. They touched down within ninety minutes in the little hamlet of Jackpot, Nevada, and were met by the sheriff, David Saunders, who had called them.

"It was a massacre, pure and simple," the sheriff began. "Eight innocent senior citizens, four married couples gunned down in our state park without any provocation." He shook his head in disbelief. "Only one of the RVs was really ransacked. It looks like only food and other staples were taken. There is no evidence that any money or jewelry was taken. Why did all of these people need to be killed? It doesn't make sense."

"Eliminate any and all witnesses," Phil said flatly, which caught both David and Kelly off guard.

"Excuse my French," David looked at Kelly first before he said, "but that's a bunch of hogshit. He's got to be crazier than a wild hare to kill innocent old people."

Phil stopped walking and turned to face the sheriff, a flare of anger evident when he said icily, "You need to understand something, David. Frank DiMocchio is not crazy, not a psychopath. He is a sociopath without a conscience, who does not care who is killed as long as he survives the encounter. He needed supplies, and this was the best place to restock. He used military tactics because that is the way he was trained. These people were considered collateral damage and that is all. He is beyond extremely intelligent, with an IQ in the 145 range, along with the best training in every form of killing. He is a tactician, not an impulsively crazed druggie you see portrayed in the movies or certain profiles." The last sentence was said with vindictiveness. He turned and walked away.

Kelly smiled weakly and shrugged her shoulders as if apologetic for Phil's brusqueness as she followed behind, concerned about his ability to continue to be objective in this situation.

The first thing Phil noted was the remoteness of the RV park. The closest large civilization was over seventy-five miles away in an entirely different state (Twin Falls, Idaho). The beautiful desert scenery that he saw flying in was evident beyond the pine trees that they were walking past. Plenty of sagebrush was scattered about; their fragrant smell when damp was quite aromatic and unique, especially when mixed with the scent of pine. Unfortunately within minutes, all he could smell was dried blood and decomposing flesh. He caught Kelly shielding her nose with her hand. He tried breathing mostly through his mouth to decrease the acrid smells, but to no avail. His stomach was instantly churning acid, which he tried to decrease by chewing two Rolaids from his portable pack. He offered some to Kelly, who took three.

As he walked about, Phil tried to imagine the sequence of events as they unfolded. The coroner's unofficial initial evaluation was that the three bodies at the campsite farthest from the entrance were the first three killed. Two of those three bodies were outdoors. The other five were killed inside their RVs. He stopped in the middle of the road, scanned the entire campground, saw the layout as Frank would have as he drove in, and began walking toward the last campsite. Kelly had read the same reports and had agreed to start with the initial murder scene and work their way back. They walked past at least fifteen police and forensic technicians. Multiple pictures were taken at all different angles.

"This body is Gregory Devine, the owner of the fifth wheel and Ford F350 Heavy Duty over there," Sheriff David Saunders said. He pulled the body sheet back, which revealed the old man flat on his back, a twelve-gauge shotgun five feet from his right hand. Phil looked down at the man, noted the single bullet wound dead center of the chest, with the pool of blood spread over the rest of his shirt.

Phil bent down and with his gloved right hand lifted the shotgun. He cracked it open, smelled the open chamber, and showed the sheriff the two fresh shotgun shells in place. "The poor bastard never fired," David said.

"He never had a chance even if he tried to fire," Phil said bluntly. "Mr. Devine could have been pointing his shotgun at him with the trigger pulled halfway back, and he still wouldn't have had time to fire." Phil stood up and went over to the second body, which lay seventy-five feet away. He pulled the sheet back. The first thing he saw was two pools of blood, a snub-nose 38 caliber pistol near the right hand, and two separate bullet wounds. He rolled the body onto its side. Rigor had started to form, he noticed and found the wound near the left shoulder. He noticed the difference in the size of the wounds and the fact that he was shot both in front and back. The back shot underneath the left scapula was probably the fatal shot and was the same size as the one that killed Mr. Devine. His shoulders slumped as the realization hit home.

Gina was now a killer, not just a victim. She had transformed herself into a persona similar to Patti Hearst, the newspaper heiress who was kidnapped by the Symbionese Liberation Army in 1975 only to become one of them, captured in a famous picture toting an assault rifle. Gina had gone one step further.

Phil stood up and found himself looking directly into Kelly's eyes. She was actually studying the sadness that was shown in his eyes. "We've got a major problem," he said.

"Two shooters"; this time it was the sheriff speaking. "The coroner didn't want to report that yet, due to the possible implication if the media found out, but his thoughts were the same."

"She shot first on this one; he finished the job," Phil said.

"She shot more than just him," David said flatly.

Phil closed his eyes, took a deep breath, and tried to alleviate the feeling of total betrayal at that moment in time. "Let's go see the rest," he said bluntly as he started to walk toward the trailer. Upon entering, they saw the old woman slumped over in her wheelchair, bullet hole in the forehead, eyes staring blankly ahead with a mouth twisted to the left. Thankfully Phil knew that Frank killed this defenseless woman, not only by the size of the bullet hole, but the shot itself. Gina wasn't that good, at least not when he knew her. Who knew what she had learned in the interim?

The place had been ransacked as far as supplies. The cupboards were bare, as was the freezer. "They never touched the money or jewelry, just food and supplies like toilet paper," David said as they walked through and saw nothing else out of the ordinary. "The other trailers weren't ransacked like this one." He paused and looked Phil in the eyes. "The killings, however, are different. Each of the men beyond what we saw outside were killed with a single shot to the head, the women in the chest and head, with a second weapon that matched one of the wounds on Mr. Christopher Johnson, the second victim you looked at outside."

Phil knew the implication as they made their way to the remainder of the trailers. The head shots were from Frank's gun; the chest and head shots were from Gina's. Sure enough, as they looked at each scene, David's assumptions were correct. The difference in bullet holes was evident to anyone who looked close enough. Plus an amateur would always shoot at the center of the mass first to ensure hitting the target, then have to waste a second bullet to finish the kill, even if the victim were already dead. Frank wouldn't need to shoot twice. She was definitely learning rapidly from Frank. Phil's worst nightmare was now reality. He hoped it wouldn't end with him having to kill Gina. He could lie to Kelly about his commitment to do what was right, but could he? His thoughts were rudely interrupted as they exited the final trailer by the guttural hiss of a few dozen vultures that circled less than five hundred feet above. Their death circle intrigued him as they waited to pounce on the dead for food.

The captain saw the same thing and raised a hand with a circling motion to one of his deputies, and with rapid movement, deputies began to remove all of the bodies. A large air-conditioned Ryder rental truck was being used as a makeshift coroner's meat wagon to tote the multiple bodies back to the morgue in Reno, where both state and federal officials would attend the autopsies. Phil already knew what they would find, and it would just add to the collection.

"He's bound to make a mistake," David said.

"The problem is by the time we discover his mistake, he's gone," Phil said dejectedly. "He's always one step ahead of everyone, leaving more carnage in his wake. And now he has a partner willing to carry out his evilness."

Kelly saw the torment in Phil's eyes and wondered how much more one human could take in his or her life before snapping. She was also concerned about his ability to continue the investigation with this change in Gina's behavior. The conflict of interest was too great. But so was her guilt about their situation, which also put her in conflict. So she kept quiet and just kept watch over him, which would cost her dearly later.

As if reading her mind, Phil said to her as they walked back to the sheriff's car for the ride back to the helicopter, "I'm fine and, no, I'm not being pulled off of this fucking case. Do you understand what I said?" His icy stare bore through Kelly.

She understood the order perfectly and only nodded her head in agreement. What she didn't realize at the time was that was the last moment of closeness that she and Phil would ever feel again. What she did realize was that he had changed. Whether it was anger or betrayal was unclear at this time. Both were great motivations for driving most people apart, but now her concern was whether Phil's emotions would push him over the edge.

She would soon discover that Phil's metamorphosis would not end with the beauty of a butterfly, but the ugliness of an evolving sadistic demon.

CHAPTER 43

The nightmare was as vivid and real as any that Gina could ever remember. It left her shaking, even though she was now wide-awake. Her heartbeat pounded both in her chest and in her ears. The silence in the bedroom made her more aware of her hyperventilation; her anxiety had now reached a crescendo. She threw the covers back, jumped out of bed, and ran across the room, through the door, and down the stairs as she gasped for air. She threw the front door open and stepped out onto the porch. In the darkness she bent over and continued to rapidly breathe in the crisp early morning air until her breathing began to decelerate. Then the sobbing began, which within seconds became uncontrollable. It came in spasms and waves that caused her knees to weaken. Then the dizziness caused her to crumble to the floor. She lay there for about twenty minutes before she finally calmed down and gathered up the strength to push herself up against the side of the house.

Gina wiped the tears from her eyes and cleared her vision long enough to find her bearings. Slowly the disorientation cleared as her conscience began to analyze her dream. The hauntings of the murders had finally surfaced in the nightmarish vision of the death of her father, replayed multiple times in slow motion. Bullets and body parts exploded in surreal detail; the smell of blood and carbine was entombed in her nostrils. What made the vision even worse was hearing her mother's screams as her father died. Then she turned and saw Frank's sardonic smile as he stared back at her over the gunsight of his rifle. The realization of what she had done had finally come full circle. She now understood her guilt and was ashamed of what she had done. The thrill of the kill had been replaced by the screams in her dreams.

The message was clear.

She stood up slowly, her knees still wobbly as she braced herself against the wall; the coldness, invigorating in its effect, awakened her further. She quietly made her way back into the house and slowly closed the front door. Without turning on any lights, she made her way to the kitchen. The digital clock lights on the coffeemaker and oven threw a faint soft blue glow to the room as she searched for Frank's cell phone, which was plugged into the charger. Before touching it, she listened for any sounds coming from the house. Being in the house for the past three weeks as they hid from everything and everybody had gone from a joy to an imprisonment. She knew every creak and crack in the house, and nothing was moving. She always kidded Frank that he could sleep through an atomic bomb. He was still asleep upstairs. In the distance she could hear his snoring.

She made the sign of the cross and said a prayer for forgiveness as she tried her best to slow her pounding heart. Her breathing was now short and shallow, so she consciously made an effort to take slower deep breaths to prevent more hyperventilation. Within a minute, her head and soul cleared and she reached for the phone. She looked over her shoulder quickly and felt her hands slightly trembling as she magically texted, "Ketchum, Idaho, overlooking Sawtooth Mountains, hurry, please, I'm sorry." She stared at the screen for almost one minute, then she hit send. Waiting for confirmation, she found the sent message and deleted the text after confirmation was received. She then downloaded the weather forecast from cnn.com and put the phone back into the cradle of the charger. She turned around and took five steps before she came face-to-face with Frank.

The rage in his eyes was evident even in the dark of night. He towered over her and snarled, "What have you done?" his voice full of pure evil.

"What?" she said defiantly, waving her hand in a dismissive manner. "Can't I look up the weather, or is that not allowed under your rules, your royal assholiness." She had hoped her bluff would be enough to assuage Frank's paranoia, but instead it reinforced his anger. He pushed her out of the way and grabbed the phone. He quickly checked any outgoing messages and found none at first. He noted the downloaded weather forecast, and his instincts told him that it was a red herring. Like any computer, he checked for recently deleted items, finally found the message that Gina sent, and saw the familiar phone number of Lieutenant

Philip DiMarco. The rage inside erupted as he turned and approached Gina. He showed her the text. Her eyes widened with total fear, and she urinated onto the floor. He threw the phone onto the floor and smashed it with his bare foot. He pulled out the SIM card, threw it into an ashtray, and burned it with his small butane lighter. The last thing he needed was a lock on any GPS signal.

"Again you betrayed me," he said with coldness like death itself. Then his right hand came out of nowhere and backhanded her across the right side of her face. The blow immediately cracked her mandible as she was lifted off the floor by its force, which sent her five feet backward. She landed with a thud, and her head struck the dining room table and knocked her unconscious. He stood over her crumpled body with balled-up fists. He realized she was out, and instead of hitting her again, walked over her body and went back to the kitchen to make a pot of coffee. He'd have to pack up and leave immediately. He looked at his watch, saw it was 5:28 a.m., thought for about twenty seconds, and figured he'd be ready by six o'clock at the latest. While he was packing, he'd plan some form of diversion to aid his escape, and figure out what to do with Gina.

Almost four weeks had passed since that massacre in Nevada, and there had been not one sighting of either Frank or Gina. With no new leads, the trail had gone absolutely cold. That all changed at 5:25 a.m. that morning. Phil had fallen asleep in his La-Z-Boy chair watching the Dodgers lose again as they fell into third place behind the Giants and Diamondbacks. Kelly was back in Washington, and he had not seen her for almost two weeks. Even though they talked on a daily basis, their conversations had become more formal, businesslike, as the wall between them grew thicker. In the meantime, he had become permanent liaison between the FBI and the CHP, and was now stationed in the Bay Area. He was renting a two-bedroom house in Pleasanton and had relocated all of his things up north, most in a storage unit since he had scaled down to 1,450 square feet from his previous 2,500. But the area was quiet, with rolling golden hills with groves of black oak trees.

He had welcomed the change from the desert southwest. Even though his bones hurt more with the damp weather, he loved the cooler temperatures and the feeling of being home. He had always felt displaced in the desert, making the most of his home but missing both New York and the Bay Area.

He instinctively rubbed his face with his hands, then slowly opened his eyes, trying to focus on the TV that was showing one of the local morning shows giving the weather and traffic. Their voices were too happy for this time of the morning, and it immediately pissed him off. He heard a buzzing noise for a few seconds. He thought at first that it was coming from the TV. After shaking off the cobwebs, he realized it was his cell phone, plugged into the charger in the kitchen. He rose up slowly from his position as his joints cracked and hurt, and he remembered his father's warning about the aches and pains in the fifties. His father's joke was always that "if one woke after fifty and didn't have any aches or pains, it meant you didn't wake up." He scratched himself as he made his way to the kitchen; the two-day-old beard stubble felt like sandpaper.

The phone number of the text was a 208 area code. He had no idea where that was, but he opened up the text while letting out a giant yawn, eyes half-closed.

Then his heart stopped, his breathing quickened, and his mouth went open and dry, all within milliseconds. There in front of him was Gina's message. "Ketchum, Idaho, overlooking Sawtooth Mountains, hurry, please, I'm sorry." It hit him like a bolt of lightning. He dialed his staff and asked them to immediately run the number and get any information on the person of ownership. Then he dialed Kelly.

"You're up early," she said jokingly.

"Gina just texted me." His words brought a gasp of breath over the phone. "'Ketchum, Idaho, hurry, please,' plus an apology to me," he said quietly.

"Do you think it's real?" Kelly asked, recovering from the shock.

"I've already asked to run the phone number, ownership, and so on," he said as he was rummaging through his old Rand McNally Road Atlas from 2005.

"Where the hell is Ketchum…" Her words were cut off by Phil.

"In the middle of the fucking state of Idaho off state route 75, which is off US 93," he replied. "Less than a hundred miles north, on the same US 93 from where the Nevada massacre occurred. He must have a second house there."

"I'll alert the agents in the Idaho office and have them contact the local sheriffs and other agencies, get something coordinated. I'll get a flight to Boise, and I'll arrange for a flight for you."

"Get the locals to block off any escape from Ketchum, put up roadblocks, and have them check everybody," Phil said hurriedly. "He's probably moving as we speak."

"Why do you say that?" Kelly asked.

"Because Gina took a big chance sending me that message," he replied, "which means she's in trouble, or they're about to leave."

"That makes sense," Kelly said. "I'll call you back in a few, let you know what's going on."

The early morning operator from the task force's Bay Area office called for Phil. "The phone is registered to a Francis DeMartini, but the application for purchase used a social security number and address that no longer existed. Federal records showed him as dying in 1998. We attempted to locate the GPS signal but were unable. We're looking for any properties under the same name or close aliases to see if we can pinpoint his location."

"It's him. Keep digging, and again, great job along with a big thank you," Phil said.

Phil now was more worried about Gina's situation and condition than ever before. The fact that the GPS signal, which is built into every cell phone produced in the world, was unable to be located meant that the device and its chip had been destroyed. That meant that Frank knew about the text and Gina's betrayal of him, which eliminated her status as a willing partner in crime. She was always expendable, but could have survived long-term if she joined forces with Satan and gave up her soul for what she felt was true love. However, as Phil had experienced, love was fleeting, whereas the soul was forever and could not be bartered. It was something that Gina probably finally realized, but too late.

CHAPTER 44

Gina awoke about minutes later with the left side of her face swollen and bruised, unable to fully open her mouth. She knew her jaw was broken, but that was the least of her worries. She sat herself up against the kitchen cabinet; her head throbbed as she moved. A wave of nausea began to build as she momentarily became lightheaded. She had a hard time focusing but was finally able to see the digital clock on the stove. The eerie blue light displayed the time of 6:04 a.m. and shone brightly in the dark space. Suddenly she heard the door of the truck being closed, followed by footsteps on gravel, then the front door opening and closing.

Frank's shadow appeared in the doorway; a hallway light outlined his massive features. She didn't move and instinctively tried to slow her breathing rate down as the hyperventilation increased her lightheadedness. Her fear of dying overwhelmed all of her senses, so she lay there frozen in fear. He bent down into a squatting position, his face now mere inches away from hers, his breathing slow and steady.

"Time for us to go," was all he said. She was bewildered, wondering what he was talking about, but could not speak without causing more pain, so she just nodded. Suddenly she felt his massive hands under her armpits as he lifted her up off the floor and swung her to a cradling position, which allowed her to rest the right side of her face against his chest. She held him around the neck as he carried her outside into the chilly morning air. He held her while he opened the truck's passenger door, then settled her gently into her seat. "Buckle up," he said as he closed the door.

They drove away, down the long winding driveway lined by tall pine trees, the stars still evident in the darkness of the early morning above their tips. The hoot of a barn owl could be heard coming from up high. They turned right onto the main road, drove about three quarters of a mile, and made another right onto a fire road that began to wind upward. Suddenly the road was bathed in bright white light as he turned on the Kay lights on the roof of the truck. He slowly made his way about a thousand feet and pulled over onto a small turnout. He got out of the truck and made his way around to the tailgate, opened up the bed, then pulled out a small paper sack and a flashlight.

He quickly made his way through thick underbrush and began the ascent up the side of the pine treelined hillside. When he was approximately halfway up, he stopped and placed the package in a thicket of dry sagebrush. He opened the bag, looked over the device in the glow of the Maglite, set the timer for five minutes, and armed the incendiary device. At the first beep of the timer and the clock showing 4:59, he took off and quickly descended back down the same path previously taken. He reached the truck in less than thirty seconds, jumped in, fired up the engine, and made a quick U-turn. He raced through the hairpin turns of the fire road. It took him almost another minute to reach the highway, and then he cut off the lights as he reached the intersection. He looked both ways, saw no traffic, accelerated, and sped north about two miles before he turned on his lights. He checked his watch and estimated that detonation would occur in ninety seconds.

He looked at Gina, curled up in a ball on the passenger seat, her head cradled in her hands against the door. He had put his anger aside for now as he planned their escape, and for the first time in his life, he actually felt pity. "Watch what happens in about a minute; it will be like the Fourth of July," he said with the enthusiasm of a child.

"What is it?" she asked through the right side of her mouth; she was now able to minimally open her mouth.

"A form of napalm in a small cylinder with a detonator," he began as he continually checked his watch, "which will cause a fireball. The weather forecast is for high winds as the sun rises, with a high building out of the east. It will fan the flames rapidly."

"Why?" Gina asked.

"Diversionary tactics," he said as he began the final countdown. "Ten, nine, eight, seven…" He reached "one" as the device ignited. A giant ball of fire burst into the air five hundred feet and spread outwardly in a circle from the blast site almost a quarter of a mile. It ignited the forest immediately. "Houston, we have ignition and liftoff," he sarcastically said, then burst into his war whoop while his fist pounded the wheel. He immediately pulled over, got out of the truck, and admired his work as the forest fire took hold and spread over the top of the hill and toward the town of Ketchum at rapid speed, fed by an abundant amount of underbrush that had grown unkempt for years.

Gina was in the truck, shaking. She had heard that war whoop before, as described by her Uncle Phil. He had heard it immediately after her father had been killed. The guilt for what she had done to put her in this position caused her such grief that she actually would welcome her own death. She was no longer afraid to die, but would do everything in her final hours to take Frank with her to the grave.

Frank's knowledge of the weather patterns and terrain had proven extremely valuable for their escape. Idaho had gone through a severe drought the previous year, with one third of the normal precipitation received. The entire area was a tinderbox ready to explode from the first lightning strikes of the coming summer. Within thirty minutes of the incendiary's blast, forty- to fifty-mile-per-hour wind gusts fanned the flames in all directions, but especially from the north. Thousands of burning embers flew in the air like butterflies; their tiny flames ignited other dry brush and trees as the cycle repeated infinitely. The flames moved so rapidly and the heat was so intense that hundreds of forest animals, both small and large, died within the first hour. Clouds of thick dark reddish black smoke rose from the hellish site, climbed to a height of ten thousand feet, and could be seen for fifty miles. The first response was within forty-five minutes from nearby Twin Falls; however, by then it was too little and too late. The four trucks with the brave twenty-five men that had arrived first on the scene stood in shock at the sight of the inferno. There was nothing they could do until the heavy equipment and air support arrived. So they watched the destruction of ten square miles of pristine land within the first hour.

The first water- and flame-retardant-dropping fixed-wing aircraft began flying over the outer reaches of the advancing flames as they tried to halt the spread. Hundreds of forest firefighters were called into action from all over the western states to begin the arduous task of clearing brush and creating a firebreak in an attempt to contain this monster before it reached any pockets of civilization. With the extremely mountainous and rugged terrain, some areas would be allowed to burn, especially if no known structures or people were involved. The area had turned into a war zone, with the only remnants of battle left being the scorched earth.

The tongues of flames spiraled into a fire tornado that reached upward of a hundred feet, fanned by winds now of hurricane force as the inferno raged onward, unable to be contained in spite of man's best efforts. Mother Nature was a force they could not conquer. The fire jumped all man-made firebreaks and obstacles, with the potential to become apocalyptic.

Because of the situation, Phil's helicopter landed five miles south of the fire to avoid any interference with the firefighting effort. He was greeted by Special Agent Fred

Thomason of the Twin Falls FBI office. After pleasantries were exchanged, a detailed update was provided as they made their way toward the blaze.

"You can really smell the smoke as we get closer; you don't have any asthma problems, do you?" Fred asked.

"No, that's the one part of my body that's in good shape," Phil replied with a chuckle. "Does anyone have any thoughts about how it started?"

"Unable to tell until they find the original hot spot, which won't be for a while with the intensity of the flames and smoke," Fred said. "But they definitely think it was set by an arsonist because of the time it started, so early in the morning with no weather disturbances noted in the area at the time, and the intensity of the original fireball as reported by witnesses."

"Frank set it, believe me," Phil said as he is stared out of the passenger window at the beautiful landscape of pine trees and sagebrush as they climbed into the foothills. "He is not only a top-notch sniper, but is just as adept at demolition and incendiary devices."

"So do you think he was covering his escape?" Fred asked.

"Hopefully, that's all he's covered up," Phil said as his thoughts and worries focused on Gina. After all of this time, to think that he could save her, only to fail once again. His reflection in the passenger window only magnified the age lines that weren't evident even three months ago, before all of this started.

By the time they reached the staging area, the extent of the devastation was just beginning to dawn on both of them. It reminded Phil of the destruction left behind in the 1988 Yellowstone National Park fires or the volcanic blast at Mount St. Helens. The smoke was thick and harsh on the lungs even from a distance of one mile. Acres of dead smoldering trees and brush with carcasses of dead animals strewn throughout could be seen in all directions. It sickened both of them.

"He truly is a monster if he started this," Fred said as they walked toward the battalion chief. Phil just nodded in agreement as he continued to scan the disaster. His mind was still wandering between worry and a sense of hopelessness, the latter becoming more evident with his mood swings.

"Are you all right, Phil?" Fred asked. But Phil paid him no attention as they came face-to-face with Lloyd Nelson, battalion chief for the state of Idaho. Phil was the first to extend a hand to shake, and introductions were exchanged.

"Our preliminary report is that it was arson," Lloyd began. "There were no natural causes that can explain the start or the blaze. Plus where the flashpoint is," and he pointed to the hillside to the west, "is uninhabited, with no squatters, and the only road in and out is a fire road, just in case," he said ironically.

"Do you have any knowledge of the type of incendiary device that could have been used?" Fred asked.

"It's still too hot to get too close for a better investigation," Lloyd replied. "There's no rain in the immediate forecast, so we'll probably take a closer look tomorrow. But I'll tell you the truth," he said as he looked at Phil, who was the same age, "the last time I saw something do this to a forest was in Nam.

"Are you thinking napalm?" Phil asked.

"Something very similar to it, I'll tell you that," Lloyd said, "with plastique explosive as the triggering mechanism would be my guess."

"That's not something that your run-of-the-mill arsonist would use, is it?" Phil asked.

"No, your amateur arsonist would just use an old-fashioned pack of matches with a lit cigarette stuck inside, so that when the butt burned down, it would ignite the matches," Lloyd answered. "This is probably the work of a major professional arsonist."

"Any structures damaged?" Fred asked.

"So far about forty homes that were tucked away in the hills south of where the fire started," Lloyd said.

"Any known casualties?" Phil finally asked.

"None that we know of," Lloyd told Phil. "Luckily a general fire alarm went off and people evacuated rapidly. Most of the people here have been here for generations, so they're prepared in case of a fire or other catastrophe. It goes back to the air raids during the Cold War since there are missile silos strewn about this area."

Their conversation was suddenly interrupted by the repeated concussions of ammunitions exploding in the distance on the far side of the fourth foothill south of them, just at the edge of the advancing fire. Shells launched upward, exploding like fireworks at a Fourth of July celebration. All three men watched in silence until it ceased.

"That would have been Frank's place," Phil said deadpan as he shook his head. It was déjà vu all over again, as Yogi Berra famously said. He turned to the chief. "He used an accelerant similar to napalm attached to some form of detonator device that was attached to plastiques in Southern California. Let me know if that's what you find." He finished with a handshake and turned to walk back to the car. Fred quickly did the same, thanked the chief for his time, and hurried to catch up to Phil.

"What the hell are we dealing with, Phil?" Fred asked as they entered his car. "He's already miles from here by now, isn't he?" Phil nodded quietly with a frown. "Why is he always one step ahead of everyone?"

Phil looked out the passenger window as they began driving and said, "Because he is the perfect blend of pure evil and brilliance. He plans everything down to the finest detail, taking into account all variables, and always has a worst-case scenario plan in place. The Marines taught him extremely well."

"And now he's teaching all of us," Fred said. Phil looked at him with admiration at having surmised in less than a few hours what the rest of the FBI couldn't for the past three months. What all of this horror came down to was power and superiority. Good versus evil added to the drama, but was not his motive. Phil flashed back to that courtroom over thirty years ago when Frank was acquitted of his mother's murder. Upon leaving the courtroom after he was acquitted of the charges, Frank said he would teach everyone a lesson someday.

His day had arrived.

CHAPTER 45

The three jagged peaks appeared to rise out of the lake; their snowcapped reflection in the crystal blue water rippled as the waves made their way to the shore. The mid-July day was warm and clear, temperature in the upper eighties during the day, dropping into the forties at night. The contrast of colors of the ominous black mountains with their white peaks against the backdrop of brilliant blue skies, with white fluffy clouds above, was ideal for either a photographer or an artist. The cry of a golden eagle as it circled in the distance was the only sound heard. Frank watched it slowly make a sweeping arc of about half a mile with grace and ease, its powerful wings pushing against slight headwinds and then gliding back around.

He watched the magnificent bird for at least twenty minutes until it finally settled in its nest in a tall pine tree. The feeling of total solitude and isolation was comforting in so many ways. It gave him uninterrupted time to think and plan their next move with attention to the most minute detail. It had been two days since they had left, driving almost nonstop until they reached this wilderness paradise.

Taking a snaking route on back roads and two-lane highways through sparsely populated areas allowed them to evade not only the authorities, but most people in general. What concerned him was the fact that evasion would last only so long.

He looked up again at the Grand Tetons and watched as the shadows of the clouds above began to appear on the face of the majestic mountains. As he watched them float by, a plan began to form in the back of his mind that would be simple yet still foil the task force to the point of their own insanity. He smiled at the thought of the total chaos he could create and the knowledge that they could not stop him. Hearing footsteps on the gravel behind him, he turned to see Gina slowly making her way toward his position, her head down, shoulders slumped, as she walked. The look of total resignation of her fate was apparent in the now-fading bruised but less swollen face, which had the sad appearance of the old Emmett Kelly clown. She looked pitiful, but he had no pity for her. In his mind, she was lucky to be alive.

She came up beside him, stood with him, and stared at the precious sight of nature's magnificent beauty. Frank pointed out the eagle's nest, and as if on cue, the eagle took off soaring and flew northwest toward Yellowstone National Park. Frank saw the sudden departure as a sign. "We need to leave now," was all he said as he turned and headed back to the truck, leaving Gina bewildered at his sudden departure. His mood had swung from total complacency to intense agitation within seconds. What she didn't understand was why. Her fear was that he was becoming more mercurial, with the extremes of the mood swings becoming worse, especially the anger and aggressiveness toward her. She instinctively put her hand to her jaw and felt the tenderness where it was bruised, not broken as she had first feared. She was able to chew and speak, but chose not to at this time. There was no reason to anger him further.

When they reached the truck, he surprised her by opening up her passenger door and helping her up into the cab. He turned and took one more look at the Grand Tetons, knowing it would be the last time he would see them in this lifetime. He quickly took a few hits off of his joint and eased the anxiety he had begun to feel. He inhaled slowly and deeply as he took in the clean Wyoming air. A feeling of tranquility enveloped him as a vision of his next conquest developed within his delusion of superiority. He climbed into the truck, started it up, and headed northwest, intent on following the same path as the other bird of prey had shown him.

"If you're wondering where we are going," he said out of nowhere, "I've had a hankering to see Yellowstone's Gibbons Falls." Then he went silent as they drove north on US 89; the last view of the beautiful spires was seen in the rearview mirror.

She looked at him with a bewildered expression. "Why?"

"Because I missed it the last time I was through, and I heard the water is really flowing this year," he replied as if he were your average tourist.

"Are you trying to get us killed?" she asked bluntly as Frank smiled.

"Just the opposite," he said with conviction. "The last place they figure we would be is a very public place like a national park as popular as Yellowstone. They're probably scouring all of the campsites in all of Idaho and Montana."

"Why Montana?" she asked.

"Because they figure I'm heading to Canada, and Montana is between the part of Idaho we were in and the northern border. Take the straight path north," he replied. "I am heading up to Canada, but through the Dakotas, not Montana. So I figured we'd spend a few days in Yellowstone, see the buffalo and hopefully a bear, just like two ordinary tourists."

"But they'll recognize you," she said.

"Not if I change my appearance again, cover up the tattoos, and steal a truck with a fifth wheel attached," he said with a shrug. "Ain't no big thing."

Her anxiety levels increased as she realized that there would be more killing. She knew now that since she already had killed, Frank would expect her to continue killing, just like him. The problem was she wouldn't be able to indiscriminately kill again. That would be unacceptable to Frank, and an admission of betrayal, which would lead to her immediate death. If she had to kill again, it would be the death of her soul. She refused to let that happen. She would rather die and face God's wrath for crimes to humanity that she had already committed than to take another being's life again.

Unless that person were Frank; then she would kill with joy, knowing God would thank her for thwarting true evil.

Phil stood there for over fifteen minutes staring at the large map of the western United States and studied every possible escape route from Ketchum, Idaho. Just as before, the massive manhunt among multiple law enforcement agencies across five states failed to catch even a glimpse of Frank and Gina. With roadblocks, air search with both helicopters and fixed-wing aircraft, and broadcasts across all forms of the media, not one hint of the couple's existence could be found. The damage they had left behind, however, could now be calculated in the millions of dollars. The Ketchum fire, which was only 50 percent contained, had burned six square miles, destroyed over a hundred homes and structures, and killed four firefighters when the wind had taken a sudden turn, trapping them inside their vehicle, which turned into a crematorium.

The reward for Frank and Gina's capture had climbed to 5 million dollars, with pledges across the country from every firefighter's budget-restricted coffers. The brotherhood was that strong. The word spread through their communication channels to watch the usage of back roads by the fugitives, something Phil had suggested all along.

So now he stood and tried to imagine where Frank would go next. He had this gut feeling that they weren't hiding at all but were out in public so they could blend in with the rest of the tourists. This could only mean that they had changed their appearance or mode of transportation, or both, enough of a change to where no one had reported seeing either of them. That's what bothered Phil the most. Had they made it to Canada? Was Gina still alive? Was she truly trying to surrender and face the consequences, or was she manipulating the system—and him? He had answers to none of the questions circulating continuously through his mind.

Phil looked for the hundredth time at the large green shaded area on the map in the corner of the area where the states of Idaho, Wyoming, and Montana met. He had an intense gnawing in his gut that this was the area where they were. He had discussed his hunch with Kelly, but she felt differently this time. Her demeanor had changed noticeably, which had disturbed Phil. She sounded just like the rest of the profilers, as if she had drunk the Kool-Aid and now her mind was brainwashed like the others had been. Everyone on the task force was betting against him in so many ways, had since the beginning of the case. He was the outsider, who had failed to get Frank convicted all of those years ago and was becoming their scapegoat now.

So the distance between him and the rest of the task force had increased, while communication had almost come to a complete halt. He knew Frank better than anyone else, but at this point of time, his opinions were spoken usually to deaf ears. He was mentally exhausted and ready to pack it in and retire, but the guilt of not completing his mission and his responsibility to save Gina kept driving the need for him to see this thing through. His thoughts were broken by the soft touch of a hand on his shoulder. He turned in time to see Kelly look at him with concerned eyes.

"They won't appear on the map, Phil," she said sarcastically. "They have disappeared off the face of the earth, just like the last time. We may not find them for weeks to months."

"So?" Phil said. The hairs on the back of his neck began to bristle at her tone and possible insinuation. "Hell, we've been after them for over a quarter of a year—what's a few more weeks?" he replied with bitterness.

"Phil," she said more quietly, "I don't want to get into an argument in front of everyone else. All I'm saying is that we may have some downtime, and I thought it would be a good time for you to go back home, take some time off. I'd call you if anything broke." Her look was sincere, but her eyes portrayed something deeper and more sinister.

Phil felt like he had been punched in the gut and stabbed in the back at the same time.

"There's no reason to stay around here." She waved her hand at the office surroundings and added, "Plus I'm going back to Washington and work remotely."

At that point of time, the portrait of betrayal had been completed. He had been relegated to lesser stature in her eyes, acknowledging her greater importance. He stayed silent while trying to gather his thoughts and respond with proper diplomacy, but he could not get past his anger. "Fuck you," was all he could say through gritted teeth. The look of death was in his eyes as he stared her down, and she cowered slightly like a wounded animal; a look of fear had now replaced her smugness. "You can fly back east, but I'm not leaving until Frank DiMocchio is found dead."

"You may not have a choice," she said firmly.

"I have a choice, and I just made it," Phil said. "Like I said just a moment ago, fuck you and the horse you rode in on." He turned and walked past Kelly, who stood with her mouth open; fifteen other agents who had heard the entire conversation stood there also. Before Phil could make it out of the door, Fred stopped him and said, "You'll need a ride," and gave him the keys to his vehicle as he shook his hand. "Where do you think he is?"

"Yellowstone National Park," Phil said.

"That's what I figured; that's where I'd go," Fred said and nodded to say good-bye. Phil did the same as he acknowledged his debt to Fred. "Good hunting."

And in a second he was gone and alone again, but this time on his own terms, which suited him just fine.

CHAPTER 46

The gray evening was eerily quiet as Frank and Gina drove north on US 191/89. The edge of a massive thunderstorm that moved in rapidly from the northwest could be seen touching the peaks of the Rocky Mountains and obliterated any sun that was left for the day. The temperature had dropped twenty-five degrees from a few hours earlier. The breath emitted from a herd of buffalo caused vapor clouds to form above their heads as they grazed, oblivious to the storm clouds above. The forecast was for hail and heavy rain overnight, with winds up to fifty miles per hour through the passes. Frank knew they could not chance getting caught in the storm and having to seek shelter at the last moment. He scanned the distance to the west of the highway and followed the Snake River as it wound through the valley floor, with the mighty mountains in the background. Besides admiring the beauty of the magnificent peaks of solid granite, he was searching for his next hideout.

The area was dotted with large ranches as horses grazed on the tall prairie grass. Spread among these large estates were smaller homes, few and far between in this yet underdeveloped territory. Most of those belonged to either young families just starting out or retirees. It was easy to tell the difference by the types of vehicles that were owned, or if there were any signs of children with toys and swing sets on the property. Finally he saw what he felt was a perfect residence.

As he came over a small ridge to the upper valley area, he saw the small cottage-style house with a fifth-wheel recreational vehicle parked on wooden studs. Smoke was rising from a single chimney in the middle of the roof. A 1999 Green Chevrolet Z71 pickup truck was parked in front of a small one-car garage that was separated from the main house by over a hundred feet. A smaller toolshed next to the garage, with a meticulously manicured three-acre front lawn left him with the impression of an older couple. He slowed down and turned into the driveway. Gina turned and looked into his eyes as if pleading not to do this.

"What if there are kids there?" she asked, as she knew his disdain for killing innocent children.

"There aren't, trust me," Frank said with confidence.

The driveway was actually a hard-packed dirt road that extended 1,500 feet to the front of the house, which was surrounded by groves of aspens. The front of the house was lined with planters full of petunias, spaced between azalea bushes that had already lost their flowers. Frank pulled the truck even with the Chevy and parked five feet away. He opened up his console and took out his Walther PPK and Gina's 9 mm Glock. He handed it to her as she obligingly took the gun, her hands slightly tremulous and sweaty.

Frank looked at her and said, "If there's any shooting, I'll handle it; just back me up, that's all I'm asking." She nodded in acknowledgment and tucked the gun in her back waistband, as did Frank. The feeling of her gun between her butt cheeks gave her almost an erotic feeling, a feeling of power and invincibility. "Just follow my lead, okay?" he asked. She nodded again. They both got out of the truck simultaneously and walked hand in hand toward the house, like a couple in love, false smiles on their faces. Frank saw the curtain of the front window pull back slightly, the hand hidden inside the fabric, but no face appeared. Then the curtain fell back into place.

They walked up to a large English Chestnut-stained oak front door that slowly opened as they approached. A shorter, well-dressed, late-sixties-year-old man stood in the doorway with a double-barrel pump shotgun in his hands, the barrel pointed in their direction but low to the ground, which was a huge mistake.

"What do you want?" the man asked. "I don't take kindly to strangers on my property." His voice was a combination of Sam Elliot with a little John Wayne and definitely local.

Frank held up his hands and faked surrender. "We were driving by and saw your beautiful house and wondered if you'd be interested in selling," Frank said. "We'd pay cash."

"Well, sorry, but the house ain't for sale, so you can just get along," the old man said with venom, using the rifle as a pointer. Second and fatal mistake.

In one swift motion that Billy the Kid would have been proud of, Frank dropped his left hand, grabbed the Walther

PPK, raised it, and fired. He hit the man square in the middle of the chest. Crimson red spread as he dropped the shotgun; he grabbed his chest as he collapsed and fell in the doorway. Frank stepped quickly over his body and entered the house with Gina trailing, her gun held out in front of her with two hands, like she saw in TV shows. They went from room to room slowly but found no one else in the house. Frank went back to the front door, picked up the dead body, closed the door, carried the body over to an area rug, and laid it facedown. He wrapped the body up in the rug, lifted it up onto his right shoulder like a sack of potatoes, looked at Gina, and said, "Clean up the mess."

He walked through the house and then out the back door. He stopped in his tracks as he gazed over another three acres of beautifully manicured yard, with smaller groves of aspens that overlooked grassy areas that separated multiple flower beds and a large koi pond with lilies in the center. He looked down at the carpet-wrapped body with admiration of the care this man had given to his home. Frank knew at that moment that he was a widower and that there was no one else at home, period. He found the center of the yard and laid the man down. Rapidly Frank went to his truck, retrieved his shovel, and returned. He looked up at the now-darkening sky, felt the wind pick up, and knew he had less than a half hour before the storm unleashed its fury. With rapid and steady motion, he began the ritual of digging a grave. The ground was well-hydrated due to an excellent irrigation system, which made the excavation easier. Even in the now forty-five-degree weather, he began breaking a sweat within the first minute of digging.

Gina watched from the kitchen window as she searched for cleaning agents and found them underneath the sink, along with sponges and a bucket. She stared at Frank as he attacked the grave relentlessly, his body motions almost robotic in nature, as if it were a ritual. His breath came in clouds of vapor with every thrust of the shovel. She stood amazed at the speed with which he worked and finally realized that he would be done before her if she didn't get moving. She passed through a beautiful kitchen with every amenity, including a center island with a professional stove and granite countertops, into a hallway lined by montages of family pictures, and finally into the foyer. She opened the massive front door and stared at the now curdling pool of blood on the floor. She turned, ran to the porch, and vomited over the railing into a row of petunias. She wiped off her mouth, slowly stood up, took a few deep breaths, went back, and proceeded to clean up another death that she could have prevented.

She finished in plenty of time and took the agents back to the kitchen. She looked out the window and saw only Frank's shoulders and head sticking out of the grave; the same robotic motion continued. The gun was still between her butt cheeks as she calmly walked out the back door and quietly strolled over to the grave site. When she was within fifteen feet, she could hear Frank's heavy breathing and the sound of the shovel as it hit the dirt in a methodical rhythm. She came around to the front as she pulled the gun from her waistband. She stared down at Frank, who briefly stopped, looked up at Gina, saw the gun, and smiled. She aimed, pulled the trigger, and heard only a click. She checked to make sure the safety was off, then pulled the trigger three more times with the same result.

"Do you really think I'm that stupid to trust you with a loaded weapon?" he asked through heavy breathing. He laid the shovel up on top of the grave, and in a move reminiscent of a professional gymnast, pulled himself out in one quick vault. He picked up the carpeted body, threw it into the grave, picked up the shovel, and handed it to Gina. "Now you can finish the job. I'm going to go see if the old cowboy has any beer lying around, relax, and smoke a joint," he said nonchalantly as he bent down two inches from her face and snarled, "Do you have a problem with that?"

Gina shook at the realization of her failure to kill him, nodded in agreement, and began the task of filling in the grave. Frank turned, began to walk away, stopped, and said, "One more fuckup like that, and it will be you down there, do you understand?"

"Y-Y-Yes," she said.

"Good," he said, turned, and walked back toward the house.

Gina looked down at the ground, saw the puddle of her own urine on the ground, her right leg wet from her incontinence, and began to pray to the Lord for mercy. Or a quick death.

CHAPTER 47

The swiftness and ferocity of the storm caught most tourists by surprise, but not the local residents, who had seen worse storms in the past. They knew what to do to survive even the worst tornado. Everyone had a storm cellar, with plenty of food in a freezer, canned goods, extra water, and wood for both cooking and heating in case of a prolonged blackout. This storm crippled a wide area from Idaho through the Dakotas at higher altitudes as it blanketed the area with twenty to thirty inches of snow with seventy-five-mile-per-hour and greater gusts of wind, which created whiteouts on all of the mountain-pass roads. In the valleys, massive torrents of rain and hail engulfed the area and caused the Snake River to rise five feet in the first thirty minutes. The Alberta clipper claimed fifteen deaths within the first two hours as drivers tried to race to their destination, but lost the fight against the forces of Mother Nature.

Phil was worried that Gina would join the statistics over the next twenty-four hours. He stood on the balcony of his hotel room in Jackson Hole, Wyoming, and watched the silver-dollar-sized hail come down hard in all directions dependent upon the wind. The howling of the winds was as loud as anything natural Phil had ever heard outside of the thunder. He held onto the railing as a gust of wind almost blew him backward; the hail felt like small rocks as they struck his face and body. It felt like a hurricane with hail, something he had never experienced before. As a kid in the Bronx, he remembered the summer thunderstorms that came rolling through the city in the late afternoons, with brief downpours that cleaned the stale air, but nothing like this. He went back into his room and watched the Weather Channel's continuing coverage of the only storm in the entire United States.

The first thought that occurred to him was that some evil force had covered for Frank, throwing this storm at the goodness side and allowing Satan to escape. At least divine conspiracy theorists would consider that scenario. One consolation was Phil knew that the passes both into and out of Grand Teton and Yellowstone National Parks would be closed for at least a few days. That meant that Frank and hopefully Gina were holed up somewhere. The question that was gnawing at Phil's stomach was where and who they had killed to secure shelter through the storm. He knew that Gina had no friends in this area and Frank had no friends at all. So somewhere in this area, there was either a hostage or a murder victim that had not yet been reported.

"Hey, Fred, it's Phil," he said as he speed dialed his only friend in the agency at this point of time. "Do me a favor and send out an alert to this area to look out for any missing person's reports of local residents from worried family members. I think they targeted a hostage and have shelter at this point of time. Usually with a storm like this, relatives will call and make sure people are okay." The instances of missing person reports increased with massive storms like this, especially when there were power outages and telephone services were down.

"Great idea, Phil," Fred said. "You know I have to clear it with Kelly," he added with some disgust.

"Tell her it was your idea, just in case Frank is up here, and it couldn't hurt to put out the bulletin," Phil said.

"And if she says no?" Fred asked.

"She won't, because it will cost her no manpower but a communication to all agencies, which can be done in five minutes," Phil said with conviction.

"Okay, I'll give it a shot and get back to you. Stay warm," Fred said with a chuckle.

"Fuck you, Fred," Phil said with his own laugh.

He walked over to the sliding door that led out to the balcony, looked out, noticed the rain coming sideways with trees bending like Gumby, and realized he was stuck for a while. He switched the TV channel to ESPN and lay down on top of the bed. He looked around the standard Best Western Hotel room and began to evaluate his relationship with Kelly, which had grown uglier and was basically dead. The problem was that it didn't bother him at first. Now this only caused him more grief as he began to ruminate about his failures in life, especially in the romantic department. He was at his lowest when he felt lonely, especially now in the late-middle-aged years. The prospect of spending the remainder of his life alone haunted him terribly. It was something his mother always warned him about as a youngster when he wished to be left alone all of the time and would lock himself in his room for hours. He had his wish granted forty years later when he least wanted it.

It's so ironic, he thought, *that the more humans crave solitude, the more they cannot tolerate it when given the opportunity.* Like Frank, he had wanted less and less of human interaction in his formative years as his anger for the stupidity of mankind grew with each passing adolescent year.

His thoughts turned to Gina and how he had let his late partner down. He had promised to protect her like his own, but had not lived up to his responsibility. For the hundredth time in his life, he cried himself to sleep.

Frank scanned the pictures on top of the fireplace mantel while he warmed his legs and torso against the roaring fire. All of them were of the man he had killed, with a woman who Frank assumed was his wife, over many years of marriage. The last one was probably recent because it showed them as much older, with the wife looking gaunt, as if dying from cancer. When he picked up the frame to look closer, a funeral card with the picture of Jesus Christ on one side and the Lord's Prayer on the opposite, with the date June 17, 2011, the name Sally Ann Cartwright, and "May God Finally Ease Her Pain," fell out. For some reason, he felt sad. Not for killing the man, for he was now with his wife, but for knowing that he would never have a mantel full of such pictures.

"What the fuck; I'll probably never make my old age anyway," he said to no one and put the picture and card back. He was relieved to see that the man he killed was a widower with apparently no children, which meant that there wouldn't be too many relatives calling to check on him. He looked out the living room window at the driving rain as the world seemingly came to a halt with the storm. This would work out better than he had once thought.

Gina was already asleep after being exhausted from burying Mr. Cartwright. Frank was just the opposite. Fully awake and energized, he had explored almost every inch of the house and grounds before the storm unleashed its wrath. He estimated that they had enough food for about four weeks and could wait at least a month before they had to venture out for anything. He had placed his truck inside the garage, which was as well-organized as the yard. A John Deere riding mower was neatly parked off to the side as he pulled in to the space where the Chevy truck usually was parked. His Dodge fit perfectly well.

No one knew where they were. He had discarded the cell phones and had disconnected any house phones. He smiled at the thought of the task force going crazy trying to locate them. Even though he had already removed the internal GPS locator on his phone, he could not trust Gina ever again. In fact, her antics earlier confirmed the need to dispose of her after her usefulness had passed or if she put him in harm's way.

He smiled to himself as he watched the rain turn to hail, which intensified and began to form a sheet of ice on the grass and driveway. This was going to be a beauty of a storm and would cripple any efforts to locate them, as long as they laid low.

Gina, who was actually wide-awake, also stared out of the window, but her view was in the back of the house, toward the mountains. Her demeanor was also 180 degrees different from Frank's. She felt total despair and isolation. But most of all, she considered herself a failure in life. She may have been successful at her job, but her personal life had been in shambles for years. She never had any children, and never attained any great wealth or true happiness. And now, she was a wanted killer and a dead woman walking. Since she was going to die anyway, she had made up her mind to make sure that she took Frank with her. He needed to die. Maybe God would forgive her for her transgressions if she eliminated this truly evil entity. The image of Sister Margaret Marie in the second grade telling her that she was heading toward an eternity of damnation for taking Jimmy Wilson's Tootsie Roll was embroiled in her mind. If she were eternally damned for a Tootsie Roll, what was the penalty for five murders?

She climbed back into the cold bed, rolled up into a ball, held her legs with her hands locked in place, began to pray as hard as she could for forgiveness, and silently wept until she finally fell asleep.

CHAPTER 48

The mighty beast, symbol of the American West, had tattered fur and flies on its back as it moved slowly along the road and came within a few feet of their vehicle. Its vision focused on Frank's eyes as it shook its head side to side, snorted loudly, then settled down and continued to walk with the remainder of the herd of buffalo. The up-and-down motion of their heads as they strutted in unison was constant, no matter what age or size. It reminded him of a platoon of soldiers during marching drills. As they pulled to the front of the herd, they came upon the most massive buffalo they had ever seen. He was obviously the "king" of the herd, with a large main, lionesque in nature, with two large curved horns that protruded forward out of its huge head. The top of the animal's shoulders came to the same height as the roof of the old Chevy truck. Suddenly the beast appeared to become agitated. Frank floored the gas pedal and launched the truck forward, pulling the fifth wheel in a jerky motion. The animal tried to gore the rear end of the RV; instead, it shoulder checked the vehicle, which caused the rear wheels to momentarily lift off the ground before they settled down with a shudder as the weight inside of the vehicle shifted rapidly and challenged the ball joint between the truck and RV.

Frank took his foot off the gas as he gained better control of the vehicle. He gripped the wheel extra firmly, kept an eye on the large side-view mirror, and made sure the RV was not about to jackknife. He slowly accelerated after the RV settled down, and he continued to drive north on US Route 191/89 through the southern portion of Yellowstone National Park. The old Chevy pulled the RV with ease. Frank had more respect for the old man after he noticed the new large-block six-liter engine and matching five-speed automatic transmissions. This allowed him to switch vehicles and pull the RV without attracting attention. The truck was in excellent shape, and the fifth wheel gave them the luxury of truly "living on the road."

They got through the entrance gate to Yellowstone National Park more easily than expected. In spite of Frank's and Gina's pictures being hung up on the bulletin board, Frank paid his $50.00 for the truck and RV, was given brochures and instructions on what was closed because of the recent storm, and handed his receipt with a smile. His appearance was entirely different as compared to the photo. His hair was cut back to short length, with the beard replaced by a thick walrus moustache with a small soul patch under the lip. His tattoos were all covered by long-sleeved clothing, and he wore Ray-Ban sunglasses, which hid his eyes. He also spoke with a local accent after studying the local TV broadcasts during their stay in the Cartwright cottage. Gina used one of Mrs. Cartwright's wigs that she had found lined up on mannequin heads in the bedroom; it was gray in color, and with her makeup, made her appear twenty years older. She felt strange being in a dead woman's wig, but had no choice as per Frank's demands.

They had stayed in the cottage house for only thirteen days as the first snowfall in the higher altitudes began to thaw. The amazing aspect of this part of Wyoming was the variety of weather with drastic extremes. It would snow one day and be sixty degrees the next, which allowed clearing of all of the main roads. It also allowed time for Frank to check out the RV and older truck to make sure they were worthy of his plan. It was time well-spent as it allowed them enough time to evade any law enforcement while he planned his next move as he tried to stay one step ahead of the task force.

He handed the brochures over to Gina who immediately began reading about the largest National Park in the United States. "I had no idea that this whole area is one large volcano" she said with amazement.

"When it blows it will be the largest cataclysmic effect ever" Frank said. "All those fancy ranches we passed just a little while ago before we entered will be gone along with who knows how much else of the western United States. It will make Mt. St. Helens look like a burp."

Gina looked at him with slight trepidation in her eyes.

"Don't worry it ain't going to blow today, and if it did, what a way to go" Frank said with a strange look of glee in his eyes. Then he let out a really wicked laugh which made

Gina squirm in her seat. "Chill, woman, I'm just fucking with ya" he said with disgust.

"Are you sure this is safe to go through a National Park?" Gina asked.

Frank looked at her with a smug look as if she doubted his master plan. "We've got three weeks of food, a house to live in, and plenty of gas," he said. "Since no one checked on Mr. Cartwright in the time we were there, it's safe to say that his whereabouts won't be known for a while. By then we'll not only have seen all of Yellowstone, but Little Big Horn and Mt. Rushmore as well before we head up to Canada."

"But I have no passport to get into Canada," she said.

"Don't worry about such trivial issues," he said with a dismissive wave of his hand. "I have enough contacts to take care of any documents that are necessary. So let's go see Gibbons Falls first, then the Upper and Lower Yellowstone Falls, Mammoth Hot Springs, and at some point Old Faithful."

"Okay," she said with a child's grin on her face. Her apprehensions were abated at that time, as his demeanor improved as they traveled. Driving was something that appeared to soothe him naturally.

He smiled, not because he was happy to please her, but because he knew he wouldn't need to get any false papers. He had enough of his own passports, but Gina wouldn't need one, because she wouldn't make Canada alive.

The minister was concerned. He had not seen Adam Cartwright for three weeks at his services. Adam hadn't missed one service in twenty-seven years, except the day his wife had died. He always sat in the same pew for all of this time, but for the past few weeks, that spot was empty. He knew Adam to be a private individual who was hardworking and respectful in the old-fashioned way. He tried calling after the service, but there was a disconnect message when he dialed the home phone number. The minister knew he was all alone, with no children or family after his wife had passed, and that no one probably had checked up on him.

So he decided to pay Adam Cartwright a visit at home that afternoon.

As he pulled into the driveway, a feeling of dread apprehended his soul. He knew Adam was dead. There were patches of flowers that had wilted from the recent storm, but what concerned the preacher most was the shape of the lawn as he noticed weeds growing wildly. He also noted that the old Chevy and Adam's beloved fifth wheel were gone. Adam never went far from home and was never gone this long. The minister parked in the spot where Frank's truck had been and got out of his car. The first thing he noticed was the silence. The second was no sign of Adam at the front door; his custom with all of his friends was to greet them with a smile and a "Good day." The minister was met by no one. He walked up to the front door, rang the bell, tried the doorknob, which was locked, and finally looked inside. Everything appeared in order, but the house was definitely empty. He walked around the house and tried the back entrance, but found it also locked. He turned around, peered over the unkempt backyard, and as if by divine intervention, was suddenly drawn to the center of the yard. In a patch of exposed earth, he saw the edge of something in his profession he had seen many times.

A freshly dug grave.

He immediately said a prayer for the dead while he wiped away the tears. He hoped that he was wrong, but his gut instincts told him otherwise. He took out his cell phone and called another parishioner, the sheriff of Teton County, Timothy McCoy.

"Hi Tim, it's Father Tom," the minister began. "I'm out at Adam Cartwright's place, and I think something bad has happened." He proceeded to tell the sheriff about his suspicions and his findings as explicitly as possible.

"Oh boy," the sheriff said, his voice one of resignation. "Don't touch anything, Reverend. I'm about thirty minutes away and will be there right away. I'll notify the lab unit, get some forensic people out there."

"I'll sit in my car and say some prayers until you get here," the minister said.

"That would be best," McCoy said and hung up the phone. He turned his light bar on as he made the left-hand turn at Moran Junction and headed south on US 191/89. He rubbed his face with his free hand and took a deep breath. He remembered talking with the FBI's task force liaison and wondered if this was the work of the West Coast Killer. He hated federal interference due to his libertarian views of states' rights, but if this monster were loose in his county, he would welcome all the help he could acquire. He opened up his Bluetooth channel, reached his receptionist, and asked her if she had the liaison's name and number available.

"A Lt. Philip DiMarco, CHP, was the man you spoke to, and I have his cell phone number," she said.

"Can you patch me through? I'm headed down to Adam Cartwright's place. We may have a problem," he replied.

"Sure, give me a second," she said, and he was put on hold. After about thirty seconds, she came back on the line. "I have Lt. DiMarco for you, sir," she said as she patched the call through and disconnected.

"Hi, sheriff, tell me you have something." The excitement in Phil's voice could not be hidden.

"I have a possible murder scene of an old-timer, a widower with no children whose truck and fifth wheel are missing. Call me Tim by the way, please," he said.

"Please call me Phil. Why do you say possible murder scene?" Phil asked.

The sheriff proceeded to explain about Adam Cartwright and the minister's findings of the empty house and missing vehicles. But then he dropped the bomb on Phil. "The minister said he found a freshly dug grave in the backyard."

"It's him," Phil said determinately. "Give me his address. I'll get the tag numbers of his vehicles out immediately nationwide, just in case he's already fled Wyoming." His heart was pounding in his chest as he rose from his hotel bed. He had remained in Jackson Hole knowing that Frank and Gina were lying low locally. It was Frank's pattern in the past, something Phil tried to relay to everyone else on the task force. But no one would heed his advice. Maybe now they would listen, especially Kelly. The sheriff gave him the address, which he wrote down and said with a laugh, "I'm an hour away at normal speed, but I'll be there in less than forty-five minutes."

"What are you driving, and I'll alert the state troopers," McCoy asked.

Phil told him, thanked him, and hung up. He immediately called Fred and relayed what had transpired. Fred would alert Kelly and put out an immediate bulletin for every law enforcement agency within five hundred miles of the area. With that Phil grabbed his holster with his official 45 caliber Remington. Then he grabbed his Italian Genitari 37 caliber long-range rifle and enough ammunition to kill an entire platoon. He left the room immediately, jogged to his car, jumped into the driver's seat of his Crown Victoria, took out the portable cherry light, plugged it into the cigarette lighter, and took off like a bat out of hell.

He was back in the hunt.

And it felt good.

CHAPTER 49

The serenity of the small cottage was shattered by the cry of a golden eagle as it flew overhead, a small animal grasped in its talons. The sound and sight caused the two of them to stop what they had been doing as each looked up with amazement at the sight of this beautiful bird of prey. They shielded their respective eyes from the midafternoon sun as the bird flew directly west toward the mountains and its nest. The slow-moving powerful wings beat rhythmically as the creature moved rapidly away from them. Once it was fully out of sight, they resumed their investigation.

Phil stood in the garage, stared at the sight of the dark amethyst-colored Dodge Ram, totally empty, with every inch cleaned to perfection. He had been searching for the occupants of this vehicle for so long; however, he came up short again. The good news was that there was evidence of Gina still being alive, but he was no closer to saving her than he was almost four months ago. He could only imagine what it had been like for her not knowing from one day to the next whether or not she would survive.

Then he thought about his own endurance and how much this mission to rescue a promise from years back had drained his own lifeblood. Right now, though, he was just infuriated that Frank had not only escaped, but killed again.

He felt a gentle hand on his right shoulder and turned around to see Sheriff Tim McCoy's sad eyes and knew what was coming. "You found the body," Phil said, and McCoy nodded his head while he looked down at the ground. Phil's anger intensified and he found himself balling his fists with force until his forearm muscles began to cramp.

"He was buried at six feet deep, just like you said, one shot to the chest, buried with a throw rug from the entryway," McCoy said quietly. "What kind of fucking animal are we dealing with, Phil?" The tears ran down his face, and his eyes started to redden. "I knew Adam Cartwright and his wife for over thirty years. She died a few years years ago, which tore him apart, but he was always the same to others. He was the first to give a helping hand, the last to take anything in return, respectful, and liked by everyone."

"To answer your question, the devil himself embedded in a sociopathic killing machine, the worst fucking human being that you will ever meet," Phil replied. "He killed his own mother at age thirteen, was acquitted, and then became a prized pupil of the US Marine Corps, who trained him in the art of killing in oh so many ways. The perfect killing machine with no conscience, who is smarter than you and I combined. Throw in a six-foot-five-inch 255-pound body with all of that evil, and that's what Frank DiMocchio is like."

"Why Adam?" Tim asked.

"He was the perfect target, a widower with no family to worry about," Phil said. "Probably shot as he answered the door, being friendly to strangers and was shot. Then they take over the residence, especially with the storm, and wait until it's the right time to leave. They probably wiped out the supplies in the house, which gave them ample food for wherever they are headed." Phil's cell phone buzzed, and he saw that it was Fred and answered. "What's up?"

"We got a hit on the Chevy and RV, but you're not going to like this," he replied.

"Where?" Phil asked with trepidation.

"Yellowstone National Park, but five days ago," Fred said.

"Five fucking days ago, after we put out the fucking bulletin three fucking weeks ago? Fucking park rangers couldn't find their fucking ass with both hands." He was now shouting and spitting with disgusted anger. "Motherfucker! They're long gone by now."

"I said you wouldn't be pleased," Fred said jokingly as he tried to calm Phil down. "Do you want the other bit of news?"

"What news?" Phil asked.

"Agent Flaherty is returning to your neck of the woods," Fred said, almost apologetically.

Phil was disappointed, but he didn't let Fred know. "And your point?" he said with a snarl. Inside, his guts were churning with the knowledge that she had not called him, but let it be known to him through other channels.

The slap in the face was too much for him at that point in his life. He was better off alone, except for his children and grandchildren. Finally he said, "Any sight of the RV or truck since five fucking days ago?"

"None," Fred said, "but we have a national alert out for the vehicles. They can't go too far with that load, Phil, before being spotted."

His optimistic voice made Phil bite his lip. They still didn't understand how good Frank was at evading capture by staying twenty steps ahead of the morons in the federal government. "He's laying low somewhere, most likely in surroundings where a thirty-foot vehicle can be hidden."

"We'll get him, Phil. Be good," Fred said.

"Yeah, you too," Phil said and hung up. He turned and began to shake his head as Tim said, "You and I know he's long gone from Yellowstone National Park."

"You have a map of the western states handy?" Phil asked.

"Sure," Tim said and pulled out a plastic five-inch sealed envelope from inside his jacket. He opened it and took out a four-inch map that he unfolded to a thirty-eight-inch size. Phil looked down at the most detailed topographical map with every inch of road, paved or unpaved, that he had ever seen since his days in the corps. But the way it was carried meant that Tim had spent a lot of time underwater.

"You were a SEAL, weren't you?" Phil said.

"For ten years," Tim said.

"Let me shake your hand," Phil said as he extended his right hand, exposing his forearm cobra tattoo. "It's always a pleasure to meet a SEAL."

"How long were you in the corps?" Tim asked as he gripped Phil's hand solidly.

"For five years," Phil said. "What made you leave?"

"Met a woman in San Diego while on liberty, fell head over heels in love, and lost the thrill for the mission," Tim said. "Knew it was time. How about you?"

"The war ended, and I moved on," was all Phil said. He still was not willing to admit fault for the atrocities he had witnessed or had carried out, so the truth behind his honorable discharge remained hidden. "So, where do you think he has gone?" he asked quickly to shift the subject.

"Are you thinking he's making his way up to Canada like you said last time you spoke to my deputies and me?"

"At some point, yes, I think he'll cross one of our borders, and I don't think it is going to be Mexico," Phil said emphatically.

Tim and Phil scanned over the map as it lay on the hood of the Sheriff's Dodge for about two minutes. Finally Tim put his finger on a campsite called Horseshoe Bend Area in the middle of the northernmost border of Wyoming and Montana. "Perfect area, elevated, with limited access, Bighorn Lake is stocked with bigmouth and rainbow, along with total seclusion. A lot of snowbirds park their fifth wheels there and travel north an hour and a half to Little Bighorn," he said. "He would also have the high ground if anyone like us came in looking for him. Take the high ground first for defense of any position."

Phil slowly nodded his head in agreement because it made sense. He remembered hearing Frank once discussing the desire to see the battlefield where Custer and the Seventh Cavalry were killed so many years ago. "I concur with your deduction." Phil thought for a second, then asked, "You want him badly, don't you?"

"I'd be honored to be the one to put a bullet through his chest," Tim said. "It's personal now. Adam Cartwright was a friend, and a SEAL never leaves a friend's killing without being revenged."

"He killed my partner at SFPD," Phil said, "and I'd be honored to have a Navy SEAL as a partner with me as we hunt down this motherfucker." They shook hands again, but this time as a sign of a silent code that few outside the military would understand. They would protect each other, no matter what. They had a common mission in their pursuit of Frank DiMocchio—his death.

"I'll let my deputy handle the paperwork and any duties while I'm gone. I've got six months of leave built up; might as well use it before some politician says I don't deserve my pension. So I am at your disposal," Tim said with a smile as Phil patted him on the back as they left the garage.

"Don't you have to talk to your wife first?" Phil asked.

"Wife, hell, she left me ten years ago for some doctor," Tim said.

"Lawyer," Phil said with a laugh as Tim joined him.

"But leave your Fed car here. We can take my truck," Tim said as he pointed to his Dodge Ram parked about 750 feet away.

"Thank you so much; I hate that car," Phil said with a smile. For the first time in a long time, he felt as if a guardian angel had just been dropped in his lap, someone who finally would understand what they were up against.

But most importantly, a person who knew how to kill someone without hesitation and someone he could trust to not ask questions afterward, just in case.

CHAPTER 50

Frank watched the black GMC Sierra as it pulled the twenty-five-foot Airstream fifth wheel into the parking stall just below and to the right of where they had been camped for the past two days since leaving Yellowstone National Park. At first he was dismayed that someone had decided to camp close to him, which ruined his total seclusion. Then he saw the truck's license plates came from "Beautiful" British Columbia, and his frown turned instantly to a smile as a new plan began to form in his head.

He assumed that by now Mr. Cartwright's absence would have been noticed by someone and an investigation would eventually lead to his truck and fifth wheel. The task force also would have been alerted, which meant national alerts, so his days of driving these vehicles were numbered. He watched an older couple get out of the truck, stretch their weary bones, and finally look around the arrangements of their campsite. Frank didn't waste any time as his plan was set and about to be placed into action.

He reached into the Chevy's console and pulled out his Walther PPK and silencer, checked the magazine to make sure it was full, and placed it into his back waistband. He closed the door, turned around, quickly walked down a small path between the two neighboring campsites, and was within twenty yards of them when the older man noticed him and turned to say hello, but never got the chance as Frank pulled out his gun and shot once. The cough of the silencer was a bit louder in the thin silent air, but it didn't matter, as the bullet struck its target between the eyes, killing him instantly. The wife came around the back end of the fifth wheel. Frank closed the distance as he ran quietly on the toes of his shoes and was within twenty feet of her when she caught sight of her husband lying on the ground. She stopped immediately and put her hands to her mouth in shock, but never had the chance to scream as the bullet severed her spine at the C2 level and caused her instant death.

Frank looked around and saw no movement anywhere in any of the other campsites. He opened the Airstream, went inside, gun out in front, and inspected every inch of the interior. He found ample supplies, but no other humans or animals. Satisfied with his inspection, he left the RV, picked up both of their bodies, and carried them into the woods behind their campsite. He laid them down on the far side of a tree, ran back to his truck, and got out his shovel. After he found a good secluded spot, he began his ritual of digging a proper grave, but this time buried two people in one to save time.

Gina watched in horror as the entire scene unfolded outside her bedroom window of the RV. She was powerless to stop Frank.

After thirty minutes, the grave had been dug and the bodies had been tossed into the bottom. Within another ten minutes, the grave had been completed. Frank entered the RV full of dirt and sweat and said, "Get up and get dressed. We've got new wheels to drive, which means reloading all of our shit." With that, he turned and walked out of the RV, slamming the door.

She immediately got up and got dressed.

Within an hour they had transferred everything into the new truck and RV. They had covered up any bloodstains in the ground by sweeping dirt over the area until they weren't noticeable. Frank took one more look around and was satisfied that they had left nothing behind. He looked back at the old Chevy and RV and gave a military salute, as if paying respect to a fallen comrade-in-arms. Gina walked over and he said, "We better get going before someone shows up looking for us." He turned around, looked at her in her eyes, and for the first time in a while kissed her gently. The move surprised her, but she responded to his offering. They embraced for almost a minute. Then they walked to their new truck and RV as nonchalantly as two people on vacation.

He climbed into the GMC Sierra, fired up the 5.9-liter V8 engine, and slowly backed out of the stall. Then he pulled forward to the entrance and located the honor box where campers left an envelope with campsite number and cash for the fee. With brute strength, he ripped off the small Masterlock of the latch of the box, lifted the lid, and removed the two envelopes that were there, his and the Canadians'. He smiled wickedly as he laid his envelope back into the box but kept the Canadians'. That would be his parting shot for Lieutenant DiMarco. Within five minutes they were on US Route 14 northbound, headed up to Little Bighorn and Custer's last battle.

The helicopter flew barely forty feet above the tree line as it came over the ridge of the foothills to the Bighorn Mountains. Dispatched from the FBI's base in Sheridan, Wyoming, the Sykorsky S-115 was equipped with the latest digital Nikon camera, with zooming capability of 1,500 meters. It flew at a speed of 120 miles per hour, reached the Plume Creek campsite within thirty minutes, made several passes at a thousand feet above the ground, and snapped over two hundred pictures. The pilot then swung the aircraft southwest and performed the same mission over Tie Plume campsite twenty miles away. Within thirty minutes of snapping the last photo, the analysts found the old Chevy and RV parked in the last stall at Horseshoe Bend Area. The excitement around the computers was palpable as they relayed their information to their superiors.

Finally Fred called Phil with the news of the sighting. Phil was elated to hear the information but was worried. "Are there any signs of life in any of the photos, any signs of defensive positions around the perimeter?" Phil asked. Fred became silent as he hit some keys on his computer and zoomed in on the photos, especially within fifty feet of the encampment.

"I don't see any kind of reinforcement or signs of life around the RV and truck," Fred said dejectedly.

"Exactly," Phil said with a slight twinge of anger. "I'll bet you my life savings that they are already gone." Tim agreed from his driver's seat with a nod of his head. "We're ten minutes away, so do I have a bet or what?"

"I'd never bet against you, Phil," Fred said. "You're the only one who's been right all along."

"Tell that to your superiors. I'll call you with an update in a few." Phil clicked off before he could hear Fred's reply.

"Fuckin' Feds," Tim said. "They couldn't find their own dicks without proper instructions and oversight."

Phil burst out laughing. His two hours with Sheriff Tim McCoy was a godsend to lift his heart. They were kindred spirits in their experiences of war and marriage. They were only six months apart in age, both raised in a strict Catholic upbringing, both the victims of war-related injuries and divorce. Whereas Phil had only been divorced once, with many failed relationships afterward, Tim was in the process of getting his second, with failed relations in between. Like so many men of their age, Tim had "fallen in love" after his first marriage with a woman ten years his junior. It was great at first until he caught her sleeping with men years younger than she. He hadn't realized that he had married a cougar. He just called her a slutty bitch and booted her and her boy toy out of the house. That was over three months ago, with final legal proceedings scheduled for three weeks down the road. Phil felt sorry for the man. This mission was actually great therapy for Tim, and he admitted to such.

They drove northwest on US Route 14, which wound through Custer National Forest; jagged nine-thousand-foot mountaintops covered with snow could be seen to the north. They began to climb as the elevation increased from a thousand feet to over four thousand feet within five minutes. The trees were predominantly ponderosa and cedar pine; their aromas permeated the air. The forest was extremely thick, with tall underbrush growth. There hadn't been any fires in that area in decades, unlike Yellowstone, which had almost been devastated in 1989. Phil tried to see any signs of wildlife, but the foliage was the perfect camouflage. As if Tim were reading his mind, he said, "I'd hate to get lost in that brush."

"Yeah, but Mother Nature's animals love it, especially the deer," Phil replied.

"We'll be coming up on Horseshoe Bend Area camp in less than two minutes. How do you want to handle this?" Tim asked.

"We could drive right up to the truck and RV," Phil said flatly.

"What if they're still there?" Tim asked just as flatly.

"He'd shoot you before you reached his stall if he saw me in the truck," Phil said.

"So you're down in front and I drive in, looking innocent as I troll around," Tim said.

"You have no markings of law enforcement, and this truck doesn't have the appearance of a black and white, so I guess, yeah," Phil replied with a shrug of his shoulders.

"Sounds good to me," Tim replied with the same nonchalance; he opened up his console and pulled out a Remington Colt 45 semiautomatic pistol with a modified clip of fifteen rounds. He checked the safety and put the gun underneath his left thigh. "If you reach underneath the backseat, you'll find a fully loaded fully automatic M-16 and a MAC-10."

Phil gave him a quizzical look, unlocked his seat belt, turned around in his seat, and reached back. He grabbed both weapons as Tim began to slow down, with the sign for the campsite indicating half a mile to go.

"Choose your weapon," Tim said.

Phil held up the M-16, his best friend in Viet Nam. "This will more than do," he said.

"I thought so," Tim said with a smirk as Phil handed him the MAC-10, which he placed on top of his lap. Phil ducked his large frame down into the passenger cab space below the level of the doorframe and dashboard. His hamstrings began to cramp up earlier than expected, and he vowed to drink more water and less coffee. He felt Tim make the left-hand turn at the entrance and felt the gravel road underneath the oversize tires. What took only thirty seconds to drive felt like an hour. Finally Phil felt the truck come to a stop, and Tim said, "I think they're gone. There's absolutely no movement inside the RV."

Phil sat up slowly and saw the truck and RV for the first time. He agreed that they looked abandoned. "No way to know unless we investigate." With that he slowly opened the passenger door, and using it as a shield, slowly got out of the truck, M-16 in the ready position. Tim got out at the same time, with both weapons pointed at the RV. Phil signaled to Tim to take the left side as he flanked to the right. They looked in the windows, and it definitely appeared empty. They met at the entrance, and Phil nodded as Tim turned the door handle and opened the door slowly. Tim went in first and headed to the back of the RV, while Phil headed to the front. As expected, it was not only empty but completely bare of any essentials.

"They definitely bugged out and cleaned this place out," Tim said. "They must have commandeered another large vehicle, probably another RV, but where are the original occupants?"

"Dead and buried," Phil said matter-of-factly. He pointed to the forest. "Somewhere out there probably." His dejection was evident, knowing that they were back to square one, again.

Again reading his thoughts, Tim said, "He has to slip up and make a mistake. When he does, we'll be there."

"That's the same thing I said over thirty years ago, and many times since," Phil said. "I believed that at first, but now I think it's going to come down to good old-fashioned blind luck. And that's something I've never had."

"I beg to differ," Tim said emphatically. "If you didn't, you wouldn't have survived Viet Nam and all of the other tribulations God has put before you."

Phil's mother had always lectured to him about his guardian angels that they would always be there to protect him. He had put his faith in that belief many times in the jungles and the swamps and survived with that knowledge. He lost his faith in humanity after seeing too many grisly murders while working homicide for SFPD. He had never lost his faith in God, but questioned the reasons behind so much catastrophe in his life. He had felt neglected and abandoned by his own God at times, especially since the discovery of all of those bodies in the deserts of Southern California. Now he felt as if God had provided yet another guardian angel, this time to help conquer the angel of death.

CHAPTER 51

Frank and Gina stood less than fifty yards from the only headstone that was covered with gold. The wind swept across the rolling hills, which were covered by long prairie grass. The tall reeds blew in the direction of the gusts in a slow rolling motion, like a wave of water on land. The sounds of the souls of the regiment's dead could be heard as they called from the great beyond, their cries echoing across the historic battlefield. The whispers of the fallen victorious warriors also called out, but as a reminder of their people's slaughter at the hand of those they had vanquished. It also was a reminder of the futility of man's own ego and arrogance. The belief that only those that were taught proper military training through an academy could understand tactical situations well enough to plan strategic battle plans was gutted with the defeat of General George Armstrong Custer at Little Bighorn.

The usage of what would become known as guerilla warfare was unheard of at that time in military history, except when dealing with barbaric cultures. The total annihilation of the Seventh Cavalry at the hands of the

Sioux and Cheyenne sent shock waves through all of the branches of the armed forces. It led to changes in future military training, but with the blunders in Viet Nam, Somalia, Iraq, and Afghanistan, all against those who only knew guerilla tactics, the lesson learned was that superiority in power and numbers did not guarantee victory. Especially against people who had a true reason to fight and die for, not just because they had to take orders.

Frank genuinely understood these facts and knew that the only way to guarantee his own survival was to maintain his own version of hit-and-run maneuvers as a means of staying one step ahead of his own enemies. He could not remain static while he was still being hunted. He was wanted by too many people now, with the reward for his head increased substantially after the killing of one Adam Cartwright. It was easy to cover up his full-body tattoo, but hard to disguise his massive size.

He wandered over to the memorial with all of the names of the soldiers who died that fateful August day in 1876. All because of an egotistical general who would not listen to reason before going into battle, and felt his superiority over "savages" would propel him to an easy victory. Only to be slaughtered at the hands of those who were fighting not only for their land, but also their independence. The same government that was founded on that one principle was trying to strip it away, as it still was today. He understood their duty to honor, but he despised the man that caused their death.

Yet his headstone was the only one in gold.

"Let's go before too many people show up," he said to Gina. She nodded her head and followed him away from the site, haunted by the sounds of the dead. She had never been there before and was truly moved with the sounds and sights of the memorial to those brave soldiers and Native American warriors. It made her think more of her own destiny, which she knew was a certain death. She just didn't know when. So at this point of time, she remained totally obedient.

They climbed into the GMC Sierra and pulled the Airstream slowly out of the parking lot as more tourists began to enter the area. Frank had already changed the license plates to Montana's from his stock of stolen plates that he always carried with him, just in case. He turned east on US Route 212 and passed a sign that said "Rapid City, S.D. 210 miles." Gina looked at Frank with a quizzical look. He had said all along that they were going to Canada, but Rapid City was actually south of where they were now.

As if reading her mind, Frank chuckled and said, "We're still going to Canada. But I've always wanted to see Mt. Rushmore. So we're just taking a little detour."

She shook her head with amazement. She knew he had big balls, but this was inviting trouble, almost as if he were asking for a confrontation. He wasn't crazy, because his look was one of a sane man, who for some reason was pissed at the entire world and the only way to satisfy his anger was to kill people. Were his morals and ideals warped? You'd better believe so, but he wasn't insane. She kept quiet, not wanting to entice an argument, and stared out of the passenger window at the rolling prairie with tall grass and wheat. In the distance she could see some more mountains as they traveled on the two-lane highway on this bright and warm mid-August day. *Another two weeks until Labor Day and the unofficial end of summer*, she thought.

She hoped to still be alive.

Phil wandered down the hard-packed road past multiple law enforcement vehicles as the local sheriff and his deputies were being briefed by Tim in their search for grave sites. They would look inch-by-inch in specific grids with a specific radius away from the RV, which was Frank's pattern. Others had been sent to canvas the two other occupied campsites at the other end, to see if anyone was witness to any of the killings. Phil already knew what would transpire. Nobody would have seen anything, and if Frank used a silencer as he always did, then nobody would have heard gunshots either. The only questions that remained were how many did he kill, what was he driving now, and where was Gina?

He looked into the distance and saw a few Cooper's hawks as they circled high in the sky, but no buzzards today. Could someone have been kidnapped instead of murdered? He doubted that theory when Tim had inquired just before the sheriff had arrived. Frank would never leave a witness alive, and he wouldn't take a hostage for ransom. It was just not his modus operandi. His thoughts were interrupted by the sound of a distant thumping of a helicopter's blades. He had heard that sound too many times in his life. He focused on the sound and localized it coming out of the south, probably from Casper. That could mean only one thing, something he had been dreading since his phone call with Fred.

The Doppler effect was apparent as the aircraft neared his position, but no visual sighting could be had until a few minutes later, when he saw the familiar white helicopter as it approached swiftly. The acid began to churn in his stomach; he reached into his pants pocket for the package of Rolaids Tim had given to him. His mouth was bone-dry as he chewed the minty paste-like tablets before gagging and swallowing. He noticed that his heart had begun to race faster, so he did the old-fashioned deep breathing exercise to calm his anxieties. Then he made a right-hand turn and hiked up into the surrounding forest, keeping one eye on the approaching aircraft as he climbed up the slope. His breathing grew harder, and his heart felt like it was coming out of his chest when he finally decided to stop. His fear had driven him almost 750 feet higher than the campsite next to Frank's abandoned RV.

After being bent over as he gasped for air, Phil straightened up slowly and peered down at the empty campsite below. He noticed something strange about an area that had a darker shaded spot, as if something were underneath the dirt. Oblivious now to the landing of the helicopter, Phil set off quickly down the hillside toward the open campsite and that spot in particular. When he was within about two hundred feet, the hill flattened out, and as he passed a small clearing, he stopped dead in his tracks. There below his feet was a freshly dug grave. He made the sign of the cross and said the Lord's Prayer as he backed up off the spot.

"Tim, I found it," he shouted through the silent forest, his voice echoing off the mountains.

"Where are you?" Tim said.

Phil turned in the direction of his voice and called, "Over here about two hundred feet into the forest above the next campsite." Within about forty-five seconds, Tim, the sheriff, and four deputies stood around the perfectly rectangular grave; all observed their own moment of silence. Phil broke the mood. "I saw what looks like covered-up blood pool in the campsite below as I was heading down the slope," and he pointed to the vacant site.

The sheriff turned and told one of his deputies to seal off the crime scene as he and the other three deputies accompanied Phil and Tim down the hill. As if drawn to the exact spot like a magnet, they slowly swept away the loose dirt, which revealed two separate pools of dried blood within ten feet of one another.

"Something tells me there are two bodies in that grave," Phil said as he looked up toward the grave site. As he turned around, the familiar white helicopter landed on the highway outside of the entrance to the campsite. Phil's mouth instantly turned dry as he saw the passenger door open and Kelly emerge. Fred got out after her, waved, and smiled. Phil grinned back and nodded.

"That must be Agent Flaherty," Tim said as he straightened up. "Now I understand even better just seeing her for the first time." He nodded in approval.

"Thanks a lot, partner; I thought you were in my corner," Phil said as Kelly and Fred slowly approached. Phil didn't move an inch, but as Kelly and Fred came closer, he held up his hand and said, "Fresh crime scene; please watch where you are treading."

"What do we have here?" Kelly asked.

"Probably a double murder scene, with a grave site found about two hundred feet up in the forest," Phil said. "They escaped in another vehicle, type unknown and whereabouts unknown," Phil finished with a slight sarcastic tone.

"How long ago?" she asked with slight irritation as she put her hands on her hips in a defiant stance and looked up at him directly in the eyes. Fred backed up a step or two, having seen this act before. Tim moved closer.

"Unknown." Phil bent down slightly with a snarl and furrow in his brow. "But we'll find him."

"And who is we?" she asked with a snippy attitude.

"Retired admiral, now sheriff of Teton County, Tim McCoy, ma'am," Tim said and extended a hand.

Phil turned and mouthed the word "admiral" as Tim acknowledged. Phil was even more impressed. "And he's ex-Navy SEAL, better trained to find and kill this bastard than a hundred of your agents."

"And who gave you permission, sheriff?" Kelly asked.

"If you'd like to call General McMurtry, I'm sure he could vouch for my part in this nationwide manhunt," McCoy said flatly.

"General Roger McMurtry," Kelly asked, "as in the chairman of the Joint Chiefs of Staff?"

"Yes, ma'am, he asked me to join up with this fine ex-marine of his and hunt down this monster who has disgraced the uniform he once proudly wore," Tim said emphatically.

Phil almost pissed in his pants listening to his bullshit, but she was buying the whole thing.

"Oh, okay, then I guess, uhm… where did you say the grave site is?" Kelly asked, all flustered.

"It is two hundred feet up the hill," Phil said as he pointed. "The murders were committed here. The areas have been cordoned off, but you are more than welcome to inspect them, as long as you stay out of the lab rats' way. I've got better things to do." Kelly was absolutely shocked at the way he spoke to her, but had no response.

"I'll show you the way, ma'am." One of the deputies led her and Fred up the hill, with Fred clearly hiding the widest grin Phil ever saw.

"Are you really a fucking admiral, and do you know McMurtry?" Phil asked after they were out of earshot.

"Yes to both," Tim said. "The last time I saw Roger was a month ago, when I beat him at Texas Hold 'Em, and he still owes me a fucking grand."

For the first time in many months, Phil actually laughed until he began to cry. "We're finished here," Phil said, "so with your permission, sir, this lowly lieutenant is asking permission to bug out."

"Permission granted," Tim said as they mock-saluted each other and got into Tim's truck. "Aren't you going to let Kelly know where we are going? And by the way, where to?"

"Little Bighorn," Phil said as if in a trance. "Frank once wrote a tactical military synopsis of Sitting Bull's victory at Custer's Last Stand, in which he praised the plan of battle as being brilliant. Being this close, I can't see him not stopping by to see the memorial."

"Is he that crazy?" Tim asked.

"He's not crazy, Tim; he's evil. There's a big difference," Phil said. "His thoughts are more analytical than yours or mine, and he has evaded numerous national and international manhunts for years. That doesn't sound crazy to me. To answer your other question, I'll call her when I get there and get over being pissed."

"Then it's off to Little Bighorn, I guess," Tim said as they exited the campsite and headed north to Montana and the battlefield where the souls of the tormented still resided.

CHAPTER 52

The late afternoon sun began to fade in the distance and the temperature started to drop as Frank and Gina pulled into the KOA campground outside of Broadus, Montana. There were only a few occupants as they slowly pulled the RV into the farthest site away from everyone. Frank slowly backed the fifth wheel into the space and made sure that he had an unobstructed view of any incoming traffic. Within twenty minutes, Gina and Frank had everything around their area secured and were ready to relax. They sat in comfortable canvas chairs that were situated at the side of the GMC Sierra, which overlooked the rolling hills that were between them and the Black Hills of South Dakota. There were blackbirds singing as they made their nests for the night, and the golden sunset began to take hold in the distant skies. The temperature now hovered around fifty-five degrees, after having been eighty degrees one hour ago. In between tokes, Frank blew vapor rings and enjoyed the chill in the air.

"Fall is coming," he said out of nowhere with a smile.

The thought did not console Gina as it had in years past. The uncertainty of her future held her captive within a self-made prison. She knew deep down that she would not live to see any of the upcoming holidays. So she took a toke herself and tried to allay her fears. She leaned back and watched a flock of crows fly south. Her serenity was broken as Frank jumped up to his feet. "What is it?" she asked.

He turned toward her and quietly said, "Shh, listen" as he turned toward the west.

As if a switch were turned on, she could faintly hear the sound of engines as they approached, but had no clue as to what caused the sound. Frank opened up the cab of the GMC Sierra, reached under the cushion of the rear bench seat, pulled out a large duffel bag, and put it on the ground as the sound of the engines grew closer. He opened up the bag and pulled out a fully automatic M-16. He made sure the magazine was fully loaded and that the safety was on before he handed the rifle to Gina, who had a most shocked look on her face.

"What's going on?" Gina asked as Frank took out a MAC-10 and more bullets for his Walther PPK.

"There's going to be a lot of motorcycles coming into camp soon, and if it's who I think it is, it could only mean trouble," Frank said. Gina shrugged her shoulders to let him know that she didn't understand. "Hell's Angels, returning from the annual big rally in Sturgiss, South Dakota, going home for the winter. But they like to party, and when they party, they get mean and loot others' possessions or kill people for the thrill."

She stood up and studied her weapon.

"Remember when I taught you, the safety is here and this thing is fully automatic, which means you can empty this full clip of fifty rounds in no time. It also has a very sensitive trigger, so don't pull it unless you're going to use it." She nodded in agreement. "One other thing: if I hear you click that safety switch before we have any trouble, I'll shoot you dead where you stand. Capice?"

"Caputo," she answered.

As the sunlight faded, the roar of over fifty motorcycles filled the canyon; their headlights illuminated the road in front as they turned off US Route 212 and entered the camp. They rode in pairs, side by side, like the US Cavalry, their black leather jackets with their club's colors evident on the sleeves and backs as the bikes rumbled into camp. The women rode on the backseats except for the bikes with two women, cleavage and other areas of flesh exposed as much as possible in the chilly evening. They pulled to a stop about 250 feet away and began to occupy at least ten campsites on both sides of the road.

Frank motioned to Gina to sit down and relax, which she did immediately. She kept the M-16 across her lap, right hand on the trigger. Oblivious to the chilled air, Frank for the first time in almost five months pulled off his sweatshirt in public. Then he pulled up the sleeves of his T-shirt to the shoulders and flexed the muscles of both arms, which caused the illusion of a flight of wings. He didn't sit down; instead, he stared intensely at the presumed leader of the pack. In the dim light their eyes locked as he dismounted from the chopped Harley Davidson. He wore shades at night, the gray hair and beard under a red bandana, as he began to walk over toward Frank and Gina. The remainder of the gang hung back and waited to see what would happen. Frank looked at Gina, handed her the MAC-10, and said, "You stay here, and I don't want to hear the safety click off unless I kill him first." He started to walk toward his opponent. Gina saw what the biker couldn't, and that was the outline of his famous Walther PPK against his lower back.

They came within ten feet of one another. Frank's height advantage of almost eight inches was very evident, but the amount of muscle definition on both of them was almost identical. The difference was the tattoos. The fire dragon tattoo on the biker's right arm matched the jacket logo, symbol of the San Jose branch of the Hell's Angels. He smiled as he stood with his arms comfortably at his side. The scar across his right eyebrow ran down his right cheek, the remnants of a knife fight years ago. He wore it as a badge of courage.

"What can I do for you?" Frank asked him without any hint of friendliness.

The biker's smile quickly disappeared. "That's not neighborly," he said.

"I'm not the neighborly type, tend to keep to myself," Frank said flatly. "Like I said, what do you want?" On purpose, Frank crossed his arms across his chest so that the red-tailed hawk's feathers were fully exposed.

The eyes of the Hell's Angel grew wider at the recognition of who he was dealing with, but he would never show any signs of fear in front of his gang. "I wanted to know if I could use your comfortable facilities and take a shit," he said.

"No," Frank said.

"You know we could take anything we wanted; we outnumber you sixty to two," he said threateningly.

"You'd be the first to die, so I don't care," Frank said as he shrugged his shoulders.

"Are you threatening me, you motherfucker?" the biker said and took a step forward. He reached into his pocket, extracted a seven-inch switchblade knife, and snapped it open; the blade sparkled in the residual light.

"I wouldn't do that if you value your life," Frank said, but to no avail as the biker began his bull rush and swung the blade through the air backhanded left to right. Frank calmly watched the arc of the blade, and with perfect timing caught the wrist of the biker's right hand as the knife was held in mid-swing, stopping any attack. Then in a show of brutal force, Frank twisted the arm violently in a clockwise fashion with his left hand, which cracked both the radial and ulnar bones of the forearm. It caused the hand with the knife to be pointed at an ugly ninety-degree angle inward. The biker grunted in pain, but then his eyes widened in fear as Frank broke into a cold smile as he drove the knife home into the biker's epigastric abdominal area and lifted him ten inches off the ground so the point of the knife would slice the left ventricle, which killed him instantly. Frank dropped the body, letting it fall to the ground like a sack of potatoes. He immediately retreated toward his RV as most of the bikers began to rush toward the body.

He caught the MAC-10 from Gina as she unlocked the safety switch; they stood ten feet apart with both rifles pointed at the gang. The bikers charged in spite of the show of force, so Frank unleashed a volley of ten rounds from his gun; the echoes of the gun sounds bounced off the canyon walls as the bullets dropped the front eight bikers. Gina then gave off her own volley of fifteen rounds, which took out another five; the remainder stopped and retreated, quickly leaving the wounded and dead lying untouched. They immediately got on their motorcycles, fired up, and left like they were trying to be the first one out of pit row.

Frank watched them go, but not before he took back his M-16 from Gina. "Good hunting," was all he said to her as he calmly put the weapons away as the roar of the motorcycles faded into the night air. "Obviously we'll need to leave, but we'll leave the fifth wheel behind. So let's load up as much as we can into the truck and bug out."

Within twenty-five minutes, as much food and supplies as they could round up and fit into the GMC Sierra was accomplished. Frank and Gina drove slowly out, with no headlights, the early evening light outlining the bodies strewn across the campsite. The smell of blood was sickening to Gina and she became nauseated. Frank lit up a joint as they pulled back onto US 212 and handed it to Gina after taking a large toke. She did the same; it immediately calmed her nerves and her stomach.

"You did good back there," Frank said with a smile. "You know, there may be a future for you after all," and with that he laughed. "But next time you have to hit more than five with fifteen rounds." He howled with laughter.

Gina didn't laugh or smile. She doubted that she ever would again.

CHAPTER 53

The massacre at Broadus became the story of the day and Phil's worst nightmare. With ten killed and four more critically wounded, the news was bad enough. But with the eyewitness accounts of a man and woman shooting randomly into the rushing crowd of Hell's Angels, the pressure from within was truly unbearable. He wanted to believe that they were firing in self-defense, but the reports that Frank had taunted the leader, coerced him into a fight he could not win, and then finally killed him went against that theory. It was murder, and Gina was just as guilty.

It was 9:00 a.m. the next morning, and Phil and Tim, along with half of the FBI agents in Montana, were at the scene. The dead were still strewn across the campsite road; the stench of dried blood, urine, and stool permeated the area. Phil bent over the body of the leader, the switchblade buried into the lower chest, his right hand still gripping the handle. The forearm was severely deformed, at almost a ninety-degree angle mid-shaft. Phil winced at the amount of pain that must have caused and knew only Frank could be capable of that much strength and skill. The remainder were all gunshot-wound fatalities, all male, all Hell's Angels. If it were a rival gang that did this, then all hell would have broken loose with a war. But he knew better.

It was Frank's message to the entire world not to fuck with him.

"So, what do you think?"

Her voice startled him. He stood up slowly, suddenly felt ten years older, and looked over the carnage. His mind wandered back forty years and five thousand miles away to a small village in Viet Nam. His unit of marines on patrol came across a village that was massacred by the Viet Cong for siding with the enemy. Women and children then, men and women now, but still fueled by the same evil force. That was during war, when civilians were considered collateral damage. Even though these victims were members of a gang of criminals, they still had the basic right to life, which was cut short.

"Frank just upped the ante," Phil said flatly.

"This isn't poker; what's that supposed to mean?" Kelly asked with a bit of anger in her voice.

"It means he doesn't think you can stop him, that he is omnipotent, or that the FBI is a bunch of stupid pussies. Take your pick," Phil said with venom.

The hurt in her eyes could be seen and Phil felt guilty for saying what he did, but he wouldn't back down now. If they had listened to him all of these times, Frank would have been dead and buried by now.

"Gina is no longer considered a victim, and the order has been given for anyone to shoot to kill," Kelly said and stormed away, but not before she raised her left middle finger in salute.

"Boy, Phil, you sure have a way with women," Tim said.

"Fuck her dead ass," Phil growled through clenched teeth.

"What are you going to do about the order concerning Gina?" Tim asked. "You tell me what you want to do, and that's how I'll play it."

"Thanks, Tim. If she poses a threat, do not put yourself in harm's way," Phil said, "but if she's willing to surrender, we do what is morally right. Frank is a different story."

"Like I said before, Phil, I have no problem killing him," Tim said.

They examined the rest of the bodies and examined the RV before deciding to leave. There was nothing more for them to do, so why stay put while Frank and Gina were on the move? The question was where. Tim asked as much.

"We had reports of the two of them visiting Little Bighorn, and then they headed south on US 212 toward South Dakota," Phil said.

"Are you thinking Mt. Rushmore?" Tim asked incredulously.

"That and Crazy Horse Memorial," Phil said emphatically. "That's only twenty miles from Mt. Rushmore, and he's a big American-Indian war nut. The Black Hills are the highest holy ground of many tribes, but especially the Lakota Sioux, and he always told Gina when they were kids that he wanted to see where Sitting Bull and Crazy Horse once lived. Once they find out the identity of the true owners of the RV, they'll have the type of truck Frank is driving, which Fred will feed to me. We'll be that much closer to nailing the son of a bitch."

"Aren't you going to tell them where you are going?" Tim asked.

"Why should I?" Phil asked. "I have already alerted the park rangers at Mt. Rushmore, and I have the backing of the chairman of the Joint Chiefs of Staff."

They both shared a hearty laugh as Tim tossed Phil the keys to his truck. "Since I outrank your sorry ass, it's your turn to drive the beast," he said with a smile.

Phil's eyes lit up like a kid at Christmas and jumped at the opportunity to see what the beast could do. They slowly pulled away from the hideous scene; Phil steered the truck away from the crime scene and Kelly. Then they laughed all of the way to the main highway. The last thing Kelly saw was arms that hung out of their respective windows as they both gave her the one-finger salute as they left.

CHAPTER 54

Frank and Gina drove slowly through the small downtown main street of Hill City, and the first thing they noticed besides the small boutique shops and the multitude of Harley Davidson motorcycles was the increased presence of law-enforcement vehicles of all types. Gina drove the speed limit, while Frank sat extremely low in the passenger seat and surveyed the entire scene. His instincts had told him before entering the city to allow Gina to drive while he hid. Unless they had already discovered the make of the Canadians' truck, there was no way to recognize Gina in her old lady's outfit. But he knew that any plans to go to either Mt. Rushmore or Crazy Horse Memorial were out of the question. He remembered the area well, so he immediately formulated a new plan.

"Once we get through Hill City, you'll pass by Harney Peak, the tallest mountain in South Dakota. It's on the right side," Frank said without sitting up or looking at Gina. "About half a mile after the sign for Harney Peak, you'll see a right-hand turn that is a hard-packed dirt road. Take a right onto that road and drive about a mile, then pull over. I'll take it from there."

Gina gave a thumbs-up sign under the dashboard so as not to speak. No one really paid any attention to her at all as she calmly drove through the picturesque town in the middle of the Black Hills of South Dakota. After five nail-biting minutes, they exited the town and headed south, away from Mt. Rushmore. Within five minutes Harney's Peak could be seen, and then came the sign that designated the height of Harney's Peak, 7,242 feet. Within half a mile Frank said, "Right there," and Gina turned onto the narrow hard-packed dirt road that appeared to travel for miles.

"Where are we heading?" Gina asked as she pulled over after the first mile. They quickly exchanged seats, with Frank taking over the wheel. He threw the gear box into four-wheel-drive and took off.

"Bear Mountain Lookout," Frank said. "Way up in the hills away from civilization, where we'll disappear for a while. There's a fire station that is now abandoned due to federal budget cuts. God bless the US government for supplying us with such nice gifts." They shared a good laugh.

They had enough food and water to last about two weeks since nothing they had was truly perishable. There would be enough small game to hunt if they craved any meat. If the circumstances were right, Gina could always go shopping as the old lady. But Frank still didn't totally trust her, even with her recent killing spree.

The area was absolutely gorgeous; the deep blue skies contrasted against the pine tree-covered, dark-soiled mountains were a photographer's dream. Frank would love to see the area in the spring, when all of the wildflowers first bloomed after the winter thaw. The road was bumpy, but the Sierra handled it well, which impressed Frank. They began the climb in elevation from 1,150 feet at the turnoff to about five thousand feet where the lookout was located. The temperature dropped about five degrees as they neared their destination.

Just as Frank remembered, at mile marker 4.5 miles, the turnoff to the fire lookout was on the right, but a chained US Forest Service road barrier extended across the gate entrance. Frank stopped the truck and got a large bolt cutter out of his trusty tool chest, quickly disabled the chains, and opened up the gate. They drove about another half mile on switchback roads as they climbed another five hundred feet to the lookout and residence. It was a one-bedroom, one-bathroom, nine-hundred-square-foot cabin. Frank slowly pulled the truck up to the front and stopped. He rolled down the window and shut off the engine. The car filled instantly with the chilled air full of a pine-scented aroma with the peace and quiet of a deep forest, except for the sounds of nature. Frank took it all in while he scanned the area for any signs of human inhabitants, but found none.

Not trusting anyone, Frank opened the truck's console and removed his Walther PPK. He slowly opened the truck door as Gina looked at him for instructions. He put his finger to his lips to encourage silence, then signaled for her to stay put as he investigated the premises. He slowly moved past the truck, looked at the few windows available, which were all covered with shades, and heard no movement from behind. The house was your typical square shape, with a chimney in the center of the structure, which probably indicated wood heat. Like all other US Forest Service structures, it was painted a pale putrid green, even the doors and window frames. Frank slowly walked around the entire structure and found a large propane tank in the back, hopefully still with gas so he wouldn't have to burn any wood. The heat and smoke could be picked up by satellites or local yokels. Satisfied that there were no human beings besides themselves present, he walked up to the front door and tried the handle, which was locked. He reached into his pocket, pulled out his own special Swiss Army knife, and opened up the skeleton key. He inserted the tool into the door handle's lock and quickly heard the tumblers click as he turned the key; the handle turned, and he opened the door slowly. Bent down in a squat, gun held out in front, he slowly made his way into the house.

As he entered, he noticed the small kitchen to the left, dining area to the right. In the center of the house was the metal, round, wood-burning fireplace, with a small living area in the back left corner and the bedroom/bathroom to the right. The furniture was simple, with a small wooden table and chairs, small two-seat coach, and metal frame queen-size bed. He walked around and noticed the spiderwebs and dust, but no signs of recent inhabitants. He found the light switch on the far right wall and flicked all of the switches. Within seconds, the rooms filled with standard fluorescent light, which magnified the dust and cobwebs. He walked back to the front door and waved for Gina to enter.

He found the thermostat to the heater unit on the far left wall in the living room and turned it up to seventy degrees. The current reading of fifty-two degrees was too uncomfortable for his liking. Within thirty seconds he heard the rush of the propane gas as the electric pilot light clicked ten times and ignited the furnace. The blower kicked on another thirty seconds later as the fan began to circulate the air. Within another forty-five seconds came the smell of a heater first being fired up after being shut down for a while. Frank smiled as he realized how stupid the government was to leave the power on and propane tank with gas after they closed the station, but that was not unusual. Gina finally entered, brought her suitcases with her, and dropped them on the kitchen/dining room floor. She looked around and said, "This is quaint."

"I'm going to go outside and start unloading the rest of the shit. See if you can start cleaning up after putting your gear away," Frank said flatly as he turned and went back out the front door. Once outside he looked around quickly and noticed that he had almost a complete 360-degree view of the surrounding area for miles. The old wooden fire lookout tower stood above the trees approximately two hundred yards away to his left, which would be a perfect spot to hang out while awaiting any approach by the task force. His binoculars had a three hundred-meter zoom capability, so he could see the hair growing on a fly's ass at three miles. He felt as secure as he could be as he began the arduous task of unloading, as the late George Carlin called it, "all your stuff."

Suddenly a rustle in the underbrush to the right startled Frank. He immediately pulled the Walther PPK out of his waistband and held it pointed at the area where the noise emanated from. To his surprise, a mother white-tailed deer and her young fawn emerged from the forest. Frank immediately lowered his gun as he stared at the pair of beautiful animals, who both stood at attention and stared back. For about a minute, the staring contest continued until the mother realized Frank was no threat and she nudged her offspring, who began eating some of the vegetation at the base of the large pine trees. Both of their heads bent down, grabbed luscious young leaves off of wild succulents, and chewed slowly while they kept one eye on Frank. He smiled, put the gun slowly away, and began to unload the truck.

Killing humans was easy and at times necessary, but harming a beautiful, innocent, and peaceful animal unless hunted for food was taboo.

CHAPTER 55

After discussion, Phil and Tim had decided to take Interstate 90 instead of the smaller two lane routes in an attempt to get to Mt. Rushmore as quickly as possible and intercept Frank and Gina. They stood in the overflowing parking lot and scanned the crowd. People passed by, oblivious of their surveillance as the sight of the four presidents carved into the granite mountainside captured each one of them in a momentary state of shock and awe. It had the same effect on Phil and Tim when they had first arrived four hours prior. Phil vaguely remembered the first time he had been there as a young boy of nine on the way to Yellowstone National Park with his parents and older brother. He admired his parents, his father an insurance agent, his mother a secretary, who both sacrificed their own necessities to save up for a yearly trip to one of the national parks. That year, the four of them had crammed into a 1963 yellow Volkswagen Beetle for the trek across the country to Wyoming from the Bronx and back. All in two weeks, with his father chain-smoking Lucky Strikes and his brother farting every chance he could.

There had been no sighting of Frank and Gina. No one even close to their description had been seen within one hundred miles of the iconic sculpture. Their last known whereabouts had been at Little Bighorn Battlefield the day before. Phil and Tim had missed them by about eight hours, but there was one park ranger who remembered a couple that matched the description of a large man with a much smaller woman. They had been at the memorial when it had first opened in the morning. She couldn't see their faces due to their having worn sunglasses and hoodies, but the largeness of Frank was unmistakable. It had appeared to the ranger that Frank had acted like he had been there before and guided Gina around before they quickly left in a pickup, type unknown, that pulled an Airstream. The vehicles had Montana plates, but she could not recall the numbers. Phil had called in their findings to Fred, who relayed the information and also requested any surveillance footage from local/state agencies near the national park.

They also waited for the identity of the two older victims found buried in the grave, but so far no fingerprints matched with any known US citizens. The search had been expanded through Interpol.

So they waited and watched.

By 2:00 p.m. they both knew their surveillance was futile and that Frank and Gina had altered their plans. Tim was the first to acknowledge the fact. "They're not coming, Phil," he said out of nowhere. "Just the timing from when they left Little Bighorn is way off by now."

"I agree, but didn't want to admit the truth," Phil said dejectedly. He also knew that he would have to admit the same to Kelly. At this point in their pursuit, Phil found himself more afraid to communicate with her than to face Frank in a firefight.

As if Tim read his mind, he said, "You don't have to admit fault to anyone; fuck 'em all."

Phil looked at his newfound best friend and smiled. Just then his phone buzzed, and he saw it was Fred calling. "Sometimes I think my phone is bugged," Phil said with a chuckle.

"It is," Tim said seriously.

"Thanks a lot," Phil answered. "Hey, Fred, what's up?"

"I have good news and bad news. First, we found the Airstream abandoned about one hundred miles from Little Bighorn," Fred began. "We ran the VIN number and discovered the RV to be owned by a Sean Mulligan of Vancouver, British Columbia."

"They're Canadians?" Phil asked.

"Yep, bought the fifth wheel in 1972, and according to the field tech, looks brand-new," Fred said. "It was cleaned out of any supplies."

"What's the bad news?" Phil was afraid to ask.

"Mr. Mulligan didn't own a pickup truck and didn't rent one, so we think he borrowed a friend's or family member's truck to pull the fifth wheel," Fred concluded.

"Shit," Phil said. "The witness at Little Bighorn said they had Montana plates, which means he stole a set or someone else is dead. So we are back to square one."

"Pretty much," Fred replied. "What do you want me to inform Herr Flaherty?"

"That I was informed and acknowledged your findings," Phil said, heeding Tim's advice; Tim gave a thumbs-up in the background.

"She's flying up to your area tomorrow," Fred said.

"Fuck," was all Phil could say.

"Yes, we are," Fred said and hung up.

Phil proceeded to explain the situation to Tim and waited while Tim scratched his three-day stubble of a beard as the wheels turned in his head. "If he dumped the Airstream and he didn't show up here in the normal amount of time, then we have to assume that he's holed up somewhere in between."

"Those were my thoughts exactly," Phil said.

"Would he double back, or change course and head somewhere else?" Tim asked.

"Not immediately," Phil replied. "His pattern is to find a safe house, settle for a period of time, usually a week to ten days, before moving on again. In the interim, he'll change his appearance if necessary, confiscate different modes of transportation if necessary, and live off what supplies he has plus what he can take from Mother Nature."

Tim was quiet for a minute as he digested what Phil had just said. He reached inside his truck, opened up the console, and retrieved another perfectly folded and encased topographic map. He quickly unfolded it and spread the states of Montana, Wyoming, and South Dakota across the hood of the truck. Phil just stood back and smiled as he watched Tim trace a finger from Little Bighorn to where they were now, his eyes focused like a lion on its prey before it would pounce. Finally he said, "He's definitely in the Black Hills. It's the only place rugged enough between Little Bighorn and here that could hide them, especially with everything else flat farmland with little cover."

"What's the symbol that looks like a guardhouse, and why are some of them colored green?" Phil asked, since Tim's maps were so much more detailed than any he had ever seen.

"Those are lookout towers for fire spotting in hard-to-get-to places, especially with forest fires started by lightning strikes. The tan ones are to designate towers alone, while the green ones have living quarters attached," Tim replied. "Most of them have been closed due to federal budget cuts."

They both reacted with instant recognition at the completion of Tim's answer; they knew where Frank and Gina were probably hidden at this time. "How many green ones are there?" Phil asked.

Tim did a quick count and replied, "Eight."

Phil took out his cell phone and speed dialed Fred, who answered on the first ring. "You have something?"

"If you look at a detailed map of the Black Hills, you will see eight fire towers with residential quarters nearby spread through the mountains. He's hiding in one of those, and I'll put my pension up for collateral on any bet," Phil said, "but we can't just drive up and knock on the door. I would send a reconnaissance chopper from Rapid City up into the hills and scout every one of those eight to make sure there are no unwanted tenants."

"I'll clear it with your friend and mine; call you back when I hear," Fred said and was gone.

"I gotta piss like a racehorse before the Kentucky Derby," Tim said, "and the prostate isn't making me a comfortable lookout."

Phil laughed, then said, "Get the hell outta here before I have to explain why an admiral pissed on himself." Tim ran like a jackrabbit to one of the seven blue Porta Potties lined up near the ticket stands, and as his luck would have it, all were occupied. He waited patiently while doing an Irish jig in the lead spot on line for the next vacant stall. As soon as the handle on the far one began to turn, Tim sprinted like an Olympic athlete, pushed his way past a startled priest as he exited the portable bathroom, and closed the door behind him. His cry of relief as the urine stream passed could be heard from where Phil stood, who proceeded to laugh so hard that he almost lost control of his own bladder.

Just then, his phone buzzed again. He saw it was Fred and answered immediately. "We have a go for your idea, and it will be done either later this afternoon or early tomorrow," Fred said.

"We can't wait until tomorrow," Phil said, exasperated again at the delay tactics.

"She said you would say that," Fred said.

"Oh, yeah? What else did she say?" Phil asked with a New York edge in his voice that sounded like Tony Soprano.

"That you wouldn't take no for an answer," Fred replied.

"Hum, anything else?" Phil asked with a grunt.

"I don't speak Gaelic," Fred said, the implication clear.

"*Testa di minghia* (dickhead)," Phil said.

"I don't speak Italian either," Fred said and hung up.

Tim returned with a bounce in his step, and Phil didn't have the heart to tell him that everyone heard his cries of relief. "They're going to send up a helicopter either today or tomorrow," Phil informed him.

"Tomorrow? Fucking assholes. Don't they know anything about rapid response?" Tim finally asked.

"They are probably waiting for Queen Flaherty to arrive so she could prove me wrong firsthand," Phil said with a bit of dejection.

"Nah," Tim said. "Knowing the way things are going, something unexpected is going to happen because they won't listen to reason, and you'll be blamed."

"Now who's being cynical?" Phil said as they both shared another laugh.

"Let's go get a beer," Tim said. "Nothing bad is going to happen until tomorrow."

What Tim didn't realize at that point of time was how prophetic his last statement would prove to be.

CHAPTER 56

Frank and Gina finished unloading and cleaning their new residence just in time to fall asleep exhausted. Frank awakened earlier than Gina and brewed some coffee. Filled with the savory brown liquid, along with powdered creamer and sugar, he took his travel mug outside and immediately felt the morning chill, which awakened him quicker than the caffeine jolt. The first order of business was to set up security and guard the perimeters. To that end he went to the bed of his truck and took out the canvas bag that held his 50 caliber rifle with its stand and another bag with other assorted weapons. He trudged his way along the path toward the lookout tower. Since it was now overgrown with weeds, he was poked by thorns on both legs and arms. He reached the tower in about ten minutes, looked up and down at the fifty-foot wooden structure, and inspected for any rot or undue wear that would make it unsteady under his weight. After that was completed, he began the climb up the narrow exterior ladder as he balanced the weapon-filled bags over his shoulder. When he reached the tower, he held onto the ladder as he lowered both bags gently to the floor, then climbed over the edge himself.

The view was absolutely breathtaking.

He stood surrounded by a thick forest of mighty green pines that covered all of the mountains and hills; the early morning sun glistened off the dew as he stood and marveled at the sight for almost fifteen minutes before he set up his arsenal. He placed the 50 caliber rifle and its tripod on the eastern section, which faced Hill City. He opened up the other bag and removed his M-16 and multiple long- and short-range Italian sniper rifles that he had used multiple times, along with plenty of ammunition. Pleased with the armory, he shimmied back down the ladder, back through the path to his truck, and pulled out his canvas chair, telescope, and binoculars, then made his way back to and up the tower. The next few days would be for reconnaissance during the day. He had figured that any attack would occur sooner, rather than later. The longer he remained isolated, the less likely they knew where he was, thereby allowing him to plan an eventual successful escape.

Gina, on the other hand, was in charge of all of the domestic chores. She had found cleaning supplies and equipment under the kitchen sink and made her way gradually around the entire house until it was spotless. The cleaning was therapeutic for her: the familiar smell of chlorine bleach and other antiseptics caused a wave of nostalgia for her nursing days. She scrubbed until her fingers cramped, then she scrubbed again. Finally after five hours, she stopped and looked around, pleased with her work. She decided it was time to visit Frank. She changed into her outdoor clothing, made her way out the front door, and called to Frank, warning him of her intentions. She heard him say, "Come on up," as she made her way to the path's opening. She climbed gingerly up the ladder and tried not to look down, which would induce her acrophobia. The climb was well worth it, as the beauty of the Black Hills was displayed out in front of her. Her first reaction was identical to Frank's as she stood gazing all around with the look of awe.

"Beautiful, isn't it?" Frank asked. "Now you can see why the Native Americans consider this area such high holy ground. The earth is dark and fertile, with plenty of natural minerals, and Mother Nature added a few of her own brushstrokes," he said and extended his arms out in display.

Gina looked at him with amazement. Here standing before her was a killer without a conscience, yet a friend to nature. He displayed true remorse to her after he initiated the Idaho fire, and now this made her realize the complexity of this man in his own twisted way.

"Shhh…" Frank said as he concentrated, turning his left ear toward the east and closing his eyes. "Helicopter," he said, handing her the binoculars as he turned the telescope in that direction. Gina didn't hear anything at first, but then faintly made out the distant rhythmic thumping of the chopper's blades. Frank pointed at the shape as it now appeared to be about five miles away, closing fast and flying just above the tree line. They both viewed it at the same time, and Frank realized that it was a reconnaissance helicopter. "They're looking for us," Frank said and pushed the telescope aside as he scrambled to his 50 caliber rifle, positioned it to point eastward, and released the safety. Gina instinctively bent down to hide and peered over the edge of the lookout tower as the bird approached their position. As she looked through the binoculars, she saw the pilot and three passengers, with the front passenger looking back at the tower with his binoculars. She didn't see her Uncle Phil.

Frank watched the helicopter pass over a distant foothill from his own crouched position, then immediately locked the sight of his scope on the front end of the chopper. When it was about half a mile out, he squeezed the trigger; the explosion caused Gina to cover her ears as the whole tower shook. Frank watched with absolute joy as the bullet struck the rotor and shattered the housing. The helicopter immediately went into a vicious death spiral as the pilot desperately tried to gain control of the aircraft with futility. It finally crashed into the thick pine tree forest, which caused the helicopter to disintegrate upon impact and it fell to the ground in multiple shattered pieces. Frank stood up and did his famous dance with his war whoop, which scared the hell out of Gina, again.

As he looked again through the telescope, Frank saw the debris, with human body parts scattered with the fragments of the chopper. He stood up and looked squarely at Gina. "Your uncle wasn't aboard," Frank said. "I would have felt his death."

Gina looked at him and asked, "What do we do now?"

"Nothing, until somebody comes looking," Frank replied. "With the amount of wreckage, it will take months to figure out the cause of the crash. With the rapidity of the crash, I doubt the pilot could get off a Mayday while he tried to fight the aircraft's descent. Plus we have the advantage as far as having the higher ground to defend, in case it comes to that."

Gina knew it would come to that and that he would defend himself to the death. Her fate, however, was already deemed expendable.

She then decided that the good-wife routine would finally come to an end; she felt the rebirth of the confidence to finally kill Frank. What Frank hadn't realized was that he had taught her to kill, almost to the point of pure enjoyment on her part. She also had no further fear of herself dying, as a feeling of serenity appeared within at the moment of her decision. Frank's death would be her own salvation.

CHAPTER 57

The identities of the Canadian couple were finally confirmed from the Canadian Ministry of Records. The Royal Mounted Canadian police further investigated the origins of the pickup truck. It turned out to be the son's GMC Sierra that he had let his parents borrow for their dream vacation all over the western United States. Now their deaths became his nightmare. The phone interview with the son almost tore a hole out of Phil's heart, but gave him valuable information, such as the truck had a Lojack unit on board in case it were stolen.

But it appeared that Frank also knew about the unit because when it was activated, the GPS settings led them back to the Airstream, where it was found attached to the undercarriage. Again Frank was one step ahead of everybody, which infuriated Phil even further.

There had been no sightings of Frank and Gina at either Mt. Rushmore or the Crazy Horse Memorial. The task force was under the impression that Frank had already crossed over into Canada, probably through back roads. Phil still thought otherwise. He figured Frank to be holed up somewhere in the Black Hills. Phil was holed up in a Motel 8 in Rapid City, South Dakota, and studied the topographical map that Tim had pulled from his map portfolio. He saw nothing but extremely rugged terrain, with plenty of valleys in between mountains and forests thick with pine trees.

"What do you think?" Phil asked Tim as he walked out of the bathroom. "Where would you go if you wanted to hide?"

"What's his pattern like?" Tim asked. "How does he like to position himself, for starters?"

"Usually isolated, taking the defensive high-ground position, with the ability to have a clear view of his surroundings while being hidden at the same time," Phil said. "He often settles in one position for a while to wait out the enemy, and is always one step ahead, moving instinctively at the whisper of trouble."

"True sniper/assassin mentality," Tim said. "He was taught well."

"Only by the best marines in the entire corps," Phil said with jaded pride. "He was severely verbally abused by his mother as a child. She was a lush and a slut, who probably caused his father's heart attack at a young age of forty-two when Frank was about ten. With his father's death, her verbal assaults became physical. However, she didn't count on him growing to be over six feet tall by the age of thirteen, at which time he killed his mother. Her body was never found. He was acquitted. My partner and I were the arresting officers at the time. He went on to murder my partner on the steps of our precinct house with a 50 caliber rifle from a mile away. He was on active duty with the corps at the time. I've been after that motherfucker ever since. He went on to become a paid assassin, then a serial killer by the names of East and West Coast Slayer."

The look on Tim's face was one of amazement as he shook his head. "How a mother can truly fuck up her own child is beyond my understanding," he said. "My wife and I may be divorced, but I was always close to my kids, just like you," he continued as Phil nodded in agreement. "This dude's pissed off at the world and could eclipse the number killed by any serial killer."

"He probably already has," Phil said. "He has this total-body tattoo of a red-tailed hawk, with each feather representing a killing. Gina says it was over 150, and that was before his massive killing spree."

Tim shook his head again as he took a portable magnifying glass out of his map portfolio. He leaned over the map and carefully studied it before he stood and pointed at a spot. "Bear Mountain Fire Lookout," Tim said. "Easy access by hard-packed dirt road, part of the US Forest Service system."

"How far is that from here?" Phil asked.

"Thirty-five to forty miles through Hill City," Tim said with a gleam in his eye. "If we're going in, we better study the layout and plan something, or he'll pick us off like ducks at a bazaar."

"I agree…" but before he could answer fully, Phil's cell phone buzzed on the dresser. He went over, picked it up, scanned the screen, and looked puzzled at the name of

Anthony Balducci. "Lefty, what a surprise. What did I do now?" Phil asked sarcastically.

"If it wasn't at this time, I'd hang you for that remark," Tony said quietly.

Phil knew Tony like a book, and his tone meant nothing good. His stomach began to gnaw as he asked, "What happened?"

"We lost a helicopter over the Black Hills today, mechanical failure they assume," Tony said. Phil's heart began to pound in his chest as Tony said, "And there were no survivors. One of them was Kelly, Phil; I'm so, so sorry."

Phil's hand began to shake as he tried to hold the phone steady; his mind exploded in thirty different directions as the shock of the news hit him. The entire world disappeared into a montage of images that faded before him. His knees weakened, and he began to go down as an iron hand grabbed him under the armpit and eased him down to sit on the edge of the bed. His eyes sought out Tim's as he tried to focus, and finally mumbled, "Where did it happen?"

"Near a place called Medicine Mountain," Tony said. "If there's anything I can do…"

"Thanks, Tony, but no. You've done enough," Phil said and hung up.

"Who and what?" Tim asked without mincing words.

"Kelly was killed in a chopper crash, probably mechanical, near Medicine Hat Mountain in the Black Hills," Phil said as he stared off into space.

Tim looked at the map and said, "Medicine Hat is a mile from Bear Mountain."

Phil leaped up off the bed and spun around to look at where Tim was pointing. "Motherfucker shot her down, didn't he?" he said, breathing hard with anger.

Tim just nodded his head in agreement. "Time to go kill Lucifer," he said.

"Let's get packed and ready; we'll go at night," Phil said. "I can get any nighttime equipment we need."

"I agree. Let's just hope our mutual adversary isn't equipped with the same," Tim said.

Phil knew Frank did have nighttime equipment, but didn't care at this point of time. His life had been one suicide mission after another, so why stop now? With Kelly's death, there was no longer any fear of him dying. In fact, he was beginning to welcome the thought.

CHAPTER 58

The arrival of the proper equipment to conduct a nighttime raid on the tower was delayed, but had finally arrived. So they decided to delay the mission until early morning, just before sunrise. Phil lay in his bed and stared at the ceiling as the red digital numbers on the room's alarm clock marched slowly forward. With the death of Kelly and the possibility of his own demise, the darkened room gave him plenty of time for inner reflection. His thoughts wandered to and from the different periods of his life, taking inventory of his failed marriage and the realization that it was half his fault, especially after the murder of his partner. He had put his career ahead of his family. He made up for it with his kids, and he was proud of the father he had turned out to be, still very close with them to this day. He had tried to correct some of his flaws as pointed out by his ex-wife and the marriage counselor, but could not change his personality.

He shifted his body as the aches and pains in his fifty-eight-year-old body started to do their regular nighttime appearance. Thirty-five years as a law enforcement officer after leaving the Marine Corps had taken a toll on his life, both physically and mentally. He knew he could take no more after this was over, even if he survived. The loss of Kelly was the icing on the cake. Even though their relationship had soured, he still had deep feelings for her. It truly bothered him that he never had a chance to develop a relationship away from work. Now he would never know, and that bothered him even more. His Catholic upbringing made him feel guilty for repeating the same mistakes that occurred in all of his relationships. The thought of eternal loneliness frightened him deeply. To counter his fear, he thought of retirement, which brought him solace. The thought of sleeping in every morning had true appeal at this stage of his life.

His thoughts were interrupted by the vibration of his cell phone. A text from Tim asked if he was awake. Obviously he hadn't slept either. Phil replied no and asked Tim if he wanted to meet him in his room to discuss tactics before departing.

Their meeting was brief, since they had had plenty of time to plan the mission. Tim wanted to explain the proper usage of the equipment so there were no mistakes made. They were supplied with not only night-vision goggles and binoculars, but also heat-sensing radar, up to a mile away, which they hoped would give them the advantage necessary to finally take Frank down without losing their own lives. Tim's explanation took all of five minutes, and they were packed and on the road within fifteen.

From their hotel they went south on US Route 16, which was empty at 3:30 a.m. There was a new moon tonight, so the stars and planets were shining brightly in the night sky. The Milky Way's fluffy appearance was clearly evident, and it appeared much closer to Phil than when he saw the same in Southern California's deserts. Thinking of that made him homesick and angry that he was still in pursuit of the worst serial killer known, without any success.

They rolled through downtown Hill City and saw nothing but empty streets, with almost all of the inhabitants tucked away in their cozy beds. The only people out would be criminals and law enforcement between 3:00 and 4:30 a.m., and tonight they saw neither. Their plan was to reach their staging point, at which time they would abandon the truck and make their way on foot by 5:00 a.m. They were twenty minutes ahead of schedule. Within ten minutes they turned onto the hard-packed dirt road that would take them up to Bear Mountain Fire Lookout. They would shut down any lights when they were within five miles of the station and drive with night-vision goggles only. They would park the truck a mile out and hike in the rest of the way. Tim was convinced they would be able to surprise Frank and neutralize him with little effort if the mission were timed right.

Knowing Frank as well as he did, Phil was much more skeptical of not only their chances of success, but also of survival.

Frank's instincts told him that the most logical time for any offensive would be early morning. It was simple military training that was always popular, from World War

II through the Iraq war of 2003. To strike at the darkest point of the day would aid in any type of camouflage and serve as the primary reason for the attack, with the added bonus of human nature's need for sleep by that time. He also calculated that the strike force would be small in number. Probably Special Operations such as Delta Force or Navy SEALs would be enlisted. His own military training prepared him for every scenario. His ego, however, welcomed the battle to prove his superiority.

He had decided to stand guard all night and spend it in the lookout. He had prepared the necessary supplies of coffee and blankets to help keep him warm and stay awake, with his own nighttime equipment, which included a nighttime telescope with thirty-mile zoom capability. Knowing any attack would come from the east, he had focused the scope in that direction. He followed every vehicle to and from Hill City, waiting for any sign of movement toward his position. Coming up on 4:20 a.m., there had been none noted. He stood and stretched and walked around a few minutes to get the blood circulating as the temperature dropped to about thirty-five degrees. Luckily there was no wind, so with enough layers of clothes and blankets, he was still quite warm. He went to his thermos and poured another cup of his strong coffee, which was still hot and smelled fresh.

He sat back down and focused the telescope on a vehicle that drove south on US Route 16 about five miles south of Hill City. He could make it out to be a pickup truck, but could not see any identification or how many occupants there were. What he was more concerned about was its direction. The truck continued to travel southbound at a leisurely speed and was the only vehicle to be seen for almost twenty miles. Then it suddenly slowed down and made a right-hand turn.

Onto the dirt road that would lead to his position.

He smiled and took a slow sip of coffee. If they were militarily trained, they would cut their lights at least five miles away and travel on night-vision equipment. If they were local yokels, they would announce their presence with lights blazing, thinking this was Hollywood and they were shooting an action movie. He carefully followed the truck as it traveled through the valley on a westward course. He reached over and removed the tarp from his 50 caliber rifle and tripod stand. He looked back toward the truck, and he suddenly knew what to expect.

The lights flicked off, but the vehicle hadn't stopped.

To follow the truck better, he switched the sensors on the scope to track anything that produced heat. The truck began the slow arduous climb up the dirt road, made slower by relying on night-vision equipment instead of good old-fashioned headlights. Frank removed the scope from its stand and attached it to a specially made part of his 50 caliber rifle. He flicked off the safety switch, put in his soft earplugs, and turned his San Francisco Giants cap backward before he settled into his one-knee shooting position with a pillow under his right knee. He felt very comfortable, drew a few slow deep breaths as he slowed his heart rate down, and refocused on the truck engine's heat. The scope's digital read indicated the truck was still over three miles out, so he followed the truck's path as it continued its slow climb. His breathing was now slow and steady, with a heart rate of fifty-five beats per minute, as he settled his right index finger lightly against the trigger. When the scope read two miles, he cranked his neck and head in a counterclockwise rotation until the customary pop occurred. Then he settled his right eye on the scope. When the truck reached exactly one and one half miles, he squeezed the trigger.

The blast echoed through the mountains and valleys, which caused sleeping birds to awaken and scramble from their respective nests with the sound of the fluttering of their wings and squawks of complaint. In spite of the tripod and the three-inch padding at the butt end of the rifle, his shoulder still felt the massive kick with the resultant pain, which was momentary. The truck came to a dead halt. He put a second shot through the center of the truck's windshield. Within a matter of seconds, both doors opened, and he saw two men scramble quickly out of the vehicle and dive behind the tail end of the truck.

Frank relaxed his trigger finger and smiled at the results. He continued to watch carefully through the scope and saw no movement from behind the truck, with both men still well-hidden. He wished he could be a fly on the tailgate of the truck and listen to their conversation right now. They would quickly devise some form of plan where there would be a decoy or diversion so one member was sure to survive and thereby continue the mission to fruition. But which one would be the sacrificial lamb?

It didn't matter because he would only wait five minutes before he shot at the gas tank and kill both of them. He would be disappointed if he couldn't kill them one by one and get in some long-range practice at the same time, but a good explosion would be a blast. He smiled at the pun and relaxed, took a sip of coffee, refocused on the scope, and continued his game of *Nighthawk*.

CHAPTER 59

They both heard the recoil of the rifle in the distance, followed by a horrible thud that shook the truck. This was followed by a violent rattling from under the hood, then total silence as the truck came to a sudden halt as it died. Tim and Phil looked at each other in total shock, which was displaced by fear as they heard the second shot, followed by a shattering of glass as a hole was blasted out of the center of the windshield. "Let's get the fuck out of here," Phil screamed as they grabbed their rifles, opened their respective doors, and dove for the back end of the truck, each crawling as rapidly as possible. They reached the safety of the tailgate and gasped for air.

"What the fuck did we just get hit with?" Tim asked.

"Probably the same 50 caliber rifle that took out all of those people in Southern California," Phil said in between rapid breaths as he leaned his back against the bumper, knees pulled up in a ball, helping him to inhale deeper, and contracted a potential target. Tim did the same.

"Obviously he has a night-vision scope, also probably heat-seeking like ours," Tim said.

"Obviously," Phil said slightly sarcastically. "Well, admiral, what next?"

"Why hasn't he shot again?" Tim asked.

"He's waiting for us to make the next move," Phil said. "With his position he can pick us off as soon as we move." They each looked around and saw dense forests that lined each side of the road they traveled on, but the closest trees were more than fifty feet away.

"If we both take off at the same time on a zigzag path to the trees, he may be able to only pick off one of us," Tim said.

Phil looked at Tim and said, "Unfortunately, that may be our only option."

"I suggest we wait him out," Tim said. "He can't stay focused without taking a break, which would help us tremendously."

"I agree, but how long do we wait?" Phil asked. "It will be dawn pretty soon, and he doesn't need natural daylight to help make the shot easier."

Tim looked at his watch and said, "We still have over an hour until sunup, so I figure we should wait at least a half hour." Phil didn't say anything because he had a feeling that Frank wouldn't wait that long. "We should call for backup. Do you have your cell phone with you; mine is still in the…"

The recoil was again heard, but this time the bullet struck the left side of the truck near the rear quarter panel, which caused the truck to briefly rock to the right. "Shit, he's trying to hit the gas tank," Phil screamed. "We have to get the fuck out of here, or he's going to blow us up. Follow me."

Phil bellied down and began to quickly crawl away from the truck, but at an angle toward the trees so as to keep the truck between them and Frank. Tim quickly followed. They were only twenty-five feet away when a second shot was heard; the ensuing concussion from the explosion of the truck lifted both of them off the ground and hurtled them into the underbrush. Dazed and battered but alive, Phil heard the war whoop in the distance. He slowly raised his head out of the thick green groundcover but was blinded by the sight of the burning truck. He got a quick bearing of his surroundings, grabbed his rifle, and began to slowly crawl backward, using the thick foliage as camouflage. He sustained cuts and scrapes as he inched backward, and it took him an agonizing ten minutes to reach the safety of the forest. He finally sat up and leaned against a massive pine tree's trunk, finally safe from Frank's deadly aim; he took inventory of his injuries as the adrenaline began to wear off and the pain settled in.

He softly called out, "Tim, hey, Tim, can you hear me?"

The only sound that could be heard was the dull roar of the dying flames of the burning truck. His night-vision goggles had flown off his head at the time of the blast, which meant he was basically reduced to being able to see from the light of the fire but no farther. It had reached the darkest point of the night. Phil also realized that if he tried to run, his shadow would be seen moving in the glare of the fire and Frank would have a perfect target. Contrary to what Tim thought, Frank never tired looking through a scope, and Phil didn't want to take the chance. He checked his pocket for his cell phone, only to find the pocket empty. Now he had no choice but to wait before trying to advance on Frank. He had already decided that if he had to advance during the daylight hours, he would. At this point, he didn't care. All he wanted to do was to kill Frank. He closed his eyes, and the post-adrenaline crash caused him to immediately fall asleep.

The rifle blast awakened Gina instantly. She threw the blankets off of her, immediately rose out of the bed, and went to the window facing the lookout tower. She arrived in time to witness the flash and blast of the second shot. She got dressed as quickly as possible, rushed outside, and stopped as the cold air hit her like a brick. She ran back into the cabin and retrieved her coat and gloves. She began to make her way toward the tower when the third and fourth shots rang out, followed by an explosion off in the distance in the valley below. She stopped frozen at the sound of the war whoop in fear, with the first thought that it was her uncle that was just killed. She broke into a full run and made her way to the lookout, screaming at Frank as she approached, "Frank, it's me, Frank, it's me." As she made her way up the ladder, she felt Frank's massive hand grab her under her right shoulder and hoist her onto the deck of the lookout.

"Fucking amateurs thought they could outfox me, but now they're toast," Frank said with a glint in his eyes.

"Who was it?" Gina asked.

"I don't know, and I don't care," Frank said. "If you're worried about your precious uncle, I don't think it was him."

His snarl scared her, and she worried that she had pushed the wrong buttons.

"To tell you the truth, I hope it wasn't him because I want to look into his eyes when I do kill him," he said. "There's nothing more here for you, so why don't you go back to bed." It was more of an order than a suggestion, so Gina lowered her head and quietly left the lookout tower and went back inside the house.

Frank looked back through his night scope and saw the flames almost completely extinguished. Looking about twenty-five feet to the left of the burning structure, he saw a body prone in the underbrush wearing fatigues. He studied the shape for almost five minutes and saw no movement, no sign of breathing either. He could not see the face, which was buried by the plants, so he couldn't tell who it was. He thought about putting another bullet through the lifeless body but thought the better of it, so as not to waste any more rounds than necessary. He didn't see the other body, which was disconcerting. He carefully studied the surrounding areas but could not find any other signs of life. Satisfied with what he saw, Frank turned the scope back toward the highway but saw no other traffic in his direction. The elation of the kill had begun to wear off; he felt more at ease, decided to take a short power nap, closed his eyes, and fell asleep within seconds.

CHAPTER 60

The rattling sound appeared in his dream, but Phil couldn't discover its whereabouts. The haze began to lift, and he slowly opened his eyes, only to look directly into the sun. He lifted his right hand to shield his eyes and heard the rattling sound come from his left. He glanced that way quickly and spied the diamondback rattlesnake coiled up only fifteen feet away from where he lay against the tree trunk. It flicked its tongue, while the golden slit eyes stared at him with bad intentions. He slowly pressed his back firmly against the tree and used his legs to quickly piston his body to the upright position while he kept an eye on the rattler. It stayed coiled up without any attempt to move or strike at this time. Even though Phil had his rifle, he dared not risk a shot, or he would awaken the beast above.

He looked at his watch and noticed it was eight thirty. He had been asleep for over three hours. No wonder he felt disoriented and stiff as a board. He slowly looked over his right shoulder at the charred remains of the truck, but could not locate any sign of Tim near the wreckage. When he looked back over his left shoulder, he noticed nothing but a thick forest and underbrush that extended as far as he could see. The snake was still in the same position, but followed his every movement with those evil eyes.

A plan began to form in his mind to attack and kill Frank in broad daylight. It involved using Mother Nature's beautiful forest as well as a good running back uses his offensive linemen to guard him from the enemy. Using the trees as camouflage, he could go beyond the lookout by outflanking his position and attacking from the least-expected direction. He felt in his jacket pocket, extracted the detailed topographic map that Tim had supplied, and noted exactly where the lookout and house were located. He compared the map to his surroundings and got an exact bearing of his current position. By his measurements, the house was about one and a half miles away. Phil was amazed at Frank's accuracy from that distance at night. That also meant that Phil had to be extra careful and avoid being sighted at all, or face the possible consequence of being Frank's next victim.

No matter which way he proceeded, it would be uphill through severely rugged terrain. It was a challenge he hoped he was up to, since the last thing he needed was to die of a heart attack in the middle of nowhere. Only the buzzards would find his carcass. His only other option was to retreat, make his way back to civilization, and call for backup. That might be the logical and safe thing to do, but he was tired of defensive maneuvering, and he owed it to Kelly to avenge her murder. It was the only honorable choice he had.

He recited the Lord's Prayer and made the sign of the cross before he bolted off the tree trunk as if catapulted by some unknown force. He broke into quick time as he was taught forty years ago. He quickly headed directly north, pushed his way through years of overgrowth of underbrush, and kept his focus on his direction by using the sun's position to guide him. After a few minutes he slowed his pace down as the edge of the foothills approached, with an extreme uphill climb for the next mile. Suddenly he stopped as he found himself entering an open area of no underbrush that stretched for seventy-five feet, which was surrounded by the tall ponderosa pines. The sun's early morning rays could be seen shining through the tall trees, giving it a spiritual feeling like the fingers of God, which gave Phil time to pause and think. He compared his position to his map and noticed his frenzied dash had taken him one third of a mile north of his previous position. He was deep enough to begin his western advance and outflank Frank.

Suddenly Phil heard a rustle come from his right, which made him freeze and listen. Multiple footsteps on broken branches could be heard, but too many for one person. Phil unclicked his safety and raised his rifle toward the sound as he took cover behind the tree. Within ten seconds a white-tailed deer doe with her two small fawns emerged from the forest, stopped, and looked directly at him. He immediately lowered his weapon and gave a nod of his head. The doe appeared to acknowledge his gesture and gracefully walked away across the empty patch. The fawns followed along but ran faster to catch up with their mother as she entered a path on the western side, which was the same direction Phil must travel. He stood and watched for another five minutes before he took off toward the trail.

After his nap Frank had watched for over three hours and saw no evidence of any movement of the fallen enemy. Therefore Frank assumed they were dead. Even though he could not locate the other perpetrator, he was confident that the blast had killed him also, and maybe his charred remains were part of the wreckage. He also hadn't seen any sign of investigation or backup by any law enforcement agency, which meant they never communicated their whereabouts or what had transpired. Since the wreckage was not visible from the main highway, no one would find it unless they came in his direction. So far there was no evidence of anyone searching for the dead soldiers.

Plus, he was hungry.

Carrying his small arms and scope with him, he descended the ladder. Instead of going back toward the house, he turned and headed deeper into the forest toward a rabbit's lair he had spotted earlier. He found two northern jackrabbits and killed both with his silenced Walther PPK. He picked them up and made his way back through the forest path to the house. As he entered, Frank noticed Gina was still asleep in the bed, and there was no coffee brewed. The lack of sleep had left him extremely cranky, and he felt like he could very well lose his fuse easily today. He marched over to the bed and knocked the foot of the mattress with his right knee. The vibration awakened Gina immediately. She sat up and stared at Frank with a blank look.

"When you get your bearings, I'm hungry and would like some breakfast," Frank said.

"Please," Gina said quietly while she rubbed her eyes and tried to wake up.

Frank walked over, stared down at her, and snarled, "Make me some fucking breakfast before I lose my temper." With that he turned and threw the two rabbit carcasses at her before he headed toward the bathroom.

She looked down at the sight of the executed dead animals and tried to scream, but instead became overwhelmed with nausea and vomited uncontrollably until she was zapped for strength and collapsed back onto her bed.

CHAPTER 61

Frank made his way back up the lookout after breakfast, satisfied at the taste of the rabbit, but agitated that he had to end up cooking after Gina became ill. He was starting to get tired of her attitude and lack of cooperation. He was ready to dispose of her since she had served her purpose and he was getting the itch to find a new hunting ground. She would only get in the way of his plans to renew his predatory existence. These thoughts began to cause internal excitement as his delusions of new conquests began to flood his brain. He climbed up the ladder and vaulted onto the floor of the lookout with renewed vigor. With a spring in his step, Frank went over to the telescope to see if anyone else were coming. He peered into the lens, looked off to the distance first, and saw no vehicular traffic heading his way. He scanned the rest of the valley and then swept the scope back toward the burned-out pickup truck and froze.

The body of the "dead" soldier was gone.

He scanned the surrounding area intensely, almost inch by inch, yet found no sign of him or the second body anywhere. The only logical explanation was that he was in fact not dead but knocked severely unconscious from the blast's concussion. He probably regained his senses while Frank was cooking and eating breakfast. For that he blamed Gina, who didn't have the guts to shear the animals. She would never survive in his world. He stood up and began to pace as his thoughts became more focused on a plan of escape, and the sooner the better. He immediately began to pack up his gear from the lookout, including his 50 caliber rifle and stand. He made multiple trips to the truck and loaded all of it as quickly as possible. He headed into the house for the rest of his gear and was stunned to find it uninhabited.

At first he was concerned about her disappearance, but then he thought the better of it and looked at the idea of her being gone in a positive light. He went about, packed up his things, and left Gina's stuff strewn around. He gathered up his gym bags full of weapons and all of the food. He loaded them into the truck. He looked over his topographic maps and figured to head west until he hooked up with northbound state route 117, which would take him beyond Rapid City. It would also be driven through sparsely populated areas. He lit up a joint, took a few deep tokes, and relaxed his anger's inner tensions. He hated calling an audible. He always preferred to have solid planning ahead of time. He jumped into the cab of the truck and turned the key to fire up the engine, but got nothing but a crank of the starter motor without any ignition. He tried it again and got the same response. He reached under the dashboard and pulled the lever for the hood release.

He walked to the front, undid the secondary latch, and finally raised the hood. He stood there in total shock as he looked at all eight spark-plug cords hanging loosely, their ends cutoff and gone. The truck was dead in the water. The anger in him grew instantly to the point where he lost control and let burst a violent primal scream that reverberated through the hills. It chased away all of the local birds and caused all of the forest's creatures to stop and listen. He opened up one of his bags of weapons, removed his favorite Henry long-range rifle, a fully automatic M-16 rifle with extra ammunition, checked the load in his Walther PPK, and began looking for foot trails that would lead him to Gina.

Then he would kill her.

Phil stopped dead in his tracks as the hair rose on the back of his neck at the sound of the roar that echoed around him. It was definitely human in origin, but full of pure anger and evil. He knew it was Frank screaming, but wondered about the circumstances surrounding the cause. He prayed that Gina was all right. His breathing was heavy and his legs were aching from climbing almost a thousand feet in elevation through heavy vegetation and rugged terrain. He listened for any more sounds so he could better triangulate Frank's position. But the forest went absolutely still, and the only thing he heard was his own heart pounding in his chest. He sat down on a large boulder under a gnarly black oak tree, took out his map, and estimated that he had traveled approximately one mile in about forty-five minutes.

He needed to rest or he wouldn't be up to the challenge of facing Frank.

He wished Tim were here to help.

But in the end he knew that it would be Frank and him in an old-fashioned bang-bang shoot-them-out scenario, or like in the old John Wayne movies. The problem was, he wasn't John Wayne or Clint Eastwood. He was an old ex-marine cop trying to avenge the death of so many and to reclaim his own soul from the devil. He looked at the map again and figured that he was just about even with the lookout, maybe at a distance of an eighth of a mile northeast. Phil decided to take five minutes and recuperate before he trudged another three quarters of a mile west and then doubled back toward Frank's position. He wiped the sweat off of his brow and wished he had a good cold bottle of water right now. He was carrying a canteen, but it was warm and he needed to save what he had, just in case. He would be crossing a river within half a mile and would get his fill there.

At exactly five minutes, he stood up and stretched everything he could so he would get past the pain quickly. Once ready, he took off through the dense brush and passed multiple mammoth pine trees. Luckily the air remained crisp and clear, without any hint of storms, which was a blessing. His uniform was beginning to get slightly tattered as he pushed through wild berry plants with their many thorns. His backpack weighed about fifteen pounds with extra rounds and high-calorie protein bars, again just in case. His bulletproof Kevlar jacket under his uniform weighed another twenty pounds but was well worth it, again just in case. Knowing his luck, Frank would take a head shot. The thought sent chills down his spine as if someone walked on his grave.

Within ten minutes he began to hear the sound of rushing water, maybe even a waterfall. With each step the sound grew closer, until he finally came upon an opening in the forest that revealed a swollen stream. About two hundred yards upstream was the waterfall he had heard. The crystal clean water cascaded downhill over large rocks and settled into pools of absolute calmness with the appearance of glass before it resumed into rapids downstream. Before he entered the clearing, Phil checked to make sure there was no sign of Frank, even though he had passed the tower a long time ago. He knelt down at the side of the creek, cupped his hands, and felt the refreshing, cold liquid for the first time. Phil took handfuls at a time as he replenished his volume depletion with the best-tasting water ever. He took the time to fill his canteen as he spotted a large bird in the distance. Suddenly he heard the shrill call as the bald eagle flew closer, its majestic wings spread fully as it rode on wind thermals. The telltale white head scanned below; its eyes focused briefly on Phil as it flew about two hundred feet overhead. He was overwhelmed by the sight. He watched it slowly fade from his sight as it continued on its journey in search of food.

Finally he dunked his head in the cold water. The physical stimulation was instantaneous as the frigid feeling awakened his senses. He shot up and sprayed the water with a twisting motion of his head like a dog. He combed his hair back with his hand, stood up, and looked for a shallow enough place to cross. Finally Phil found a narrow area with plenty of rocks one hundred feet south, which he crossed over with minimal wetting of his boots and lower pants. He began to go more southwesterly as he began to sweep around the hills to reach his destination from the rear position. He remembered his training all of those years ago in North Carolina. His tour of duty in Viet Nam taught him more about guerilla warfare than he cared to know at that time, but it came in handy now.

All of that changed as he suddenly heard Frank's voice screaming with evil intentions, "Gina, I will get you and kill you, and no one can help you now." Then he heard a single blast of a powerful rifle echo through the trees, but different from the recoil he had heard earlier that day. It probably came from a smaller caliber rifle. It came from his right about a half mile away.

Then he heard, "Fuck you, Frank, you cocksucking motherfucker killing son of a bitch, come and get me if you've got the balls," in Gina's voice. But it came from behind him to his left. At first he was glad to hear her voice and began to make his way toward her voice as quickly as possible. Gina had just committed the worst error in her battle with Frank. She gave up her position, so now not only did Phil know where she was, but so did Frank. Phil's only hope now was to find her before Frank did. His only prayer was that her blunder would draw Frank out into the open, where Phil would have the element of surprise. He was not the caliber of sniper that Frank was, but knew the capability of his rifle and his own skills.

A sense of total serenity enveloped Phil as he drew closer to the end of his quest than at any other time over the past thirty years. He knew that one way or another, the final episode would be played out here in the beauty of the Black Hills, and that death would follow. What was unclear was whether that death would include his own. Yet he was at peace with himself at that very moment, as he felt, then knew, that the end was finally here. So be it.

CHAPTER 62

Phil charged through the forest as quickly and quietly as possible given the present circumstances. He had no clue exactly where Gina was, but he went in the general direction of her initial expletive-laden scream. All of his plans for a surprise flank assault was for naught, as Gina would need his help first since Phil had no clue where Frank was now, especially after her academy-award performance. He was incensed at her stupidity of revealing her whereabouts after she escaped the grasp of the worst serial killer in the history of mankind. Then he thought otherwise. He knew what she was capable of doing, and he wondered if she were trying to draw him toward her. Was she armed? Did she have the higher ground? It wouldn't matter because she was outmatched. Her trying to defeat Frank DiMocchio was today's version of David and Goliath, with Goliath having the military genius of General George Patton.

He increased his pace until his knees began to cause more pain than he could stand. Phil had to slow down, especially as he began to climb in elevation and the ground grew rockier. He stopped and scanned all around him and tried to make out any type of traceable movement on the ground in the midst of the dense forest of pine trees. He also wanted to slow his heart rate and breathing down, so he could concentrate and listen for any signs of movement, such as breaking branches. All he could hear, however, was the constant call of a flock of crows at first, followed by the high-pitched shrill of a bird of prey, such as an eagle or hawk, in the distance. Then it grew eerily quiet as the breeze stopped blowing and all of nature's sounds stopped momentarily. If he were in California, Phil would have thought an earthquake were coming.

Instead, it was the force of evil that was about to disrupt everyone's lives.

Suddenly a flash of light almost blinded him as he was hit by the sun's reflection off of a metal object. It came from up higher on his left. It had to be Gina. It was her second mistake, but gave him clearer direction to her location. He knew Frank had probably seen it and was not too far behind. He adjusted his route and was about to move toward her when he heard the first shot from behind him and to the right ricochet off the rock where he had just seen the flash. Then a return shot was fired from above ten feet to the right of the original sighting. The exchange of fire surprised Phil, but was good for him, and hopefully Gina. Frank had no idea that he was there, so he had the element of surprise on his side again.

Phil made his move toward Gina as he tried to be as quick and quiet as possible. He hoped it wasn't too late.

Frank didn't think Gina would respond when he had hollered at her and to the world, which was purely out of anger. But her reply made him smile. He located the sound immediately. It came from up above and to the left. She was truly an amateur, but at least she had learned to take the higher ground. It didn't matter what her defense was like because he would expose her weakness, then attack and kill. He moved quickly toward the other side of the valley and up the mountainside. If necessary, he would capture her first, get her to the point where she would beg for death, and then finally kill Gina. The feather tattoo for her death would extend up to his left middle finger. He smiled at the thought as he rapidly made his way through the underbrush and began to climb in elevation.

A sudden movement caught him by surprise to his left about five hundred yards away. He stopped and scanned the area where he thought he had sighted something and waited. After almost two minutes, he hadn't seen anything when he was hit by a flash of light. It was a reflection from the same area the voice had emanated from. Rifle barrel was his first thought, so he raised his Henry and fired a round at the very spot, hoping for a wild shot. He never expected the return fire, which came from about ten feet to the left; he heard a bullet strike a tree about thirty yards to his right. It was closer than he had expected, and that meant he had to be more discreet until he caught up with her. It also meant she was on the move. Another tactical error was made on her part.

With the skills he learned over the years, he ran toward Gina through the underbrush and forest with nary a sound. Even though he was huge, Frank was extremely light on his feet and agile. He was able to dart around large bushes and sapling growth as if he were a halfback in the NFL. He began up the incline with the same long stride. His rigid physical training had left him in excellent cardiovascular condition, with the ability to beat any younger man in competition. Within five minutes he had covered half of the distance between them when he stopped and rechecked his position and bearings.

That was when he caught a glimpse of someone dressed in military fatigues in the same direction as he was, but a hundred yards ahead and to the left. Could it possibly be the "dead" soldier whose body suddenly disappeared after lying still for hours? More likely it was the second soldier, who had escaped any injury when the vehicle exploded. Frank was upset at himself for not locating the second body and for not putting another bullet through the first. Self-reflection would come later. Right now he needed to think of a way to eliminate the intruder.

The soldier stopped and turned as if he sensed something. That's when Frank realized who he was chasing. A smile came slowly across his face as the thought of his destiny set so many years ago in a house in San Francisco was coming to fruition.

He would finally kill both Gina Androcelli and Lieutenant Philip DiMarco simultaneously. That would be the epilogue to this chapter of his circle of death.

CHAPTER 63

Phil sensed that Frank was very close, but he could not see anything out of the ordinary. The thickness of the forest and the underbrush made it impossible for Phil to see anyone even as big as Frank. He felt as if he were being watched and feared that his cover had been blown. At this point it didn't matter, because he had to rescue Gina at any cost. Total reclamation of his guilty conscience depended upon his success. He stopped again, listened intensely for a full two minutes, but only heard his own breathing. He resumed his relentless climb up toward her last spotted position. His breathing was labored, and there was burning pain in his chest, which he chose to ignore.

Suddenly he saw her less than a hundred feet away, but was afraid to call out her name for fear of being heard. He moved his aching legs and back a little faster and closed the distance within a few minutes. When he was within twenty feet, she turned and stared right at him, rifle leveled at his chest with her finger on the trigger. Phil noticed the safety had been released.

He looked at her, held out his hands in a peaceful, friendly gesture, and smiled.

The shock on Gina's face was evident as she froze for ten seconds as she mouthed the words "Uncle Phil" to him and lowered the rifle. They raced toward each other and finally hugged fiercely, as if it would be their last.

"I knew you would come for me, no matter what I had done," she said quietly as her head was buried in his chest. "I don't know how to ever say I'm sorry for what I have done."

"Let's worry about that later," he said in a hushed tone. "The first thing is to get you out of here now before it's too late."

They immediately began to make their way west, away from where Phil had felt Frank's presence. They moved quickly in silence and tried to avoid being heard as much as possible. The pains that Phil had experienced on the climb up had entirely disappeared with the adrenaline rush caused by his rescue of Gina. Even if she spent the rest of her life behind bars for what she had done, he felt vindicated and relieved. Within fifteen minutes, they had descended over 1,500 feet and were in sight of the river and, hopefully, safety when they crossed.

Phil found his original path to cross the river and led Gina quickly across the rocks, then back into the woods. They finally entered the cathedral of trees where Phil had followed the family of deer. Gina paused as she came upon the opening, with equal wonderment as Phil had felt. Phil stopped as much to catch his breath and to once again take in the beauty of this place before they moved on. He looked back at Gina, who was staring like the little girl she used to be all of those years ago when they went to the Marin Woods with her father; he wished he could go back in time. For now he would take in this moment of serenity in his otherwise chaotic life.

As if in a real church, Gina felt the need to confess her sins at that moment, to cleanse her tortured soul. "I'm so sorry for what I did and what I put you and everyone else through," she said with tears streaming down her face. Her pain and grief were evident to Phil, as was her genuine feeling of remorse. "I don't know why I did some of those things, maybe to save my life at first, but not in the end. I figured that to beat Frank at his own game, you had to become like him, think like him, and finally act like him in order to destroy him. The problem is the destruction was of me, not Frank."

Phil hugged her as hard as he could as he tried to ease some of her pain and suffering. It also helped to heal some of his inner wounds. They both shed some tears as they held on tightly, afraid to let go for fear of letting life's misery in.

Suddenly as if on cue, hundreds of birds from crows to sparrows scattered from their nests and perches in the tall trees that surrounded them. Phil sensed the evil nearby and looked at Gina. "We need to move quickly," he said. With that they darted out of the silent center into the surrounding thick heavy underbrush. They ran for about a hundred yards, at which time Phil stopped abruptly, pulled Gina down to the ground, and with one finger held up to his lips, gave her the universal sign for silence. From about two hundred yards to the east, he could hear the definite crunching of branches on the ground. As he listened to the sounds, which appeared to draw closer, Phil sensed that whoever or whatever it was that was out there was not trying to hide its presence. That was not like Frank, thought Phil, unless he had lost his mind and twenty years of marine training. Then he heard the grunt and knew it wasn't human. He looked at Gina and motioned for her to be completely still. She had the look of questioning him about what was happening, but his facial expression told her not to say anything.

Within a minute the black bear passed within fifty yards of them, but being upwind from Phil and Gina's position, did not catch their scent of absolute fear. The massive beast kept on westward, as if on a mission. It was probably looking for one good final meal before it settled down for the night. Phil had no intention of being its last supper, so when the sounds had finally faded, he stood slowly and looked in the direction of the animal. He noted no further sight and motioned Gina to stand up slowly, with her rifle ready to fire. They both stood perfectly still for what appeared to be an eternity and watched the area to where the bear had disappeared. The air was completely stagnant, without any breeze whatsoever, as the silence in this part of the forest suddenly felt like a coffin had closed upon their faces and shut out the world.

"I don't like this one bit," Phil said.

"What is it?" Gina asked, the fear evident in her eyes.

"He's here," Phil said as he changed the settings on his M-16 to fully automatic with the flip of a switch. "Keep your weapon ready to fire, and don't hesitate to shoot first if you spot him."

"Where do you think he is?" she asked as quietly as possible.

"Right here," the booming voice of pure evil echoed across the forest.

Phil and Gina turned toward the area where the voice emanated from and came face-to-face with the direct descendent of Satan.

"Well, what do you know, even the bears are afraid of me," he said with a huge grin on his face. The true sense of his evil, however, could be seen in the coldest, darkest eyes ever imagined.

Gina shrunk at the sight of the monster who had tormented her for so long. Phil, however, stood taller, as the anger that had been contained under the surface suddenly rose in volcanic proportions. But instead of rage, a sense of absolute darkness enveloped him as all of the goodness that was within suddenly disappeared. He felt omnipotent and unafraid of anyone or anything. He locked his eyes, filled with a vision of death, onto Frank, who for the first time appeared unsure of his own superiority.

Two highly trained dogs of war stood at an impasse, their weapons locked onto each other as if they were two old gunfighters from the Old West. Each waited for the other to flinch first.

Death hung in the air as it waited to choose its next victim. Unbeknown to both of them, the circle of vultures began to appear above as they awaited death to arrive.

CHAPTER 64

The smile faded slowly from Frank's face as he eyed them cautiously from fifty yards away. The laser sighting from Phil's M-16 was pointed directly at the center of his sternum, and ultimately his heart. He stared into Phil's eyes, which had morphed in those few minutes to a mirror image of his own, which unsettled Frank. Phil took a few steps to the right as he increased the distance between Gina and himself, which would decrease their risk of both being shot and killed. They stood their ground as the beast hesitated, unsure of his next move. Phil's actions had unnerved Frank and caused momentary confusion, of which he tried to quickly gain control. Phil's eyes were now the color of death, which caused a shiver to streak down Frank's spine. Frank knew that they were at a standoff as he stood defiant. At that distance, he was the better marksman for a kill shot than Gina ever would be, but he was unclear about Phil, which caused him to hesitate.

"So, here we are, one nice big happy family," Frank said with a sarcastic cackle.

"We're family; you are not," Phil said with a snarl as he motioned to Gina. "My sister was her mother and married to her father for over twenty years until you killed him. You are not from our blood and never will be family."

"Sorry to hear that, Uncle Phil," Frank said with the emphasis on uncle.

"Again, I'm not your uncle, you fucking piece of subhuman shit," Phil said with such venom that even Gina flinched. "I'm here to make sure you burn in hell after I end your miserable life. That's it in a nutshell." His demeanor could only be described as equally satanic, with ice water for blood. He had reached that stage in his life where he didn't care one way or another whether he lived or died. He was raised a good Catholic. He had always believed in God and a judgment day, but now preferred to be the judge, jury, and executioner. With that said, Phil moved laterally another ten feet. The Henry rifle in Frank's right hand didn't budge as he kept it targeted on Gina's chest, but the Mauser in his left hand followed Phil's movement as the red laser dot from Phil's weapon remained static and centered on Frank's chest.

"Nice try, Uncle Phil," he said, "but I wouldn't move anymore or I'll have to end this nice encounter before time is over. I hate ending games too early, takes away the thrill of the chase."

"Is that all it is to you, a game?" This time it was Gina, and she was definitely showing her anger.

"Isn't that what life is, a series of games?" Frank asked. "Survival of the fittest, as Darwin described in his writings."

"Is that why you killed your own mother?" Phil asked. "She certainly wasn't fit as a mother. Look at what she raised." The last statement was a calculated gamble on Phil's part to further drive Frank over the edge, where mistakes would be made.

Frank looked directly at Phil as his evil smirk disappeared. "Uncle Phil, Uncle Phil, when are you going to let that one go?"

"You didn't answer the question, fuckwad," Phil said. "Only a man with true balls owns up to his kills."

"No, no, I guess you are right. That is not too much to ask," Frank said. "I've got all day—you don't—so which death of the 232 that I have killed do you want to know about?" His casual answer was made as he tried to regain superiority in this final chess match. The remark made Gina cringe at the thought of her once loving this monster. The number impressed Phil, but he didn't move a muscle or bat an eyelash at the statement of fact.

"Start with your mother," Phil insisted.

"Jesus, you are a pain in the fucking ass," Frank screamed as his irritation increased. "Did anyone ever tell you that?"

"My ex-wife and all of my friends have suggested as much," Phil replied with a stoic facial expression.

Frank looked straight at Phil and said, "Do you know how much my mother tortured me after she caused my father's death?"

"I saw the cigarette burns; I remember," Phil said.

"That was nothing," he said with another short cackle. "She locked me in the closet when she was fucking someone other than my dad, sometimes overnight. She gave me enemas when I didn't need them and other things that I cannot talk about. She deserved to die for what she did to my dad and to me. It was easy to just snap her neck by twisting her head from behind while she was seated at the table and ate lunch."

"Where's the body?" Phil asked.

A smirk appeared on Frank's face as he remembered under which tree in the redwoods of Marin County she was buried. "That will be my secret until the day I die," he said.

"What about my father?" Gina asked as her anger grew with Frank's cavalier attitude toward death.

"What about him?" Frank answered as he lightly applied pressure to both triggers in anticipation of her next question and his response. Phil saw the slight movement and did the same.

"Did you kill him, like Uncle Phil has said all of these years?" she asked with more intensity.

Phil tensed more as he heard the agitation in Gina's voice and knew that she would react with pure anger and cause a catastrophe. He didn't have time to say anything before Frank answered.

"Your dad hated me and tried to stop me from seeing you," Frank said, "and that wasn't right."

"But you were in Okinawa at the time, according to the Marines," Phil said as he tried to have Frank fill in the blanks that were always missing from the investigation due to classified information protected under "national security."

"I was actually on loan to the company to assassinate one of the leaders of the larger drug cartels in Mexico," Frank said proudly. "That job established me as the best at what I do and boosted my ratings, along with financial gains from the CIA, KGB, FRCA, MI-6, and the Mossad," he boasted. "Anyway, I finished that job early, so I had layover time until the next assignment."

"So you killed him?" she screamed.

"He always paused on the steps of the precinct when he exited, as if taking in the fresh air," Frank said. "That made it real easy even from over three blocks away," he said with an evil laugh.

Everything happened so fast, with devastating consequences. Gina erupted with a primal scream and fired a round a millisecond before Frank and Phil opened up with their respective weapons. Unfortunately Gina's shot went wide left, but Frank's blast with the Henry was dead center, which lifted her up and knocked her backward. His first shot with the Mauser caught Phil in the left upper chest area at the same time Phil's hit Frank dead center. The blast to Phil's chest propelled him slightly backward and to the right as the vest underneath took most of the blow. Phil's finger never released from his weapon as he stumbled backward. Frank's second shot grazed the left side of Phil's neck as he struck his head on a boulder. All the while, his weapon continued to fire as the laser beam moved up the target. Just before everything went black, Phil thought he saw Tim's smiling face covered in camouflage paint look down at him and smile.

It was reminiscent of a scene straight out of a Martin Scorsese film, with a twist of surrealism by Stanley Kubrick. No one knew Tim was still alive, which allowed him to remain unaccounted for. After the initial blast of his truck that early morning, he had lost consciousness for the better part of two hours. When he awoke, he crawled from his prone position into the underbrush away from where Phil had settled. They had lost all communication with each other, but Tim had never lost sight of his compatriot. He had followed Phil on a parallel path for the past mile through all kinds of terrain at a safe distance, but had closed the distance quickly after he heard the first volley of obscenities.

All of his tactical training with the navy SEALs came into play that fateful day.

He had flanked Phil to the rear and right as they had made their way past the fire tower. When Gina and Frank exchanged their first unpleasantries, Tim was able to triangulate their positions compared to Phil's. Tim also knew that Phil would do everything to save Gina, which meant he would move directly toward her voice's last position. That was his tactical error. He knew Frank would try to outflank both Gina and Phil, which meant circling farther to the right and beyond that point before he gained level ground. Frank would never attack from below.

So Tim decided to outflank all of them to the left and took off. He just hoped that he would get to the point of confrontation before it was too late. He suffered the same cuts, scrapes, and bruises as Phil had as he moved as quickly as possible through thorny bushes and thick underbrush. He climbed almost five hundred feet in elevation over less than a half mile in under four minutes. His heart pounded in his ears as his thighs screamed in pain from his climb, but he continued on adrenaline alone.

Especially after he caught sight of the black bear as it passed him one hundred yards to his right. It ran faster in the opposite direction, away from the impending gun battle. *And they call humans the more intelligent species*, he thought as he ran toward danger, whereas others ran away. If he had the breath, he would have laughed, but he couldn't.

The last quarter mile was the hardest as he climbed over massive boulders and ascended through wild berry bushes that dotted the forest haphazardly, their thick vines lined with hooked thorns that shredded his sleeves and pants. He felt no pain even though his tattered clothes were stained with his own sweat and blood.

He stopped briefly in an attempt to locate Frank and to catch his breath. In spite of excellent binoculars along with his best efforts, Frank could not be located. Suddenly, however, almost a dozen large turkey vultures, their small ugly pink heads tucked under massive wings, began to circle above a point less than a quarter mile to the east. The bodies and wings of the birds of prey created a tornado-like image as they circled, with the downward funnel pointed at the next site of death.

He ran as quickly as he could toward nature's vortex.

The heated words could be heard as they echoed through the mountains. He heard Frank scream at Phil, the raw, evil emotion evident even from afar. Phil's ice-cold response caused the hairs on Tim's neck to rise. Phil wanted Frank to vault over the edge of rage so as to cause mistakes. Tim understood, but did not agree with the method. It was almost as if Phil invited the gunfight. He knew that Phil wanted to kill Frank, but that would cause Gina to die first in this battle of lifetime enemies.

He reached the pinnacle of a large boulder that gave him a partial view of the scene as it unfolded below. Tim scrambled to the front of the rock and threw himself down as quickly as possible. He located the combatants below, with Frank at the tip of a perfect triangle, a laser target on his chest. Tim readied his rifle and sighted his target just as Gina's primal scream erupted, with her weapon's blast the exclamation point. The volley of fire that followed caused her to be lifted off the ground as Frank shot her dead center. Then Frank and Phil were both catapulted backward as each bullet found its target. But no blood was seen on Frank's chest as he was hit multiple times in succession in an upward fashion. Tim aimed his rifle for the head shot and pulled the trigger. He watched Frank's head explode twice as both Phil's and his bullets struck different sides of the monster's head simultaneously. The lifeless corpse fell immediately to the ground.

Tim immediately looked toward Phil's last position and saw him down against a boulder and saw that he wasn't moving. Tim jumped off of the boulder and ran directly toward him. Gina was dead as far as he knew. If she weren't dead yet, she would be soon, especially with the blast she took. Phil, however, had worn a vest, so hopefully he was still alive. As he approached his friend, Tim noted a small pool of blood near the left side of the neck, but also noted movement of Phil's legs. He reached Phil in time to see his eyes fluttering into unconsciousness. Tim smiled with relief that the mission was over and that they were both alive. He inspected the neck wound, which was a through and through only an inch above the subclavian artery and vein. Phil had lost about one to two units of blood, but would not bleed to death from this wound.

Tim wouldn't let Phil die. He immediately opened his backpack and extracted military first aid supplies. He placed a pressure dressing over the wound, which had already stopped bleeding, grabbed Phil's rifle, and slung it over his left shoulder. He then lifted Phil up over his right shoulder in the fireman's position and began to make his way down the mountainside.

He checked on Gina just to make sure. He stood over her remains, a crimson stain across her chest and underneath her upper torso. Her cold, lifeless eyes looked heavenly as they guided her home. Tim stood silently for a minute, said the Lord's Prayer, and asked God to care for her tortured soul. He would notify the task force to retrieve both bodies before the vultures left only the bones after he had Phil's condition secured.

So he turned, shifted Phil's body on his shoulder, and began the long journey down. The irony of the entire situation was not lost on Tim. In spite of the pain, suffering, and deaths that had occurred, for the first time in years he felt alive and smiled.

CHAPTER 65

The deaths of Frank DiMocchio and Gina Androcelli in the Black Hills of South Dakota became the blockbuster story of the week. The finality of the most massive law enforcement manhunt in recent decades came with both relief and anger. The FBI's task force at first took front and center stage, along with all of the credit. When further investigative reporting by the *Washington Post* and *New York Times* unearthed the truth behind the debacle that was the execution of an innocent man in the East Coast Slayer case, lawsuits were immediately filed by all of the relatives involved. Then an internal investigation by the FBI revealed the shortcomings of their esteemed profilers' unit, with the discovery of their numerous mistakes and missteps. The final straw was the revelation that the helicopter crash in which Kelly Flaherty had died was not caused by mechanical failure; it had in fact been shot down by the individual they pursued. Congressional hearings were held as the blame game in Washington was in full stride. In the end, Lieutenant Philip DiMarco was finally given the credit for his unrelenting pursuit of the monster who had terrorized an entire nation for so long. With help from Admiral Timothy Riley, the worst serial killer in modern-day history had been cornered and killed. For that fact, they were made national heroes. The final report to the public by every committee and every form of media gave the FBI a huge black eye. It led to the immediate forced resignation of Assistant Director Anthony Balducci.

The story behind Admiral Riley's brush with death after the explosion and subsequent pursuit of his comrade and the perpetrators was great for the ratings. But the icing on the cake was when it was discovered that Tim had carried Phil back alive over mountainous terrain for seven miles to the highway on a fractured fibula, which made him an instant celebrity. He made the obligatory rounds on both the late-night and morning talk shows. He walked in a moon boot with a hand-carved cane while he flashed his smile and bright blue eyes. He became the face of rugged handsomeness across the country and enjoyed his newfound fame. He also resigned as sheriff, moved out of Wyoming, and settled in southern Florida.

The total absence of Lieutenant Philip DiMarco from any of the up close interviews was a mystery to all of the media agents who had requested his appearance. The only word about his condition came from Phil's oldest daughter, who requested privacy while her father recovered from his injuries from the gun battle, but did not elaborate further. Phil had experimental stem cell surgery to help heal his left brachial plexus, which had been severed by Frank's bullet and had caused left arm paralysis. He spent two weeks in an unknown hospital and then was shuttled to a private rehabilitation facility for intensive physical therapy.

What was never told to anyone outside his immediate family was the deep, dark depression that Phil had fallen into as part of post-traumatic stress disorder. The death of Kelly, the deaths of all of the people at the hand of Gina, and her subsequent death in the Black Hills overwhelmed him with guilt at not having prevented any of the catastrophes. Especially since he had been after Frank for so long, just to find out that he had lived in his territory for all of those years in Southern California. Phil never became suicidal. He just chose not to communicate with anyone beyond his children. He was even tight-lipped with them and exposed only the bare essential facts.

Only Tim knew the truth of what had happened in the forest that day. The autopsy on Frank was compromised due to severe tissue destruction from the bullet wounds and the vultures who had a field day after Tim had left with Phil. As if guided by a hidden force, Gina's remains had not been touched by the voracious birds of prey, which was not the case with Frank. In spite of Tim's denials, Phil knew he did not fire the shot that killed Frank. He likened the story to the old John Wayne western movie *Who Shot Liberty Valence,* in which Jimmy Stewart was credited with gunning down the evil Liberty Valance, played by Lee Marvin. Unbeknown to the townsfolk, it was actually John Wayne who had fired the fatal shot from the shadows across the street. But he never took the credit, which led Jimmy Stewart to eventually become US Senator after he rode his wave of fame. Phil did not request or desire any fame or credit for something he had not done.

All he wanted was to be left alone.

The months passed by as fall progressed to winter. The movement slowly returned to Phil's left arm and hand, along with increased strength. He was finally released from treatment in the rehabilitation center to continue home exercises, which was his first step to total recovery. The second step was to sell his house in the desert, move closer to his children in San Luis Obispo, and retire from the CHP, with commendations along with a nice pension.

For the first time that early spring, he heard the birds chirp as the sun rose without the usual pale of fog; no mist rose from the ground. A slight fragrance of early jasmine filled the air. He looked out his back window. The grounds that had been unattended over the winter had grown a few weeds, the rosebushes hadn't been pruned, the bird feeders were empty, and the paint on the garage was peeled.

He got up with caution as his back and shoulder cried out in pain, a residual of that fateful day in South Dakota. He took the first five steps slowly. Finally the pain subsided, and he could walk like a normal person. He opened up the cabinet, took his vitamins, stared at the bottles of painkillers, still unopened, and closed the door. He turned on the shower and waited for the steam to rise before he got in for his morning ritual of isometric stretches of his muscles, followed by active movement of all of his joints. His mind felt different today, as his focus of purpose had returned. Once done with his exercises, he quickly dried off and dressed.

Phil grabbed his backpack, coffee thermos, and blanket as he headed out the front door of his new house. He found the morning paper, tucked it into his bag, and began the one-mile walk on his private path, which wound around tall pine and eucalyptus trees. He reached the outer edge of the dunes and emerged from the forest alone. He scanned the beach and saw another high tide, with waves up to ten feet in height. The roar of the surf as the curl unfolded drowned out any dark thoughts he had and brought a brief feeling of serenity.

He laid his blanket down, opened up his backpack, and retrieved his camera and his stash. He sat perfectly still as he admired the day and knew that spring was near. He lit up his joint and took the first four tokes of the day, which allowed the feeling of warmth to spread throughout his body. The colors around him exploded in pinks and purples as the first wildflowers of the year were in bloom. He immediately began to snap pictures of the flowers and waves. On a lark, he turned the camera on himself and snapped one last shot.

The warmth of the sun began to be felt on his back as the sun rose higher in the eastern sky. Even though it was only fifty-five degrees out, he removed his T-shirt so he could start an early spring tan. With the rehabilitation for his injuries, his body was in the best shape of his life since he was a young marine, his muscles cut and defined, with only 3 percent body fat. He had to be careful not to overexpose his skin, so as not to fade the new tattoo of the golden eagle on his upper back, which was not yet fully completed. He reviewed the pictures he had just shot on the camera's LED monitor and was pleased until the last shot appeared. The face that stared back at him was that of a stranger in his body. The lines that used to appear as a permanent smile were now deeper and turned downward. The anger that was deeply ingrained in his soul could be seen through the eyes. The once bright baby blue irises were now a steel gray, which matched the entire flock of his gray beard and shoulder-length hair.

For the first time in six months, he looked at himself and the world in an entirely different light. He had become more disillusioned with society as a whole outside of his immediate family. The guilt that had caused his depression had been followed by a period of intense anger that he had originally turned inwardly.

But not anymore.

He had made peace with himself over all of the consequences that had occurred. But that was not the case with those he considered fools and idiots inside the multiple layers of the justice system he had dealt with over the past thirty years. If those in charge of one investigation after another had only listened, none of the deaths after Frank's mother would have happened. The names and faces of those he considered the most malfeasant, along with the most derelict of duty, were forever ingrained in his bitter soul. He remembered the saying from the streets of the Bronx that "Paybacks are a bitch, but revenge is a motherfucker."

He had made a promise to himself all throughout therapy that those responsible would someday pay. The nonchalant manner in which Frank had admitted the number of kills had always haunted Phil. Not because the statement had bothered Phil or that Phil felt sorry. The problem was that Phil felt admiration of the feat, which provided the motivation for his recovery.

He paused in mid-thought as an older man with a golden retriever appeared on the empty beach a quarter of a mile from his position. Phil watched them intensely for about five minutes to make sure he would not be disturbed or recognized by anyone. When the pair appeared to move closer, Phil reached inside his backpack, removed the gun from its hiding spot, and placed it into his lap. He looked down at the Walther PPK with the silencer attached and smiled at the inscription engraved on the undersurface of the barrel: "Use only for bad intentions, Tim." It had been given to Phil late one rainy night while he lay in his bed at the rehabilitation center. He never questioned how Tim came into possession of Frank's favorite weapon, but cherished the gesture as only comrades-in-arms could understand. To this day, no one outside the two of them knew of its existence.

As the dog drew closer, Phil scanned the beach to see if anyone else were nearby, just in case. He watched the young male dog as it ran after a wayward seagull, its tongue hanging out the side of the open mouth as it frolicked forward. When it came within five hundred feet of Phil, the animal stopped dead in its tracks as they made eye contact. Its look of happiness faded into one of recognition of an enemy as it bared its teeth and growled. Phil gripped the handle of the weapon, flicked off the safety, and stared at the animal with a higher degree of animosity. As if propelled by mental telepathy, the dog sensed defeat, lowered its tail, and retreated in a full trot past a stunned owner, who turned to chase. The dog only glanced back at Phil once as it headed quickly up the beach toward the stairs and safety.

Phil clicked the safety back on, placed the gun back into the backpack, and smiled. He never would have shot the dog. That would have been inhumane. Its owner, however, was fair game and would have made a great practice run, especially since there were no witnesses around.

Just as he had learned from the best.

ABOUT THE AUTHOR

Robert Abatti is the pen name for Robert J. Abatecola, MD. Born and raised in New York, he graduated from New York University and New York Medical College before completing residency at University of Southern California. He is a practicing family physician with over thirty years of medical experience, who began writing as a medical student. He resides in Northern California with his wife, children, and grandchildren.